A SWIFT BRAND OF JUSTICE

HEATHER AMES

CHAPTER ONE

"You failed your proficiency again," Hal Shaw said.

"By five goddamned points." Brian Swift paced back and forth in front of the chief's desk.

"Five or fifty, I still can't put you back on active duty." Hal leaned back in his chair and tapped his pen. "There are other options, Brian. I need someone to head up Cold Case. You've got great attention to detail, and Christ knows you're relentless when you're working a case. It'd be a good fit."

"Cold Case? That's a desk job, Hal." Brian stopped and slammed his right hand down flat on the desk. "I want field work. Put me back into Homicide."

Hal looked at the hand. "Careful, Swift. I know you're angry, but this isn't the place to get out of control. And stop calling me Hal."

"Why? Because you're behind that desk?" Brian threw himself into one of the brown leather chairs. "I've got to call you Chief, even when we're alone? I've always called you Hal. What the hell *is* this crap?"

"You need the practice." Hal's voice was measured. "I can't have a detective yelling at me and calling me Hal. It's insubordinate." He shook his head. "You're still a discipline problem. If you'd get your temper under control, you could be looking at getting promoted to captain someday."

"At least you're telling me I'm still on staff." Brian tried to calm himself, but it didn't do much good. Inside, he was cooking like an oven set to 500 degrees.

"Of course." Hal frowned. "No one's even talking about placing you on permanent disability. But you've got to face facts. It's been four months, and you can still barely hold anything in your left hand, let alone a gun."

"I've worked damned hard at that firing range. How many other guys have you got who can even come close to my score when they're forced to switch hands?"

The corner of Hal's mouth quirked. He shook his head. "No one."

Brian glared at the chief. "Then put me back on duty."

"No. You still couldn't react quickly enough in an emergency."

"I managed to arrest Sean Hastings with my arm in a sling."

Hal sighed. "I realize that, but he was a basket case junkie who weighed forty pounds less than you." His pen tapped more forcefully. "Do I really need to remind you his father had the drop on you and almost took you and Kaylen out before Sean shot him?"

Hal was getting exasperated, Brian thought warily. Pissing off the chief would almost certainly shut down any further discussion. He rubbed his right hand over his face to give both of them a moment to lower the intensity and possibly redirect the debate. He felt the scratchy texture of the beard he'd allowed to grow because it was easier than shaving and tried employing the deep breathing technique that Dr. Fleming, the psychologist he had been forced to consult, had maintained would help control his hair-trigger temper.

He figured it was time to test out the most reliable of the hokey relaxation tricks Fleming had insisted would work better than giving in to the outbursts that had alienated Brian's coworkers at Miami-Dade Police Department as well as intimidating witnesses. Brian could see the benefits of controlling his anger within the department, but he thought the guy was completely off the mark in counseling his interrogation techniques. What did a shrink know about getting a confession out of a suspect?

He truly hated his sessions with Fleming. The man was, Brian grudgingly acknowledged, insufferably astute. He was also unwavering in his demands. After Brian took a boat charter instead of attending one of their preliminary meetings, the psychologist had told his reluctant patient that if he truly wanted to return to active duty at any time in the foreseeable future, then he'd better plan on attending every one of his remaining sessions. He'd also have to complete all homework assignments and evidently, along the rocky and treacherous path to the shrink's concept of enlightenment, confront every demon he had firmly shut away deep in his psyche.

The day Fleming laid down that demand, Brian had slammed out of the doctor's office planning never to return. He'd take a different career path; join his friend, Jim, as a private investigator. *Fuck* the department.

Three people intervened. Hal tore up his resignation and called him a goddamned idiot, Jim advised him to reconsider with quiet words of reason, and Kaylen's unwavering support and common sense finally curtailed his rashness. He put the brakes on ending his career with MDPD, despite his feelings about the department's choice of psychologist and his methods.

At the thought of Kaylen, tension flowed out of Brian. She'd urged caution and patience when he became frustrated over the requirements for his return. Her caring concern had stopped him spiraling deeper into the depression that had dogged him since his injury.

But neither his brother Tim's death nor the extended leave from Brian's career could hold a candle to the potential horrors of returning to confront the demons of his childhood. He had long ago bolted the door on those nightmare memories, only to have them dredged up in the weeks following Tim's disappearance and murder.

The last thing he wanted was another trip down memory lane, returning to Baton Rouge and the trauma of those years. Maybe he *hadn't* healed more than the physical effects, but he damned sure didn't want to reopen the psychological wounds. He was secretly afraid he'd lose not only his career, but his burgeoning relationship with Kaylen. He didn't deserve her, he knew, but dammit, he wasn't going to risk losing her because Fleming insisted on opening Pandora's box, either. Cool and detached were workable. Any alternative definitely wasn't.

Brian took a sip of water and leaned back in his chair, another of Fleming's tricks. Incredibly, it seemed to work, too. He felt the tension flow out of not only his shoulders, but his back. "Give me a break, Hal," he said, listening for any hint of the Louisiana drawl that still surfaced when he lost control. "I'd recently been released from the hospital."

"Fair enough." Hal sighed again. "You're right. We don't need to rehash the mistakes of that night."

"No," Brian said. "We definitely don't. I learned my lesson."

"Did you?" Hal's expression looked about as dubious as his voice sounded.

Brian knew he hadn't presented his case in anything close to a convincing way. Fleming might have some merit, he thought grudgingly. Maybe his emotions *were* still on the ragged side. Maybe he did need to work on better coping skills in his private life. But he knew he could handle the demands of his job. He'd done so successfully for years. *It was the interpersonal skills that were lacking.* The sudden insight surprised him. Fleming again, the bastard.

"Yes," he said. "And I've got a clean bill of health, except for this arm. I'm still going to outpatient P.T. twice a week. I'm running three to five miles a day. I'm taking boat charters…"

"Why in hell are you taking charters?" Hal's tone was uncharacteristically sharp. "You don't need to work at anything except regaining the full use of your damned arm." He started frowning again. "I know as an adrenaline junkie you've got to be bored out of your skull, but for Christ's sake, can't you try for once in your life to relax and put all your energy into getting well? I know you're serious about coming back to the department— that's never been in doubt. But the bottom line is, and continues to be, you're not ready."

I'm stifled, Brian wanted to say. *Every day I have to force myself out of bed.*

But telling Hal the truth was too painful. Too humiliating. Way too revealing.

He reluctantly cracked open a door. "I *need* my job. I can't go on dealing indefinitely with charter clients or worse, Tim's fu…friggin' tenants. They're driving me crazy."

Brian carefully placed the water bottle on the table, watching for any sign of shaking. He knew Hal was looking for it, too.

"Listening to those people in Tim's buildings with their constant complaints about leaky plumbing and peeling paint," he said, the pressure cooker inside him heating up again. "Then going out on charters and having clients tell me I'm going too fast or too slow, or I haven't gotten them to the best fishing spot, or it's too choppy and they want their money back because all they've done is get seasick…"

Hal leaned forward, about to interrupt him. Brian refused to stem the tide of his semi-controlled outburst. "I'm a detective," he said. "Not a travel coordinator or a goddamned landlord. Working for the department's been more than a career to me; it's been my life for the past fifteen years. It defines me." He felt a surge of pain as his left hand cramped harder than the knot balling in his gut.

"I know." Hal's voice was quiet and horrifyingly sympathetic. "But I can't and won't let you come back until you're physically and mentally ready to handle any situation. Until that happens, you need to hire a manager for those buildings and keep yourself busy helping Jim out with the PI business, as long as you're taking phone calls or doing research. No field work."

Brian heard pity in Hal's voice. *Shit!*

"I'm not asking for a favor," he said, determined to clarify his position. "If I didn't think I was ready, I wouldn't be here."

Hal shook his head. "You never know your own limit. Your biggest fault, and mine for not recognizing it before Tim's death. I'm not going to make the same mistake again."

"Give me a chance, Hal…Chief. I won't blow it." Brian swallowed his pride, and it went down like bile. "Please."

Hal pointed to the proficiency test. "Bring your skills up to passing or take the Cold Case position."

"This is bullshit." Brian gave up, at least for that week. He got to his feet and walked over to the door.

"Don't slam it on your way out this time," Hal cautioned. He turned to his computer, effectively ending the meeting.

Brian felt like taking the door right off its hinges. Instead, he closed it quietly behind him and watched Hal's secretary, Alicia Solis, avert her eyes as he walked past her desk.

CHAPTER TWO

KAYLEN ROBERTS LOOKED up from scanning the weekly club reports. "We've got to do better with the liquor requisition," she told Rob Diaz, Bannisters' manager, seated in one of the red leather club chairs opposite her desk. "I want to include Julio for that part of our meeting. We've got to make better projections. I don't like having to buy extra cases of wine at retail prices, which we've done twice in the past few weeks. Last month, we catered three large private parties, and they bumped up the consumption of hard liquor. Neither you nor I allowed for that. We've both got all the chops for restaurant management, but Julio's the one running the bar."

"I agree." Rob nodded. "The restaurants I worked at before catered to a happy hour crowd who mostly drank wine, beer, martinis or margaritas. The thirties theme here presents unique challenges. Julio's developing specialty drinks, which adds to the club's revenue, but also results in these underestimated hard liquor numbers."

Kaylen smiled. "He's so inventive. The Red Bomber, Chillin' Clam Rock-Out. Where he comes up with these names, I don't know, or the combinations, either."

"Experimentation. Research. The wide range of sources he taps through the internet and his buddies," Rob said. "I knew Julio was good by reputation, but you've allowed him free rein here, and he's developing a knowledge of mixology unparalleled in Miami. Several times lately, I've met patrons coming here specifically to spend time in the bar, sampling Julio's concoctions. I've got a suspicion they're either sent by rival clubs or they're bar owners wanting to spice up their own offerings."

"Or trying to steal Julio away from us," Kaylen interjected, frowning at the thought of her head bartender being wooed away by a better financial offer, or even a stake in a rival club or restaurant. "Does he ever talk about leaving here and going somewhere else?"

Rob shook his head. "No. He used to talk about opening his own gig, but now he says you pay too well to even consider that seriously."

"Well, thank goodness for that." Kaylen drank the last of her Diet Coke and stood up, placing her hands in the small of her back and stretching kinked muscles. "I need a break."

"You should take one." Rob glanced at his watch. "You should eat something, too. You've been here all day. You want me to order you a sandwich from the kitchen?"

Kaylen thought of Emrico, the head chef, having to switch gears from dinner preparations to getting a sandwich made. Never one to gracefully take on even minute challenges to his rigid schedule, she could imagine how well that digression would sit with him. "No, thanks."

"Let me know if you change your mind." Rob headed for the door.

Sending one of the busboys out to get her a sandwich was a better option, Kaylen thought, but she had more pressing things to think about, and they didn't involve work. Brian had met with Hal that morning, regarding his return to active duty.

She glanced at her smartphone, sitting silently beside her laptop. Brian hadn't called. Her stomach churned uncomfortably, and it had nothing to do with hunger. She knew he'd had to go straight from the meeting to a charter, but if the news from the meeting had been good, surely he could have spared two minutes to call and let her know. Even a text, although less personal, would have been better than nothing.

The landline rang, startling her out of her musings. *Brian,* she thought, relieved. But he always used her smartphone, not the club line, she reminded herself as she answered.

A pleasant male voice informed her Ziggy Stavros was calling on behalf of his family. His father owned a Greek restaurant, The Corinthian. Perhaps Kaylen had heard of it?

"Of course." She stifled frustration and disappointment. "It's famous for its award-winning food and wines."

The Stavros family was legendary in the Miami community. They had started with a tiny hole-in-the-wall café and built it into an eatery that was mentioned prominently in all local travel guides. Although Kaylen had never been inside it, she knew from others that the decadence of the menu was equaled by the opulence of the décor. Why would Ziggy Stavros call in the middle of a weekday afternoon?

"You must be wondering what I want," Ziggy said.

He echoed her thoughts so closely, Kaylen wasn't sure if she wanted to laugh or shudder with apprehension. "You're right."

"My family is taking on an expansion. Something completely different from our traditional restaurant. We would like to speak with you regarding you acting as a consultant on this new project. Of course, you would be generously remunerated for your contribution."

Who used words like 'generously remunerated?'

Kaylen was intrigued by the presentation and Ziggy's formal use of language. She couldn't remember even one member of the Stavros clan attending any promotional events for Bannisters. She didn't remember seeing them when she'd gone with George to any of his frequent philanthropic happenings, either. She did remember a photo in a local newspaper a few years back, showing a father and several children, both boys and girls, standing in front of The Corinthian when it celebrated a milestone anniversary, but no wife or mother. Perhaps Mrs. Stavros had passed away. Kaylen couldn't imagine a divorce—she'd heard the Stavroses were as traditional in their thinking as their restaurant and menu, which had not been changed in the last twenty years, according to the ads they ran infrequently on TV.

"I'd be interested in hearing your proposal," she said. "When would you like to meet?"

"The sooner the better. Would you be available in say, an hour?"

Kaylen glanced at her watch. Julio didn't arrive on the premises until 4:00 P.M., since he stayed after hours to restock and inventory for loss prevention. Brian's charter didn't end until 3:00 P.M., and she never called him until he came back into port. She knew he didn't like being disturbed when he was working, and neither did she, even for a pleasurable call.

They had agreed any contact between them during working hours would only be for emergencies. Kaylen counted Brian's return to Miami-Dade Police Department as an emergency, but maybe he didn't. No, he would have called, she decided. His job was way too important to him. Maybe he'd been running late from the meeting and had to rush to be on time for the charter....

"Why not?" she told Ziggy, still waiting patiently for her answer.

She could arrange to meet with Julio the following day. Twenty-four hours wouldn't make much of a difference in the bar's bottom line. "Could you can make it any sooner?" she asked Ziggy. "I've been working in my office all day, and I'm ready for a break."

"Yes," Ziggy said, all business suddenly. "Twenty minutes?"

"Great," Kaylen said.

They hung up in unison.

A consultancy position really did sound enticing. With the liquor situation resolved, she could back out a little from closely supervising Bannisters. Rob's hand kept the club running on oiled wheels, and she was getting tired of spending every evening working. Her social life was practically non-existent, even though she had a boyfriend with whom she really wanted to spend more time.

Brian's charters were mostly daytime commitments. He refused to come to the club on more than an infrequent basis, and he kept their relationship under wraps. When she'd asked why, he told her plainly that being the girlfriend of Tim Madison was one thing, but being the girlfriend of Tim's detective half-brother was another thing entirely.

Did she really want to have to be more careful than she already was, he'd asked? Did she want to start carrying a gun? Detectives had more than their share of disgruntled people wishing to exact revenge on them or those closest to them. He didn't want to worry about her getting involved with his problems on more than a fringe basis. The cartel could still be an issue too, fractured though it had been by the damaging evidence Tim's case had revealed.

Reluctantly, she had admitted that, no, she didn't want to start looking behind her again on a regular basis, and she'd stopped pressing Brian for steady dates. He thought spontaneity was the way to go. She didn't. But she demurred to his experience and his sensible approach. Temporarily, at least.

She'd asked to attend department functions with him, particularly informal ones, where she could tap other wives and girlfriends for advice. Brian told her they'd go when he returned to active duty. Stalemate, she thought, chagrined. She felt less and less important to him, and today's failure to call her only compounded her sense of him quietly drifting away from their relationship.

Kaylen shook herself out of her despondent daydream. Her spur-of-the-moment meeting with Ziggy Stavros was going to mean skipping lunch, unless she could eat with Brian when he got back. Her stomach growled in rebellion at the thought of waiting several more hours for food.

"Shut up," she told it, grabbing one of the cracker packets she perpetually munched on when working at her desk. She should take out stock in the crackers' manufacturing company, she thought, ripping open the wrapper. She took a bite and followed it up with a swig of water from a bottle sitting beside the phone. Warm. Yuck!

She grimaced and headed for the mini fridge. Maybe something more substantial than crackers lurked inside, along with a fresh bottle of water. She found a take-out container with coleslaw from yesterday's lunch and two hardboiled eggs she remembered bringing with her a couple of days before. The slaw was still edible, and she had cooked the eggs herself at home, so they were, too. She peeled an egg and ate it standing up. A couple of mouthfuls into the coleslaw, she tossed that in the trash.

Kaylen wasn't in the mood for marginal leftovers. She wanted a real meal. She picked up her phone. If Brian wasn't back at the dock, she'd leave him a message. Even more than food, she wanted to spend time with him, and the mood she was in, they'd either come to some agreement over their mostly-off relationship or they'd end up in one hell of a fight.

CHAPTER THREE

IT WAS 2:15 P.M. when Brian guided his 50′ motor yacht, the *Need to Know*, toward the Coconut Grove Marina. A strong tailwind had propelled them back to shore a lot faster than they had left.

"You're really getting better at this." Jim Paxton, Brian's friend and neighbor at the marina, nodded encouragingly.

Wearing sharply-pressed shorts and a spotless white sport shirt, he stood beside Brian as he maneuvered between buoys and speedboats, yachts and jet skis.

"Don't say that too loud. The new clients'll hear you. They don't know I haven't always been like this." Brian brought his left hand up and with difficulty, hooked his fingers onto the wheel. "You'll make them nervous."

"Sometimes, your steering makes *me* nervous." Jim's weathered face crinkled into a wide grin. "A lot less these days. Want to dock her?"

Brian wanted to try his luck, but knew he wasn't ready to place the boats in the adjacent slips at risk while he attempted to bring the *NTK* into port. Jim's own *Fanciful Folly* sat to starboard. To port, the *Naughty Nautical* bobbed serenely at anchor six days out of the week. On Sundays, the Summerfields, her seventy-something owners, brought what looked to be their entire family down to the water so they could chug around the bay before returning to spend the rest of the afternoon preparing and then eating dinner on deck. Unfortunately, it was only Friday, so he'd have to avoid both boats.

The Summerfields had already made it clear they thought Brian should have moved to another marina after the *Destiny* exploded in what they described as 'a ferocious ball of flame.' Despite the fact that Brian wasn't responsible and his insurance had restored their less-than-pristine boat with brand new seats, sails and a paint job, they hadn't warmed to the idea of him remaining in the same slip, and thought even less of him replacing the *Destiny* with a larger vessel.

Mr. Summerfield had come over soon after the *Need to Know* was delivered, not to bring good wishes for Brian's recovery, but to complain the *NTK* was limiting their view, their access to sunlight, and was no doubt polluting the bay as well as the entire marina. After delivering that speech, he returned to Mrs. Summerfield, glowering from her perch amidst her grandchildren, all sitting on their new seats, and started the engine, which belched out clouds of reeking black smoke. They continued their disapproving glares as *Naughty Nautical* puttered away, leaving a trail of oily residue all the way from the marina to the open waters of the bay.

"Nope," Brian said. "I'll work on my maneuvering a couple more weeks first."

"Let me guess—no teeing off the Summerfields," Jim said.

"You've got it." Brian relinquished the wheel. "I don't want to risk bumping their damned boat. I don't think my insurance agent could handle another claim from them. He said they about took him out of his twelve-step program. It doesn't seem to faze Summerfield one bit that I'm licensed to carry a gun, either."

Jim took the wheel. "Summerfield's an old coot. That wife of his is no peach, either. I know that well. *Fanciful Folly* used to occupy your slip."

Brian stared at him. "You never told me that."

"Yeah, well, I don't tell you everything." Jim pulled his cap down over his eyes. "I wanted a slip on the opposite side of the marina after a couple of run-ins with them over diddly-squat stuff like me hanging my washing in the stern. They told me it was against marina policy."

Brian couldn't help laughing at the image of Jim fighting with the Summerfields over his freshly starched shorts.

"You laugh all you want," Jim said. "Now I have to drag everything to the laundromat. Those machines ruin your clothes."

"Not mine."

"Your old clothes had already been ruined by years of use," Jim said. "Their replacements are another story. If you take what Kaylen picked out for you to a laundromat, you won't be able to get into them afterwards. They'll all shrink and get lint balls."

Brian tried not to laugh harder. Jim looked and sounded like he was getting pretty perturbed. His appearance was almost as important to him as his boat. He spent a good deal of his day cleaning and polishing. Brian thought Jim's fingers must itch to do the same thing whenever he came onto the *NTK*.

"Kaylen'd be really mad at me if I ruined those clothes," Brian said. "She let me know how much time she spent helping me pull together a new wardrobe as well as replacing everything else I lost when the *Destiny* burned."

"She's got great taste, your girl." Jim powered down as they closed in on the marina and the traffic built up, as it always did early on fall afternoons.

Brian raised his voice above the whirring motor. "She's got expensive taste. Much like Tim's. He always wore designer duds. Mine were more like Salvation Army specials."

"And looked it." Jim smiled, belying his words. "One of the few good things to come out of that fire was the loss of your belongings, such as they were."

"You give me the hardest damned time," Brian said. "Remind me again—what is it I like about you?"

"I'm useful," Jim said. "And witty. And I keep you on your toes while you're on disability."

"Thanks for clarifying that." Brian stared at the buoys marking the entrance to the marina.

"Things didn't go well today with Hal," Jim said.

It was a statement, not a question, but Brian shook his head. "No. I failed the proficiency by five points. He won't let me back in."

"You'll get there, buddy." Jim's voice was quiet as he guided the *Need to Know* toward the dock. "It's only a matter of time."

"Too much time. Christ, I'm bored."

"How can you be bored? You've got the boat, Kaylen..."

"Charters," Brian said. "I can't even manage those alone. And Kaylen's got the club. She's always busy."

"She's never too busy for you, and you know it."

Brian left that comment unanswered. Jim slowed the boat to a crawl, alternating short bursts of power and controlled coasting as he eased the *Need to Know* into her slip. Brian left the upstation to join Carlos, the deckhand he'd hired for all his charters after purchasing the larger vessel. Carlos was already on the dock, having secured the first line. Brian tossed him the remaining ropes and helped secure the moorings. Jim shut down the engine.

The familiar sights and smells of the marina welcomed them home. Seagulls whirled overhead, their cries reflecting their search for fishermen returning with their catches. A mass of people carrying fishing poles, coolers, towels, and even beach chairs walked toward the parking lot while they chattered and called out to errant children lagging behind or running too far ahead. A concentrated salt tang wafted up from the dock. Boring, maybe, but soothing—definitely.

Brian settled up with his middle-aged clients as they gathered their belongings.

"We had such a wonderful trip," the woman said. Pleasant-faced, with salt-and-pepper hair pulled back into a loose pony tail, she clutched a straw hat and beach bag. Despite having liberally applied sunscreen, her skin glowed with a rosy tint. "Thank you so much."

"And thanks to your crew, too," the man added. Bald as an egg, he wore a Hawaiian print shirt, flapping open over his tanned and hairy chest. With two towels slung over one shoulder, he pulled out his billfold, gave Brian a check and added some wadded up bills from his pocket. "The rest of your fee and tips for them," he said, nodding toward Carlos and Jim, making his way down from the upstation. "We'll definitely be back."

"With friends next time, maybe," the woman said. She smiled at her husband. "Or just us again. This was better than our honeymoon cruise. Do you make moonlight trips?"

Brian thought they looked like the perfect couple. Well matched. Happy. Something he'd always wanted for himself, even though he'd believed it to be an unattainable goal. "I can do an evening trip for you," he said. "It'd be a pleasure," he added. He watched the man escort his wife off the boat. He turned away as they walked hand in hand through the throng on the dock.

Jim was right about Kaylen and her business, Brian thought. *He* was the one who was always busy. He worried that if she spent too much time with him, she'd see him for what he really was, and they'd break up. Sometimes, when they were alone out on the water, with her arms wrapped around him and her head resting against his, he knew moments of happiness. But always the doubts crept in.

Even after they made love and she was asleep, curled up against his side, he'd tried lowering the protective walls that shielded him, but found he couldn't leave himself vulnerable. Overwhelmed by emotions, he quickly shored the walls back up.

The meeting with Hal had brought too much crowding in. Uncertainty, disappointment... Brian stopped staring into space. He'd spent way too much time reflecting and regretting over the last few months. Something he hadn't done since leaving Baton Rouge at the age of sixteen.

He ducked instinctively as a soccer ball flew past his head and landed with a plop in the water.

"I'm so sorry!" Standing on the dock, shielding her eyes with her hand, stood a woman and a boy, maybe 8 or 9 years old. "Are you okay?"

"Fine." Brian watched as she lowered her arm to reveal an attractive, concerned face and warm smile. Early to mid-twenties, with a pale complexion. Definitely not local.

"No harm done," he said. "Unless you count the ball. That's gone."

"Mom!" The boy jumped up and down, pointing. "It's leaving. I've gotta get it!" He started toward the edge of the dock.

His mother grabbed the back of his shirt. "Oh no, you don't. Tell the detective you're sorry." She smiled up at Brian again. "You're Sergeant Swift, right?"

Brian nodded. He jumped onto the dock and extended his hand. "And you are?"

"Shelley Summerfield. Another granddaughter. The one they never talk about." She laughed. "I'm one of the two black sheep of the family. My mom's the other. I guess we're trying to get back into the fold." She kept her grip on the boy, who still looked like he wanted to jump off the dock into the water and chase his ball. "This is my son, Teddy. Named after his grandfather. We just moved here from North Dakota. I'm helping my grandparents with the other kids while their mom's working, but I've gotta look for a real job. Grandma thinks room and board's pay enough. I can't run a car on that or buy the things we need."

"We're moving to an apartment right near my school," Teddy said. "I'm gonna play soccer."

"Is that right?" Brian wondered why Shelley was telling him the story of her life.

"I missed my own mom while we were so far away, too." Shelley pushed stray hairs away from her face. "Mel. Have you met her? You two'd get on real well." She smiled widely. "Mom's a pistol."

Brian wasn't sure whether Mel being a pistol was a reference to his career or his personal likes and dislikes. He chose to ignore it and started to edge away. "I should get going."

"I'm a waitress," she said. "Do you know if anyone around here is hiring?"

Brian knew of someone who hired on a regular basis, but he wasn't going to enlighten Shelley he was dating a popular club owner. "Not around the marina," he hedged.

Shelley wrapped her arms around Teddy's neck and gave him an affectionate squeeze. "I could really do with a break. We need to get out on our own, but I don't have a lot of references."

"Mom." Teddy squirmed. "You're choking me."

"Sorry, honey." She let him go.

Teddy watched his ball bob away on the current. "Can we buy me a new one?" He sounded doubtful.

"Maybe grandpa's got another one in the garage," Shelley said. "We'll look when we go home."

"Are we still going out on the boat?" Teddy scratched his lower leg, which started bleeding.

"Stop that," Shelley told him. "Scratching never helps." She looked back at Brian.

"Mosquito bites," she explained. "My mom never said the bugs here were the size of jumbo jets."

"There she is." Teddy pointed, jumping up and down. "We're going. We're going!"

Brian saw a woman striding purposefully toward them. Red-gold shoulder length hair shone like a halo around her very attractive face, an older version of Shelley's. Her tan definitely looked like a Florida native's. She wore tailored shorts and a tight pink top with a low scooped neckline. Large sunglasses shielded her eyes.

She smiled at Teddy and Shelley, took off her glasses slowly, her shirt riding up to expose an equally tanned midriff, and held out her hand to Brian. "Sergeant Swift. I'm Mel Summerfield. So good to meet you. I've followed your recovery in the news, like everyone else in this marina, I'm sure. How are you doing?" One of the spaghetti straps of her top slid partway down her upper arm. She left it there.

Brian saw no tan lines anywhere on her. He questioned how she could possibly be related to the dour, rude Summerfields who owned *Naughty Nautical*. "I'm doing well, thanks." He watched Teddy climb onto the *Nautical*. "I don't think I've seen you around here before, have I?"

"No." She tucked the sunglasses into a big white purse she carried slung over one shoulder and casually slid the strap back up her arm, the motion more a caress than anything else. "I've been living in St. Pete for years. Until Shelley moved back here." She put an arm around her daughter. "We're going to move in together. I can get to know my grandson better."

Shelley looked uncomfortable, but she managed a smile when she looked up at her mother. "We'd better get going," she said. "Teddy'll get cranky if we stay out too late."

"Mom and Dad would wonder where we are, too, and probably get crankier than Teddy." Mel looked at Brian. "I bet they've given you a bit of a hard time, Sergeant. My parents have never gotten over my brother's death. They blamed the police department for not solving his murder." She smiled a little crookedly. "He was my only brother. It was tough on the whole family, but people have to move on."

She handed her purse up to Teddy. "Here, stow this in the cabin, and be careful. I don't want it going overboard, or we'll be diving in after it. My car key's in there." After she stepped onto the boat, she turned and gave Brian a frank once-over. "Very good to meet you. I hope we get to see more of each other."

Brian found himself watching Mel's shapely legs as she climbed behind the wheel and gave himself a mental shake. She looked like potential trouble, and he planned to keep her at arm's length.

He had a feeling their supposedly-random meeting wasn't. Those two women had tried to play him like a violin with sex and innuendos.

Naughty's engine rumbled to life. Shelley untied the moorings. Both women waved as the boat eased out of her slip, like they expected Brian to be watching them. He questioned whether the elder Summerfields knew the *Naughty Nautical* was going out for a cruise. Their strict Sunday afternoon-only boating schedule was being broken without them present.

Naughty came pretty close to the *NTK* before heading into open water. Brian wondered how long it had been since Mel had taken a boat out, and hoped that she wouldn't put a hole in the *NTK's* hull when she came back into port.

CHAPTER FOUR

No DOUBT ABOUT IT, Brian decided. Mel had left him slightly on edge. Partly due to her direct manner, but mostly because of those shapely legs.

Kaylen had continued to wear capris right through the summer. She still hadn't come to terms with the tattoo Tim had inked onto her leg before his murder. Brian decided the only time he got to see her gorgeous thighs were when they were wrapped around his waist. With that thought, the edgy feeling turned into something else entirely.

In desperate need of a cold shower, he fought the visual that had popped into his head and settled up with Carlos, whose mouth gaped open at the sizeable tip he'd been given. Leaving his deck hand to finish cleaning before the caterers arrived to pick up their equipment; Brian went in search of Jim.

Beer in hand, ropy legs crossed at the knees and one foot twitching rhythmically, Jim looked completely at ease as he lounged in a deck chair facing the stern. He'd taken out a soda for Brian, who had abandoned his staunch refusal to control his pain with anything but Advil, and now always took a dose of Vicodin before going either to Physical Therapy or on a charter.

Jim waved away the tip money. "You already paid me more than enough. Give it all to Carlos. Sit down and have a cold one, even if it's pop. We've both earned a break. What a jewel of a day that was." He held out the can.

Brian took it, placed the wadded up bills on the table next to Jim's chair and sat beside his friend. "Yeah," he agreed, popping the top of his soda, which responded with an explosive fizz. He took a quick sip. "Peaceful, calm. No seasickness complaints, the caterers outdid themselves with the food, and we got back into port on time." He clinked cans when Jim held his up in a salute. "Thanks for your help again. I couldn't do these charters without you."

"I'll enjoy crewing even when you *don't* need me anymore," Jim said. "Hope you'll keep me on. Saves fuel and wear and tear on the *Folly.*"

"Hal told me to cut out the charters," Brian said.

He took a long drink of the soda. He missed a beer, good and sharp, chilled to perfection, after a day out on the water. But any kind of booze wouldn't mix well with Vicodin. He told himself he'd almost weaned back to over-the-counter pain relievers during the last couple of weeks, but there were still times when they weren't enough.

Jim's eyebrows rose. "Why would Hal say that?"

"He told me I didn't need to work on anything but my health if I wanted to go back to work anytime soon. I thought the shrink was bad enough, issuing ultimatums."

"They've both got your best interests at heart," Jim said. "Even though you might not see the sense of what they're telling you right now."

"There's a bunch of crap." Unwelcomed anger stirred in Brian's gut. "You're beginning to sound like them. Don't you turn on me, too."

Jim turned his chair around to face Brian. "I'm always in your corner. You should know that by now. But even you have to admit you're a mite too stubborn to listen to good advice sometimes." He paused a moment, evidently monitoring Brian's reaction. "Maybe most times," he added, when Brian didn't respond. "But that's also what's kept you on your feet and functioning since the business with Tim and your injury."

"Damn right it has." Brian felt at least partially validated, after being told off by everyone around him. The self-prescribed authorities on both his medical condition and his life had multiplied as the weeks passed, and he was sick of pontifications.

His anger amplified at the memories of well-meaning but poorly-delivered pep talks and advice to sell the *Need to Know,* retire from MDPD, or even hire a live-in caregiver to help him 'since his left arm was paralyzed.'

"That's not to say Hal's arguments aren't merited," Jim added, destroying his good faith with the next breath. "You've been taking more and more charters lately. You're out of port more than you're in it some weeks. Maybe if you'd rest up more, your pain wouldn't trouble you as much, and you'd get off the narcotics."

"Are you fixing to give me yet another round of advice?" Brian stopped slouching and sat upright. "I'm not a drug addict, Jim. And if helping me out is too much for you, then say so. I'll hire someone else."

"There you go, jumping to conclusions again." Jim grimaced. "Buddy, I'll gladly help you out, any time, any day. But you've been cancelling your P.T. sessions lately to take charters. And I always see the Vicodin coming out of the cupboard before we sail."

"I've tried handling the boat on Advil. Doesn't work well. I'm in pain for hours afterward, and I don't sleep that night."

Brian couldn't stay seated. He mashed his empty can flat against the table, got up and leaned against the rail, right arm folded against his chest. Jim took another sip of his beer, completely unflustered by his friend's agitation.

"As for cancelling P.T. sessions, something's gotta give," Brian said. "I can't cancel my appointments with the shrink or he'll rat on me to Hal. I'll lose business if I keep telling charter clients I'm unavailable." He looked out at the crowded marina, boats bobbing gently on the swell. "With Thanksgiving coming up fast, the charter business is slowing down. If I don't take advantage of all the opportunities this good weather's giving, clients'll forget my business even exists by next spring."

"You won't have time for charters by then," Jim said. "You'll be back wearing your badge and grilling suspects."

"Not if Hal has anything to do with it. He's determined to keep me right where I am; wasting my time at the gun range, fucking with Tim's tenants, and taking charters so I don't go completely crazy."

"I'm going to say it again: If you rested more, you'd get well faster," Jim said.

"Jesus. You *do* sound like Hal today." Brian ran his hand through his hair and felt his fingers unexpectedly snag. "I don't need another lecture. Back off."

"I'm not backing away from anything you need to hear, buddy. It's time you took stock of what's really keeping you from going back to work."

"Give it a rest, Jim. Please. I don't want to get into an argument with you, too." Brian felt like throwing something, anything, but he knew that would only make him look even more out of control.

Jim wasn't going to be silenced. He waved his hand around, as though he was giving a tour of Brian's life. "Things are getting out of control, but you're not seeing it. Like the boat. Stuff's everywhere."

He frowned and pointed to the charts Brian had once treated so carefully. Now they were loosely folded and crammed into pockets beside the seats in the salon.

Brian had to employ his calming techniques twice in one day. "You know damned well I can't put knife-creases in those charts with one hand."

"It's not just the charts. The only time you tidy up below is when you've got a charter or Kaylen's coming over, and then you still pretty much leave most of that to Carlos." Jim jerked his head in the direction of Brian's deck hand, busy packing up the last of the dishes from the clients' lunch.

Carlos glanced up at them, his expression anxious. Jim and Brian had never disagreed in front of him before. He started moving faster, china clinking.

Brian's fraying temper snapped. Jim had overstepped his bounds again, sounding more like a father than a friend. He tossed the calming techniques overboard. "No, I damned well don't," he retorted. "Sometimes my bed's not made. It's not a crime. I close the door so the clients never see it. I always clean up before Kaylen comes over. You *know* how difficult some things are for me, so don't give me a hard fu...," he drew in a deep breath, "a hard goddamned time."

He'd promised Kaylen he'd try to curb his swearing, and Jim would probably report any lapses to her, like any good pissing informant.

Jim didn't even blink. "You never iron anything, these days, either," he said, as though Brian hadn't even spoken. "Even though I gave you a new iron...."

He maintained eye contact despite Brian's darkest warning scowl.

"You look scruffy, too," Jim continued, completely unintimidated. "Your hair's too long. So's that beard. If you weren't so young and good looking, you'd never get half the clients you do, let alone keep Kaylen as a girlfriend."

Brian chose to ignore the comment about Kaylen. She was an even more complex problem than his ongoing battle with MDPD. He preferred to let his temper rip. "Goddamn you, Jim. You interfering, judgmental bastard."

Jim nodded, encouragingly. "Go on. Get it out of your system."

"Out of my system? What do you think this is? A fuckin' intervention?"

"If that's what you want to call it. I'm ready to take whatever you want to get off your chest. It's past time, and you're not opening up to anyone else. It's not just your injury that's got you derailed. Your whole life has been turned upside down, and you're keeping it all inside, pushing us all away when we're here, more than ready to help you heal."

"I don't need anyone's help, pity or do-gooder intentions." Brian felt the tension in his left shoulder climb from painful to biting, like a hot knife turning in the joint. He had to stop and draw deep breaths to keep from grinding his teeth.

Jim jumped right back in. "Everyone needs help at some point." He stayed seated, but he had uncrossed his legs, leaning forward to give Brian an intense and frankly uncomfortable stare.

"I've done without anyone's help for close to forty years," Brian said.

"Which is way too long to be alone." Jim patted the chair across from him. "Sit down. It'll be okay. Everything'll work out."

Brian's anger deflated, like a pricked balloon. Jim's calm, unflustered nature and forthright gaze always seemed to do that to him. He sat. "You're a shit," he said.

"If that's what you want to call your best friend, then I guess I'll have to deal with that label for now." Jim took another soda out of the cooler and offered it. "You might want to put this on the back of your neck before you drink it," he suggested. And then he smiled.

"Before all this happened, I'd have done a lot more than call you a shit," Brian warned. "You know that, right?"

Jim nodded. "I'd probably have lost a few teeth before getting thrown overboard." He looked past Brian and waved.

Brian turned. A group of boaters standing at the rail two slips away waved back and dispersed. He almost shot them the bird, but resisted. He'd done enough damage to his reputation for one day.

"I feel like I'm on the end of a short fuse most of the time," he told Jim, turning back to face his friend. "I'll apologize for some of the things I just said, but not all of them. I've done without a father my whole life. I don't need one now. You're a great friend. The best I've ever had. But don't overstep your bounds like that ever again, or we're through."

"Everyone needs a father, buddy," Jim said. "Even you." He got up. "Your objections are duly noted. We're still figuring out our roles in this friendship of ours, so try not to get so uptight when I hand you advice."

"I'll try, but no guarantees. I'm better left alone, but you and Kaylen won't listen to me when I tell you that."

Jim smiled again and gave him a friendly clap on the right shoulder, invading Brian's personal space like he'd never spoken. Brian fought the impulse to shrug away Jim's hand. The older man's friendship was more valuable than anything else in his life, apart from Kaylen.

Jim stretched and yawned. "Time for me to get washed up. I've got a dinner date at seven. You should be getting ready for a date yourself. Kaylen needs to see a whole lot more of you than this boat does."

He walked over to Carlos on his way to the dock and gave him the wad of money Brian had left on the table. Carlos stared at the bills in total disbelief before wishing Brian a good day and following Jim off the boat.

"See you tomorrow," Jim called. He and Carlos both waved.

Brian waved back, settled into his chair and closed his eyes, dry and scratchy behind the lids. He deserved the drumming headache that had started when he sounded off at Jim. A shower was definitely a necessity, but before going inside, Brian allowed his friend's words to filter through his mind. He wanted to compartmentalize and contest everything Jim had said, but deep down, he knew the truth had been laid out that afternoon. He was fighting against overwhelming odds, trying to regain a life that was as irretrievable as his brother.

And while he was grasping at that lost future, he admitted he was also jeopardizing the possibility of building another. Something completely different, but with infinite possibilities, if he didn't continue fucking them all up.

He *should* be spending more time with Kaylen, but how could he ever measure up to Tim? His younger brother had charmed everyone with whom he came into contact, including her. Brian knew he was severely lacking in the charm department, and wondered whether she drew comparisons with the way Tim had kissed her, the way he had made love to her...

Brian opened his eyes and sat bolt upright. He refused to go to that dark place. Hell resided there, along with unbridled jealousy and self-hatred. He reminded himself that if Kaylen didn't want to be with him, she would have left, and that without Jim's well-intentioned and frequent interference, he would be in sorry-ass shape.

He had never shared his secrets with anyone, but since Tim had dumped him in Kaylen's bed, so much of his private life and inner doubts and misgivings had been turned into an open book. Brian's left hand cramped from its wheel work and the recent tension, adding another discomfort to the knife already sawing away at his shoulder. He massaged his stiff fingers before getting up and going inside.

Walking into the salon, he ran a hand over his beard. Reluctant to admit Jim might have been doing more than picking at him about his appearance, Brian told himself the reason it felt straggly was because it was covered with salt.

He decided to make a pot of coffee before getting cleaned up. While he waited for the brewing cycle to finish, he sat at the breakfast bar to work on some exercises. He tried picking up the lid of the coffee canister. He almost succeeded, but the effort took too much energy, his fingers refused to cooperate, and the lid dropped back onto the polished teak surface.

Shit. That pretty much summed up his life in a nutshell.

His phone rang.

"Hi," Kaylen said. "Are you at the marina, or is this a bad time?"

"No, hon, your timing's great. We docked about thirty minutes ago." The unsettled feeling that had plagued Brian ebbed at the sound of her voice. "I thought you had a meeting with Rob this afternoon, to work on the accounts for the club?"

"We already finished. We decided a meeting with Julio would give us a better handle on ordering for the bar, but that can't happen today. Instead, I set an appointment with someone who wants to use me as a consultant for a new restaurant." She sounded excited. "I think I might like to do it, as long as the project's got decent funding and a good location. Do you have time for a late lunch? I'm pretty hungry, and I should be done with that appointment in an hour."

Brian's spirits took a sudden updraft. "Sounds great. I didn't feel like eating earlier. And I could do with some company—especially yours."

He heard the smile in her voice. "I can pick you up."

He thought about what Jim had said and looked at his crumpled shorts. "No, that's okay. I'll shower and change, then drive over. That'll give you time for your appointment."

"If you're getting naked, I'll cancel and be there in five minutes." She giggled.

"Promises, promises." He checked his watch. "I'll see you around four-thirty."

"Great." Her voice sounded like warm honey.

He wanted to tell her he *really* missed her, but that sounded corny as hell. "'Bye," he said instead.

"'Bye." Now she sounded wistful.

She hung up.

Brian cursed himself for being an idiot, decided to drink his coffee after his shower and walked into the bedroom. He wanted to tell Kaylen how he felt, but somehow the words never came out.

He glanced in the full length mirror on the back of the closet door and stopped. Jim was right—he *did* look scruffy. He'd been hanging out on the boat way too much. His tangled blond hair almost touched his shoulders and the beard, grown originally to cover the scars from the broken glass that had hit his face during the shooting, was more than straggly. If he didn't do something about it, very soon he was going to resemble Rip Van Winkle. An untidy Rip, at that.

He returned to the galley and searched around in the drawers until he found a pair of scissors. Careful not to catch his skin in the blades, he chopped the beard down to a more manageable length before pulling his razor and shaving cream out of the grooming kit he'd stowed under the bathroom sink and lathering up.

What was he doing? He'd turned into some beaten-up version of himself who went to P.T. so he could sweat and strain in a painful effort to regain the use of his left hand and arm. When he wasn't suffering at the clinic, he was using Jim as a physical crutch to keep the boat running and Kaylen to fill the emotional void. He'd become all take and no give.

After managing to give himself a fairly close shave without nicking his face, he turned on the water and stepped into the shower. He'd also better start using that brand new iron Jim had given him. He'd left it in the box and stored it at the bottom of a cabinet, because ironing, like most other things in his life, took too much effort.

No more leeching off everyone around him, he promised himself. Jim's lecture had awakened him from a long nightmare. He decided he was done with mourning, both for Tim and for his job, as well as indulging in self-pity. He scrubbed himself thoroughly and pulled on a bathrobe because, like so many other things he had once taken for granted, wrapping a towel around his waist with one hand was too difficult.

He opened the closet. He'd been living in shorts for the past few months. All but one of Tim's designer suits he'd had altered hung in plastic bags and most of the sports clothes he'd purchased with Kaylen were lined up with the tags still on them. The only times he had put on a suit were for the fights with Hal and infrequent dinner dates with Kaylen. He'd stayed away from her club during open hours, because he wanted to keep their relationship under wraps. He'd wanted her to ease back into her life without complications. Kaylen deserved that. If he hung around Bannisters too often, pretty soon people would be asking how she had become involved with Tim Madison's brother.

Brian chose a pale gray suit and a blue shirt. The last thing he wanted was to look like a bum when he picked Kaylen up. Then he remembered he had to wear a tie to get into the club. *Damn, damn, damn.* He'd have to go find Jim to get the thing knotted.

He opened the closet back up and found several options already loosely tied, hanging on a rack at the side of the door. Wondering who was thinking ahead, he selected one with a pale gray background and faint blue stripes. Pulling the tie over his head, he was able to tighten the knot relatively easily.

Another check in the mirror showed a thinner, dressier version of himself. The pale skin over his chin contrasted with the rest of his face, but a few days in the sun would soon remedy that. The scars on his left cheek were barely visible. Less so than his scarred lip. Splitting it open twice had resulted in a lengthy and uneven healing.

Whatever. He'd survived being shot because Kaylen had stopped him from bleeding to death. *Better scarred than in the cemetery.* He stepped away from the mirror.

Brian wished his psychological scars would heal. Then Fleming would leave him alone. Gathering up his keys and billfold, he locked up the *Need to Know* and walked across the parking lot to his new car, equipped with adaptive controls. Jim took Brian's beloved Camaro out for short spins to keep the battery charged. Her manual transmission barred Brian from driving her anywhere. As he slid behind the wheel of his Mercedes, he wondered again whether he should offer the Camaro to Jim or sell her for whatever he could get. Another depressing thought. She was another symbol of the unavoidable changes in his life.

Damn Tim, he thought. And then he felt guilty, blaming his dead brother for all his troubles.

CHAPTER FIVE

KAYLEN HAD JUST FINISHED her call to Brian when Ziggy Stavros knocked on her partially-open office door.

"Hi." His smile showed two rows of even, very white teeth as she looked up. "Thanks for seeing me on short notice." He stayed in the doorway, silently asking permission to enter.

Kaylen appreciated the gesture. He was respecting her position as Bannisters' owner.

She stood up and extended her hand. "Hi Ziggy. Come in. Your project sounded really interesting."

He crossed the room in long strides and took her hand in a warm, strong grip. Up close, his eyes were the color of rich espresso coffee and almost a match for the curly hair tumbling around his shoulders. His suit, charcoal gray, was as exquisitely-tailored as the ones Tim had worn. His white shirt was conservative, but the yellow and white polka-dotted tie hinted at a nature much more in keeping with his hairstyle.

"So nice to make your acquaintance," he said.

Kaylen was curious. "Is your name really Ziggy?"

He smiled and shook his head, curls bouncing. "No, my given name is Constantine. My brothers nicknamed me when I was little. They said my wild hair looked like Ziggy Marley's."

Kaylen returned his smile. "I used to get teased about my hair, too. My father told me I looked like I'd stuck my finger in a light socket. He had my hair cut really short, and I frequently wore a hat."

She gently pulled her hand away from Ziggy's. It wasn't that he made her feel uncomfortable. On the contrary; it felt like she had known him for years instead of moments.

But she didn't want to give him any false impressions. This was strictly a preliminary business meeting, not a social event.

"How about something to drink? Coffee? Tea?" She gestured toward the kitchenette. "I've got both."

"How about a glass of white wine instead?" Ziggy looked around. "Nice office. My father's is very cramped and full of files. It's behind the bar at the restaurant, so he can keep an eye on the staff at all times through a one-way mirror. He had cameras installed in the kitchen a few months ago, too."

"He doesn't trust his employees, then."

Reluctantly, Kaylen took a bottle of Chardonnay from her wine cooler. She didn't like the idea of drinking alcohol during a meeting. She had a feeling she would have to set the tone and make it formal. Ziggy was way too chatty as well as personable. When she turned around, he was standing behind her desk, checking out the photos of Brian on his boat, with Jim and the boat, and with her arms wrapped around Brian on the dock, in front of the boat. A lot of boat pictures, she thought. They should have photos of themselves in other locations. But the other locations were pretty infrequent, and Brian stayed away from Bannisters.

Not today. Her mood lightened considerably. Today he was coming to pick her up from the club, and they were going to have a leisurely lunch, hopefully followed by lovemaking.

She smiled to herself as she used a bar towel to give two long-stemmed wineglasses a quick polish. She could leave the club in Rob, Julio and Marvin's more than capable hands and spend the night with Brian. If it was on the boat, then so be it. The *Need to Know* was like a third person in their relationship, anyway.

Until Brian returned to active duty. She crossed her fingers after placing the bar towel on the counter and sent out a silent plea for good news. For Brian to have his career back. For him to be able to concentrate more on their relationship, and for his full recovery from the gunshot wound that had stalled so much in his life.

A surge of emotion forced her to keep her back turned while she blinked away tears. She opened a drawer and selected her favorite bottle opener from a neat row of samples left by wine salesmen.

"I hope this is okay." She plastered a smile onto her face and showed Ziggy the bottle before opening it. "I don't keep much in stock back here."

He put down the photo of Brian standing beside the *Need to Know* and walked over to read the label. "According to the wine magazine I just read, it's supposed to be a very good year. I'm trying to study *Wine Advocate,*" he told her. "My father says it's a must if you are in the restaurant business. I see you have a copy on your desk, and *Wine Spectator,* too." He took both bottle and opener from her. "Allow me."

Kaylen reluctantly stood aside and watched him. She didn't want any wine, but she didn't want Ziggy to feel awkward, either, drinking alone. "A small serving for me," she told him as he drew out the cork.

Ziggy poured a bare inch into one of the glasses. Kaylen thought he was over-reacting, and felt suddenly awkward. "So," she said. "What location are you thinking of for the restaurant?"

"We already bought the building." Ziggy picked up the glass by its stem and swirled the wine around before presenting it for her to sample. "*Is* it a good year?" he asked.

Relieved she had misread him, Kaylen swirled the pale liquid again, inhaled the bouquet and sipped, rolling the wine across her tongue. She swallowed a little quickly for a wine connoisseur, but after all, she thought, this was not supposed to be a test of her abilities as a sommelier. Or maybe it was. After all, he was asking her to consult on a new restaurant, and her advice might be sought for stocking the wine cellar as well as recommending optimal pairings of wine and food.

"It *is* a good one," she said.

Ziggy took the glass back and poured two liberal servings. Kaylen wondered if he had ignored her request for a small amount, or whether he was used to drinking a bucket of wine before lunch. She thought about her empty stomach and took a box of crackers out of a cabinet. She tipped some into a dish and offered them to Ziggy, but he shook his head. Kaylen munched, swallowed the cracker and started choking on the crumbs. She took a big sip of wine and a surge of heat followed the cracker down her throat, bringing a flush to her cheeks.

Ziggy pointed to the photos. "Your boyfriend and his father?"

Kaylen cleared her throat. "My boyfriend, yes. But Jim's a friend. They both have boats at the Coconut Grove Marina."

"Ah." Ziggy nodded. "My family has a motor yacht there, too. A hundred footer. A bit large for a short cruise, but my parents like to invite relatives and friends to join them. We had to hire a captain and crew." He picked up the photo of Brian and the *NTK*. "Do you know the size of this one? It looks smaller."

Kaylen wasn't sure if she should take Ziggy's comment as an insult or not. "Fifty feet. Brian had a thirty-eight footer before. I liked that one a lot. Much easier to handle. Older, but that was part of its charm." She thought of the *Destiny* with affection. The first night she'd spent with Brian had been on that boat.

The night he got beaten, she reminded herself, unpleasant memories threatening to well up. She still had flashbacks. Several sessions with a psychologist had taught her some valuable coping techniques, which she would need to use if she didn't steer the conversation away from Brian and the *NTK*. She wasn't planning to spend an hour reminiscing about anything to do with why he was now the owner of a new boat while drinking too much wine and possibly making a fool of herself by crying. She'd been there and done that a few too many times already.

"Have a seat." She sank into her office chair while Ziggy sat on one of the club chairs. "So, you said you bought a building?" She put down the wine glass and ate another cracker.

"Yes."

Ziggy's eyes narrowed a little as he watched her, but he didn't comment about her abruptly clamming up.

"It was a restaurant before, but it had fire damage, so it was very reasonably priced," he added after a few noticeable beats of silence. "My father likes a bargain, and the location's good. People expect the Stavros name to be linked only with Greek cuisine. I thought it might be good to change that, and to increase our bar traffic, too, which you have been able to do very successfully at Bannisters. There's more money in liquor than dinner." Ziggy held out his glass. "Here's to a successful collaboration."

"A bit premature for that, but I'll drink to your success, whether I participate in it or not." Kaylen clinked glasses with his and took a tiny sip of Chardonnay, but a weird feeling had stirred in the bottom of her stomach at the mention of fire damage. "Where's this restaurant located?"

"Close to the Coconut Grove Marina. We seem to be talking a lot about that marina, today." Ziggy swirled his wine, sniffed appreciatively and took another sip. "This really is excellent. I must recommend it to my father."

"It's our biggest seller," Kaylen said automatically. Her mind was buzzing, and it wasn't from the effects of the alcohol.

"You may know of this restaurant, if you frequent the area," Ziggy said. "It used to be called The Hideaway."

Kaylen downed the rest of her wine in one big gulp and stood up, feeling slightly dizzy. She leaned on her desk for support. "This meeting has to be over. I won't get involved with that place. The former owner and I used to be very good friends."

Ziggy rose, too, his dark eyes suddenly sympathetic. "Sam Wilson," he said.

"Yes. My former mentor. He's a criminal. I won't discuss him." Hands shaking, Kaylen tried to put down her empty glass. It tipped sideways on the desk top.

Ziggy scooped up the glass before it rolled off and fell to the floor. "I'm sorry. I do remember reading news accounts about possible arson and Mr. Wilson fleeing the country. But that was several months ago. I thought you wouldn't have a negative reaction now." He reached across the desk and placed his hand over hers. "After all, the restaurant will be completely remodeled. It won't look like The Hideaway. Depending on how much damage was done by the fire, the building may even need to be demolished."

"No; I don't care." Kaylen pulled her hand away as she fought back memories of three murders, of Brian's boat in flames, her panic when she thought he was on board, and of Sam's betrayal.

A sickening feeling churned her stomach, joining the dizziness. She sat back down in a hurry, afraid she was either going to pass out or vomit. Maybe both.

"I had no intention of upsetting you." Ziggy looked worried. He sat down, too. "I have no experience with negotiation. My father was right in telling me not to contact you."

They both turned at the sound of angry voices in the hallway.

"My son is back there!"

Kaylen looked at Ziggy's face. His chin had a noticeable tremor.

"There!" An older man, dark hair liberally streaked with silver, immaculate in a white suit, strode through Kaylen's door, a younger man behind him.

"I tried to stop them." Rob pushed his way past both men and halted their momentum by placing himself in front of Kaylen's desk. "Short of punching them, that wasn't going to happen."

"Ms. Roberts." Ziggy's father sounded both apologetic and volatile at the same time. "I beg your pardon for the interruption, but my youngest son doesn't have the authority to negotiate anything with you." He scowled at Ziggy.

Kaylen saw sweat roll down the side of Ziggy's face. She felt empathy for him. She well knew what a roaring, angry parent could do to a child, regardless of age. She had plenty of memories of Preston Grant, her own father shouting at her on the family farm up in Maine.

She followed her instinct not to be in a subordinate position and stood. "It's okay, Rob," she assured her manager.

Rob's fists were clenched at his sides. He had become very protective of her after all the drama surrounding Bannisters' opening. But she didn't feel any need for protection, despite the threatening demeanor of her latest visitors. Ziggy was the one on the receiving end of the waves of anger, not her.

As she watched, Ziggy's father hid his wrath in an astonishing show of control and turned toward her with an expression of affability that almost made her mouth drop open. Rob unclenched his fists and stepped aside, but warily kept watch.

"I must apologize for this unwarranted intrusion, Ms. Roberts." Stavros smiled, showing teeth almost as white and even as Ziggy's. "I'm Peter Stavros." He shook Kaylen's hand with a grip even firmer than

Ziggy's. "This is my eldest son, Apollo." He gestured toward the man behind him.

Apollo barely glanced at Ziggy, but that glance was filled with contempt. "Ms. Roberts." He inclined his head and held out his hand.

"I don't know what this is about." Kaylen perfunctorily shook the proffered hand while glancing from one visitor to the next. "But I'm not getting into the middle of a family feud."

"No feud, Ms. Roberts." Apollo smiled at her.

Another set of even, white teeth. Kaylen felt like Red Riding Hood, surrounded by deceptively friendly Big Bad Wolves.

"However," Apollo shot another icy look at his brother, "Ziggy should have waited for us, instead of taking this meeting himself."

"Yes." Peter Stavros placed himself in front of the open club chair and sat.

He glared at Ziggy, who sprang out of the other chair. Apollo sat down in his brother's place while Ziggy sank into the background, hovering next to the wine cooler like a vanquished wraith.

"Please." Peter waved, encouraging Kaylen to sit back behind her desk. "May we continue, but this time with my own plans for the new Stavros venture?"

Kaylen watched Apollo's smug expression. He ignored his younger sibling, as though Ziggy didn't even exist. She empathized with Ziggy's humiliation. Peter and Apollo were truly dredging up memories of her father's hurtful and frequently-manifested disappointment in having a daughter instead of a strapping son to help him with the heavy chores.

She sat. "Very well." She locked gazes with Peter. "I'll listen, but let me tell you up front, I'll only act as a consultant for your project if Ziggy's my contact."

All three men looked startled. Peter recovered first. "Let me present my ideas before you make that decision," he suggested in a calmer, less confrontational tone. "Then if you're interested we can work out details agreeable to us both, including Ziggy acting as a liaison."

Ziggy took several steps forward, an expression of shock filling his face. "Papa…"

CHAPTER SIX

KAYLEN DETECTED a slight movement at the corner of her eye. She turned to see Brian standing in the doorway and wondered how long he had been there. She knew she wouldn't have seen him unless he wanted her to do so. One of the many things she appreciated about him. No muscling into her territory unless she asked for help or looked like she was in some sort of physical danger.

She winked at him. Brian's presence always calmed her.

His eyebrows rose in response. He mouthed *'What the hell?'*

Kaylen knew better.

'What the fuck?' was more like it, but so far he'd kept his promises: no lies, and curb the swearing. She smiled broadly and beckoned. "Hi, Brian. Come and join the party. The Stavros family came to talk to me about a consulting proposition for their new business venture."

Rob headed for the door. "I think you've got this in hand now without me. I'll call the electrician to take care of those burned out circuits in the hallway." He nodded at Brian as they passed and closed the door behind him.

Ziggy rushed forward. "Pleased to meet you." He energetically pumped Brian's hand. "I saw the photos on Kaylen's desk. You must be her boyfriend. You're a detective, I believe. Haven't I seen you on the news?"

"Yes, but I haven't been newsworthy for a while. You've got a good memory." Brian managed to pull his hand out of Ziggy's grasp. "And you are?"

"My youngest son, Constantine," Peter Stavros said.

"People never call me that." Ziggy avoided looking at his father. "I'm Ziggy."

"Good to meet you." Brian smiled briefly. He eased around the desk to stand beside Kaylen's chair.

Kaylen's attention shifted from the Stavroses now Brian had left the relative gloom at the entrance to her office. The first thing she noticed was his chin. He'd shaved! *Was that a sign he'd returned to active duty?*

Her pulse sped up. His hair, although the same overgrown length, now rested on the collar of an immaculately-tailored suit that molded his body in such a way, her breath caught in her throat.

A flush crept up her neck, and it had nothing to do with any hastily-drank glass of wine. She wished the Stavros clan were anywhere but right in front of them. She wanted to throw her arms around Brian's neck and nestle her cheek against his without feeling the roughness of that beard, to kiss him and revel in the softness of his lips without the inter-ference of a moustache. She wanted to run her hands all over that exquisite suit and feel his rock hard body beneath…

Kaylen pressed the heel of one shoe onto the toes of her other foot, the momentary pain redirecting her focus to the three other men inside her office.

"I'm Peter Stavros, the restaurateur," he told Brian. "I own The Corinthian. You may have heard of it, or walked past when you are on the beat."

Why had Peter's tone shifted from cordial to icy? Kaylen felt more flustered than she had with Brian's appearance. She cringed at the insult so easily delivered it almost could have been missed. She knew Brian's detective status left walking a beat far in his past. There was also a subtle suggestion that he couldn't afford the likes of The Corinthian. The rude-ness puzzled her.

Peter might be correct in guessing Brian had probably never been inside The Corinthian, but it wasn't because he couldn't afford Peter's eatery. Rather, it was because Brian's culinary tastes started at fast food burgers and stopped at an occasional Mexican dinner, something Peter certainly couldn't know. Between the poverty of Brian's childhood and the eat-on-the-run lifestyle of his adult years, Kaylen knew Greek restaurants weren't anywhere on his wavelength. She hadn't tried to change his mind by insisting he move out of his gastronomic comfort zone. She figured he'd had enough adjustments to make in his life over the months since Tim's murder without being asked to revamp his diet.

"I know of the place," Brian said, his tone and expression neutral.

He shifted his attention to Kaylen, and she felt the dismissal of Peter Stavros as much as she knew Peter did.

Brian looked over at Ziggy. "So what are you trying to cook up with Kaylen, no pun intended?"

Kaylen didn't know why she'd felt defensive of Brian, even momentarily. He might not have his brother's charm or social graces, but it would take a lot more than rude Peter Stavros to make him feel insecure. He'd also brought Ziggy into the conversation as more than a peripheral observer, which Kaylen appreciated and knew Ziggy must, too.

"Well..." Ziggy seemed to have lost the ability to finish a sentence after she'd dropped the bombshell of insisting he be the front man for any further discussions with his family. "I...that is to say, we..."

"We were discussing me acting as a consultant on a new restaurant venture the Stavroses are putting together," she said, carefully easing the attention away from Ziggy. "Very preliminary. In fact, I was leaning toward refusing." She rocked back in her chair and saw Ziggy's expression change from expectant to hangdog. Again, his desolation tugged at her emotions. Kaylen felt herself waffling, despite her dislike of both Peter and Apollo, or her aversion to even seeing the burned-out remains of Sam's restaurant, much less becoming involved with its reincarnation.

"You haven't heard my own vision for The Hideaway yet," Peter said. "Perhaps this is a bad time for such a detailed conversation. You obviously had other plans with your...uh... friend, that are far more important than any highly lucrative business proposition I had for you this afternoon."

His tone was a rebuke. Kaylen got up. "Since you feel this was a waste of your time, the meeting's over. I had a few minutes to talk with Ziggy before Brian arrived. My plans didn't include an extended discussion with three people who aren't even on the same page."

"And we didn't have a contingency plan for interruptions from your boyfriend." Apollo stood, the club chair scraping against the floor. "A crippled detective who took a bullet and got a commendation must take precedence over any business in this club."

Peter looked quizzically at Apollo.

"He shut down an entire drug cartel, single-handedly," Apollo explained, his words sounding more patronizing than informative.

"That's incorrect," Brian said. "It was my brother's information that brought the cartel to justice. So you're mistaken as well as...," he paused and his eyes glittered as they rested on Apollo, "...fucking rude." He turned toward Kaylen. "Sorry, hon."

Ziggy's intake of breath was audible in the ensuing silence.

Peter found his voice first. "Apollo, what is wrong with you?" He asked his eldest son, as though his own remarks had been far from insulting. "I thought you looked familiar," he told Brian. "It's rare to meet a hero." He looked at Kaylen. "You must be very proud."

Kaylen didn't know what to say. She couldn't figure out the dynamics in this strangely dysfunctional family.

Totally unexpectedly, Ziggy laughed. "I'm sure you feel very safe when the detective's around," he said, smiling widely at Kaylen. Suddenly, he winked.

What a family, Kaylen thought, completely astonished. *The snob, the brown-noser and the inappropriate flirt.* She had lost all control of that meeting, if she'd even thought she'd really had it in the first place.

"I definitely do feel safe," she said. "When Brian's not around, my staff watches out for me." She placed both hands on her desk and leaned forward. "Look, I'm not really sure what all of you have in mind, but obviously, you're not in agreement with who should be giving me the details, or who I'd even be dealing with." She looked from Peter to Apollo and back again. "You also have an appalling lack of manners, especially when you came here uninvited."

"Ziggy knew he wasn't authorized to come here by himself and negotiate anything," Peter said. "Apollo is my second in command with all business matters."

"To do with The Corinthian." Ziggy sounded defensive. "I thought you were going to give me more responsibility with the new restaurant. It was my idea to make seafood the main focus of the menu, and I was also the one who suggested making the bar more of a feature than it is at The Corinthian."

"I realize that, Ziggy." Peter waved his hand dismissively. "But you don't have the experience to helm a project of this magnitude. Apollo does. We'll find a smaller, more appropriate venture for you at this stage in your training. Perhaps a food cart."

Ziggy initially looked as though he couldn't decide whether to jump up and down like a five-year-old or stomp out of the room. But as his father continued to give him a look of extreme displeasure, Ziggy's face took on a look of defeat that broke Kaylen's heart. She felt aligned with his frustration.

"I liked Ziggy's ideas," she told Peter. "I would never deal with Apollo, or you for that matter, after your offensive behavior and hostility." She stood up straight, very determined not to fold her arms across her chest or look in any way intimidated by the glares from Peter and his firstborn. "You can show yourselves out."

Peter blinked, as though he couldn't believe what he'd just heard, and rose slowly to his feet.

"I'm going to get a beer and chat with Rob," Brian said. "You know where to find me if things get rowdy again." He grinned at her as he walked out the door.

Kaylen relaxed. The disrespectful and strange Stavros family would be gone in moments, and she'd be able to tell Brian that things were going to get *really* rowdy after they'd eaten and she had him alone in a bedroom, whether it was on the *Need to Know* or at her condo. Very rowdy indeed, she decided, thinking of his smooth face and that awesome suit.

CHAPTER SEVEN

KAYLEN SNUGGLED CLOSER and Brian pulled the comforter over them both. "It's colder on the boat," he said. "You're gonna regret staying the night."

"Uh uh." Her arm came across his chest and held him close. "We can always crank up the heat. Besides, you'll keep me warm." She kissed his neck, her lips soft and inviting.

A thrill shot through him. He loved the languid caresses she gave after lovemaking, when she was half-asleep and draped across him. She felt like an erotic blanket that night, one long leg thrown across his hips, breasts pressing against his chest, and her face nestled in the crook of his neck.

"Sure you didn't feel cheated by picking up take-out?" he asked.

Lunch had turned into a quick hunger-sating meal in the *NTK's* salon before they pulled off their clothes and fell onto Brian's bed in a tangle of arms, legs and mouths. In the two hours since they'd arrived on the boat, they'd made love twice. Amazingly, he felt himself hardening again as her fingers drifted across his chest and circled one flat nipple.

"No way," she said. "This is where I wanted to be as soon as I saw you. I don't know what prompted you to shave, but I want you to know how much I appreciate not getting scraped. Anyone who says beards are soft has never touched yours. Not that I would allow anyone else to touch it."

Kaylen's lips left his neck, drifted across his cheek and settled on his mouth. Her kiss started light but deepened quickly, her tongue meeting his. She shifted on top of him, arching her back and rising up. She teased him, straddling his hips and sitting upright, her breasts rising as she lifted the hair from her shoulders and pulled it into a knot on top of her head. She reached for a rubber band on the end table and wrapped it around the knot to anchor it.

"My only regret is that we were both so hungry, we had to stop to eat." She giggled, the sound light and airy, filled with fun. The palms of her hands ran down his body as she inched lower. She rimmed his belly button first with one index finger, then with her warm tongue. Her breasts brushed against him, the nipples erect.

"You're planning on killing me this evening if you're going for three times," he said, but he was already reaching for her as she rocked gently against him.

"You know, if we moved in together, we could enjoy ourselves on a regular basis. Maybe I wouldn't be so demanding then. I can't get enough of you, and I've got to make up for lost time when I only see you a couple of days a week." She kissed him again, without any trace of gentleness.

Brian welcomed the newly-aggressive Kaylen. She'd found she really enjoyed initiating sex, and it turned them both on regardless of how tired they were. But behind her playful aggression that evening, he sensed more than a desire for intimacy. He detected a note of desperation, even sadness.

No doubt a result of the taxing meeting with the Stavroses, he decided as he succumbed to passion. He didn't comment on the subject of moving in together. Kaylen had broached that topic the last few times they had been together, and obviously, she wasn't going to let it drop.

He'd talk to her tomorrow, he thought, as he gripped one slender hip and the rhythm began.

The tempo of Kaylen's breathing increased. She started making soft noises.

"Take that damned rubber band out of your hair," he told her. "I want it all over you and me."

"You do, huh?"

Movement ceased. She leaned over and flipped on the lamp, bathing the cabin with its soft radiance.

"You're swearing again," she said, but she smiled at him. "Makes me know you're losing your cool. I like that."

She tugged and the band came loose. Her hair tumbled down, cascading across her shoulders, gliding around her face.

"Better?" She wriggled provocatively.

"Yeah. Much." He ran a handful of thick chestnut curls through his fingers. "Now we're gonna make your hair wet, sweaty and tangled."

"Oh, yes," Kaylen said. "We sure are."

CHAPTER EIGHT

RIGHT AFTER KAYLEN finished her first mug of coffee the following morning, Brian knew he had underrated her tenacity. Dressed casually in a pair of tight black pants and a red open-knit sweater over a black lace camisole she had left on board the last time she had visited, she looked very much at home on the banquette.

It was a blustery day, clouds playing peekaboo with the sun. A constant background drone of metal rigging slapped against masts, competing with gentle creaking as the *Need to Know* lifted and fell rhythmically at her moorings.

"So what happened at your meeting with Hal?" she asked.

Brian had kept the conversation light while they prepared breakfast, in the hope she wouldn't talk about filling up his limited closet space with her clothes or ask him to start spending more time at her condo. But while Kaylen *might* be willing to drop the subject of cohabitation, she wasn't going to let his meeting with Hal skate by her. Where his job with MDPD was concerned, she was like a worrisome terrier.

Brian stuck to basics: "I failed my proficiency by a slim margin. Hal refused to put me back on active duty."

"I thought so." Kaylen placed her empty mug back on the table. "When you didn't call." She scooted a crust of toast around her plate.

"You know, it wouldn't have hurt you to call and tell me that yesterday. It's important to me, too."

He put down his own mug, still half full but cooling rapidly. "Hal made me angry. We didn't part on good terms. Then Jim brought the subject up on the way back to port, and I jumped all over him, too. I'd had enough discussions about my shortcomings by the time I got to the club."

"Oh, honey." Kaylen slid over next to him and put her arm around his shoulders. "I'm so sorry."

Brian stiffened. He hated commiserations, even from Kaylen.

She sensed his withdrawal and only held on tighter. She kissed his cheek, her hand sliding over his as it rested on the table. "You're so close," she said. "It's only a matter of time."

"Time that's running out." He sighed, resigned to not pulling away from her.

She'd damn well follow him if he did. He was sure of it. Shaking off Kaylen was impossible, and he really didn't want to distance himself from her. The last few months, she had turned his life into something so much better, he felt like pinching himself to make sure he was awake. He didn't plan on ruining it by being surly or flat out rude, like those damn people in her office yesterday.

"You're making progress," she said.

Brian shook his head. "Remember what Doc West said—whatever I've got back in six months is the end of it. I'm over halfway there, with a weak arm and a useless hand. If I can't improve my proficiency with my right, then I'll be out of a job." Saying it aloud seemed to make that six month deadline creep even closer.

"Hal said that?" Kaylen's eyes widened. "God, that's horrible."

"No, it's the truth, that's all."

Brian looked at their hands. He could feel the pressure of hers, but the sensation was dulled in places, like his had fallen asleep and needed shaking around to restore circulation. His grip was still fucked, too.

"Hal offered me the Cold Case Squad," he told her reluctantly. Just the thought of it made him angry again. "A damned desk job. Like that's supposed to appeal to me." He gently pulled his hand away from hers.

Kaylen stared at him. "He offered you the squad? Heading it up?"

"Yeah."

"That's a promotion, isn't it?"

Her expression had taken on a look of hope he hadn't seen since the day he had gone to her apartment to tell her she wasn't in danger any longer, and he believed they had something more than friendship between them. But he couldn't raise her hopes when his were so dashed.

"A back-handed one. More like a compromise." He had trouble looking at the disappointment flooding her face as she heard the resignation in his voice. "Makes Hal feel better about himself, and maybe keeps me busy an' off his back." Brian couldn't sit still any longer. "I'm gonna check the lines." He slid off the banquette and stood. "Wind's picking up, and I wanna make sure everything's tight."

He walked out of the salon into a biting wind, Kaylen right behind him.

"It's freezing out here." She shivered, but wrapping her arms around herself, she continued to follow him. "What's your problem with the position?"

"Cold Case is pushin' paper around. Looking for somethin' that got missed. Evidence gets lost or discarded. Witnesses die. It's thankless." He pulled on one of the lines, found it secure and moved on.

"Not for the families and friends of those murdered people, it's not."

Kaylen's teeth were beginning to chatter, but she continued shadowing him as he checked the remaining ropes. The few people on the dock all wore windbreakers and knitted hats. A couple of them waved as they passed and Brian nodded to them. Kaylen got in front of him before he could climb off the boat.

"Those people were killed by someone. They need justice," she said. "You could get it for them. Tim's case still hasn't been solved. If he wasn't related to you, how hard would the detectives be working on it now, when they've got more recent cases with witnesses who can still remember what they ate that day, who they met and what they saw that looked out of place?"

"That's damned unfair, Kaylen, an' you know it." Brian's ready temper threatened to flare.

"It's nothing of the sort." She stood her ground. "Those people whose files are in Cold Case have just been dead longer. They're still murder victims."

She touched Brian's cheek with a hand as cold as ice. He flinched. It was like one of those victims had reached out from the grave. "Christ, Kaylen." He couldn't watch her shivering. "Let's go back inside and get you warmed up. To hell with the lines. If we hit Jim's tub, I can take the griping."

"What if you hit the other one? You don't get on with the Summerfields."

He steered her back inside, closed the door and turned up the heat. "I'll throw money at them." He shrugged, winced as pain slammed into his shoulder and bit back a curse. "I've got that, at least." He hated the venom in his tone, but he needed some space from her questions and a dose of pain medication. It was time for Kaylen to go home.

"You've got a lot more than money these days." She sounded offended, but as she gathered up their breakfast dishes, evidently not enough to leave immediately.

He'd hurt her, yet again. Something she never deserved, Brian sharply reminded himself. She'd been his biggest cheerleader and supporter since his injury. Even bigger than Jim, which was saying a lot, he thought, still amazed by their refusal to be put off by his caustic manner. Instead of allowing himself to say the first thing that came into his head at that moment, he paused before delivering yet another zinger.

Fleming had told him to use phrases that validated people's feelings. He needed to use one of them right then, unless he was planning to alienate Kaylen and her good intentions.

"I've got a whole lot more," he said, carefully watching her expression, which was closed and defensive. "I've got you. And when you're not letting me know what a pain in the ass I am, you make me very happy."

Her face brightened. *Good.*

"Then make me a promise," she said.

Well, so much for fucking tact. Fleming's advice had landed him on shaky ground again.

"Another one?" He tried to make his tone light, but she started frowning.

Damn it; she always wanted more than he was capable of giving.

"Yes. It's what people do when they're in a good relationship." Kaylen placed her cold hand on his bare arm that time. "And we are, Brian, whether you believe it all the time or not."

And then she nestled up against him, her breath warm against his ear, her arms sliding around his waist, trapping him. He remembered a time when she would have waited for him to initiate contact, and was glad she no longer did, even if he wasn't always comfortable with so much closeness, like right at that moment.

He would have preferred her to become angry and leave the boat, but somehow, she saw right through his defense mechanisms, like she was channeling Fleming. Kaylen was beginning to know how to diffuse his anger, interpret his moods and adjust her behavior to them. She was one smart woman, he thought, admiring her tenacity and thanking her silently for refusing to back down and give him his space at a time when he really didn't need to be alone with his doubts and frustrations.

Her height could be disconcerting. Instead of looking up at him, she was eye-to-eye when she raised her head, and her gaze was direct and unwavering.

"I want you to consider Hal's offer. Think about it really hard before jumping to a refusal." She shook him lightly. "Talk to Jim if you can't talk to me. Or Mills. Even one of the other detectives in your squad. You can't always go it alone. I thought you'd learned that much, but you always surprise me, and sometimes not in a good way."

"Oh, hon. You don't know what you're askin'…"

"I love you," she interrupted. "I was trying to hold off telling you, hoping you'd say it first, but I can't see the use of not sharing my feelings with the one person I absolutely should be telling everything, anytime I need to."

Brian had trouble getting his breath. He wasn't sure if he felt stifled or elated. The very thought of Kaylen falling in love with him was so foreign; he couldn't seem to grasp the concept.

She was watching him intently, trying to gauge his reaction.

He couldn't get any words out. Inside, his emotions were churning in a way they hadn't since his brother was found dead in the Everglades. When he'd had a complete meltdown in front of Hal—twice, he reminded himself. And then again at Tim's funeral, with Kaylen holding him.

He felt her arms fall away from him. Then he watched her pick up her purse from the end of the breakfast bar and pause, watching him.

"You've got a lot to think about," she said. Unshed tears sparkled in her eyes. "You know where to find me when you've made those decisions, but don't wait too long, or I'll feel humiliated as well as alienated." Then she bit her lip and turned away. She walked rapidly out the door without looking back or waving, as she usually did when she left the boat.

Brian turned away himself, to stare at whitecaps racing across the water beyond the *NTK's* stern.

He'd really messed things up now. Shit!

CHAPTER NINE

THIRTY MINUTES AFTER KAYLEN LEFT, Brian pulled himself together enough to finish making sure the *NTK* wasn't going to swing around and hit either Jim's *Fanciful Folly* or the Summerfields' *Naughty Nautical*.

He still felt numb and off-kilter, and definitely not in the mood to talk to anyone.

"Glad to see you're making sure your boat's not going to smack mine." Ted Summerfield's grouchy tones boomed out as he walked onto the dock from the parking lot.

Of all people. Brian swore profusely under his breath. "Good to see you're here to take care of your own boat." He tried hard to keep the animosity out of his voice. "Looked like Mel needed more practice when she took the *Naughty* out yesterday. She mightn't have tightened the lines enough when she brought the boat back, either."

"She took the *Naughty* out?" Summerfield looked shocked. "By herself?"

"No. Shelley and Teddy were with her."

Ted Summerfield's complexion paled. "They shouldn't have done that. Mel hasn't been at the helm for years. We had a little fishing boat she handled fairly well. But this bigger one's harder to steer. They could have gotten in trouble…Teddy could have fallen overboard…"

Ted didn't look at all well.

"Why don't you come and have a cup of coffee?" Brian suggested. "I'll help you check the lines afterward."

Ted nodded. He took a small pill box from an inside pocket of his windbreaker and slipped a tablet under his tongue. "Nitro," he said.

"Come on." Brian took his arm and steered him onto the *NTK*. "Let's get you out of the cold."

Ted sat and looked around the salon. "Very nice. I bet you like this one a whole lot better than your old boat." He shrugged out of his coat.

"I still miss the *Destiny*." Brian walked into the galley. "But with Kaylen staying over now, it was gonna be too small for both of us, even if it hadn't burned."

"Short on space for all those clothes women want to bring with them." Ted nodded, like he knew all there was to know about women.

Brian didn't disagree. Ted's color had improved from pasty to slightly pink. "Should you have coffee after taking Nitro?"

"Probably better make it decaf if you have it." Ted rubbed his hands together. "A good warm drink would really hit the spot."

"Sorry we got off on the wrong foot." Brian kept an eye on Ted while he poured water into the coffeemaker.

Ted nodded. "Me, too. I know I sound like a grouch most of the time. That family of mine is enough to make any sane man wonder why he ever got married." He stretched out his legs. "You're the sensible one. Keeping that beautiful girlfriend just that—a girlfriend. No responsibilities other than those you've got right now." He smiled. "Wish *I* could have taken early retirement."

Brian almost dropped the canister of decaffeinated coffee he was getting out of a cabinet. "I haven't retired. I'm out on disability until my arm heals."

Ted watched him pry the lid off the canister and fill the coffeemaker. Brian felt completely self-conscious and spilled grounds all over the counter. He bit back yet another curse. Good thing he hadn't promised not to swear under his breath.

"How much longer's that going to take?" Ted asked. "You've been off work for a while now."

"Damned if I know." Brian pushed the button to set the brewing cycle in motion. "I'm mulling over a couple of options right now."

"Options are good." Ted nodded again. "I had none, myself. Once I was diagnosed with a bad ticker, I was pretty much forced to retire. I had a job in a plant, running machinery. Bad place to have a heart attack. People's lives depended on me keeping my attention on what I was doing." He found some mark on the tabletop and rubbed at it with one large, blunt thumb. "So I exchanged one racket for another." He made a sound like a wheezing snort. "From deafening plant machinery to a pack of grandchildren. Believe me, it's a toss-up which is worse."

"I hear you on that one. I can't even imagine what it must be like having children underfoot." Brian took mugs out of the cabinet. They were all neatly lined up by size and color. *Kaylen,* he thought. The living part of his quarters had never looked so orderly. Maybe he should have her tidy the bridge to shut Jim up.

What would come next if he agreed to Kaylen moving in? He stared at the coffee rapidly filling the carafe and tried to imagine life with another human in his personal space.

She'd do a lot more than tidy cabinets. She'd want to get married, and then she'd bring up the subject of children, even though she knew he didn't want any.

No repeats of his own childhood, he thought grimly. Brian had no idea how he'd react to a crying baby, let alone a screaming toddler or a willful teen. Would he turn into his abusive stepfather? He refused to ever take that chance.

Enough introspection, he told himself. He saw a packet of cookies between the cups and the coffee canisters. Chocolate chip with walnuts. His favorite kind. Kaylen must have brought them over. Her little touches were beginning to invade his space whether she lived with him or not, and to his own surprise, he suddenly decided that didn't make him feel trapped or annoyed. He slit the packet open by stabbing it with a knife and put some cookies onto a plate, which he took over to the table.

Not so long ago, he'd have put the whole packet on the table. *Kaylen was rubbing off on him. He was getting soft, or domesticated, or some such shit.*

"Thanks." Ted took a cookie and bit into it, munching loudly. "Boy, these are tasty." He finished the cookie and took another. "Feels good to talk to another guy. I've got so many women around me right now, I feel hen-pecked." He accepted the mug of coffee Brian took over to him.

"Cream? Sugar?"

"Nope. Black's fine." Ted was eating a third cookie. "Cheers." He crammed the rest of the cookie into his mouth and lifted the mug.

Brian lifted his own mug. It seemed like the makings of a weird day. First Kaylen had told him she loved him. Now he was having coffee and cookies with someone who had barely given him the time of day before that morning. He sat and sipped.

"Shelley told me she and Mel moved back to Miami to help you and your wife with the grandchildren," Brian said.

"They did, bless them." Ted put down his mug. He looked longingly at the cookies but didn't take another. "The wife's been doing her best, but having four children around at our age hasn't been easy. Those kids are five, seven, nine and almost eleven. We were glad to send them home after having them for an afternoon, but now they're with us twenty-four hours a day unless they're in school. And we recently added Teddy to the mix. I can't wait for the five-year-old to go to kindergarten next year. She just missed the deadline for this school year." He shook his head, and the corner of his mouth sagged. "By three days."

"Sounds like me missing my proficiency on the firing range," Brian said. "A miss is as good as a mile on both counts."

They chatted companionably for a while about fishing, boating and the state of the economy.

"Wish my youngest daughter hadn't decided to remarry," Ted said. "And then have four kids followed by yet another divorce. Her ex picked up and moved out of state. Alaska of all places. We haven't had much contact with him since. He sends money, but not enough to keep their lifestyle intact. She let the house go back to the bank and moved in with us. Thank goodness we've stayed in our family home all these years; otherwise we wouldn't have had the room."

"So how come you and your wife are babysitting?" Brian asked.

"My daughter, Alice, works. She's a bank teller. Needs the income and the health benefits. She's trying to provide for the youngsters with life insurance and one of those 401K things, but it's real hard on her."

"Hard on you all." Brian took another sip of his coffee. *How was it*

Kaylen's tasted better? Maybe because this was decaf, which he rarely drank. "What happened to your son? Mel said he'd died."

Ted put down his coffee. "Murdered in a botched robbery at a grocery store he managed in Tampa. Years back. The wife's never gotten over it. The police department gave us all a bit of a rough time, and then they let the case go colder than a goddamned tit in an ice storm, if you'll pardon my French. Anyway, it's all water under the bridge some days, but others..." Ted blinked and wiped his eyes with one of the paper napkins Kaylen had left neatly piled at the back of the table, along with salt and pepper and the hot sauce Brian liked. "You never get over losing a family member." He looked at Brian. "I guess I don't have to tell you that. You probably know it more than most."

CHAPTER TEN

"BRIAN, your phone's turned off or busted." Jim walked into the *Need to Know's* salon and stopped abruptly when he saw Ted Summerfield.

Brian got up from the banquette. "I think you know Ted already."

Jim nodded, barely making eye contact with Brian's guest. "You've got a pile of messages from tenants at Tim's buildings. I stopped by the office and the manager gave them to me."

Ted checked his watch. "I'd better go. I told the missus I'd be back by now."

"You go on home," Brian said. "I'll check the lines for you."

Ted smiled. "Thanks, so much. I'm going to have a chat with Mel and Shelley."

"Good thinking." Brian returned Ted's smile before his new acquaintance walked out the door, his back slightly bowed, his steps slow. Ted held onto the *NTK's* rail and stepped onto the swim platform. He looked slightly unsteady, and for a moment Brian thought he was going to have to sprint outside to save Ted from falling into the water, but thankfully, Ted recovered his equilibrium, stepped onto the dock and waved before walking away.

Jim came over to stand beside Brian. He jerked his head in Ted's direction. "There's something I never thought I'd see; Ted Summerfield having coffee with you on the boat. What's going on? Did the sky fall in the night and somehow I didn't notice?"

"He's got a bad heart. I thought he was going to pass out and need a 9-1-1 call an hour ago."

"Oh." Jim put the message stack on the counter. "You want me to help you check his moorings?"

"That'd be a nice gesture on your part."

"Smart ass." Jim chuckled. "But you'd better see to your phone and those messages first. I could do with a cup of coffee, anyway." He made a beeline for the coffeemaker.

"It's decaf," Brian warned.

"You? Drinking unleaded?" Jim took a mug out of the cupboard.

"Didn't think it wise to give Ted's heart too much of a jolt."

Brian turned on his phone. He hadn't wanted or expected to be disturbed during Kaylen's visit, but forgetting to turn it back on afterwards was a mistake he'd better not repeat. He checked his messages. Sure enough, there were 10 new ones. Tim's crappy buildings were always in need of maintenance, and Kaylen's visit meant he'd probably left at least a couple of tenants without some service they thought they should be enjoying, if that was a word he could even use in regard to Tim's real estate holdings.

"I hate being a slumlord." He checked the handwritten messages against the ones on his phone before making calls.

Luckily, they all corresponded, with three from tenants in the same building and four other calls from one tenant at another location...a number familiar to Brian. It belonged to a crotchety eighty-year-old man with poor eyesight who kept thinking the reflections from swaying branches outside his windows were actually bugs crawling on his walls. The man didn't speak English and Brian's rudimentary Spanish was less than understandable to his tenant, who also had bad hearing. Brian circumvented frustration by calling Rob and explaining the situation.

"Sure," Rob said. "No problem, Brian, you know that. I'll run by his apartment and take some groceries, too. That always calms him down."

"You need more money?"

It was a familiar scenario for both of them. Brian had understood the worth of gifting groceries after sending Tim's nosey neighbor, Mrs.

O'Grady, out to shop while he broke into Tim's apartment when his brother went missing. A woman who rarely exited her apartment was dressed, down a couple of flights of stairs and into a cab within fifteen minutes of the call telling her she'd won a drawing.

"Nah," Rob said. "If I go over the sixty dollars you gave me last month, I'll send you an invoice. I know you're good for it." He laughed. "I swear you're paying that old guy to live in your building instead of the other way around."

"He's got no money to go anywhere else, and that place has been his home for the last twenty years," Brian said. "Hopefully, the neighborhood won't turn around so fast it makes more sense for me to sell the land and let the buyer tear down the building. I'd like Mr. Pacheco to die in familiar surroundings, even if he thinks he's sharing them with cockroaches."

"You and your brother, you're good men." Rob said.

Brian figured Rob was referring to the tenants' stories of Tim helping them out financially on a fairly frequent basis. A habit Brian had continued. Praise always sat awkwardly on him. Luckily, Rob hung up before he had to figure out a response.

Jim had finished his coffee and was rinsing out the mugs. He smacked his lips. "Not bad for decaf. I'll get started on the lines. As long as Mrs. Summerfield's not in the vicinity of the *Nautical*, I'm okay. Otherwise, you wouldn't get me anywhere close. That woman's a dragon." He zipped his jacket up. "I'll leave you to make the rest of your calls."

He laughed a little too gleefully for Brian's taste on the way out. Resigned to an unpleasant next few minutes, Brian ran down the list according to the times the calls came in and listened to repeated rants about plumbing issues from three tenants in the same building. One definitely needed a plumber to fix a cracked pipe, but the other two, a leaky faucet and a stopped-up toilet, Brian could have fixed himself if he'd had two good hands and sufficient patience. Lacking both, he called in a plumber he seemed to have on retainer before joining Jim outside.

"I'll never get the hang of all this," Brian said.

"All what?" Jim tut-tutted over the loose moorings that had the *Naughty Nautical* rocking and swinging as well as bucking on the increasing swell. "I thought Ted Summerfield had more sense than this."

"Ted wasn't the one who took the boat out last. And I mean Tim's businesses. I'm no mogul."

"Maybe not, but you're beating yourself up for no reason." Jim secured one rope and moved to the next. "You'll figure things out. Just watch that the manager you hired keeps his hands out of the pot."

"It's a big pot." Brian walked over to check the *NTK's* hull. She could easily have been damaged by the *Naughty Nautical's* loose moorings, but luckily for the Summerfields, everything looked intact.

The pot was even bigger than anyone but he and Kaylen knew. The attaché case filled with Tim's escape money was still undeclared and undiscovered except by them. Even Jim didn't know what the case had held, and he'd minded it for weeks after the roundup of cartel members started.

Brian had finally decided to stash the contents in a safe deposit box he'd rented in Savannah, Georgia. The money worried him frequently. He wondered if it was drug money, either syphoned off by Tim or collected as fees for courier work his brother had done for the cartel. Until Brian figured out its origins, he'd leave it at the bank. He already had so much more than he'd ever need, as well as the headaches to go with the completely unexpected windfall from Tim's will.

"Are you okay?" Jim asked. "You're even more preoccupied than usual. I haven't seen you like this since, well, since Tim's case wrapped up." He watched Brian with concerned eyes.

"Yeah. I'm okay." Brian ran a hand over his chin, feeling strangely exposed without the beard.

Jim didn't look convinced, but he shrugged. "I'll be back late afternoon if you want to talk. I'm going to get cleaned up and take Vera to lunch," he said, referring to a waitress he'd met at one of his favorite sandwich shops in Coconut Grove and recently started dating. He dusted minute specks of lint off his jeans. "Then I've got a two o'clock appointment with a prospective client the agency wants me to check out. Some woman who wants her husband followed. She thinks he's cheating on her." He shook his head. "Seems that's all I hear these days...men or women cheating on their partners. I thought I'd be doing something more meaningful as a PI."

"You watch yourself," Brian said. "Those people are usually pissed off and out for revenge. You could get shot, and it'd be a toss-up whether it was the husband or wife who put a hole in you. Whoever's got the most to lose."

"Listen to you...Mr. Sunshine." Jim shook his head. "What are *you* doing this afternoon?"

"Going to the range. I'm not giving up. Hal can hang up *that* hope."

CHAPTER ELEVEN

BRIAN TOOK a detour on the way to the shooting range. He felt as unsettled as the weather. Going to Tim's gravesite might have a calming effect on him. Otherwise, his performance at the range could well end up as lackluster as the rest of his day. He couldn't afford to remain distracted, but Kaylen's words kept buzzing around his brain. He hated people giving him deadlines or ultimatums; they hung over him like heavy black clouds wherever he went.

He passed the Cielo Azul Apartments on the way to the cemetery. The financial advisor he had hired was convinced Tim's investment would pay off in spades in some not-so-distant future. If Brian sold the building, he'd be going against his brother's savvy business sense and the advisor's, but he'd also get rid of ten tenants and their assorted problems. Two paid late, two called at least a couple of times a week to complain about one thing or another, and then there was Mrs. O'Grady.

Brian grimaced at the thought of her. She'd apparently come with the building when Tim bought it, and she'd probably still be clinging with her dirty, broken nails to the last brick that fell when the Cielo Azul finally got demolished. Her and her four cats. Brian shuddered at the memory of her blue-veined legs and the smell of cat urine when he'd last encountered her. He almost missed Woodlawn Park Cemetery, braked hard and slowed to a more respectable speed as he passed through the gates and parked.

The sun came out as he strolled down paths between mausoleums and regimentally straight rows of headstones. He watched visitors arranging flowers in urns as they kneeled or squatted beside graves. Some prayed. Others sat on benches strategically placed for rest and reflection. The wind didn't blow with such intensity in the manicured grounds, but it still managed to fly the flags around tombs of Cuban revolutionary war heroes. Leaves rustled in the trees, while muffled traffic sounds provided a steady background drone.

Brian felt the effects of the peaceful atmosphere. Tension drained from his back and shoulder, taking them from painful to mildly achy. In the quiet serenity, Tim's specific instructions regarding his last resting place didn't seem so self-indulgent, despite the fact that he'd made it clear his goal was to provide those who knew him with a constant reminder of his presence.

Brian noticed the flowers when he was still one row away from Tim's white marble headstone. Red roses. A dozen, by the look of it.

The flowers were fresh and tastefully arranged. Brian decided Kaylen must have been there. She went to the cemetery at least once a month, and she always placed the same flowers Tim had sent to her when they were dating. Her visits usually didn't disturb Brian, but both of them going that day did.

He sat on a bench beneath an old, spreading oak tree and stopped trying to push aside Kaylen's ultimatum. Without knowing whether his career with MDPD was over, he couldn't make any long-term decisions. Kaylen should know that, he told himself angrily. She shouldn't press him.

Brian ran a hand over his face and tried to regain his objectivity. He shouldn't blame her for wanting answers. It had been four months, and he wasn't the only one who couldn't plan ahead; the only one affected by the uncertainty. *Damn it to hell,* he thought, trying to keep his swearing on the milder side even when thinking of Kaylen, and particularly while sitting in a cemetery.

He reluctantly allowed his doubtful thoughts to expand. His misgivings didn't end with Kaylen. Where Tim's business holdings were concerned, he was on a steep learning curve. He'd worked for others, never himself. He'd had no wish to become an entrepreneur, and he thought he was floundering in his new role. Jim was right about watching the financial manager, but if the guy was cooking the books, Brian wondered whether he wouldn't realize it until checks started bouncing. He didn't know how Kaylen ran Bannisters without looking and acting continually stressed out. She was one smart woman. He felt like a failure, and he didn't like it one bit.

He walked over to Tim's grave, squatted down and spoke to his brother for the first time since Tim's death.

"You're a jerk," he said. "Or maybe I should be saying 'were?'" He paused, feeling slightly stupid. What did he expect? An answer?

The wind ruffled his hair in response, and the roses swayed in the urn.

"I'll take that as an agreement," Brian said. "Look, I don't know what Kaylen told you when she came earlier, but she's painting me into a corner, and a good part of that's your fault. You could have left me clues to solve your disappearance without involving her. And I could have gotten things cleared up a lot faster without taking care of Kaylen, too."

He paused again. If he was being honest, then he had to admit that at least part of the time, Kaylen had taken care of *him*. She'd saved his life.

"Don't think I'm ungrateful," he added. "I know what she did. I even think I may understand why you did what you did, but you know… knew…damn well I've never wanted to get into a long-term relationship. It's too damned complicated, and now she's really made things difficult. She wants everything, and I can't give it to her. *You* couldn't even give her that, you shithead."

A gust of wind whipped dirt up to pepper his face.

"Goddamn it, Tim."

Brian got up and strode back through the cemetery. He didn't care if getting a face-full of dirt was coincidence. He vowed he'd never spend time at that gravesite ever again.

CHAPTER TWELVE

KAYLEN STOOD in the shower and held her face up to the stream of hot water. She knew she'd pushed the issue with Brian, but what choice did she have? She'd spent the last four months nurturing their relationship, but he still wasn't ready to commit to anything or even give her hope that he could.

She stayed under the water for a long time, hoping she'd feel less worried. Less panicked, if she was really willing to admit it. What if Brian *didn't* give her the answers she wanted? What if he said they were too different, too far apart in too many areas of their lives to find common ground except in bed?

"I'm such a fool," she said, and then she was crying, like she had so many times since Tim's disappearance. She turned off the water and pulled a towel off the rack, plunging her face into its soft, billowy depths. The bathroom was a mass of white, swirling steam.

The heavy air made her leave quickly, flipping on the exhaust fan on the way out. She left the wet towel hanging over the bedroom door and put on a robe as she walked into the kitchen. Pulling an open bottle of Bannisters' house Pinot Gris out of the refrigerator and a large wine glass from a rack over the breakfast bar, she filled the glass halfway.

Kaylen took the wine with her to the couch. Legs tucked under her, she sat and drank, watching palm trees sway outside the balcony doors as her mind took her on completely unwelcomed trips into multiple futures without Brian.

Her heart ached. He infuriated her with his single-mindedness and refusal to accept that his future might not include a return to investigating homicides. But his ability to struggle forward with the enormous responsibility of managing his brother's business holdings, his determination to run charters and handle a fifty-foot motor yacht with a skeleton crew and a disability, and even his stubborn refusal to accept defeat in any shape or form, only made her love him more.

She carried her empty glass back into the kitchen and glanced at the clock. She still had at least two hours before she needed to be at the club. She texted Rob and Julio, scheduling a 4:30 PM meeting over the bar receipts, then threw her swimsuit into her gym bag with a sarong to wrap around her waist to hide the wretched rose tattoo Tim had given her both as a parting gift and a clue for Brian. A punishing session of lap swimming would clear her head, tire her out and shorten the time she had to spend reflecting on and dissecting her relationship with him.

She did a mental walk-through of clothes she knew were in her office closet at the club. At least three outfits, she decided. She had picked up a couple of cocktail dresses from the dry cleaners a week ago and forgotten to take them home. She always kept several pairs of shoes and sandals there, too.

No need to return to the condo after her workout. She had a fully-stocked bathroom attached to her office. Remembering how cold the morning had been, she added a sweatshirt to her gym bag and a black jacket for the drive home after work. She stuck wrap-around sunglasses on top of her head and shoved her feet into white sandals, slid the strap of her purse onto her shoulder and grabbed her keys.

"Damn you, Brian Swift," she muttered as she slammed the front door behind her.

She took the stairs instead of waiting for the elevator.

CHAPTER THIRTEEN

BRIAN NOTICED a pair of shapely ankles hanging over the edge of the rail as he stepped onto the *Need to Know*. Not Kaylen's. She'd never wear hot pink flip flops decorated with big turquoise flowers. As he approached, Mel Summerfield came into view. Catching sight of him, she casually lowered her feet to the deck and smiled up at him.

She wore skin-tight white capris that fell just below her knees, molding to her tanned, well-developed calves. "Hello," she said. "It's cold out here. I've been waiting for you for over an hour."

Brian was in no mood for any more rebukes. "Maybe you should make an appointment next time," he told her as he unlocked the door to the salon. He held it open against the strong breeze and waited impatiently for her to get up.

Although Mel was complaining about the cold, he noted the zipper of her sweatshirt was half open. He got a good view of a pale pink lacy bra and a lot of cleavage as she leaned forward, taking her time about getting out of the chair. She was barking up the wrong tree if she thought that was going to turn him on, Brian thought, especially that day. Kaylen had satisfied all his urges and then some. She'd also drained him emotionally.

All he felt was fatigue when he looked at what he figured Mel was offering. "What do you want?"

She pouted, her lips forming a perfect, glistening pale pink oval, and placed her hands on her hips. "My daddy was pretty upset with me. You snitched about Shelley and me taking out the boat." Her breasts jutted out, straining the lowered zipper, which descended a couple more inches.

"Didn't know it was a secret." Wondering if he was inviting more trouble than he was ready for, he motioned her inside. "You'd better come in out of the wind, before you blame me for getting you sick."

She smiled, revealing white, slightly crooked front teeth, and walked past him, wiggling shapely hips. The capris were skin tight from the back. No panty lines. She unzipped her sweatshirt completely, revealing a t-shirt even tighter than the capris. "Dad really lit into me." She slowly peeled off the sweatshirt, thrusting her breasts out even further in the process. "He thought I hadn't been on a boat since I was a teenager."

"The way you took the boat out yesterday, I wouldn't blame him for thinking that."

Brian tossed his keys onto the breakfast bar as she bent over to throw the sweatshirt onto the back of the couch. Her t-shirt rose up, exposing her tanned midriff. She made no attempt to pull it back down.

Annoyed, Brian thought about telling her to leave, but she must have another reason for hanging out on the boat in the cold, other than trying to seduce him. "You about clipped my boat when you left," he told her, making no attempt to hide the bite in his voice. "You didn't secure the lines tight enough when you got back, either."

Mel's eyes flashed. "I wasn't even close to your boat. As for the ropes, I told Shelley to take care of them, but I didn't check after her, so I guess that was my bad." The momentary show of anger disappeared into a winsome smile. She glided more than walked over to him and placed cool fingers on his arm. "Are you going to write me a ticket, detective?"

Her voice had lowered, almost to a purr. When he felt her thumb stroke his arm, Brian pulled away and walked into the galley, placing the breakfast bar between them.

"Right now, your boating skills are your dad's problem," he told her, making sure his voice was sharp and authoritative, despite his growing agitation. *What the hell was she trying to do, and for what reason?*

"Bet you could give me some pointers." Mel batted her eyelashes.

Too much, Brian thought with relief. She'd played him wrong. "If you pull either or both of the same stunts again, you'll be hearing from the marina management. Hit my boat, and your dad will be contacted by his insurance agent."

Mel rolled her eyes and pursed her lips. "Are you always this grouchy?"

"I'm a cop who didn't get much sleep last night."

She abandoned the provocative act. "Sorry. I didn't, either. Living in a house with a bunch of little kids as well as four other adults is beginning to wear on me." She sighed heavily. "I really did get ripped by my dad, too. It's not good for his heart to yell like that." She plunked herself down on a bar stool. "I could really do with a cup of strong coffee."

Brian relented. She looked a lot more approachable. "I can make us both a cup."

"That would be great."

He filled the coffeemaker and got it started. When he turned back, Mel was on her feet again. She ran her fingers along the breakfast bar. "I love your boat. It's so much prettier than my dad's." She drifted back to the salon and circled the coffee table.

"That's because it's brand new and hasn't had the wear and tear of a family."

He watched as she sat on the couch, spreading her arms across the back and leaning into the plush cushions, her red-gold hair cascading across them. She really was attractive, he thought. Annoyed, he took the half-full carafe from the coffeemaker and filled two mugs.

What was the matter with him? Was he really that much of a guy that he'd fall for Mel's open display of sexuality after spending half the night making love with his girlfriend?

Mel smiled at him. A knowing smile, as though she'd read his thoughts. "Maybe you could give me a refresher course on boating," she purred. "Show me what I'm doing wrong and help me fix things."

She kicked off her shoes and sat cross-legged. The effect was unsettling. Brian, in the middle of putting the top back on the coffee canister, dropped it into the sink. He fumbled for it, his eyes unwilling to look away from Mel's golden skin and thrusting breasts, nipples prominently visible against the pale pink fabric all the way across the room, as though she had played with them while his back was turned.

A mental picture came into his mind, so sexually stimulating that he had to force himself to get the lid out of the sink and press it clumsily back onto the canister. "Your dad could show you that," he told her as he tried to decide if his hand was steady enough to take her coffee mug from one side of the galley to the other. He knew he wouldn't be able to carry it into the salon without spilling half of it.

The last thing he needed was to be with Mel out on the open water. There was a recipe for disaster in his relationship with Kaylen, and no mistake. "It'd be better for you to familiarize yourself with the boat you'll be using," he told her. *Damn it, even his voice sounded breathless.* He cleared his throat. "Besides, the *NTK's* bigger and harder to handle." The moment he said that, he regretted it.

Mel giggled and stepped right into the opening. "Like its owner?"

"You're a bad girl," he said. *Dear God, he was flirting right back. What in the hell was the matter with him?*

Appalled at himself, Brian hit the brakes. "I didn't mean that. Forget the coffee. You should get going. I've got a lot of things to do today, and hanging out on the *NTK* with you will make me late for my appointments."

He had no appointments, but lying seemed the easiest way out of what was developing into a situation he wasn't handling at all well.

Mel sat up. "If that's what you really want." She stared at him. Hard.

Brian found himself avoiding her direct gaze. "Yeah," he said. For some reason, he felt regret and hated himself for his reaction. "I do."

Mel fluffed out her hair. "Do you mind if I check myself in your restroom first?"

"No problem." He would have preferred her walking right out of the salon and onto the dock, but he didn't want another Summerfield mad at him for being himself. "The head's off the bedroom."

His eyes stayed glued to her as she leaned forward, yet more baby pink lace and cleavage spilling out of that low neckline. He mentally lashed himself while he did it, but even better than that, visualizing

Kaylen's reaction brought things into perspective like the slap of an ice-cold towel, and his partial erection abruptly departed, leaving Brian relieved in more ways than one.

He wiped down the already-clean counter as Mel hip-swayed through the open doorway of his bedroom. She paused momentarily in front of his bed and ran her hands over her hips before walking into the head. *Christ! She must be dynamite in the sack.*

He shook his head, more at his own thoughts than Mel's actions, and checked his watch. Four o'clock. He wondered if Jim would stop by and save him from Mel before he had to do it himself. Two Summerfield visits in the same day were well on the way to being more than he could handle without back-up. He turned off the coffeemaker and emptied the carafe into the sink. No more coffee for him. He'd had enough stimulation for one day.

"Brian?" Mel's voice drifted out of the bedroom. The doors were closed. She must have done that while he wasn't looking.

"What?"

Annoyed, he threw the cloth into the sink.

"Can you come here for a moment?"

Had she blocked up the head? If he found water all over the bedroom floor, he'd toss her into the bay.

He walked rapidly across to the closed doors and slid one back to find Mel lying across his bed, her clothes in a pile on the floor. She was wearing one of his dress shirts.

"What in the hell are you doing?" He felt slightly panicked and changed his mind about Jim dropping by. That would be the makings of a disaster more than a potential save.

Angered instead of aroused, he knew his reaction wasn't at all what she was expecting. He picked up her clothes and flung them at her. "I don't need any more complications in my life. Put these back on and get out. If you don't, then I'm going to throw you out of here in what you're wearing. You'll look like an idiot."

Momentarily startled, she quickly recovered. "No." She unbuttoned the shirt a lot faster than she'd done anything else up to that moment. "You'll be the one in trouble. I can cry attempted rape." The shirt slid off her shoulders as she got up onto her knees, fully exposing herself. She sucked one index finger before running it slowly down between her breasts. "Now why don't you come over here so we can have some fun?" Her finger continued on its downward path, across her flat stomach, into the thatch of auburn hair at the juncture of her open legs. She stroked herself, eyelids half closing, pink lips moist and puckered.

Brian ignored the incredibly erotic sight after one awed look. His professional training came to the rescue and he welcomed the shield with open arms.

He took out his phone. "You're a conniving slut," he told her. "I'm fully dressed. I'm calling 9-1-1 unless you're in your clothes and off my boat by the time I count to thirty." He turned and walked out, continuing onto the dock without looking back.

It took her slightly more than thirty seconds to get back into her clothes and reach the deck, but she looked sufficiently crestfallen for him to put his phone away.

"That's better." He kept his right hand in his pocket. "Now, let's take a walk on the dock, in full view of everyone, and you can tell me why you tried to seduce me."

Mel zipped her sweatshirt all the way up to her neck and avoided looking at him as she stepped off the *NTK*.

"I don't think I like you," she said.

"A lot of people don't."

The look she gave him was probably supposed to send him to his knees. Brian stared right back at her. She turned away, brushing hair out of her eyes. They began walking slowly, parallel to the parking lot. Brian waited her out. He wasn't going to make things easier for her by initiating any further conversation. Mel pulled up the hood of her sweatshirt. Brian figured she was trying to recover her poise more than warm herself up. After a couple of minutes, her strides lengthened and she folded her arms across her chest, shoving her hands inside the sleeves of her sweatshirt. He matched her pace.

"I want you to stay away from my family." She spoke without looking at him.

"No shit?" Brian stood still.

Mel kept walking, halfway past her parents' boat before she realized he was no longer beside her. She faltered and turned.

"You picked a screwed-up way of accomplishing that," he said into the gap between them.

Mel came back, her teeth worrying her bottom lip. The wind whipped around them, whistling through the space between the dock and the cars in the parking lot. Brian waited her out again.

"I thought if you got involved with me, you'd stay busy and keep away from my dad." She gave him a quick glance before fixing her gaze on the *Naughty Nautical,* rocking at her moorings. "After I hooked you good, I intended to dump you."

"Is that right?" He looked down at her, so sure of her allure, so egotistical that she never even considered that he might not be attracted to her overt sexuality.

Her gaze met his, her expression seductive yet sweet. "You'd be so mad about losing me; you'd ignore all of us after that," she said, her voice low and intimate. She rocked back onto her heels and then slowly forward onto the balls of her feet, bringing her face closer.

Her hazel eyes held unshed tears Brian wasn't buying. The red-gold hair tossed around her face, uplifted to his. She ran the tip of her tongue over her full lips. Despite himself, he felt yet another stir of desire.

He knew all she wanted was for him to seize her and take her to his bed for sex as rough as he could dream up. Nothing romantic and sensual, like his lovemaking with Kaylen. He almost wanted what Mel was offering. Almost... He found his breathing had accelerated and calmed it.

Mel smiled, her face flushed. "I'd have to force myself to break up with you," she said. "I wanted you so bad back there on the boat, I couldn't think straight." She remained on tiptoes and leaned toward him, lips parted. "Can you forgive me?" She asked, her voice quality breathy, her eyes dreamy behind half-closed lids. "Maybe we could go back inside and start over?"

"No way."

He didn't step back, but he knew she sensed the wall he threw up between them as she closed her mouth into a firm line and lowered herself back down.

"I'm not interested in you. I don't like sure things."

Anger tightened her face. She didn't look as youthful or pretty as she had a moment ago. "You really are a bastard," she said.

"I've been told that before." He shrugged. "Tell it like it is."

"I can't believe I threw myself at you." Cheeks flaming, Mel flung herself onto a nearby bench. She stretched her legs out and crossed them at the ankles, her hands still jammed deep into her pockets. She stared intently at her pink-painted toenails, poking out beyond the turquoise plastic flowers on her sandals. "I've always been a bad judge of character."

She sounded genuinely contrite, and Brian thought that might be the first truthful thing she'd said to him. He sat on the other end of the bench, keeping a good distance between them.

"Why d'you do it?" He asked. "I've got everything a man could ever need in Kaylen. I'm not available. Of course, if you *are* a nympho, you wouldn't care about that."

She glared at him.

"Bastard; I know."

"You are." She nodded. "But even if you aren't interested in having sex with me, you can't blame me for trying to protect my parents. They're vulnerable. Especially my dad. My mom has tried to move on with her life, but she's never been the same. She's always got a short fuse, and she won't trust anyone outside the immediate family."

Mel pulled the hood back off her head, like she wanted him to see her sincerity as well as hear it. "They've never stopped looking for my brother's killer." She stopped; chewed at her bottom lip. "It's complicated." She wiped the corner of her eye with the tip of one finger and sniffed. "I don't want my dad to get you snooping into something that's never going to get resolved."

"What makes you think I'd even want to do that?" He watched her carefully.

Mel took out a tissue and wiped her nose. Brian thought crying might well be another act she was putting on, but he waited while she collected her thoughts or prepared her next lie, depending on what her real motive was in trying to get him arrested for attempted sexual assault.

"My dad'll try to make use of you if you get friendly with him," Mel said. "He'll start pestering you to dig around my brother's case. He's done it before with the police up in Tampa. They still remember his name. Not just the ones who retired, either. Even cops who hadn't started working for the police department when Chad died."

Another strong gust of wind hit them. Mel shivered and hunkered down. "My dad had a heart attack from the stress of my brother's death. I don't want him having another one. He told us he had to take Nitro this morning. That was after talking to you."

"No, that was before he talked about your brother," Brian corrected. "It was after I told him about you and Shelley taking Teddy out on the boat." He wondered why Mel had stopped making eye contact again after she made the comment about things being complicated. "Your dad was so worried about the kid falling overboard, I think it caused his chest pains. We didn't even discuss your brother's case, beyond him telling me Chad died in a botched robbery."

Mel let out a profound sigh. She seemed to deflate, her chest falling in and her shoulders slouching. "Thank God."

Brian almost felt sorry for her, but he was too wary to be swayed from remaining detached. "So you can stop playing games with me." He heard the sharpness in his voice and softened his tone. "Go home, Mel," he urged her.

He left her sitting on the bench, the wind buffeting her. She didn't look up or say anything else.

He went straight to his car, pulled out of the lot and parked in sight of the exit. A few minutes later, he saw Mel in an older red convertible Mustang, top down, drive out of the lot and turn toward Coral Gables.

Brian drove after her, keeping enough distance between them to prevent her noticing him. He took advantage of a long stop light to call Jack Mills. "Who do we know in Homicide up at Tampa PD?"

"And hello to you, too," Mills said. "Your extended leave hasn't done much for your social skills."

"Sorry." Brian watched Mel's hood blow back, releasing her red-gold hair to swirl around. "I'm driving. And distracted."

Annoyed with himself, he gave Mills a brief rundown of Mel's visit and his earlier conversation with her father.

"Damn," Mills said. "I'd be distracted, too. What the hell?"

"That's what *I* said." Brian drove around a rental furniture delivery truck and saw Mel turn down a side street. "I'll call you back." He swore under his breath. If he'd had two hands on the wheel instead of one, he wouldn't have missed the turn. Either that or he was losing his touch. He made a U-turn. The truck driver braked, honked and flipped Brian off.

"Yeah, yeah."

Brian couldn't drive safely and gesture back. He had to let the moment pass and concentrate on making a slow turn onto the side street Mel had taken. Shaded by mature Queen Palms, pastel-painted bungalows with plantation shutters lined both sides of the street. Built somewhere in the 1970's or 80's, they were shaded by lush vegetation. Older cars filled driveways and spilled over to populate curbs outside the homes. Brian thought of long-term homeowners with families who had grown up on the street. Most of the cars were between five and ten years old. Brian figured them for hand-me-downs, their drivers the teenaged children of parents whose newer cars occupied the garages.

He spotted Mel's Mustang parked curbside in front of a white bungalow with yellow shutters. A couple of brightly colored plastic Big Wheels sat on the lawn. Brian remembered envying children who rode them when he was a kid. Evidently, they had never gone out of style. One was predominantly pink, the other black with bright yellow, red and blue trim.

Bicycles and tricycles of various sizes littered the area in front of the open two car garage, where a couple of Toyota sedans sat side by side. Brian glimpsed several overflowing laundry baskets on top of a washer and dryer at the rear of the garage, an overhead strip of fluorescent lighting illuminating the clutter.

He drove slowly past, turned at the end of the street and coasted back, parking a couple of houses away, in front of the only shabby home on the block. Oleanders on the perimeter needed trimming. They overshadowed the lawn and partially obstructed the driveway. Several flattened foil snack bags littered a weed-choked flower bed beneath the front windows. Peeling paint on the front door revealed red under dark green. He glanced at his watch: 5:15 PM. Shadows had lengthened as the winter sun coasted toward the horizon. The unseasonably cold day promised to become an even colder evening. He rolled his window all the way up.

Maybe the house was empty, but there wasn't a For Sale sign on the lawn. Then he spotted a number of boxes and furniture items clustered around garbage cans beside the garage. Foreclosure, he decided. They'd left in a hurry and dumped what they couldn't pack or didn't want anymore.

He called Mills back. "Sorry," he said, before his coworker could start complaining. "It was either hang up on you or lose her."

"What are you doing?" Mills asked. "Tailing that chick? Are you crazy? Besides, I thought you were told to rest and recuperate..."

"...or some such shit." Anger surged again at the thought of being placed on the sidelines. "No, I'm waiting for five fucking points on the proficiency test and trying to figure out whether I'm dealing with a psycho woman or there's more to this cold case up in Tampa than's been uncovered in the past. Enough about me for one day. Can we concentrate on getting me a contact at TPD?"

"Whoa. I touched a nerve, huh?" Mills cleared his throat. "Okay, so why don't you tell me exactly what you're working on in your supposed spare time?"

Mills always managed to exude calm; even during interrogations. He was always the low-key good cop with the soft voice. But he also carried the proverbial big stick, and his attention to minute details had continually boosted the squad's success rate in solving homicides.

Brian appreciated his colleague's expertise. "Something's not right with this family, Jack. For once, I didn't go looking for trouble—it came right to me. Are you willing to help me out? Try to find out what happened to Chad Summerfield? His family says he died in a botched robbery, but I get the distinct impression that his over-sexed sister is trying to throw me off what should be an exceedingly stale track for some reason."

"Yeah, you're right. Something stinks. I'll help." Mills sounded somewhat resigned, but not disinterested. "I already checked with TPD after you hung up on me. The guy you want to talk to is Fred Engelhardt. He's one of the lead investigators, and he's got the most seniority. How old's the Summerfield case?"

"No idea. The way the dad talks, it must have gone cold some time ago, but the family's never recovered from their loss. I don't want to have to move my boat to get away from this nympho and her crazy family. I like the marina's location, and Jim keeps an eye on the *Need to Know* when I'm not around."

"Okay, I hear you. What else do you need from me?"

"Maybe only what you just did," Brian said. "But I'll let you know. I appreciate it, Jack."

"You want me to run a background check on them?"

"Well, yeah, okay. If you can handle that as well as your caseload. Otherwise Hal'll give me grief for that, too. I'm gonna get in contact with Engelhardt. See if he's got any info he's willing to share. Maybe I'll poke around the case."

"Off the record?"

"If he *is* willing to talk, I'll leave it that way for now. If it looks like more than a dead end, I'll take it up with Hal." Brian hesitated. "He offered me a backhanded promotion, heading up Cold Case, but I know he didn't mean me to get involved in something outside our jurisdiction."

Silence on the other end of the line told him Mills was pretty surprised. Brian watched a dog-walking couple grow closer in his rearview mirror. The dog stopped to sniff a bush.

"What did you say to that?" Mills asked.

Brian saw the couple split apart. The woman reached up and they kissed before she ran across the street and walked rapidly over the Summerfields' front lawn. Without looking back at the man and the dog, she stepped inside the house and closed the door. Brian couldn't get a good look at her face, but he thought her build resembled Shelley's.

"I wasn't receptive," he said. An understatement, maybe, he thought as the dog pulled his owner past the Mercedes and up the driveway of the house next to the empty one. The dog's owner pulled keys out of his pocket and stopped to look at Brian's car. He jerked the leash and checked his pet's precipitous rush toward home.

Brian waved at him. The guy waved back and stepped onto his front porch. Brian watched dog and owner go inside. The front door closed and none of the window coverings moved. He relaxed slightly, but divided his attention between the Summerfield house and the dog owner's.

"I bet you weren't receptive," Mills said. "No adrenaline rush? No one trying to shoot your fool head off in an alley while you're working on finding out who killed some drunk?"

"Yeah." Brian had to smile. "You know I live for that shit."

"I'll do some checking on my own time." Mills grunted. "We're up to our asses in unsolved cases. No one cracks suspects with your speed and efficiency. Your fan base has been growing. The brass didn't like your methods, but they definitely got results. Our stats reflect that."

Brian felt a satisfying shot of vindication. He'd never been sure the complaints about how he got confessions weren't sometimes tinged with envy. "Good to hear you guys might even miss me." He started the car back up. "Nothing going on here. I'm heading home. Thanks for offering to help. I'll keep you posted after I talk to Engelhardt." He noticed a chink of light in one of the dog owner's front windows as the Mercedes rolled away from the curb.

"Take care of yourself," Mills said.

"Thanks."

Brian called Tampa PD. He didn't expect to catch Engelhardt, but the detective was on duty, and amenable to Brian taking a trip up there to talk with him. Brian omitted the fact that he wouldn't be there in any formal capacity.

After hanging up with Engelhardt, he called Jim. "What are you doing?"

"Thanking my stars Vera had to work the afternoon shift." Jim sighed. "Boy was she boring. We had nothing in common."

"Serves you right. I told you not to step out on Sue."

"Sue was in the marina office more than she was out of it. Checking up on me. I felt like I was under surveillance." Jim snorted. "Anyway, I have to admit you were right about not getting too close to Vera. Now I won't be able to set foot in that restaurant ever again, and it's one of my favorites. I love the turkey club."

"Jim…"

But Jim wasn't in the mood for interruptions. "Look, buddy. I hate to say it, but you're batting two for two. You were also right on the money about the new case I was offered. I talked to the woman who called about hiring me. She wanted me to dig up anything and everything I could on her estranged husband. She asked if I knew any prostitutes I could set him up with, and how good was I with digital photography. Then she asked if I carried a gun and was prepared to use it. I hightailed it out of her house ASAP."

"Good."

"Good?" Jim sounded incredulous. "What's good about my day? I barely escaped with my life from some vengeful hellcat, and I blew my relationship with Sue by thinking Vera's more exciting. Instead, she's got the personality of wet blotting paper, which is something you probably don't even know existed, much less saw or used."

"I know what blotting paper is. I grew up in the seventies." Brian shook his head. Jim's problems seemed to have become his, and he was the last person to guide anyone's dating life. "I warned you about losing out on good meals at that restaurant if things with Vera didn't work out. But I also see your point about Sue always being able to keep an eye on you from the marina office." He thought of Kaylen. "Women want too much."

"That they do." Another deep sigh conveyed Jim's frustration.

Brian could feel a sharing moment coming on, and he was going to avoid that at all costs. He didn't want to involve Jim in one of the most important decisions of his life. He needed to make that one on his own. But at that moment, Kaylen's ultimatum needed to be put onto a back burner, to simmer for as long as he could leave it there.

"Let's move past that," he said quickly. "And forget the psycho divorcee. I've got a proposition for you that'll soften both blows. How about packing a bag and coming to Tampa with me for a couple of days?"

"What are you getting yourself into now?"

"I'll fill you in on the way up there. I need a partner. A second set of eyes and ears. I'll double whatever that crazy bitch was willing to pay you as a retainer."

Jim laughed. "You're something else, Brian. You have one helluva way of putting things into perspective. Okay, I'm your man. But I'm not sharing a hotel room with you. Those weeks on my boat were enough. Your mess...."

"Fine." Brian cut his friend off before a dissertation started. "I'll book two rooms, but in return, no complaining about me and my bad habits." He thought of Mills' comment. "Or my methods on the job, either."

There was silence while Jim ruminated, as he always did before making decisions. Brian waited, trying to remain patient. He pretty much knew the answer, but wasn't going to put words into Jim's mouth that the older man could dredge up later if they got into some jam for which Brian hadn't prepared.

"Fair enough," Jim said. "We leave first thing tomorrow?"

"No, we leave tonight. Meet me on the dock in...." Brian checked his watch, then glanced in his rearview mirror and saw his long hair. *Engelhardt wouldn't buy active duty or an undercover assignment being connected with a years-old cold case.* He'd better get a haircut. "Two hours."

He had one more thing to do before leaving Miami...much more important and problematic than looking department-regulation ready. Dressed in jeans and a windbreaker, he wasn't even close to meeting the dress code for Bannisters. He felt he had more than a reasonable excuse to put off talking in detail with Kaylen about her revelation that morning, but he wasn't at all sure she'd think taking what could be a wild-goose-chase trip up to Tampa was even close to reasonable.

He dialed her smartphone. She didn't pick up. Either she was in the shower or at a meeting. He left her an unusually detailed message, telling her about his trip and that they'd talk when he got back. He wasn't at all sure that would be enough, but part of him felt relieved he had a legitimate reason not to end up promising something he couldn't deliver or worse, lying to Kaylen when he had sworn he never would again.

He hoped the unsolved Tampa case was a way out of his depression and a chance to use his detection skills to finally bring some measure of closure to the Summerfield family. He'd also gain much-needed breathing space to mull over what he wanted for the future both with MDPD and with Kaylen.

He told himself this trip wasn't an excuse to skip out on responsibility and emotional involvement yet again, but he wasn't at all sure that was true, which bothered him a whole lot more than he was willing to admit, even to himself.

CHAPTER FOURTEEN

BRIAN'S MERCEDES made short work of Highway 75 as it passed through Alligator Alley then curved northward, close to the Gulf coast. Darkness alternated with bright flares of tungsten light as they flew past truck stops and gas stations with brightly illuminated convenience stores that were sucked back into the vacuum of the night. Glowing motel vacancy signs materialized like flashcards and disappeared into blackness as thick as tar. Brian kept the speedometer between 75 and 80 miles an hour as he shared with Jim what little he knew of Chad Summerfield's murder.

Detective Fred Engelhardt, Brian's liaison with Tampa PD, wanted to combine talking about the Summerfield case with breakfast at a local coffee shop once his shift ended. Jim's first order of business was researching local newspaper archives for clippings, old photographs of the area and anything else of interest at the time of Chad's death.

When the clock on the dash showed 2:00 AM, Jim's participation in the conversation dwindled from actively-engaged to intermittent grunts. Brian still missed the roar of his Camaro, which tended to keep him awake and alert. The Mercedes purred like a big cat, lulling Jim to sleep, his head leaning against the window. Beginning to lose concentration himself, Brian turned to the radio for company. He kept the volume low as he listened to a variety of stations from pop to country. They faded in and then out of range, annoying him with half-finished comments or songs that ended in static shrieks. He tried Sirius instead, finally sticking to NPR after a steady diet of Springsteen left him nodding, the Fox News Channel told him nothing new and he decided Howard Stern was more annoying than the static of the FM stations. As dawn trickled pale pink into the horizon and the black of night became a silvered shape shifter, they entered the outskirts of Tampa. Brian flipped back to Howard Stern and raised the volume to a level that would have awakened a corpse.

Jim shot upright, blinked and looked around. "What the hell?"

Brian got a perverse kick out of disturbing his friend's sleep. If he was awake at dawn, then his partner should be, too.

"If you patent that as a wake-up call, the next time I take you out fishing on my boat, I'll drown you in Biscayne Bay," Jim threatened.

"Would you rather I took my one working hand off the wheel to poke you?"

"Not at the speed you usually drive." Jim rubbed a hand over his face. "Are we there yet?" He cracked a smile that turned into a grimace as shifted in his seat. "I've got a crick in my neck. What in the world are you listening to?"

"Howard Stern. I couldn't think of anything more annoying to get you up."

"Good choice. I'm wide awake. How long was I out?"

"About three hours."

"You shouldn't have let me drop off. It's dangerous to drive at night without company."

"I'm okay. I could do with a shower and a change of clothes, though."

They arrived at the Grand Hotel right as the lights in the parking lot cut off. The sun had risen high enough to change the half-light into a muted yellow. Brian pulled into the first available space, turned off the engine and threw open his door. He felt stiff and bleary-eyed. After they both got out of the car, he glanced at his friend across the roof.

Jim stretched, winced and grabbed his back. "We should have gotten out and stretched our legs." He yawned widely and did a careful back bend. "Ah, that's better, but I feel hung-over without the benefit of the booze."

"You need more sleep." Brian popped the trunk. A uniformed bellboy came running across the parking lot to take care of their luggage as Brian dumped his bag on the ground. He watched Jim yawn widely again. "You should have breakfast and take a nap before you start checking out the archives."

"Do you have a reservation, sir?" The bellboy hoisted Brian's bag onto the cart he had brought with him.

"Yeah. Two rooms."

"Follow me, sirs. I'll take you to the reception desk." The bellboy placed Jim's bag next to Brian's and pushed the cart back across the lot to the forecourt of the hotel.

Jim lightly tapped Brian on the back. "Why didn't you use the valet parking?"

Brian shrugged. "Didn't even cross my mind. I'm used to dingy motels."

He had already warned the hotel they'd be arriving early. The lobby was almost deserted, a couple of bellboys talking with the concierge and a housekeeper polishing woodwork. Brian and Jim were checked in immediately and given their room cards. Jim took a complimentary newspaper from the front desk and they followed their bags up to the third floor, where their adjacent rooms looked out onto the pool.

Brian generously tipped the bellboy, who trundled off toward the elevator. Jim popped his head through the communicating door. "How about *you* lie down for a couple of hours after your own meeting? You look pretty tired."

Brian ran his hand over the stubble on his chin. A clock on the bedside table showed 6:45 AM. "Maybe." He doubted he'd want to sleep after meeting Engelhardt. His adrenaline had surged for the first time in months at the thought of investigating the Summerfield case, as old and cold as it was. "I'll see how things go this morning."

He looked around his suite. The luxury blew him away. How far he'd come from his childhood at the rental shack beside the railroad tracks in Baton Rouge. The bellboy had opened the blinds and a door leading onto the balcony. Sheer curtains billowed in a breeze created by the cross-draft from Jim's suite. Gentle sunlight, filtered by the sheers, spread across plush beige carpeting and the bed, beckoning with snow white linens, a mass of plump pillows and a comforter that looked like it had been pumped full of air. Brian thought of Kaylen, and how much she would have loved everything.

"That bed's calling your name," Jim said. "I already tried out mine. Fabulous." He smiled when Brian shook his head. "I know. You don't have time right now. But don't worry about me over-sleeping. I'll set the alarm or ask for a wake-up call. Maybe both. I reckon it'll be kind of hard to get back up."

Brian gave his friend a stern look, although he felt like he should let Jim sleep through the afternoon. "You'd better get up, or I'm docking your pay. I'll call you at noon to see what progress you've made."

"You would. That's why I'm so sure I'll be calling for a cab to take me over to the library before then." Jim patted Brian on the shoulder and left, closing and locking the door behind him.

Brian turned his back on his own bed, ordered a pot of strong coffee from room service and took a long, hot shower. He drank three cups of the coffee, delivered on a silver tray with cream, sugar, artificial sweetener and several packets of biscotti that he shoved into a drawer in the event Jim needed a snack at some point.

Forty-five minutes later, dressed in a pale gray suit, white shirt and black tie with a herringbone pattern, he walked briskly out to his car, gave the address to his on-board navigation system and followed the voice instructions all the way over to the Kozee Kaffe. No checking maps, poorly-marked street addresses or using an app on his phone, as he'd had to do when in his Camaro.

The Mercedes definitely had some perks, he grudgingly acknowledged as he looked for a parking space close to the coffee shop, strategically placed on the corner of a busy intersection.

If he continued to feel as energized as he did right then, he decided he'd do a quick tour of the murder scene after his meeting. Engelhardt should be able to tell him whether the grocery store still existed or had morphed into something else, and how much the neighborhood had changed over the years. Once Jim had done the archive search, they'd be better prepared to start the real leg work.

Kaylen hadn't returned his call, which was completely unlike her. He hoped she was sticking to her plan of giving him space to make a decision about their relationship versus being angry. Something other than hunger stirred deep in his gut at the thought of calling her again. It felt uncomfortably similar to the one he got prior to his meetings with Hal; something closer to dread than anticipation.

An SUV pulled away from the curb a couple of stores away from the diner. Brian quickly activated the parking assist and let the car maneuver itself into the space. He locked up and walked past an old neighborhood store with a recessed entrance, newspapers in racks standing on a black and white tile floor. Through the open door, Brian glimpsed a crowded interior. That quick glance revealed a counter whose register shared a space with Plexiglas containers of donuts and breakfast sandwiches, while hot dogs rotated on a nearby warming rack.

So much for the nostalgia of the façade carrying into the store. Customers juggled Styrofoam cups, lottery tickets and paper bags as they waited in a line that snaked all the way to the soda machines on the back wall. The inside looked more like a 7-Eleven than that neighborhood mom and pop's. As Brian passed the shoe shop next door, a middle-aged woman in a flower print dress turned the 'Closed' sign to 'Open,' smiled and waved. Brian nodded to her and waved back, feeling slightly silly. That particular part of Tampa was more like he imagined Main Street in a small Midwestern town to be. No wonder the Kozee Kaffe had such a kitschy name.

When he pushed open the door to the little coffee shop, a bell jangled overhead. Tables with red and black checkered cloths and chrome stools at the counter were filled with everything from business people in suits to workmen in overalls. A heavy representation of retirees, probably drawn by the 'Early Bird Special' advertised prominently in the front window, filled booths of knotty pine. A printed sign on a pedestal advised him to wait to be seated. He obediently stood behind it, focusing his attention on the back of the dining room. Cops usually liked to stay away from windows and keep the front door in plain sight. He doubted Fred Engelhardt was any different. A silver-haired man in a conservative charcoal gray suit sat alone in a corner booth close to the kitchen. He was studying the headlines on a neatly-folded newspaper as he sipped from a brown china cup.

A waitress carrying a half-full coffee pot grabbed a menu from a wooden pocket beside the cash register and walked over to Brian. "Table for one?"

"No, I'm meeting someone. I think that's him in the back."

She stepped up close. "Is your name Swift?"

"Yes."

"This way."

She led him over to the silver-haired man, who put down his cup and extended his hand as Brian sat.

"You made good time." Tired blue eyes were warmed by a ready smile. His chin was covered with a thin layer of white stubble.

The waitress slid the menu under Brian's arm as he shook Engelhardt's hand. She hovered, pot poised. "Coffee?"

Brian nodded. "Please."

She turned his cup right side up and filled it to the brim. "Need a couple of minutes?" She'd already whipped a notepad from a pocket in her red and white checked apron. She put down the coffee pot and took a pen from behind her ear.

Brian glanced at the menu. Small photos of loaded plates showed pancakes, hash browns, bacon and eggs in about any style he could imagine. Kaylen would be tut-tutting louder than Jim if she saw what he was about to eat. But Kaylen was nowhere within griping range.

"Nope. I'm ready."

He ordered a short stack, bacon, and eggs over-easy. Engelhardt took French toast with strawberries and scrambled eggs.

"My wife'd have a fit about the sugar and cholesterol," he told Brian. "That's why I come here for breakfast a couple of times a week. Otherwise, she'll have a dish of oatmeal waiting for me and decaf tea." He wrinkled his nose. "She must want me to live to be a hundred. I quit smoking and drinking a couple of years back, she nagged me so hard. I'm the oldest damned detective on the squad. You'd think I'd at least have the sense to retire before I get shot." He grinned, his creased face amiable and open.

Brian felt a glimmer of hope. Engelhardt might remember details from the Summerfield case, and he was as friendly in person as he'd sounded on the phone. "I don't even know how far back this case really goes," he said.

Engelhardt took a sip of his coffee. "I don't usually meet people sight-unseen when they call me on the phone, but I made an exception for you. Some cases stick with you more than others. I was a newbie back then. We're talking twenty-five years ago. Most of the other players in the department have long since retired. The store where the crime went down is still there, but it's changed hands a few times. It went through several other incarnations besides groceries: Electronics, furniture, even did some time as a thrift store. Right now it's a bargain market...mainly housewares, seasonal stuff, bed linens. Close-outs."

"How's the neighborhood?"

Engelhardt shrugged. "About the same. What you'd expect a close-out store to do well in."

"How about the employees who worked there at the time?"

"Retail's transitional at the best of times. You interview staff, go back several weeks later, there's a bunch of new faces. The manager already wanted to leave before the shooting. He took a buy-out and moved away. Jacksonville, if I remember rightly. He was good at keeping in touch. Wanted to be available for any follow-up questions. Then he notified us he was moving to Tallahassee, where he had family. He'd married one of the associates by then. She was close to twenty years his junior, but it seemed like the trauma of that day had drawn them closer together over the following months. Last address we had for them may or may not still be good. It's been a long time since anyone looked at this case. What's your interest? Do you have a new lead?"

Brian shook his head. "No, but family members are neighbors of mine." He gave Engelhardt an abbreviated version of the last couple of days. "If there's a way to help them get closure, I've got the time and the inclination to look for it." He told Engelhardt about Tim and, much less easily, about how that loss had affected him.

"So you're looking for some healing yourself," Engelhardt said.

"In a way," Brian acknowledged. "I've got some heavy decisions to make, and working this case may help. Seeing the long-term effects on this family up close and personal could put things into better perspective for me. In my brother's case, the perps probably fled the country, so I doubt I'll ever see convictions, regardless of how much time and effort's put in."

"That's a tough thing to live with." Engelhardt beckoned the waitress and pointed to their cups.

Brian's left arm was throbbing. In his haste to arrive for his meeting looking pulled-together, he had forgotten to take his pain medication. His growing discomfort made him wonder what could have possessed him to jump into his car to drive up to Tampa and get involved with a death that had happened so long ago. Twenty-five years. He was 14 years old when it happened. Living in Baton Rouge and hating it.

"Are you going to take the Cold Case position?" Engelhardt asked. "Is that why you're really poking around up here? Trying to make a decision about your career?"

Brian pushed his water glass around beside his plate, watching a ring of condensation widen. "Maybe. But what if I got the use of my arm back? I'd put my chief in a less than charitable frame of mind if I accepted the Cold Case position and then wanted to back out of it. Homicide's been a great fit for me. I miss it."

Engelhardt nodded. "I did some reading up on you. Sorry about that 'getting shot' comment. That was pretty thoughtless of me."

Brian managed a tight smile. "I didn't take it personally. I've developed an even thicker skin over the last few months. And don't believe everything you read. A lot of it's exaggerated. I did my job. End of story."

"More than your job by what I saw." Engelhardt stopped talking as their breakfasts arrived. He waited until the waitress had refilled their cups and left the checks beside their plates before slicing through the French toast. "Best ever," he said, popping a forkful into his mouth.

Brian found his pancakes light and fluffy, the eggs perfect. He nodded. "Good place. No wonder you come here regularly."

Engelhardt grunted agreement and swallowed. They ate in companionable silence until their plates were empty.

"So, let's talk generalities." Engelhardt laid his silverware across his plate. "After that, if you want access to the evidence and the box of statements and other papers related to the case, you'll have to make a formal request."

Brian knew the Tampa detective had watched him intently under those bushy eyebrows as they ate. His left hand had stayed at his side the entire time, as there was no point in trying to make it do anything functional. It would only reveal how clumsy his movements still were.He drained the last few drops of coffee from the bottom of his cup. "I'll get that paperwork in motion. I've gotta talk to my chief about this, now I know it's worth pursuing. I wondered whether anyone still remembered the case. I didn't expect to find someone still working at the department who was around when it happened."

"You'll get full cooperation from my end." Engelhardt took a pad out of his pocket. "These are the addresses of the store, the old Summerfield home, Chad's apartment. They'd pretty much be public record, so I'm not breaking any rules by giving them to you. Once you get clearance, you can see all the file info, make copies, do whatever you want." He pulled off the top sheet of paper and passed it to Brian.

"Thanks." Brian saw neatly printed addresses. "I really appreciate you taking time out to help me on this."

"We want cases closed, regardless of how old they are." Engelhardt pushed his empty plate aside and dropped his neatly folded napkin on top of it. "A murder's a murder, no matter how much time's passed."

"That's what my girlfriend said." A flush spread through Brian. Even speaking about Kaylen affected him.

"Smart woman." Engelhardt smiled. "Sounds like my Mary. She's something else, but I'd be in bad shape if she wasn't home waiting for me at the end of the day. She's always had my back. Thirty years we've been married."

"Lucky man." Brian couldn't imagine being in close proximity with anyone for 30 years.

"You could be, too. It can happen, even to us cops." Englehardt took out his wallet.

"I've got this." Brian pulled the detective's check over to join his own.

Englehardt took out his business card and inked in two additional numbers. "My personal cell and home phone numbers," he told Brian.

"Call anytime, but if you do it in the middle of the night for less than a conviction, I'll make sure you talk to Mary."

"I'll keep that in mind." Brian felt relief. Engelhardt was on board with whatever came of the Summerfield case. He extended his hand. "I'll be in touch."

Engelhardt gave him another strong grip, got up, buttoned his suit jacket and leaned in. "Let's catch this killer finally," he said in a quiet, firm voice.

CHAPTER FIFTEEN

OUTSIDE THE CAFÉ, Brian checked his watch again. 9:00 AM. Way too early to call Kaylen, who usually stayed at the club until closing and didn't get up until midday. No sense in waking her out of a dead sleep and risk making her irritable. If she wasn't when she woke up, no doubt she would be when he told her he was spending the next few days up in Tampa. Even to him, it sounded like he'd taken the trip to avoid her.

Sitting in the Mercedes, he drummed his fingers on the wheel. He wasn't scheduled to meet up with Jim until noon at the earliest. Despite some fatigue, he knew sleep wouldn't happen if he returned to the hotel. Brian took out Engelhardt's printed list and gave the navigation system the address of the close-out store. At least he could take a look at the location of the robbery and scope out the surrounding neighborhood.

The system took him on a trip down narrow streets through tacky neighborhoods. He wondered how much had changed since Chad Summerfield had lived and worked in town. Hopefully, Jim's trip to the archives would shed more light on that. As he approached his destination, Brian drove into yet another run-down area with rows of small bungalows on barely-larger lots, most properties surrounded by chain link fencing. Dogs ranged behind the fences, running along bare paths their paws had cut through overgrown grass. Awnings hung over slatted windows, tattered plastic blinds obscured porches. Children's toys littered cracked concrete driveways.

The close-out store dominated a small strip shopping center, flanked by a Chinese restaurant on one side and a bike shop on the other. Brian pulled into an open space midway through the parking lot and turned off the engine. He sat watching people coming and going for a few minutes as he sized up the clientele. A predominantly older crowd might remember the robbery. A younger group would not. He doubted their parents would have spent time discussing the day a young assistant manager got shot to death in what had been a neighborhood market at that time. He wondered what stores had flanked the market when Chad Summerfield worked there.

After deciding the people frequenting the store were pretty eclectic, both in ages and ethnicities, he pulled closer and strolled into the store. Remodeling had probably made it unrecognizable, but he walked through anyway, noting the locations of the cameras and heading for the exit sign at the back of the store. He pushed open the door and stepped through, seeing the manager's office on one side of the hallway, a large window strategically placed opposite a time clock on the opposite wall. The stock room sat to the left; a cool, cavernous space devoted to neatly marked boxes and shelves stacked with miscellaneous piles of plastic dishes, out-of-season decorations and linens. A group of plastic palm trees forlornly clustered together in one corner, dimly illuminated by a shaft of light from the hallway.

"What are you doing back here?" A man strode out of the manager's office. "No customers allowed back here. No public restrooms." He barred the narrow corridor leading to another door with a red neon exit sign over it.

"I'm with the police department." Brian pulled out his badge and flashed it at the guy.

The man held out his hand, palm up. "Let me see that. It doesn't look like a real one."

"It's real all right; but not local." Brian kept a grip on his badge, but held it out for a longer and closer inspection. "I'm from Miami."

"Then what are you doing in the back of my store, detective?" the man asked.

"Depends on who's asking."

"I'm the manager." He stood up straighter and tapped his name tag, which read: Tab Benford, Manager, Best Pic.

"I'm investigating a crime that happened when this was a grocery store. I wanted to see what was back here. Even though the store was remodeled, I figured the storage and employee areas weren't."

"The Summerfield case," Benford said.

"Yeah. I'm surprised you remember."

"I used to come here with my mom as a kid. It was a grocery store, then."

"It was." Brian nodded. "How about giving me some details of what happened that day? What you remember about it?"

Benford's gaze skittered away, fixing on a pile of boxes resting on a pallet outside the stockroom. "I'm in the middle of annual reviews. You'll have to come back some other time."

Brian wondered why the boxes had suddenly become so interesting. "This won't take long."

Benford walked over to check the labels. "I'm busy doing my job," he said without glancing at Brian. "You're in a hurry to ask questions about something that happened, what, twenty years ago?" He shook his head. "I'm paid to take care of the store, not cooperate with an out-of-town cop."

Brian sensed more than work obligations were occupying the manager of Best Pic. "If you don't want to talk while you're working, then we'll meet on your lunch break. We can chat in your office or I'll buy you a meal close by and we can talk outside of this place." He waited a beat for the offer to sink in.

Benford took out a box cutter and slit open a couple of containers without checking the contents or responding to Brian.

To hell with being diplomatic. "I'm working with Tampa PD on this," he told Benford's back. "I can send the locals over if you want to go that route. Won't make 'em happy. There'll be more than one, and they'll hang around a lot longer. Doubt your customers will like that, but hey, no skin off *my* nose."

He shrugged and turned away, striding toward the door leading back into the store. He heard rustling and glanced back to see Benford had straightened up.

The manager jiggled around on his heels for a moment and checked his watch, as though he had no idea what time of day it was. "Okay, okay," he capitulated. "My lunch is at one-thirty." He scowled. "I get thirty minutes, and I bet you want all of it."

"No guarantees I won't. Depends on how fast you talk and how much info you give me. I know bullshit when I hear it, so a clear memory will go a long way to making my time with you a whole lot shorter."

The manager muttered something under his breath that sounded like "Shit."

"Your choice," Brian said.

"Okay." Benford shoved his hands into his pockets. "I brought my lunch with me, so we can talk in the office. I don't want my employees hearing anything about a robbery, even if it was a long time ago, and I don't want to sit in a restaurant with you. No offense, but you *look* like a damned cop."

Brian pushed back a smirk. He'd dressed in one of Tim's remodeled Armani suits for his meeting with Engelhardt. While it wasn't on the average detective's budget, he didn't figure it made him look conspicuously like a cop. Certainly, when Benford had first encountered him, cop hadn't been the first thought he'd had, Brian was willing to bet.

Close to three hours until the meeting and still two and a half before getting together with Jim. His arm was aching and his head felt like it was filled with cotton. Returning to the hotel for a power nap followed by a briefing about Jim's research sounded like a better use of his time than scouting the neighborhood when he was tired and likely to miss some important details. He'd put in many long days and nights in Homicide, but he realized he wasn't back up to his full potential when he had to stifle a yawn. He hoped Jim had remembered to set that alarm.

"I'm Detective Sergeant Swift," Brian said. "You can call Miami-Dade PD to check that out if you've got doubts." He glanced at the guy's name tag again.

Benford evidently saw the second look. "My mother was a big fan of Tab Hunter, the actor."

His direct look challenged Brian to either laugh or make a comment. Brian thought the guy had a big chip—Tab Hunter's popularity had waned long ago. He vaguely remembered some movie called "A Summer Place" and a theme that went with it. His mother had bought the record and played it when his stepfather wasn't around. Then he wondered if his memory was faulty. Wasn't the actor in that movie named Troy Donahue?

Brian sharply rebuked himself for allowing his mind to ponder inconsequential garbage. If Benford thought his name was unusual, he should see some of the ones that came through MDPD on any given day. He turned his back on Best Pic's manager.

"See you later," he said over his shoulder as he reentered the store. A cluster of retirees searched through comforters and matching sheet sets all prominently marked 50 % OFF. One lady who looked incapable of lifting a pair of standard sized pillow cases hefted a comforter set into her cart and began tottering. Brian was relieved to see a young Hispanic woman drop her own comforter to steady the woman. He hurried out into the bright sunlight of mid-morning and drove quickly away from the parking lot.

As he turned toward the hotel, he decided it was time to call Hal, before Englehardt or someone else at TPD did.

"What the *hell* are you doing up in Tampa?" Hal didn't sound at all supportive.

Brian explained, keeping to the facts.

"Couldn't you work some unsolved murder down here?" Hal's tone held more than a trace of exasperation. "We've got more than enough to go around. Oh, that's right...you're out on disability. So, I repeat, what the hell are you *doing?*"

"This is personal. I know the family involved." Brian tried hard not to react to Hal's impatience. "I've got a good contact in the local PD, and an interview lined up with someone who lived in the area at the time of the robbery. Still lives and works here. Jim's with me, working on research. It's a good case, Hal...er, Chief. It'll give me a chance to kick the Cold Case tires. I know you don't want me accepting a position I'm not going to stick with."

"That's for damn sure." Hal stopped tapping his pen. "All right. What do you need? Formal cooperation between our department and

TPD? The case files? You're not going to expect me to get you temporarily assigned up there, are you?"

"You and I know I wouldn't last two days in any other department." Brian found himself cracking a smile. "I should be back in town by the end of the week."

"It's Monday," Hal said. "You can get into a pack of trouble in a five day week. I've seen it."

"This is a cold case," Brian pointed out. "Twenty-five years cold. I doubt I'll be chasing more than dead ends."

"We'll see." Hal didn't sound convinced. "I'll get you hooked up with TPD. Don't screw things up. Keep your contact with them to a minimum and mind your mouth."

"I've cleaned up my act," Brian assured him. "Jim's with me, too. You know what a real straight arrow he is. I can't see myself getting into any trouble with him around."

"Good."

Hal hung up.

CHAPTER SIXTEEN

"You know," Jim said on the way back to the close-out store, "I bet we can make some in-roads here. There was a lot of press on this case. Local elections were about to take place, so there was probably more coverage than normal on this murder. The councilman for the district Chad lived and worked in was in a contentious race. He stirred things up and gave heaps of quotes. It kept the case in the news far longer than a lot of similar ones, according to news sources."

"Didn't seem to have made much difference at the time." Brian eased the Mercedes through a busy intersection cluttered with buses, pedestrians and delivery trucks as well as cars. "You said tips and what initially looked like promising leads went nowhere."

Traffic had thickened considerably in the last couple of hours. Brian hadn't needed to use the navigation system for the return trip. Since his days in a cruiser, he'd used landmarks very effectively. He turned at a liquor store with a distinctive sign out front declaring "35 Craft Beers" onto a less congested side street.

"That's a pretty accurate summary from what I read in the news reports," Jim said. "But maybe the police reports will shed more light. You would think someone should know *something*. The guy was shot in broad daylight in the middle of a crowded store. The shooter ran out the back into the alley and according to reports, no one saw where he went after that. The murder weapon was never found."

"People were more prone to turning a blind eye in those days. That's happening a little less now, although retaliation's still a big issue. Maybe he was a gangbanger, or maybe everyone thought he was—that would be enough to keep them quiet."

Jim shrugged. "I suppose. He wore a ski mask. It was mid-July. He must have been sweltering inside it."

"I wonder why no one noticed that before he even got inside the place? He must have come through the front door from the parking lot. Who doesn't think that's weird?" Brian stopped at a red light. "We're getting close. A couple more blocks and you'll see the store coming up on the right."

Jim looked around. "This is one seedy area. Good place for a close-out store. Did you cruise the neighborhood?"

"Some." Brian hit the gas as the light turned green. Several people standing on the corner watched them pass. "I feel like this damned car stands out. My Camaro never did." He glanced in the rearview mirror. They were still watching. "While I keep the manager busy, I want you to talk to the rest of the staff," he told Jim. "See what you can find out about him. I've got a feeling he's hiding something. See if any of them worked there at the time of the murder, or they know anyone who did. Let's try to interview someone who knew Chad."

Jim nodded. "Will do. If I get done before you, I'll go check the other stores. The pics I saw of the grocery store showed a bike shop on one side and a barbecue joint on the other."

"There's still a bike shop, although it may have a different owner. The barbecue's a Chinese restaurant now."

"I'm real partial to Chinese," Jim said. "Lunch?"

Brian had forgotten about lunch. Regular meals didn't mean much to him, and hadn't for a long while. But Jim ate on a schedule. "Sure." He fought back frustration. "Something fast. I want to walk the neighborhood. We'll ditch the car and start with Chad's apartment building."

"Fair enough." Jim tapped an area map. "I marked all the locations I thought we'd be interested in. Chad's place is about a mile away from the strip mall." Jim steadied himself with a hand on the dash as they drove over a big pothole at the entrance to Best Pic's parking lot. "I'm loving this area already," he said, grimacing. "Looks like somewhere I'd want to get away from if I had the misfortune to live here."

Brian pulled into a space in front of the bike shop. "The store's a real winner. The stockroom looks like it's still holding merchandise from when Chad was alive."

"I'll give you a couple of minutes before I come in," Jim said. "No sense in giving any of the employees the idea we might be working together."

Brian walked straight through the store. None of the associates gave him more than a quick glance. He was dressed casually in a short-sleeved blue shirt and brown cargo pants with a beige jacket. He'd figured that outfit would blend into the neighborhood a lot better than the Armani suit and maybe make Best Pic's manager a little less jumpy.

Tab Benford was still camped out in his office, a plastic container with a half-chewed ham and cheese sandwich on wheat bread in front of him, a can of off-brand cola to his right and a bag of potato chips next to it. He looked up as Brian stood in the doorway.

"Come in." He looked at his watch. "You're prompt. I finished up my paperwork a few minutes early."

"Did you check my credentials?" Brian took a seat on the straight-backed metal chair in front of Benford's desk.

"No." Benford took a swig of cola. "I was too busy. So what do you want to know?"

"Let's start with you telling me more about yourself. Were you born around here?"

Benford frowned. "I thought you wanted to know about Summer-field? Why would you want to know anything about me?"

Defensive again, Brian thought. He shrugged, feigning disinterest. "If you grew up around here, you can give me some background on the neighborhood and the people who shopped in this place when it was a grocery store."

Benford rattled the cola can, found it empty and pitched it into the trash can beside his desk. He crumpled up the chip bag and threw that in, too.

"I was born in St. Pete," he said. "My mom and dad split up when I was two and I moved here with her. She got work as a waitress, but the hours were long and hard, and it was difficult for her with a kid, so she took a job behind the counter at a sandwich shop, which worked out a lot better. She worked eight to four and got home right after I came home from school. We lived in a walk-up about eight blocks from here, so we shopped here often. She knew all the clerks, and because she was pretty, she got a lot of attention from Chad Summerfield, who was the assistant manager."

Brian's senses went into high alert. "Did she like the attention?"

Benford put the lid on his plastic container. He took his time mashing it down until the sandwich was in a completely air-tight environment, like he was going to finish it later, instead of pitch it into the trash with the rest of his lunchtime debris.

"I wouldn't know," he said without looking at Brian. "I was just a kid."

"You were old enough to notice the attention," Brian pointed out. "And it sounds to me like you didn't much care for it."

Benford opened the top right hand drawer of his desk and slid the container inside. "I suppose I was jealous. I was what, ten or twelve at that time? And the only man in my mom's life since she and I moved from St Pete."

"Did they date?"

"A couple of times." Benford dabbed at invisible crumbs with his index finger and sprinkled those into the trash, too. "It didn't come to much. And then we stopped shopping here and took the bus over to another, bigger shopping center instead."

"Did he come to your home to pick her up?"

Benford shook his head. "Mom was always real careful about not letting her dates know where she lived. Right up until she married my step-dad."

"When was that?"

"A couple of years after Summerfield's murder." Benford still wasn't making eye contact. His gaze wandered around the room as though he was searching for something he'd missed. "We'd moved away then. I didn't come back here until recently."

"And you ended up right where your mom used to shop." Brian leaned back in the uncomfortable chair.

Evidently it was Benford's turn to shrug off a comment. "Familiar territory." His tone was dismissive.

"Friends?" Brian prompted.

"A few."

"From your childhood?"

"Some."

Benford inspected his pants, presumably for more invisible crumbs. Brian reached over and turned a photo frame around. An attractive, smiling woman about Benford's age stared back at him, her arms around a couple of tow-headed children, the boy slightly older than the girl. In the background, Disneyworld beckoned. "Your wife and kids?"

Benford took the frame away, studied it momentarily and set it back in its original place. "Yes. I met her when I was on vacation. Disneyworld. We're both roller coaster freaks." He smiled briefly. "Spent half our honeymoon on one. When we took our kids, one threw up, the other screamed the whole time, and not with excitement, either. Go figure."

"You live around here?"

"Nah. No place to bring kids up. I drive in from the 'burbs."

"You see a lot of the people you grew up with?"

The corners of Benford's mouth tightened. "Like I said: A few. A lot of the kids I knew moved away years ago. On to greener pastures."

Talking with the manager was like pulling hen's teeth, but Brian refused to give up and leave. He sensed that's what Benford wanted. "Give me names and addresses," he pressed.

Benford looked startled. "They'd really love me for that. Sending a cop to their doors? No way."

"So you *do* prefer talking at the precinct, then." Brian stood up. "Fair enough. My car's right outside."

Panic flickered in Benford's eyes. "Sit down." He gestured like a trapped bird flapping its wings. "Maybe you could leave my name out of it when you talk to them? Tell them it's a routine investigation or something?"

"Maybe." Brian wasn't committing to anything. He pushed a yellow legal pad from the edge of the desk over to within an inch of Benford's hand. He noticed a smear of sweat when the manager slid his hand forward to grasp a pen.

"There's Wally Malone." Benford's voice sounded borderline shaky. "He still lives in the same apartment building he did when we were teenagers. Only on a different floor."

Brian nodded slightly to encourage more cooperation. "Who else?"

"Chico. Chico Ramos. I don't know where he lives, but he works at the garage two streets away, on the corner." He pointed behind Brian. "Next to the Burger Shack."

"How long have you known him?" Brian asked.

"We go way back." Benford scribbled judiciously on the pad. "Grade school." He wiped one finger across the space between his nose and upper lip. "And Tommy Spiro. He never moved away, either. He works at a café, opposite side of the street from the parking lot. Four blocks."

"Keep writing," Brian sat back down. Slowly. Keeping his eyes on Tab Benford the whole time.

Benford was sweating like an Eskimo in a sauna. His fingers slipped on the pen. "I only know a couple of other guys slightly. I can't even tell you their last names, but I'll put them down, anyway. They both live in the area. They come in here once in a while, but we don't stand around chatting."

The temperature in the office with the door closed must have been over eighty degrees. Brian's shirt was sticking to his back, and he was dressed in light clothes. Benford wore long sleeves, the pale blue shirt buttoned at the cuffs and all the way up to the collar.

"Roll up your sleeves," Brian said.

Benford stopped scribbling and sat with pen poised over paper. "Why?" His voice was as tight as the lines around his mouth.

"Why not?" Brian leaned his forearms on the desk. "Hiding gang tats?"

"No. Eh...tats, yes." Benford dropped the pen and looked squarely at Brian for the first time. His eyes held fear. "I don't want any trouble. My bosses know about my past. I've built a reputation for turning around stores on the line to close down. But when they wanted me to come here, I tried to get out of it." He looked as defeated as he sounded. "My mom moved us away because I was getting affiliated with a gang." He shook his head. "I didn't go through initiation. For me, it was belonging in the neighborhood. Coming back could bring retaliation."

"For what?" Brian felt a prickle along his skin he hadn't felt for too long.

Benford unbuttoned one cuff, rolled his sleeve up to the elbow and gave Brian a brief look at some poorly crafted faded black and blue letters before jerking the sleeve back down. He shrugged. "Mistakes. I was too young to know better, but around here, kids were expected to make adult decisions long before they were old enough. I got some tats, and I went along when friends jacked a couple of cars..." He stopped and closed his mouth, his gaze skittering away again.

"You get busted?" Brian knew Tab was hiding more than a history of boosting cars.

"Nah." Benford seemed to have made some sort of decision. He noticed a mark on his watch face and rubbed at it, his finger slightly shaky. "I guess we were real lucky. We certainly weren't that smart." He shook his head, his eyes still downcast. "Then things turned bad. The group I hung out with decided to rob a local convenience store." He looked up, his face bland but the volume of his voice lower, conspiratorial. "One of them had a gun. I'd never even seen one." He gave a short, barking laugh. "Thought I was hot shit until then. But when we pulled up outside the convenience store and that gun came out of the glove compartment, I realized I was terrified." Tab's head dropped. "I thought I was going to wet my pants."

"I bet," Brian said quietly. He tried to imagine Benford as an adolescent, looking at participating in armed robbery with a real weapon. He remembered the first time he had seen a gun himself, in his step-father's nightstand drawer, wrapped in a dirty rag. Tim had found it while looking for change. The brothers had both handled it. How they avoided blowing at least one of their heads off, he'd never understood...

"And then, as we were all getting out, leaving Tommy Spiro behind the wheel, ready to get us all the hell out of there when we were done, I saw my mom walking toward the store."

Tab Benford's quivering voice pulled Brian away from his own half-forgotten memory.

"I ran at her, shouting for her to get away." Benford was no longer looking down. He was leaning forward, caught up in the moment. "Tommy panicked and drove off. The doors were swinging around, and because Tommy had only driven maybe a half-dozen times in his whole life, he crashed less than a mile from the store. He got patched up in the ER and left there in handcuffs."

"What happened at the convenience store?"

"People saw the gun and started yelling and screaming even louder than me. Chico and Wally were standing on the curb. One of them was holding the gun in plain sight. I don't remember who. They were both looking down the street like they couldn't believe Tommy had ditched us. The other kid, Mix I think his name was, had taken off running down the street like a bat out of hell before the rest of us got out of the car. He kept on running right past my mom and got clean away."

"What about you?"

"My mom grabbed me when I ran to her and dragged me away. We went straight to the bus station. She bought tickets for Mobile, Alabama and called my grandma from a payphone to let her know we were on our way. She picked us up when we got there. We never came back."

"Do you know what happened to Chico and Wally?" Brian asked.

"I heard they ran around the side of the store, thinking they could escape down the alleyway, but they'd waited too long. I guess they were so surprised at what Tommy did, they kind of froze. Patrol cars came, they got chased and caught."

"How did you find all this out?"

"My mom called a friend."

"Name?"

"I don't remember, but I know she died some time ago, so you wouldn't be able to talk to her, anyway."

Convenient, Brian thought. *The information source was dead?* He pointed to the legal pad. "Put your mother's address and phone number on there, too. I know you'll call her as soon as I leave here, but I'm gonna verify your story, anyway. See what details she comes up with that you missed. Does she still live with your grandmother?"

Benford nodded. "That second marriage ended in divorce and she moved back in." He looked nervous again. As he wrote, he started prattling along, determined to finish up his story as quickly as possible.

Brian figured his fingers were itching to get to his phone so he could warn his family.

"The first time I ever came back here was a month ago, when I finally agreed to manage this store on a temporary basis," Tab said. "I moved my wife and kids out to the 'burbs, and I'm here from open to close, firing and hiring, moving merchandise out to make room for new stock, updating fittings and getting the place painted. The bottom line's already out of the red. Sales are up twenty-five percent. I figure I can get out of here in another month, with a new manager in place. The company's promised to ship me and my family up to South Carolina, where we're planning to stay."

"You'd better hope I close this case within that month, then," Brian broke in.

He had no way of stopping Tab Benford and his family from going anywhere, but he figured Tab wouldn't know that.

"If you come in here making waves, I could get killed. Then who would take care of my family?" Tab leaned forward again, his voice dropping. "Or my family could get hurt. People don't forget getting sold out. Those kids got arrested and did time."

"But they never ratted on you, or Mix, either."

Tab shook his head. "We all stuck together in this neighborhood. Maybe that's why. My mom also got our names changed as fast as possible. Maybe they couldn't find me."

"So then why are you creeping around here but keeping tabs on their whereabouts at the same time?" Brian had to smile and shrug when Tab Benford glared at him. "Sorry, but it was the best word to describe what you're doing."

"I don't look like I did back then, but I'm still afraid of retaliation. I could get a visit one evening after my shift. Kind of a delayed roughing up, only with bigger and heavier fists." Sweat trickled down the side of Tab's face to drop in little beads on the desk top. "Those other two, the ones who come into the store? I've been giving them gifts once a week since they recognized me."

"You've been stealing from the store?"

"No way. I've given them gift cards. Twenty bucks a piece every time they come in. I told them we're doing promotionals, but I've been paying for the cards myself. I figure it's an investment in my future."

"Okay. I'll buy that," Brian said. "Look, I'm not trying to make trouble for you or anyone else who isn't a suspect in Chad's murder, but I'm never going to find the killer if I don't ask questions and insist on getting answers. Something got missed, or it would've been a closed case long before this."

Benford nodded curtly. "Yeah, I get that. But I'm walking on eggshells the whole time I'm in this store; this neighborhood. Even when I drive home at night. I take different routes and keep looking in my rearview mirror. I make my wife take the kids to and from school and stay inside the house as much as possible. She thinks I'm crazy taking all these precautions, but memories are long around here…"

"Which may work in my favor solving this case," Brian interrupted. "Look, if it makes you feel better, I'll give you my word I'll try to keep you out of this unless I need more information from you or I need you to testify." He took out his card. "If you feel threatened in any way, call me. Night or day; makes no difference. I've got the cooperation of the local cops, so if I can't get to you fast enough, someone from TPD will." He slid the card across the desk. "I mean business, Tab. And by the way, what the hell was your mother thinking when she changed your name? If she wanted to keep a low profile, she should've picked something like Billy or Dave."

Benford's scowl eased. "She wanted to name me Tab when I was born, but my dad wouldn't go for it. Divorce changed all that. After what she did to keep me out of the system and safe, I wouldn't dream of calling myself anything else." He managed a brief smile. "I love her a lot. When we move up to South Carolina, she and Grandma are joining us."

Brian stood up. He picked up the legal pad. "I'll take these with me. Thanks, I'll be in touch. Anyone asks questions about me, give 'em a cover story. They know the store's in trouble. Tell 'em I'm from Corporate."

Benford looked like he'd just been told he could keep his balls instead of getting castrated.

Brian decided to dispense with unnecessary pleasantries, but before leaving he turned back at the door. "What happened to the gun?"

Benford looked confused. "The gun?"

Brian wasn't buying it. Tab knew too many little details he probably couldn't have gotten from any newspaper accounts of the time, and that story he'd cooked up about the now-deceased friend of his mother giving so much information sounded like a lie. He'd got a friend in the neighborhood. Someone he'd been close with before and was close with again. Maybe even an old girlfriend he'd hooked up with after all these years.

"Yeah." Brian stared Tab down. It didn't take much. The manager's eyes shifted away to a contemplation of his half-full trash can. "You told me all about what happened to the rest of your little gang and even told me about the car, but you didn't say whether the gun was found on Chico or Wally."

"It wasn't," Tab muttered.

"So what happened to it?"

"No idea." Benford carefully placed his pen back into a black cup filled with other pens and pencils.

"A lost gun in this neighborhood?" Brian folded his arms across his chest. A little awkwardly, since the left arm took longer than the right to get there. But as Tab was still looking at other places in the room, it didn't much matter. He widened his stance. "Pretty unbelievable."

"That's all I know." Tab's mouth formed a hard line. "I've got to get back to work, or I won't finish on time."

"Those annual reviews, huh?" Brian wasn't buying the lost gun, but he knew Tab was done talking for the day.

"Yeah."

Tab did look up to watch as Brian went out the door and closed it behind him, giving the manager one last long look before turning away to walk back through the store. Jim was nowhere to be seen.

Brian pushed open one of the heavy glass doors and stepped out into welcome sunlight. He took a few deep breaths of gasoline-laced ozone before walking over to join Jim at the Chinese restaurant. It felt good to be back in the saddle, even in what he considered to be a lesser capacity, interviewing a potential witness whose memory may well have been distorted by the years and the transition from adolescence to maturity as well as his belief in some neighborhood code of conduct that may not even still exist.

In one sense, it even felt weird, he decided. Disjointed. He wondered how reliable his own memory was. What would he remember if someone came up to him out of the blue and asked him for details of an event that had happened 25 years before?

Some things were never forgotten, he decided, pushing back those old dark memories that still returned to haunt him. Others, not so much, although random thoughts or odors could remind him of everyday events: His mother standing at the sink, her arms up to the elbows in soapsuds as she washed clothes and hummed under her breath. Tim outside the house on Webber Street, sitting in the dirt and peeling an over-ripe banana, his bare feet covered with dust. Yes, Brian decided, those memories were still there for him, and Tab Benford's would be, too. Especially when it came to what had happened to a gun that was either in Wally Malone or Chico Ramos's hand while they were running away from the convenience store.

CHAPTER SEVENTEEN

WHEN BRIAN ENTERED the China Star Buffet and Restaurant, a bell jangled discordantly overhead. A young Asian girl with a big smile looked over a cash register and hit another bell on the counter. A wall obscured most of the dining room, but Brian caught a glimpse of a slowly revolving ceiling fan over a table to one side of the entrance. Either the sun was shining very brightly outside, or the interior was really dark, because the waiter who responded materialized out of the gloom so suddenly, Brian almost reached for his Glock.

Even marginal fieldwork had made him jumpy. Hal wasn't blowing smoke, Brian realized, when voicing concern over his readiness to return to work.

The waiter beckoned. Brian followed him past a lot of empty tables. A couple of booths were occupied by men in gray or navy overalls. They looked like mechanics from the plentiful supply of auto repair shops Brian and Jim had passed on their way to the close-out store. Brian wondered why they hadn't left their uniforms at work and if all the seats in the restaurant were greasy. If so, then that might account more for the lack of customers than bad food.

Jim waved from a back booth. "Have a seat."

A black iron teapot stood in the center of the table on a Lazy Susan. Jim took a sip from a white china cup as Brian joined him.

"Danny Cho, the owner's joining us for lunch," Jim said. "He lived in the neighborhood as a kid, and he knew of the Summerfields. He and his family left before Chad's murder, but he recently bought this restaurant and moved back."

A thick-waisted Asian man in an open-necked white shirt slid into the booth next to Jim. Aged somewhere in his forties, with thinning hair and a moon-shaped face with heavy jowls, he extended his hand across the table to Brian. "Detective. A pleasure to meet you. How's your investigation going?"

"Fair." Brian's hand met a firm grip.

The waiter offered a large menu.

"You'll find we serve a wide variety of dishes," Danny said.

"I already ordered," Jim said. "I didn't know how long you'd be. Danny recommended the Won Ton soup, shrimp fried rice and Moo Goo Gai Pan."

Brian closed his menu. "That'll work for me, too."

Danny beckoned the waiter over and gave Brian's order, rapid fire. "To drink?" He glanced at Brian.

"Iced tea."

The waiter left, returning moments later with the tea and three bowls of soup. Jim blew gently on the broth before taking a sip and nodding enthusiastically.

"Jim said you may have information on the Summerfields," Brian said.

"They lived next door for a while." Danny gently stirred his soup and peered into it, evidently looking for won tons. "I didn't know them that well. I hung out sometimes with Harry, the younger son, when we were in high school together. Chad was already working at the grocery store and doing so well, he got promoted to assistant manager before I convinced my father to let me go to culinary school. He wanted more for his son than being a chef or even owning a restaurant. I couldn't see why —I always loved to hang out in the kitchen and watch how the dishes were prepared."

"So what can you tell me about the neighborhood in those days?" Brian asked.

"Pretty much what you see now. Lots of small businesses, not making much money but somehow holding on. There used to be a couple of small local markets and convenience stores, a post office that closed some years back, from what I've heard, and some pizza joints that went away because the chains started delivering. My dinner business is never as good as lunch, and lately, that's been off, too." He looked around the almost deserted restaurant. "A sign of the times, I guess." He shrugged. "My parents used to own this place. My dad was upset with the way the next owner did business and convinced me to buy him out. I should have listened to my wife when she said the place wasn't worth saving."

Danny talked on as their entrees arrived; painting a picture of a neighborhood that had changed little over the years. The parents of his youth had turned into grandparents and great-grandparents. The kids had grown into adults and had families of their own. Many had stayed on, some had moved away. He remembered how torn-up Ted and Doris Summerfield were when their son, Chad died. He remembered the funeral, and how the grocery store had never seemed to recover from the two weeks it was closed for the investigation. Even remodeling made no difference. Shoppers continued to avoid it.

By the time the fortune cookies arrived, his narrative was winding down.

"So, you have any ideas on who killed Chad?" Brian asked.

Danny shook his head. "None, man. He had a reputation for playing the field with the ladies, but I never heard about any angry husband confronting him. I think he broke a few hearts along the way, but I couldn't see one of those women pulling on a ski mask and doing the deed, either."

"What makes you think it could have been a woman?" Jim placed the wrapper from his fortune cookie onto the plate before cracking open the cookie.

"The reports. They all said the person who did it was thin and pretty small."

"There's a new theory for you." Jim looked at Brian.

"Certainly worth thinking about," Brian conceded.

"Well, here's something to guide our search." Jim held up the fortune from his cookie. "You will meet someone new today."

"We just did." Brian took out his credit card. "I'll get this." He looked at Danny. "We'll probably need to talk to you again before this investigation's over."

"I hope you'll try my broccoli beef next," Danny said with a slightly uncertain smile.

CHAPTER EIGHTEEN

KAYLEN CRUMPLED her lunch wrapper and tossed it into the trash can. Sandwiches from her favorite kosher deli unfortunately reminded her of Sam Wilson. She still worried that one day she'd look up from her desk and see him standing in the doorway. Probably carrying a white bag with pastrami on rye, she thought, trying to shake the melancholy feeling that had persisted all day.

Involuntarily, she glanced at the open doorway. Sometimes she felt like she was being watched, but she could never figure out by whom, and voicing her unease to Brian would somehow give it substance, instead of only being residual paranoia from the fall-out surrounding Tim's death. *Flashbacks,* she told herself firmly when goosebumps crept across her skin. *Nothing more.*

Chilled, she drew a jacket from the back of her chair and draped it across her shoulders. The doorway was empty, the hallway beyond brightly lit with new fluorescents, the club quiet. Reassuring sounds reached her only when she strained to hear them. Normal, muted sounds of preparations going on for the evening: Voices, clinking silverware and china, the swishing of kitchen doors. They had become such a routine part of her day, she realized she no longer heard them unless she really concentrated.

Kaylen got up to check the thermostat. As usual, the air conditioning was set to 75 degrees. She sighed, undecided what to do with the rest of the afternoon. Normally, she would have called Brian, but after giving him some sort of half-baked ultimatum, she didn't want to appear weak and dependent. Or worse, she thought with a shudder that didn't come from feeling cold or spooked: He'd probably think she was only calling to check up on him and force the issue.

She sat back down and kicked off her shoes, leaned back and stared up at the ceiling as she mulled over the real source of her discontentment. Why had Brian suddenly felt the need to leave town to investigate some long-ago homicide related to his neighbors at the marina? It was the first time he'd been more than a short distance away from her since Tim's disappearance, and there was little doubt his absence had contributed to her anxiety. No wonder Sam's name had come into her head.

There were no bogey men lurking in the shadows. No hit man behind a shower curtain in her bathroom. Nothing bad was going to happen.

Life had returned to normal, Kaylen told herself. And after finally starting to have days when she didn't think about Tim, Sam or even Captain William Hastings holding a gun to her head, she refused to lapse into panic-mode because Brian's reassuring presence was more than a short trip away.

She took a key on a chain from inside her purse and unlocked the right bottom drawer of her desk, pulling out a metal box. She took another key from amongst the clutter of pens and pencils inside the top drawer and unlocked the box. Lifting the lid, she looked at the Sig Sauer P238 she had purchased on a trip to a gun shop after weeks of arguments with Brian.

Her dislike of firearms persisted. If she had fully cooperated with him, the gun would have been on her person instead of available only by using two keys, neither of them in the same place. But that day, without Brian's strong and ever-vigilant presence, she felt vulnerable. The gun had been cleaned by him two days before. Kaylen wondered if she should bolster her courage by keeping it with her until Brian got back into town, but her refusal to give in to fear made her lock it back up and leave it where it couldn't become the main ingredient in an accidental shooting. She was too jumpy to be rational, and the possibility of killing or injuring some innocent bystander was uppermost in her mind.

She wondered again why Brian would suddenly take off with Jim at a moment's notice. What interest could that case possibly hold for him? He'd told her he didn't want the Cold Case position. There had to be some other reason.

He wanted to avoid her.

Kaylen teetered between anger and disappointment. Her relationship with Brian wasn't going anywhere, and her attempt to force him into a commitment had failed miserably.

She had to face facts: Her entire day had been completely anti-climactic, including the meeting with Rob and Julio. Filled with statistics and projections, all of which they had in hand, she had come to the conclusion that Bannisters was operating in the black with less and less assistance from her. The frantic months since the opening had been replaced with the day-to-day operation of an established business.

She should be feeling satisfaction, but if she was brutally honest with herself, she was actually feeling bored and dissatisfied. The abortive meeting with the Stavros family had made her realize she needed both a new challenge and a constructive diversion from her frustration over the stalled relationship with Brian.

Months ago, when Brian had told her he wanted more than friendship with her, Kaylen had felt joy and stability were finally on the horizon after the weeks of terror following Tim's disappearance and death. Instead, she now found herself still in limbo; Brian's girlfriend, nothing more. Even after they made love, she lay in the dark and felt Brian's separation at a moment when she should have felt closer to him than at any other time.

She opened another drawer and took out Tim's photo, the one that had sat beside her bed at her previous condo. Tim's smile was frozen in time, his handsome face unmarred by the dark secrets he carried within himself. She traced the outlines of his eyes and mouth, searching again for any similarity with Brian's features and finding none. A deep sadness overtook her spirit.

Her landline rang, startling her. She dropped the picture. It slid off her lap into the drawer and landed with a clatter. The glass cracked, a diagonal fissure appearing across Tim's face. She closed the drawer and picked up the receiver.

She couldn't even find the energy to answer the phone properly. "Hello?"

"Ms. Roberts? Kaylen? May I call you that? This is Ziggy Stavros."

Kaylen planted her elbows on the desk and pushed her hair away from her face. His cheerful voice made her feel less sad. "Hi Ziggy. How are you?"

"I'm calling to apologize for the tone of our last meeting."

"You don't need to. It wasn't your fault. Your father and brother overreacted. They interrupted what was only a meet and greet." She thought of their interactions with Brian. "They were so rude. I can't even begin to imagine why."

"They were," Ziggy agreed. "I have not dared to discuss with my father the reason for his outburst toward Sergeant Swift, but I know he has no love for law enforcement. I have two other brothers. One of them was arrested for driving under the influence of alcohol and crashing my father's Lexus into another restaurant owner's car. Despite my father hiring a very competent lawyer, Markos spent time in jail. My father said the police did not perform the breathalyzer test correctly, and that it was actually the restaurant owner who backed recklessly into Markos after an argument over who owned a family recipe that resulted in us winning an award for our Avgolemono soup."

A vision floated into Kaylen's head of a younger version of Peter Stavros ramming his car into another while screaming obscenities at the top of his lungs, his breath smelling strongly of Ouzo. She fought back a sudden desire to laugh. "I could see your family being involved in something like that."

"Yes, unfortunately, I can, too," Ziggy said. "Again, my apologies. I do not know what else to say, except perhaps I should extend those apologies to Sergeant Swift."

"Better to leave that alone," Kaylen said. "Brian moves past some things very quickly."

She thought of the time she had been so angry with Brian she had slapped him, and how well he had controlled himself. She still felt guilty about it, especially after learning about the abuse he had suffered at the hands of his stepfather, but Brian had shrugged off the incident, and refused to even discuss it when she tried to bring it up later, after life returned to normal. The new normal, she thought, unsure whether she would ever get used to the shift in her own personal cosmos.

"Kaylen?"

Ziggy sounded as though he thought they had been cut off.

"Sorry. I got distracted by something. If you called to apologize, then I accept and we're all set."

"No, that's not all I called about." Ziggy stopped speaking again.

Kaylen wondered if he expected her to be a mind reader. "So what *did* you call about?"

He let out an audible sigh. "Would you be so kind as to give me a second chance?"

Kaylen felt puzzled. Ziggy was as long-winded as his father was short-tempered.

"At what? Your family made it very clear that any discussions about the restaurant would have to go through them, which I refuse to do. I'm not getting in the middle of a family fight."

"I don't want to talk about that restaurant," Ziggy said. "I've been doing a lot of thinking since yesterday. I want to go out on my own. I have an inheritance from my grandparents; a small trust fund. I would like to ask you to mentor me. You have backers for your club. I'd like to know how to approach potential sponsors for my own venture."

"Oh." Kaylen felt a bit lost for words.

"I know you're probably wondering whether this is a good idea. I want the opportunity to persuade you. It would demonstrate to both of us that I could do the same thing with others. And I need to understand how much it really does take to open even a small café or restaurant. I have no experience, and I do not know who else to go to for advice. The only other people I know are friends or business associates of my father. I don't want him to know about this until it has already happened."

"I see," Kaylen said, although she didn't.

But she was sure of one thing...pursuing anything with Ziggy wasn't a very good idea. He didn't seem ready to step out on his own, or he would have been more forceful about having been the first one to make contact with her and then having not only his father but his older sibling take the meeting right out of his hands.

"Unless you've discussed this with your father, which it doesn't sound like you have, I think I have to say no..."

Ziggy cut her off.

"I haven't." He sounded defensive. "It is really none of his business what I do with my trust fund, or the rest of my life, as long as it does not impact The Corinthian or any other restaurant he and Apollo are involved with."

"That's not the way you seemed to react yesterday," she said.

"I had all night to lick my wounds. This morning I decided I wasn't going to be the baby of the family any longer. I want to have my own career, not spend the rest of my life being grateful for whatever is tossed to me as an afterthought. Will you help me, Kaylen? I respect your business-sense very much. I want to emulate your success, but on a much smaller scale. I'm not planning to be your competitor, at least not any time soon."

He sounded stronger and much more decisive about what he wanted. Kaylen remembered her own struggles, coming out from George's shadow and being taken seriously. "Well, I don't see what harm it could do to meet informally."

"That's terrific. Thank you very much."

"Do you want to come to the club?"

"No. Not after yesterday." Ziggy laughed. "Let us meet on neutral ground. How about South Beach?"

"Okay. I know of a great little bakery and café. One of my favorites. The Maison Rouge, right off Ocean Drive."

She gave him the address, and they arranged to meet in an hour. Suddenly, she didn't feel so gloomy. She went into her bathroom to freshen up before the drive and decided to change clothes, too. She pulled out a pair of fuchsia pink capris and a white sleeveless cotton top with a boat neck that she had left in the closet a couple of months ago. Her makeup looked pale and lifeless when she brushed out her hair. She brightened her blush and put on bubblegum pink lipstick, found large white hoop earrings and a black beaded necklace in a drawer. She finished the outfit with a white cotton sweater, in case the late afternoon turned chilly.

Rob's eyebrows rose slightly when she told him she probably wouldn't be back until later that evening. Then, before analyzing her spontaneity too closely, she got behind the wheel of her BMW, drove down Collins Avenue and onto Ocean Drive, the water sparkling on her left and the wind whipping through her hair. The cold spell had left, and she felt a welcome sense of optimism and underlying excitement away from the club and her self-doubts.

The fact that Brian had nothing to do with these feelings was a little unsettling, but Kaylen brushed that aside when she found a parking space only steps from the café and spotted Ziggy sitting at an outside table, chatting amiably with a waitress, his wide smile reminiscent of Tim's.

CHAPTER NINETEEN

"So tell me more about your idea for a business," Kaylen said when they had ordered coffee and croissants, hers filled with chocolate, a rare indulgence she knew would add another half-hour of exercise to her usual regimen.

"There's a café for sale on Calle Ocho," Ziggy said. "The owner's retiring, and his daughter doesn't want the responsibility. The price seems very reasonable."

Kaylen's café au lait arrived, its rich aroma enhanced by the heavenly croissant, freshly baked and still warm. She took a sip and smiled her appreciation to the waitress, who returned the smile as she placed Ziggy's order in front of him, then left quickly to seat another couple.

"How busy is that café?" Kaylen asked.

"Pretty empty the day I saw it." Ziggy dunked one sugar cube slowly in and out of his espresso. "But it was the middle of last week at two in the afternoon, which I suppose was not the best time to see how popular it could be. I didn't think about that. I was worrying about what my father or Apollo would say if they heard."

"You worry about everything they say, don't you?" She watched him drop the cube into the depths of his cup and stir slowly.

"Of course. They are family, and my own experiences up to now have been limited to college, travel and competitive sailing."

Kaylen had always wanted to travel, but George, who had traveled extensively in the past, showed little interest in leaving Miami. Then he became terminally ill, and Kaylen's dreams of seeing Europe had been placed on a remote backburner. "That sounds more exciting than limiting," she said. "Where did you go?"

"I attended college in Athens. After I graduated, I stayed on another year, teaching. But I had always been an avid yachtsman, and I was asked repeatedly to crew. The offers were too tempting. I gave up academics to crew all over the world for the next two years. Last year, the yacht I was crewing came in third at the America Cup. My father said that was enough. I needed to be here, learning the restaurant business. My English is even a little rusty because I've been speaking Greek for eight years." He smiled. "Sometimes, I have to think before I talk. It seems silly, even to me. Apollo gets really angry with me. He told me I sound like some third world reject."

"I didn't like him yesterday," Kaylen said. "I like him even less now."

"He had my father to himself for the time I was away." Ziggy took a small sip of his coffee. "My sisters are all married and do not live in Miami. Markos moved to the Midwest after he got released from jail, and my other brother has been managing a chain of small hotels in the Cayman Islands for years." He blew on the surface of the espresso before taking another sip. "Very hot and very well made. Almost as good as you would get in France."

"What's the difference?" Kaylen asked.

"The water, I think. Everything else can be duplicated." He bit into the croissant. "Ah, now that tastes as good."

"I'm glad something here is up to par," she said. "I'm joking," she added, in case he thought she was being sarcastic.

"A lot is up to par. And things are improving all the time." Ziggy smiled engagingly. He had a small dimple in his right cheek. "Can you go with me to look at the café?"

Kaylen ignored the brilliance of his pearly whites and that dimple with a little more effort than she would have liked. "Now?"

It was six o'clock. There was plenty of time to get back to Bannisters and change into a cocktail dress. She decided she wasn't going to back out of anything just because Ziggy was coming on to her. She was used to men's reactions to her, and felt she could handle his flirty nature. He was too predictable and friendly to be scary.

"I know they serve breakfast and lunch. I don't know if they serve food in the evenings," Ziggy said. "Perhaps tomorrow would be better. Lunchtime, when it should be at its busiest."

"I think lunchtime tomorrow would be a great time to see it, but I'd like to take a look at the place now before going any further. There's not much point in giving you a lot of information about backers if I'm going to advise you against purchasing it. The fact that it was empty when you went there is worrying. If I was selling a restaurant or café, I'd get prospective buyers over to view when it was at its busiest."

He nodded. "That makes sense." He beckoned the waitress and took out his wallet. "Would you like to drive there with me instead of taking two cars?"

"I'd have to drop mine at the club. I'm not going to come back here in a cab at two in the morning."

"We can do that." He paid the check and stood.

When Kaylen started to get up herself, he cupped her elbow and guided her to her feet, the gesture warm and charming.

"Thank you," she said. "I could get used to this chivalry very quickly."

"I'd like you to."

Ziggy tucked her arm through his and escorted her back to her car.

CHAPTER TWENTY

"IF I EVER QUESTION YOUR methods again, tell me to shut up," Brian told Jim as they walked down the street where Chad Summerfield had lived.

Jim took a toothpick from his mouth and grinned. "Wish I'd brought along a tape recorder. Or maybe I could use my cell to make a video of this conversation. In case it's the only time I hear praise from you."

"I'm not throwing out crap compliments," Brian said. "I got frustrated when you wanted to eat lunch...burning to go check out locations and interview potential witnesses from the list Tab Benford gave me, but Danny Cho had so much good info. He's got some memory for details. He even remembered what he was wearing the day he heard about Chad's murder."

"Events like that stick in your head." Jim's voice had lowered. "I remember what I was wearing the day my wife died. Bet you've got memories like that, too."

"No." Brian involuntarily stiffened. "I block them the hell out."

"Hmm." Jim looked aside at him before placing the toothpick back at the corner of his mouth. "Moving on...like we always do when things get too personal for your comfort zone. You sidestep just about any question about your past. It must drive Kaylen nuts, if you do that with her, too. Do you?"

"Probably." Brian refused to take the bait. Despite Jim's well-meant prying, he wasn't in a sharing mood. Never was. The past belonged in the past, and with Tim gone, there was no reason to revisit it outside of his own mind. He checked the address neatly printed in a notebook his well-meaning new partner had handed him before they started walking Chad's route between work and home.

"There it is." Relieved to find a legitimate excuse not to offend Jim by telling him to shut the hell up, Brian stopped and nodded in the direction of a rundown apartment building on the opposite side of the street. Heavily chipped dark green trim and a battered and dingy purple door at street level made the building appear even less hospitable than its grimy neighbors.

"Christ" Jim let out a low whistle. "I wonder if it looked any better during the days Chad lived there? The place is a dump."

"You didn't find any pics of it when you were researching?"

"Not the outside. A couple of grainy photos showed Chad inside his apartment. In one he was holding a beer and hanging out on the couch with a couple of young guys, the other showed him getting a six pack out of the fridge, a cigarette dangling from his lip. He looked like he'd already had more than the legal limit. Of course, the press fell on that and questioned his management skills with his history of alcoholism." Jim shook his head. "Damned character assassination, if you ask me. If you went through my own snapshots, you'd probably find me holding either a beer bottle or a highball glass in a couple of them, too."

"Sensationalism's always been a big seller," Brian said. "Nowadays, thanks to the 24/7 news coverage, people think they're more at risk of getting shot buying a gallon of milk than they are of getting hit by a car while crossing the street."

"Life gets more and more complicated."

Brian noted ever-tidy Jim placed the toothpick in his pocket for disposal later instead of dropping it on the dirty sidewalk with the rest of the litter strewn around their feet.

"Now I really sound like an old geezer." Jim shook his head. "Kind of sneaks up on you. One day you think you're still current. The next you realize you're not."

"An hour with Sean Hastings convinces me of that," Brian said.

"When I leave him at the prison, I have to check in the mirror to make sure I didn't turn into my grandfather while I was there."

"How's Sean doing?"

"Pretty good. His mother standing by him really helped."

"Your support, too." Jim took a mint out of his pocket, unwrapped it and popped it into his mouth. "How long's his sentence?"

"He'll be out in three to five with good behavior. Hopefully, he'll stay clean. No promises with his background of dealing. Having a crooked cop as a role model was a recipe for disaster. But if Sean hadn't killed his father, I would have died that day. Kaylen, too. I owe that kid a lot."

"Damned mess." Jim sucked energetically on his mint. "My friends say there are no guarantees, anyway, however hard you try to show kids the right way to live."

Brian didn't have an answer for Jim's statement. He visited Sean because he didn't want the teen's defining moment to be shooting his own father. "What else did you see in the photos?" He asked, guiding the conversation back to their investigation.

"Chad didn't seem to own much. He had one of those old chrome-legged dinette sets that may have been a hand-me-down, an ugly floral print couch with an orange crate in front of it as a coffee table, and a small TV on top of a chest of drawers. I bet he slept on the couch."

"Sounds like the sort of place I had when I worked on the docks," Brian said. Sharing information about his early days in Miami was a whole lot easier than reminiscing about Baton Rouge. "Damned depressing to some, but I was on my own and able to afford the rent, so I figured I was doing okay. A couple of the guys I worked with gave me some old furniture they were throwing out. I picked up a mattress on sale. No box spring. It went on the floor."

"Hard to take dates there," Jim said.

Brian shrugged. He had no intention of painting a better picture of his later teen years and early twenties. They'd been rough until he became a longshoreman. Many times he'd gone for days on very little in the way of food, and had to walk everywhere because he couldn't even afford bus fare. Now he was driving around in a Mercedes and dating a socialite. *Life was one strange ride.*

He sensed a presence behind them.

"Hand over your wallets." The voice sounded like a dialed down version of a growl. *Young,* Brian thought. *Trying to sound older and tougher.*

He moved fast. One minute the kid thought he had the upper hand, the next, his knife was in the gutter and he was holding his wrist and yowling in pain.

Jim took a handkerchief out of his pocket and picked up the knife. "Kitchen," he said. "Does your mother know you took this?"

The would-be mugger danced from one foot to the other and glared. "I got it from work." He winced as he carefully opened and closed his hand.

"You're old enough to hold a job?" Brian looked down at him. "What are you...twelve?"

"I'm fifteen." The kid drew himself up. "You were lucky I didn't stab you."

Brian shook his head. The younger the punk, the smarter the mouth. "You're the lucky one. I could've broken your arm."

"He's a cop," Jim said. "A badass one."

"Yeah, right." The kid stopped holding his wrist. "You don't look like a cop to me. You're walking. Where's your car?"

"What's it to you?"

"Bet it'll be stripped when you get back to it." The kid was regaining his bravado.

"Is that what you do when you're not trying to mug people? Boost cars?"

"You an' grandpa better watch your backs." The kid grinned insolently. "Strangers ain't welcome in this 'hood."

"Is that right?" Brian took the knife from Jim and dropped it into a graffiti-covered mailbox.

"You'd better believe it." The kid looked around. "People here don't want strangers on their turf."

"We're not looking for trouble," Jim said. "Just information. About someone who lived here a long time ago."

"Who?" The kid had jammed his hands into his pockets.

"Some guy named Chad Summerfield."

"Never heard of him." The kid started to sidle away.

Brian grabbed one ear. "Not so fast."

The owner of the ear let out a holler. A couple of guys wearing hoodies stopped hanging out on the opposite side of the street and headed across it, their progress respectably fast for people holding up low-slung jeans.

"Shit. So much for keeping a low profile. Here…" Brian handed the kid, ear first, over to Jim. "Keep a hold of him."

Jim had his burner phone out.

"Don't hit 9-1-1 unless I tell you." Brian stepped forward and unbuttoned his jacket. "Nothin' to see here. Move on."

"Who you think you are?" Asked Hoodie Number One, visible gold teeth, a diamond nose ring and lower pants than his companion.

"Your worst nightmare if you don't get the hell out of here."

"'s that right?" Hoodie Number Two stood two paces behind his companion.

"Yeah," Brian said. "Fuck the hell off."

Hoodie Number One reached for his right jacket pocket, which hung lower than the left. Without waiting to see what he planned to bring out of it, Brian kicked him right where the sun may never have shone. Jim let go of the kid's ear and pushed him right into Hoodie Number Two.

All three went down like a pile of dirty laundry out the bottom of a chute.

"Come on, partner. Let's get out of here." Brian started jogging away. "Hit that button and get the cruiser rollin'."

Jim gave the information as they ran. "Pretty bad start to a walk-through of the neighborhood," he said, puffing and panting as they rounded a corner. "You know we'll probably never be able to come back here without a police escort."

"I'm all the escort you need." Brian glanced over his shoulder. Fortunately, no swarm of gangbangers was burning up the street behind them. He slowed to a brisk walk.

"I was afraid you'd say that." Jim put his phone away. "Maybe we should rent a compact car to cruise in and try to be less visible."

Brian shrugged. "Whatever. They're a bunch of punks who think there's safety in numbers."

Jim unbuttoned the top of his Henley. "Which probably worked for them until you came along."

"And you. Good move throwing that kid into them."

"I had to show you that you don't have to worry about me if we get into any more scraps." Jim took off his cap, slapped it against his thigh, creased the brim and set it back on his head.

"I never doubted you for a minute." Brian pointed to a corner store a block away. "Let's go get a soda, grandpa. Running makes me thirsty."

"Now I'm beginning to see why your methods get you into trouble." Jim watched a cruiser pass, lights flashing and siren screaming. "Grandpa." He shook his head. "Never call me that again or I'll have to show you how well I can handle myself."

"I'd like to see that." Brian laughed, glad he hadn't chosen to travel alone.

Jim's burner rang.

"Wipe it off and toss it in the trash," Brian told him. "I've got more back at the hotel. Let the locals figure out what happened back there."

"Won't those punks give descriptions of us?" Jim looked doubtful. "We'll get made in the neighborhood."

Brian didn't care. He'd had the first rush of adrenaline he'd felt in way too long. It was a high to be savored and repeated. "Maybe that'll get us some answers," he said. If not, then he didn't mind stirring up more trouble.

"Maybe it'll make us target practice, instead." Jim said.

"You've gotta stop looking at the glass as half empty." Brian pulled open the shop door and motioned Jim inside. "Shaking the tree may make something drop."

"Or bring down a lot more local punks. With guns." Jim glanced back over his shoulder before leaving the sidewalk.

"Yeah, well, sometimes there's a downside to kicking up dirt."

Jim shook his head. "No wonder you exasperate Hal."

CHAPTER TWENTY-ONE

AFTER BRIAN and Jim had wasted the better part of two hours canvassing a different part of the neighborhood only to learn that no one remembered Chad Summerfield or his murder, Fred Engelhardt called.

"I've been told to give you full cooperation, but keep you out of the building as much as possible," he told Brian. "After talking to my supervisor, I'm still not sure whether yours likes you but thinks you're a giant pain in the neck, or whether he really doesn't like you but appreciates your results."

"Maybe both." Brian mouthed 'Engelhardt' in response to Jim's raised eyebrows.

"So I got permission to get files copied," Engelhardt continued. "There'll be a box waiting for you. Ask at the front desk." He sounded half-asleep. "When you're done, everything has to come back. All items had to be checked, stamped, numbered and itemized. The clerk's pissed off. Too much extra work. He complained to my partner, who called in the middle of me trying to get some sleep. I'm on duty tonight. If you've got questions, give me a call any time after eight. Right now, I'm going back to bed."

"Thanks," Brian said. "Sorry about your disturbed sleep. I'll go pick up the box right now."

"Okay." Engelhardt yawned and hung up.

"Hal's really not happy with me." Brian put away his phone. "Neither's at least a part of TPD. But I got access to Chad's case file."

"Did you really expect Hal to be thrilled you're poking around up here after he ordered you to go home and rest?" Jim finished his coffee, pushed the cup aside and took a packet of gum out of his pocket. He offered some to Brian.

"No, thanks. Let's get the box and regroup. It's almost four, and apart from the list of names I got and the info at lunch, all we've done is wear out shoe leather." They turned in the direction of Best Pic's parking lot.

"Don't forget the mugging attempt." Jim stopped in front of a newspaper box, counted out change and inserted it into the slot. "The more exciting part of our day." He pulled down the door and took out a copy of the Tampa Bay Times.

"The last thing I'd want to do after reading through a bunch of paperwork is read something else," Brian said. "You're not going to have any eyesight left for tomorrow."

Jim checked the headlines. "I always read the daily paper. Never miss."

"I bet you can pick up a copy of the Miami Herald."

"I want to get a better feel for Tampa," Jim said. "What people are interested in. What they do for fun. How much crime and which areas are the worst. That sort of thing."

They crossed the street and passed the auto repair shop Tab had mentioned. Brian glanced into the dim recesses of the shop. Four bays, occupied by three old cars and a pickup. He smelled grease and heard drilling, hissing and banging, as well as swearing from the bay with the pickup.

"Can't fault you for that," he told Jim as he slowed to a saunter.

He checked out the location of the office and spotted what was probably a breakroom at the top of a set of rickety wooden stairs. A glass-fronted door showed a worker in grease-stained gray overalls feeding coins into a vending machine.

Brian picked up his pace as another mechanic emerged from behind an old dark blue Oldsmobile Cutlass with all four tires removed. The mechanic glanced up from wiping his hands on a red rag as Brian and Jim disappeared from view on the other side of the doorway.

"We need to check if any other Summerfields are still in the area," Brian told Jim as they crossed a side street.

Jim nodded. "I'll do a search when we get back to the hotel."

"If there are, and you can locate a phone number, call them," Brian said. "They might be relatives. Give me a list of the rest. I can ask Engle-hardt for help. He's got access to a lot more info than we do."

Jim nodded. "A mite frustrating for you, working outside the depart-ment, isn't it? Cell phones and Wi-Fi have made tracking people down more complicated on one hand but easier on the other. Soon, people will forget a time when everyone had a phone plugged into a wall jack." He chuckled. "With one of those damned cords people tripped over when their teenagers hid in the hall closet for privacy."

He scanned the headlines, flipped the paper over and read the bottom of the front page. "I don't think we've missed much while we've been trying to live in the past. The usual fare: Shootings, terror threats, Congress deadlocked. The promise of a new recipe for banana bread that'll knock the socks off some overworked husband."

"On the front page? What is this, a hick town in the middle of nowhere?"

"No. There's a small paragraph about the cooking section. What are we doing about dinner?"

"Jim, it isn't even five o'clock. What time are you eating these days?" Brian wished he'd told his friend to stock up on snacks while cruising the aisles at Best Pic. Lunch hadn't been that long ago, even if Jim held to the belief that Chinese food only lasted a couple of hours before hunger returned.

"Calm down, buddy." Jim laughed. "All I'm thinking is that if we're going to spend the rest of our waking hours with a box of paperwork, then we might want to order room-service this evening. I can change into shorts and a t-shirt and get comfortable that way. Just trying to plan ahead."

"Sorry, I'm getting irritable. I thought we'd be further along than this. Tomorrow I'm talking to all those guys on Tab's list. What we did this afternoon got us nowhere."

"I wouldn't say that." Jim chewed reflectively on his gum, the newspaper neatly folded and nestling into the crook of his left arm. "We've got oriented to the neighborhood, we've seen where Chad lived and worked, we've been given an oral history of the area, and you've got that list."

"When you put it like that, I've got to admit you're right."

"Grudgingly admit," Jim said.

"Damn right." Brian had to smile, despite his mood. He'd started the day a whole lot more optimistic than he was finishing it. Hopefully, the evidence box would give them more to go on. He wondered whether his detection skills had blunted along with his physical ones.

After picking up the box and returning to Brian's suite, they pored over the material until after midnight, only stopping to eat hamburgers, fries and, at Jim's insistence, tossed salads.

Jim finally yawned, stretched and declared he was seeing double at 12:40 AM. "Time for me to hit the hay." He pushed his chair away from the table. "I'll set my alarm for seven and go through the rest of my research notes with you over coffee."

"Fair enough." Brian rubbed his eyes, which felt as dry as the proverbial sandpaper. "I don't have much left in me, either."

"What did you get; two hours sleep in the last forty-eight?"

"Probably." Brian drained the last few drops from a bottle of water beside the pile of papers on his side of the table. "I have to call Kaylen. I meant to do it earlier, but I even put her on a backburner once I opened this box."

"I know what you mean." Jim shoved his feet into his sandals and stood up. "I didn't finish my burger. It was half-cold by the time I got through reading all the accounts of the murder." He put his plate and napkin onto a tray already containing the remains of Brian's meal. "I'll leave these in the hall on my way out."

"Thanks, Jim. You're a great housekeeper as well as a good partner." Brian smiled at Jim's pained expression. "Go get some sleep. Don't worry about setting an alarm. I'll get to work on this until you're ready to go."

"Yeah, well don't work all night." Jim stepped out into the corridor and set the tray down. "And we're going down for breakfast in the morning."

"Uh-uh. Count me out. I can't eat three meals a day." Brian attached the Do Not Disturb sign to the door handle. "I only ordered dinner because you insisted. I'll brew coffee up here."

"We'll see about that in the morning." Jim took out his card key. "I locked the communicating door earlier, so we've both got our privacy in the evenings."

"Did you talk to Kaylen before we left?" Brian asked.

"Why d'you say that?" Jim opened his door.

"Because you sound like her; nagging me to eat."

"That's because we both care about you and your health." Jim walked inside his room, but stuck his head back out. "We'd both like to see you put back the weight you lost. Regular meals do that. I'm setting my alarm. I'll knock on your door at eight-thirty, and we'll go down. Goodnight." The door closed behind him.

Brian heard the lock click. He closed his own door quietly. *Breakfast.* He didn't know whether to be pleased or pissed. Whether he wanted it or not, he was surrounded by well-meaning but invasive friends.

He looked at the clock as he laid his billfold beside it on the nightstand: 1:00AM. Dammit, he'd better call Kaylen and go to bed if Jim was coming back in a few hours.

He turned off all lights except the one on the nightstand, brushed his teeth and washed up before stretching out on top of the covers. He punched the pillows into a more comfortable position. Things at the club would be winding down. Kaylen should either be in her office or on the way home.

He pulled out his smartphone. She answered on the second ring.

"Hi," she said. "Have you been avoiding me, or are you giving me a taste of how communication with you is going to be when you're back on active duty?"

CHAPTER TWENTY-TWO

No DOUBT ABOUT IT, Brian thought. He'd hurt Kaylen's feelings.

"I've been busy," he told her, careful to keep any edge out of his voice. "I'm calling to apologize for leaving a message on your answering machine yesterday instead of talking to you in person. Jim's with me. We drove up last night."

"And you'd rather talk to Jim on the way up to Tampa than me, huh?"

Yep, she was pissed all right. Unusual for Kaylen, who was always so even-tempered and understanding.

"No. But I couldn't talk to you the way I'd want to with him sitting right next to me."

"Was he with you all day?"

"No, but you sleep during the day."

"I've been awake for hours, Brian. You just don't think sometimes. And you take me for granted."

More than pissed. He'd really screwed up.

"I'm really sorry," he said. "I've told you before...."

"You're not good at relationships. I know. I've heard that excuse too many times. We can all learn, you included." Kaylen sighed. "You can do better. Especially after I told you I love you."

He heard the tremor in her voice and hated himself. "I know. I've been putting this off since you left the boat because I don't know what to say."

"I shouldn't have told you. I put you on the spot, and you're not ready. But I can't take it back. I don't want to. We'll have to get past this somehow."

"Agreed." He felt relief. She was going to be reasonable and stop acting like she owned him.

"Have you thought about us moving in together, at least?"

So much for reasonable.

"That's a huge step," he said, treading carefully. "I've been alone since I was sixteen. I'm a slob of a housekeeper." He paused. Kaylen didn't comment, so he plowed on with the stock excuses. "I keep weird hours; I'm short on conversation and grouchy sometimes…"

"I don't need a laundry list of your short-comings, Brian," she interrupted, and suddenly, unexpectedly, she laughed. "I've known about most of them since I met you, you shit. Honestly, I think you're trying to drive me crazy. And have me give up on you. But that's not going to happen."

"That's reassuring. I'm really sorry."

"For what? Being a chronically poor communicator or driving me crazy?"

"Both."

"Can't you at least *try* to change?"

"I *have* changed. Before I met you, I wouldn't have picked up the phone until I got back to Miami."

"No wonder you have trouble keeping girlfriends. If I didn't love you, I would have given up on you, too."

"Don't," he said, suddenly more than a little concerned. Life without Kaylen wouldn't be worth much, he thought. If only he could break through the wall he had built around his emotions. Even a little. But he couldn't risk it. Kaylen was way out of his league, and one day, she'd wake up from whatever dream she was living in and realize it. *Then she'd leave him.* He didn't even know how he'd cope with that on top of everything else.

"So what are you working on?" She asked into the silence. "Something you can't tell me about?"

"No. Since it's a cold case, the rules are bit different. Unlike Tim's, where even I can't get information that's not available to the general public."

He hadn't been able to tell her anything when Tim went missing. It had caused a lot of misunderstandings between them and left Kaylen frightened and resentful. Brian didn't want that to happen again. He filled her in on his conversations with Ted, Mel and Shelley, then, after a brief hesitation, about his encounter with Mel on the *Need to Know*.

"Wow," Kaylen said after a long minute. "I don't know what I want to do first: Punch Mel, scratch her eyes out, or jump straight to taking her out for a long ride on the *NTK* and throwing her overboard with weights around her ankles and her hands tied behind her back."

"I'll keep that in mind when you're really mad at me," Brian said.

"Don't joke about this. It's serious. Thank God you're not like a lot of other guys, or you'd have taken her up on the invitation, and we'd both be dealing with that instead of your monumental lack of communication."

"No way, especially after what you just said. And you've got a gun now. You told me once you should have shot me yourself."

"I was joking. You know that. But I'd never even think about it, no matter how mad I get at you. I'm not much for physical confrontations." She cleared her throat. "Sometimes that's an asset, but since the business with Tim, it's also been somewhat of a liability."

So much for lightening the tension with a joke, Brian thought. He really was hopeless at figuring things out when it came to Kaylen.

"I appreciate you no end, Brian," she said. "I don't think you'd ever willingly make me jealous or feel like I wasn't important to you, but our relationship is more of a struggle than I even guessed it would be when we got together. You've got so much baggage. I wish we could work through it and get to the *us* part of things."

"That's the truth." He wished he could come up with some more meaningful comment at that moment, but he couldn't.

"Let's change the subject," Kaylen said, as silence lengthened between them again. "Whenever I throw too much emotional stuff at you, I shut you right down." She took a deep breath.

Brian did, too. He closed his eyes and hated himself for being so screwed up. He doubted he'd ever be the man Kaylen wanted or expected him to be, no matter how many sessions he had with the shrink.

"How *are* things going up there, anyway?" She asked.

Her voice still sounded slightly shaky around the edges, but it had that determined tone Brian recognized from previous trying situations.

"Slow. But Jim's convinced we're making progress." He shifted down on the pillows, getting more comfortable. Talking about the case was far easier. "I'm not so sure of that. I've got names of people to interview tomorrow, but I'm not holding out much hope of anyone giving me anything useful. I'm learning how frustrating a cold case can be. It's harder to trip people up when they've had years to rehearse alibis and polish up their bullshit. I'm beginning to feel like people talked together at the time of Chad's murder and agreed to close ranks."

"Some sort of conspiracy?"

"No. More like protecting someone, maybe. I don't know. I'm not used to dealing with either the well-rehearsed scripts or the old, blurred and maybe inaccurate memories. Things are usually sharp, fresh and raw in my world."

"So it's tougher going," she said. "You're up to it. If anyone can figure this out, it's you. I bet that's why Hal wants you to take that new position. I doubt he ever thought about pushing you into some basement to keep you away from where you could get hurt or cause others to be."

"Maybe," Brian conceded.

"I wish I could be of more help. I never thought I'd say this, but I miss seeing you working a case. The exciting part, that is. Not the dangerous part..." She stopped speaking.

He sensed why she had faltered, but he didn't want to ask her outright. "Are you all right, hon?" He asked gently, instead.

"I got another flashback. I hate those."

His senses hadn't failed him. "They'll go away with time," he reassured her, wishing he was there and able to hold her instead of talking at the end of a phone line. "What was it?"

"You. Getting shot. I smelled the blood."

Damn.

"Is it gone?"

"Mostly. I've still got a metallic taste in my mouth. I think that's worse than the visuals sometimes."

"I'm fine," he assured her. "You *know* that. Let it go."

"I will; I am."

She was crying. Brian closed his eyes, and for a moment, he felt the impact, the sharp pain in his face when flying glass hit... He forced the memory away, opened his eyes and sat up. He heard Kaylen discreetly blowing her nose.

She cleared her throat again. "It's gone. Funny how that reassurance phrase works. I wish I was right there with you, though. Nothing like your warm body to send away those horrible memories."

"I miss you, too" He felt relief. She was getting better, he told himself. The flashbacks weren't triggered as frequently.

"I would have come up there with you guys, if you'd given me the chance. I still can. I could take a flight."

"You're something else," he said, astonished at her willingness to drop everything at a moment's notice.

"You'd better believe it. Don't short-change me." Kaylen's voice sounded much stronger. "I was your partner for a while, remember? I can help. Tell me what to do, and I'll do it. I want the *real* you back. I've been dealing with your depressed and mixed-up twin for the last few months. He's okay, but he's not you."

"I know. I'm not liking him much, either, and I'm with him 24/7. I've told you before; you'd get better faster if you weren't around me."

"Don't even think about going there."

Her voice was quivering again. Brian gave himself another mental kick for his never-ending foot-in-the-mouth behavior. He searched desperately for something Kaylen could do to help that wouldn't place her at risk, however remotely.

"Didn't you say Mel's daughter needed a job?" she asked. "What can she do?"

"Let me think..." He rewound his memories of their first encounter.

Teddy's ball going into the water. Shelley saying she'd just moved down from North Dakota...

"Waitressing," he said. "She plans to go to college, but she wants to wait tables so she and her son can get an apartment instead of staying with Ted and his wife."

"And that job I can give her." Kaylen sounded a lot less emotional. "I'll get Rob to interview her, and unless she can't provide references or she's been up to something illegal in the past, she can start training. That'll give me a chance to pump her indirectly for information. I'll get him to make friends with her."

"Better tell Rob what he's about to get himself into," Brian said. "But that's a great idea. Thanks. You're great, Kaylen. I mean that. No kidding around."

"So move in with me. If I'm so great, why are you hesitating?"

"I'm a loner. I need my space."

"So you'll still have the boat. You can go there any time you want."

"You say that now, but you'd be upset if I spent most of my time on the *NTK*."

"You can't prove that unless it happens," she said. "I'm not trying to put you on a short leash. I understand it's going to take time for you to adjust after living alone for so long, but you can do it. Don't pull that 'I'm too old' thing again."

"Let me think about it a little longer," he told her, making sure he said it gently. "I'm a lot less depressed now I'm working this case. It feels more normal to me than chartering. More fulfilling, even though right now I'm frustrated, and Jim friggin' wants me downstairs by eight-thirty for breakfast." He glanced at the clock: 1:45AM.

Kaylen laughed. "Good. He listened when I asked him to take better care of you when I'm not around."

"I'll gain back the twenty-five pounds I lost and forty more if he keeps forcing food on me the way he did yesterday."

"I'll keep any extra pounds off you." Her voice had dropped to an intimate tone. "You can work it off in bed with me."

"I suppose you want phone sex now." He found himself smiling, and the tightness in his shoulders relaxed. He lay back down, sinking gratefully into the pillows.

She giggled. "No, I'm too tired for that. Maybe tomorrow. I'll take a rain check."

"We should get off the phone. It's almost two a.m."

"Hmm." The tension over, she sounded like she was beginning to drift. Kaylen had developed an ability to go from completely awake to completely asleep in a matter of minutes after the sleep deprivation they had both suffered at the beginning of their relationship.

"Goodnight, hon," he said. "I miss you."

"Miss you, too." She hung up without saying she loved him.

Even though she was gone, he lay with the phone against his ear a few moments longer before he placed it on the nightstand.

CHAPTER TWENTY-THREE

BRIAN AWOKE to insistent ringing coming from the hotel phone. He picked it up. "Hello?"

"Mr. Swift, this is the concierge. Your traveling companion, Mr. Paxton has requested the purchase of a large amount of office equipment for a short stay at the hotel. I wanted to get your authorization before I put in the order."

"Mr. Paxton's authorized to request anything he wants." Brian looked at the time: 8:15 AM. He'd forgotten to set his alarm and slept like a rock for the first time in months. He sat up. "What did he order?"

"Let me see."

Brian heard rustling paper. He got out of bed. He'd slept in his clothes. Amazingly, he didn't feel as stiff and painful as usual.

"A copy machine. Toner. Copy paper. A camera. Notepads and pens. A separate scanner. A laptop and a tablet. A recording device..."

"...All of it. Authorized. How quickly can you get it here?" *Jim was setting up a mobile office, and he wanted to start by copying every one of the files in that box from TPD.*

"You want it expedited?"

"Yes, but call me with the total before you get it sent."

"Very good, sir. Will that be on your hotel bill?"

"No. I'll pay with a credit card. When you give me the info, I'll make the call."

"Yes, sir. I should have that for you shortly. We can handle everything through our business office. Do you want me to call you in the room or on your mobile?"

"Mobile."

"Yes, sir. Thank you." She hung up.

Brian smiled to himself. He was liking not having to scrape for every penny, although he still felt uncomfortable about just how much money Tim had left him.

He turned on the shower, thought about having all that equipment cluttering up his or Jim's hotel suite and turned it right back off. He called the concierge. "Can you find me a small office to rent for a month?"

"Yes, sir. We can do anything here at the Plaza."

"Good." Brian felt a surge of optimism. "Better the equipment gets delivered there."

"I'll get started on this right away, Mr. Swift."

Brian headed back to the shower. Not even 8:30 AM and progress had been made. Bringing Jim on board was definitely paying off, even if it meant he'd have to eat three meals a day.

CHAPTER TWENTY-FOUR

TWELVE MINUTES LATER, Brian heard a knock at the door. *Prompt as ever,* he thought, shrugging into his jacket while grabbing his key card and phone.

Jim was dressed for work in khaki pants and a navy blue golf shirt, with a cream jacket. "Morning. You look like you need coffee."

"You've got that right." Brian closed the door behind him. "Your truckload of crap may be ready to go into an office by the time we get back from those interviews."

Jim's expression took on a look of satisfaction as they bypassed a large group of people in suits waiting by the elevators and took the stairs. "I figured the concierge would call you before going ahead with that order. Better than an alarm clock. So you're renting an office? Good. I think we should also hire a temp to manage it. Get a phone line in, that sort of thing."

"You're right. I've authorized you to get anything you want. I'll leave you to follow up on all that." Brian followed Jim as he pushed open the door at the bottom of the stairs and entered the lobby.

A throng of people moved back and forth between the reception desk and bank of elevators. Uniformed bell boys pushed carts loaded with luggage. Lines snaked into three restaurants. Brian wondered if he could convince Jim they needed to find a diner on the way to the interviews instead of wasting time waiting around for a table.

"I thought we'd try the grill this morning," Jim said. "I already made the reservation."

"You're pretty damn devious when you want to be." Brian followed his friend as Jim gave his name and they were escorted to a table in the crowded restaurant.

"You'd better believe it, buddy. I knew you'd want to skip breakfast if you saw a line. As well as making a reservation and starting the office supply order yesterday, I made a list of our accomplishments before I went to bed, and it wasn't even close to a wasted day. I'll pull out my notepad after you've had your first cup of coffee and we'll go over them. We need to decide the order of the interviews, so we don't waste time going back and forth. But first, you can tell me how Kaylen's doing."

Brian figured he'd need to drink a pot of coffee, not a cup.

CHAPTER TWENTY-FIVE

KAYLEN'S PHONE rang as she was putting on lipstick. She took a quick look at the caller ID. Angela Crossfield. What could the wife of one of her primary backers want before lunch on a weekday?

"Hi," Angela said. "Your friends miss you."

"I know; I'm sorry. I've been really bad at keeping in touch." Kaylen sat down on the couch. She wondered how much information about the last four months Angela would need to hear before she was satisfied. Even giving a bare-bones account felt too exhausting to tackle. Unpleasant memories started to well up...

"What are you doing?"

. "Now?"

Kaylen had decided to treat herself to a cup of coffee she hadn't brewed herself. Not much of a goal, but until she met Ziggy at his prospective restaurant, she was at a complete loose end.

"Yes," Angela said. "Right this minute."

"Er...nothing really. Getting ready to go out for coffee. I'm meeting a client in a couple of hours. A consulting job." Kaylen liked the sound of that. She didn't feel so adrift.

"Then you've got time for coffee with me."

"I don't know, Angela." Kaylen felt wary. She still felt bad about ruining Angela's shoes by vomiting onto them the night of her club opening, and she'd purposely kept away from most of her former acquaintances. After her best friends had deceived her, she couldn't bring herself to open up to anyone else in her social circle. How could they possibly understand what her closest friend, Sandy had done? How Sandy and Sam had betrayed her trust? How badly Kaylen felt she'd been used? She refused to even think of the consequences to both those people, once so important to her life: Sandy had been murdered, probably by the drug cartel. Sam had lost his business and become a fugitive on the run in some South American country...

"Oh, come on. You can spare me a few minutes, can't you?" Angela wasn't going to be put off, and Kaylen knew she shouldn't be discourteous and risk unpleasantness. Not if she wanted to keep Jonathan Crossfield happy. "All right. Where do you want to meet?"

"I'm only about ten minutes away. How about Mizelle's?"

Kaylen really liked the little coffee house nestled between a florist and a chocolatier. "You know I've got a soft spot for that place."

Angela laughed. "I remembered. I'll see you there." She hung up.

Kaylen finished applying her lipstick, picked up her purse, keys and sunglasses and made sure her front door locked behind her on the way out. She decided to walk instead of drive and put on her sunglasses as she exited the building. The doorman nodded to her and watched as she went through the security gate and headed off down the sidewalk.

Out of habit, Kaylen glanced around several times as she walked the two blocks, then again before and after she crossed at the light. Nothing out of the ordinary. No cars pulling away from the curb and cruising at a snail's pace. No other pedestrians following along behind. She had learned from Brian over the intervening months. Maybe he'd made her exceptionally cautious, but she preferred that to being blissfully ignorant and a possible target.

How vulnerable she had been. Anyone could have grabbed her when she was married to George. He'd been worried about her, but she'd brushed his concerns aside. Not anymore. Not after what she'd been through.

Kaylen pushed open Mizelle's door and inhaled aromas not only of coffee, but chocolate and baked goods. Little white metal tables with single roses in stem vases beckoned. Their white wicker chairs held green or blue seat covers.

"May I help you?" asked a girl in a pink apron with frills around the edges as she carried a tray of scones through white saloon doors at the back of the shop. Her name tag read 'Dina' in large black letters.

"A table for two." Kaylen smiled at the girl. "And I'd like a mocha, heavy on the chocolate."

"Large or small?"

"Large. With a scone. What flavor are those?" She pointed to the tray Dina had placed on the counter.

"Blueberry. We also have lemon poppy seed, cherry almond or vanilla with a chocolate swirl."

"We should have one of each, don't you think?" Angela said from behind.

Kaylen jumped before she could stop herself. Angela looked gorgeous in a pair of bright white capris, a baby pink silk shirt and her blonde hair caught up in a loose chignon. A flush threatened to creep up Kaylen's neck. Her heart was pounding. She'd let down her guard as soon as she walked into the shop and mentally berated herself. Brian would be shaking his head at her, his frown reproachful, and rightfully so.

She struggled to return Angela's warm smile. "Definitely one of each. Sorry not to have waited, but as soon as I got here, I realized how hungry I am."

"I'll have a double espresso, please," Angela told Dina. "Kaylen, it's so good to see you. Have you been hiding?"

"Some," Kaylen acknowledged as they sat at a corner table bathed in dappled sunlight courtesy of the leaves from a Ficus tree in a huge sea-green ceramic pot.

"We all heard something went on, of course. Tim, then that terrible thing with Sandy…" Angela looked anxiously at Kaylen. "Are you okay? I'm sorry; I shouldn't have brought that up first. What's the matter with me?" She bit her lip. "But I don't really know *where* to start."

"Me, neither. That's why I haven't called anyone. It's too complicated to explain."

"You don't have to explain anything." Angela reached out to pat

Kaylen's hand. "Are you doing okay? Jon said you looked so thin and pale after everything happened, but you don't now."

Kaylen had to smile. "No, I bet I don't. I've been sunbathing and eating far too much fast food."

"You?" Angela's eyebrows rose. "What's got you eating burgers and fries?"

"The man I'm dating."

They waited while Dina deftly placed their scones, seated in a raffia bowl lined with a starched white napkin, into the center of the table. She followed that by placing white plates, forks and napkins folded into little fans in front of each of them, then the coffee. The presentation was as professional as any five star restaurant.

"Will there be anything else?" Dina asked.

"Not for me." Angela looked over at Kaylen and took a sip of her espresso.

"Me, neither. It all looks wonderful." Kaylen smiled again at the girl, who gave her customers an intense once-over before walking quickly back across the room. She stepped behind the counter and stowed her tray on a shelf.

"So, tell me about this man," Angela said. "Do I know him?"

"No," Kaylen shook her head. "I met him through a friend." She wasn't lying, she told herself. Just stretching the truth a little. If it wasn't for Tim, she'd never have met Brian.

"And you really like him a lot, don't you?" Angela pointed to the plate of scones. "You choose first."

Kaylen selected the cherry almond and bit into it. She nodded at Angela while she chewed and swallowed. "I do, yes. He's very different from George or Tim. My life has changed a lot in the last four months. Brian's one of the good things. The club operating in the black is another. I like the condo I'm leasing, and as you said, I look and feel much better."

"So when can Jon and I meet Brian?" Angela was tenacious, like a sophisticated terrier. She took the vanilla scone, drizzled with white frosting, cut it into pieces and popped one of them into her mouth.

"I don't know." Kaylen thought she shouldn't have mentioned Brian, but he was such a big part of her life. She was tired of hiding their relationship, even if he thought it best. "He's very private. He doesn't want his photo taken and plastered all over social media."

"If he's dating you, he should get prepared for that." Angela took another sip of espresso and dabbed her mouth with her napkin. "He's not going to be able to hide forever."

Kaylen knew that, and so did Brian. But he didn't want her associated with Hastings' death or the cartel. He wanted her safe and unafraid in her daily life. If only she could get to that point, she thought, involuntarily glancing out the window as a shadow passed across the table. It was nothing, she told herself. Someone jogging, a cyclist...but she felt exposed in front of the window, despite the Ficus that provided cover as well as shade. She was really grateful they were meeting close to lunchtime, when people were more apt to go for a sandwich than coffee with a scone. The little shop, so busy at breakfast, was empty except for them.

"Have you heard anything from Sam?" Angela asked.

"No, thank God." Kaylen had finished her mocha. She beckoned to Dina. "Can I have a glass of orange juice, please?"

The girl was crouched down behind the counter. "In a moment," she mumbled.

Kaylen's level of anxiety crept up a notch. *Stop it,* she told herself, angry with her jittery behavior.

"I can't believe he left Miami so suddenly," Angela said. "Why didn't he defend himself?"

Because there was nothing to defend.

"He must have realized the police had a good case against him." Kaylen glanced out the window again and saw a man leaning against a palm tree, beneath a flapping banner that announced a winter special for boat storage. Was it her imagination, or did he look straight at her?

"Jon and I wanted to go to Tim's funeral, but we were told it was a private affair."

Kaylen forced herself to watch her companion instead of the scenery beyond Angela's left shoulder.

Angela selected another piece of scone. "We couldn't even send flowers or a card. We were so worried about you, but here you are already with a new man in your life, and looking, well, at least somewhat happy." She peered at Kaylen. "But I'm still concerned about you. You're looking anxious."

"Some days, I'm concerned about myself." Kaylen tried smiling at Angela. It wasn't easy. She took another bite of her scone, even though her appetite had vanished. Chewing and swallowing with difficulty, she realized what had tasted feather-light only moments before had turned into cardboard. "It was a rough time. I still have flashbacks. Yesterday while I was in my office, I looked up and swore Sam was standing in the doorway."

Her orange juice arrived. Dina slopped juice from the overly-filled glass, didn't stop to mop it up or ask if they wanted anything else before bolting back behind the counter.

While Kaylen placed a couple of napkins under the glass to sop up the spill, she watched Dina from the corner of her eye. The girl went back to fumbling around behind the display case.Angela prattled on. "How horrible," she said, eyes wide. "Are you having some sort of hallucinations? Because of what you went through?"

Kaylen nodded and smiled ruefully. "Apparently it's a form of PTSD. Post-Traumatic Stress Disorder. Unsettling, to put it mildly. A lot less frequent now, but I still feel better when I'm not alone."

"No wonder Jon said you've been spending a lot of time at the club."

"Not because of that. I couldn't be a hands-on owner when the club first opened." Kaylen took a deep breath. "I'm so sorry about your shoes. I'll pay the replacement cost."

Angela looked puzzled for a moment. "Oh," she said. "Those? Gone and almost forgotten." She smiled, her eyes warm. "You were so ill. Tim was so good with you."

"He was the one who made me ill, unfortunately." Kaylen drank half her orange juice in steady gulps. "He put something into my champagne. It was supposed to make me pass out, but instead, it made me violently sick. Thankfully, it did take away my memory of whatever happened next, but it took three terrible weeks before my life got back to anything like normal. The club was one place I could count on being the same as it was when I left it."

"Oh, Kaylen." Angela put down the scone.

"I'm okay," Kaylen said. "If I don't talk about this now, I don't think

I'll ever be able to, and the psychologist I consulted told me I needed to unburden myself, as he put it, to someone other than Brian."

Angela nodded. "You can trust me. I won't say anything to anyone other than Jonathan if you don't want me to."

"Trust. There's a word." Kaylen took a sip of her juice, her throat dry. "I'm really short on trust these days."

"I'll have to earn it, then." Angela smiled thinly. "I want to do that. You need to be able to count on some of us."

"I know a few I wouldn't count on." Kaylen managed a small smile, herself.

"You've got that right." Angela nodded. "So, let's move past that horrible period for now. You're living somewhere else, too."

Kaylen nodded. "My condo was ransacked, and my housekeeper was murdered in the bathtub. I know you heard about all that. You must have. I couldn't possibly live there afterward."

She stopped, took a moment to deep-breathe and swallow the lump forming in her throat. Angela waited silently, her expression open but her mouth pinched.

"So now I'm leasing a nice place only a short walk from here." Kaylen tried to sound positive. "Fourth floor, with a view of the pool. Sunny, but not hot. It's pretty nice." Angela's hand patted Kaylen's lightly, the contact comforting. Kaylen wiped a tear from the corner of her eye with one finger. "Everything's slowly improving. Can we talk about something else?"

"Of course." Angela withdrew her hand and eyed the blueberry scone. "Want to split it? I can't eat the whole thing."

Kaylen looked at her own half-finished scone. "No, you go ahead. I'm still working on this."

"I thought you were hungry." Angela's brow furrowed. "I took your appetite away with my probing, didn't I? I should have let you tell me on your own terms, whenever *you* wanted to."

"Talking about Tim always makes me sad and kind of angry, too." Kaylen abandoned her efforts to eat the scone, which was sticking in her throat. She finished the orange juice. "He was a good guy in many ways, but he had a lot of secrets, including a bunch of bad connections. I was so worried that would affect the club, but it doesn't seem to have done any damage."

"Not much came out in the local media," Angela said. "It was one of those small news items at the end of a broadcast, which never resurfaced the following day, like an afterthought."

Kaylen thought Hal Shaw must have pulled some very heavy strings. "It's all in the past," she said. "And it has to stay there."

"Fair enough, but I want you and Brian to come for dinner next week," Angela insisted. "Jon will be thrilled to have male company when we see you. He didn't get on well with Tim, but I'm sure Brian's going to be different."

"Jonathan never got over George's death." Kaylen felt a pang of sadness, talking about her late husband. "He couldn't see me with anyone else."

"I don't think he'd agree," Angela said. "He's tried to keep an open mind. After all, you're a young woman. But he told me he thought Tim was a player, and he didn't want that for you."

"He *was* a player," Kaylen said. "But then he apparently reformed. He'd been in a lot of trouble in the past, so I've since found out."

"Do you think that's why you fell for him? Good girls always do like the bad boys."

"Maybe. He was so handsome and exciting. Generous, too. He bought me presents all the time." Kaylen managed a half-smile. She still didn't like talking about Tim, either. She knew she hadn't dealt with her feelings. Instead, she'd swept that relationship under a rug because she didn't want to hurt Brian. She didn't want him to think she compared him with Tim, even though she had to admit she had done so in the beginning.

Brian had tipped the scales in his own favor many times over, she thought, except Tim knew how to make a relationship progress, while Brian had drawn some invisible line in the sand, over which he wouldn't step.

She looked up to find Angela patiently waiting her out, sipping espresso.

"Brian's out of town right now." Kaylen took a deep breath. Time to open up, at least partially. "He's a homicide detective, and he's working a cold case. I'll ask him about dinner when he gets back."

"A detective? Really?" Angela put down her scone. "That's a change for you. Did you meet him while the police were trying to solve Tim's case?"

"Yes." Kaylen could just imagine what Brian would say about her blabbing even a partial truth, but she was tired of keeping their relationship under wraps. "Actually, he's er, well, related to Tim, but nothing like him."

Angela's eyebrows shot up. "Related how?"

Kaylen knew she should have kept her mouth shut, but it would only have delayed the inevitable. They'd never get through dinner with the Crossfields without answering questions from both Angela and Jonathan.

"They're half-brothers. Brian's four years older and doesn't resemble Tim in any way. He's really tough and fairly abrasive on the outside, but he's not that way with me. Not now." She smiled, thinking how much Brian had changed over the last few months. He'd begun to show a more vulnerable side. Only slightly, but it was progress, and she clung to that.

"Boy, are you a surprise." Angela finished her coffee. "How long's he going to be away?"

"I'm not sure. He didn't get assigned to the case. His neighbor's son got killed in a robbery up in Tampa some years ago. Brian's investigating as a favor."

"Well." Angela pushed her empty cup and the partially-eaten scone aside. "Your life really *has* changed. And I sense you don't want to talk any more about those changes today, am I right?"

"You are." Kaylen felt a gush of relief and gratitude. Angela wasn't as pushy as she'd appeared during their previous encounters.

"My treat," Angela said when Kaylen took her purse from the back of the chair. She pulled out a credit card and placed it inside the black leather folder the waitress had left. "Maybe you'd like to have a girls' day out sometime soon? Shopping and lunch?"

"That sounds great." Kaylen missed her friendship with Sandy very much. Nowadays, she always seemed to be surrounded by men. "A day of clothes, perfume and maybe a salad at Vinny's, by the water in South Beach?"

"Now you're talking." Angela laughed.

The sun had swung around while they chatted. Kaylen saw a flash behind the counter. Then she saw something in Dina's hand as she held it out in front of her, level with her face.

Kaylen's flashbacks collided with reality, and she reacted out of instinct. "Get down!"

She grabbed Angela on her dive for the floor. The metal table toppled over, bringing china and silverware raining down on them. Kaylen wished she had listened to Brian and carried the Sig in her purse.

Dina screamed. A glass cake stand fell from the counter and the object she was holding flew with it. The cake stand shattered on the black and white tile floor. A smartphone skittered across the tiles.

Out of the back of the shop, Mizelle, the owner came running. She made straight for Kaylen and Angela. Shaking from head to foot, Kaylen was already getting up. Angela opted for sitting on the floor, dragging her hair off her face and trying to shove it back into her chignon.

"My God," Mizelle said. "I came in the back door and heard screaming and breaking glass. I dropped an entire flat of strawberries on the kitchen floor." She looked from Kaylen to Angela and swung around to face her waitress. "Dina, what were you *doing?*"

Dina was crying like a two year old, mouth wide open and hands trembling as tears streamed down her face. "T...t...taking a photo of them with my phone." She grabbed a handful of napkins from a holder on a table and jammed them against her mouth.

"For *what?*" Mizelle helped Angela to her feet.

"To...to...post on Facebook." Dina picked up her phone.

"You should have the sense to never, ever do that without a customer's permission," Mizelle said. "You're fired." She held out her hand. "And you are to give me that phone."

"It's mine." Dina held the phone against her chest.

"Not with photos of Angela and me in it," Kaylen said. "Give it to me right now. Did you post anything?"

Dina shook her head. "No. I didn't have a chance to. My boyfriend told me to do it. He thought we could get some money maybe, for the pics."

"Not after posting on Facebook, you couldn't." Angela straightened her shirt and brushed crumbs off her pants.

"My customers come in here assured of their privacy," Mizelle said. "Celebrities come to buy my pastries on a regular basis. I told you that when I hired you."

"But Kaylen Roberts is different." Dina used the wadded up napkins to wipe the tears from her blotchy red face. "My boyfriend said she hasn't been seen in public since her lover was murdered and her mint... ment...friend left the country so he wouldn't be sent to jail. No one's taken any photos of her in *months*. He said I'd have an exclusive thing and TV and The Enquirer would pay to have them."

"The word you were looking for is mentor," Angela said. She walked over and glared down at Dina, who was several inches shorter. "And you and your boyfriend are idiots. If you post any photos, Kaylen and I will sue you. Not Mizelle. You, personally." She leaned forward.

The girl took a couple of steps back. Angela snatched the phone out of her hand, threw it onto the floor and stomped on it with her Jimmy Choo sandal before grinding her heel against the glass screen.

Kaylen heard cracking.

"I'll give you fifty dollars to buy yourself a prepaid until you get this one replaced," Angela said. "If you ever even mention our names or Mizelle's café, and I hear about it; remember, I'm suing you." She picked her purse up off the floor, took out a fifty dollar bill and handed it to the waitress.

"Now, get out," Mizelle said.

Dina started for the back of the shop. Mizelle followed. "I'll be right back," she assured Kaylen and Angela. "I want to make sure this girl and her belongings are in the alley before I lock the door behind her."

Kaylen turned to Angela. "I'm so sorry. I feel like such an idiot."

Angela surveyed the chaos. "No harm done." She picked up Dina's phone and put it in her purse. "Jonathan will take care of destroying everything," she said. "This table looks too heavy for Mizelle to pick up by herself. Want to give me a hand getting it upright?"

"I need to do more than put the table back where it belongs." Kaylen looked around at the mess she had inadvertently created. "I'm going to help Mizelle clean up."

Angela wrinkled her nose a little, but after they righted the table and put the chairs back in place, Kaylen brought a plastic tub from behind the counter and Angela started placing broken crockery into it.

Mizelle reappeared with a broom and dustpan. "I can't believe the nerve of that girl." She swept in short, purposeful strokes. "I have to apologize for her, and for me hiring her." A pile grew of soiled napkins, glass shards, and crumbs.

Angela placed the last piece of china into the tub. "Definitely the most exciting morning I've had in a long time." She looked from Mizelle's frown to Kaylen's widened eyes and laughed.

Kaylen decided she liked Angela a lot. Her companion's white pants were spattered with coffee, her hair had refused to be anchored back into place, and yet she looked cheerful as she took the plastic tub behind the counter.

"It's been a long time since I cleaned anything. The real newsworthy pics would be me carrying a tub full of broken crockery or standing in front of a sink."

"Oh, Angela." Kaylen had to laugh.

After a long moment, Mizelle managed a smile. "Would you accept a dozen scones and coffee to go?"

Angela shook her head. "No need. And don't worry, we'll be back, won't we, Kaylen?" She brushed one particularly grimy area on her pants. "Well, I'm going home to change. This outfit needs to be trashed."

"This was all my fault." Kaylen ran her hands through her tangled hair and watched more crumbs fall onto the floor. "Mizelle, at least let me pay for the broken china."

Angela shook her head emphatically. "There's way too much apologizing going on here. Mizelle's going to have to wash this floor and the one in the back, where all those strawberries are, and hire another waitress. That's more than enough punishment for Dina's bad behavior. Kaylen, you're going to need to get cleaned up, too. Maybe you haven't noticed, but your capris are covered in blueberry scone. I think we should all declare this meeting over, but get back together in a few days to have a really good laugh about it."

"Deal," Kaylen said.

"Deal." Mizelle held the door open and turned the sign to 'Closed.'

Angela stepped outside. Kaylen followed.

"Lunch and shopping," Angela said. "I'll pick you up. What about the day after tomorrow at noon?"

"It's a date." Kaylen felt profound relief as the rest of the tension flowed out of her body. "I'll be in the lobby waiting for you."

Angela paused beside her convertible. "Let me give you a ride back. You're not going to keep a low profile looking like you do right now."

Kaylen glanced down and saw the blueberry stains. "Thanks." She climbed onto the cream leather passenger's seat of Angela's blue Porsche Boxster. The top silently rose over them, settling into place.

"No sense in giving any more people something to take a photo of." Angela glanced in the rearview mirror. "We're a bit of a sight."

"Angela, I'm so sorry...," Kaylen began.

"Enough apologizing." Angela winked as she pulled away from the curb. "No worries. But I'm going to try never to scare you."

CHAPTER TWENTY-SIX

KAYLEN DECIDED to throw away her clothes. She doubted she'd ever get the stains out of them, and she didn't need reminders of her over-reaction. So much for thinking she had almost recovered from the mayhem surrounding Tim's murder.

She showered, dressed and reapplied her makeup. She had just enough time to get to her meeting with Ziggy without being more than a few minutes late.

After reviewing her behavior, she had decided not to call Brian. Unloading on him seemed selfish as well as cowardly. He'd worry about her when he should be concentrating on his case. She'd send Mizelle flowers and explain her reaction to Angela in more detail. Angela looked like she could deal with a lot more than Kaylen had given her credit for prior to the coffee shop incident.

She gazed at her reflection in the mirror. "Get a grip," she told herself. "You've got to stop thinking there's an assassin hiding every-where you go." In Brian's attempt to make her more aware of potential dangers, she decided he'd turned her into a nervous wreck.

When she arrived at the restaurant in Little Havana, she saw Ziggy standing outside, anxiously checking passing traffic. Kaylen found a parking space a few doors away.

"Hi," she said as she walked up to him.

He peered at her. "Kaylen?"

She removed her sunglasses. "Of course. Who else around here's five-eleven in bare feet?"

"True." He kissed her on both cheeks.

Very European, but a bit invasive for Miami, she thought, pulling away. "Is the owner here?"

"No, but I've got better news." Ziggy took her arm and tugged at her. "Let's talk in my car."

"How about we talk in *my* car?" She pulled out of his grasp. "I thought you were set on this place?"

"I was until I talked to a friend yesterday."

Ziggy walked beside her to her car and waited while she unlocked it. He sat in the passenger's seat and smiled his wide smile at her. Kaylen felt the effect, even while she reminded herself that she was only being asked to consult on a business. He really did remind her of Tim. Friendly, outgoing, easy company…she gave herself a mental reprimand when she started comparing him with Brian. *No comparison,* she thought, annoyed with her reversion to shallow, socialite behavior.

Brian had raw courage and incredible depth. What he lacked in charisma, he more than made up for in other ways, Kaylen sharply reminded herself. And his ability to turn her on with little more than a look wasn't something any other man had even come close to emulating.

"You're a little distant and tense today," Ziggy said. "Are you okay?"

"Yes, of course," she snapped, before she could stop herself.

Shallow and shrewish was more like it. Brian's absence had made her more than tense, but she wasn't about to admit that to a virtual stranger, however friendly he appeared to be.

"I'm a bit short on time," she said, as though that explained her behavior. She ignored Ziggy's slightly bewildered expression. "And you're telling me you've changed your mind yet again. I don't think this collaboration's going to work."

"I haven't changed my mind about owning my own restaurant," Ziggy said. "But I've got a partner now. A childhood friend I ran into yesterday evening. He's willing to put up as much money as I do, and he believes his father will back us with anything else we need until we can turn a profit and pay him back."

"You need to schedule a meeting with your friend and his father as soon as possible," Kaylen said. "Find out how much you'll really have for a restaurant. I don't think Little Havana's a good location for you. This area's very ethnic, and you're not going to fit in unless your friend's heritage is Cuban."

"I agree. After we had our meeting in South Beach, I walked around the area and decided I would like my restaurant to be there, instead. I would have preferred Coconut Grove or Coral Gables, but my father and Apollo would then be in competition, and too close. They would come over and tell me what to do, or more correctly, what I was doing wrong, on a daily basis."

"Isn't that the truth?" Kaylen could imagine them both strutting through Ziggy's establishment with their deprecating comments. "What's your friend's name?"

"Louis Gilman."

"His father's Leonard Gilman?"

Ziggy nodded.

"If Louis isn't giving you lip service, this could potentially solve all your financial issues," Kaylen said. Leonard Gilman had been a close acquaintance of George's. He owned the Colonial Sports and Activewear conglomerate. "But why would Louis want to join you in the restaurant business when he could work for his father?"

Ziggy gazed through the windshield at the throng crowding the side-walk. "He is in a similar situation to mine. He has two elder siblings who are already making their mark in the family business. He wants to do something independently, where he can earn his own money and stand apart from the others."

"It must be tough sometimes, being a younger member of a large family," Kaylen said. "I'll never know that; I'm an only child."

"But you could marry into a large family and see the drama first-hand."

"I don't think that's going to happen."

Kaylen thought about the fact that Brian now had even less family than she did. None, in fact. She felt a pang of sorrow for him. Tim may have infuriated Brian, but they'd had that family bond. She had a father, but he hadn't contacted her since she'd told him she was marrying George Bannister Roberts. Preston Grant had told her in no uncertain terms how stupid she was and slammed the phone down in her ear. He had refused to attend her wedding to 'the old man' as he had dubbed George.

"Why don't you have that meeting with Louis and Leonard, and then call me if you get an agreement in writing?" She told Ziggy. "Until you've got something concrete, there's no sense in us looking at any potential restaurant sites."

"Okay." He nodded. "Thank you for meeting me. Would you let me take you to dinner? To thank you?"

"I don't think that's a good idea. It's too much like mixing business with pleasure, and I already have a boyfriend."

"It would only be a friendly dinner," Ziggy said. "Your boyfriend is in law enforcement. I wouldn't take the chance of making him angry with me."

"You'd better continue to keep that in mind." Kaylen shook her head. "You're too young for me, anyway."

"I'm twenty-eight. I have a youthful face."

"I'm thirty-two," Kaylen said. "I'll be thirty-three in a few months, and I feel a lot older than that sometimes. Especially lately. Life's really complicated."

"I'm a good listener," Ziggy said. "It's one of my best assets. I've been listening to my family all my life, except for the years I was in competitive sailing. It wasn't easy to communicate when I was moving around so frequently."

"That must have felt weird at first. But after you adjusted, maybe a bit of a relief, not having people telling you what to do all the time."

Ziggy nodded slowly. "I suppose you could say that. But I missed everyone, even Apollo. Being alone can also be very lonely."

"Yes."

She thought of Brian again. She couldn't stop thinking about him. She felt obsessed, and supposed he'd be upset with her if he knew. He liked her to be strong and independent, not clingy and high-maintenance. Sometimes it was a strain to live up to his high standards, or her own.

Much as she loved being a club owner, she worried constantly that without Sam Wilson's expertise and input, she'd make a mistake that would seriously impact the financial health of Bannisters, and jeopardize both her backers and her employees.

A flutter of unease stirred in her gut. What was she thinking, trying to tell Ziggy what to do? Where did she get off thinking she was an expert because she'd managed to stay in the black for the four months Bannisters had been open?

"Well, I had better go; I have to call Louis." Ziggy opened the door carefully, to avoid bumping pedestrians on the sidewalk. "Thank you, Kaylen," he said as he got out. He leaned into the car before closing the door. "I hope you will change your mind and take me up on my dinner invitation. I'm quite trustworthy, and I would never try to get between you and your boyfriend."

"That's good to hear." Relieved, Kaylen sat and watched him walk away, down the sidewalk toward the restaurant he had wanted to buy only twenty-four hours earlier.

Ziggy didn't know what he wanted, she decided. Until he did, she was not going to spend any more time on this consulting project, and she should have told him that. But she liked him, and she didn't want him to lose his inheritance because of a bad decision. When she had managed Sam's restaurant, everything had seemed so easy to deal with. The difference was that she was playing with her own money now, she told herself, instead of Sam's.

She decided to drive over to the club instead of going home. She wanted to review the menus Emrico, the head chef, had compiled for the week. His choices were usually in keeping with the 40's-era club, but a couple of times he had tried to sneak some contemporary dishes past her. As she pulled away from the curb, something made her look at the little restaurant again, and her heart contracted painfully, skipping a beat. She had no more time to look at anything but the traffic as a loud honk caused her to check her rearview mirror. She saw a bus bearing down on her car, accelerated and pulled into a space barely big enough to accommodate her Beamer, causing more honking.

Completely rattled, she managed to avoid sideswiping a cab. "Sorry, sorry," she mouthed to no one in particular. She gripped the wheel tightly as she accelerated and maneuvered her way through to the expressway. Inside, she was quaking like an aspen leaf in a high wind.

Thirty minutes later, she opened the menu plan on her laptop, but she couldn't concentrate. The print swam, and she seriously thought about asking Julio or Rob to fix her a strong drink from the bar. But if either of them saw her, they'd know something was wrong, and she certainly wasn't going to discuss her fears with her employees.

Kaylen tried to convince herself she was being silly, being paranoid, seeing things that weren't there, but she couldn't do it. Finally, after a completely non-productive hour, she admitted she felt an overwhelming need to call Brian and tell him about her day, in the hope he'd tell her she had been acting like an idiot, and reassure her nothing was wrong. From the incident at Mizelle's to what she thought she had seen in that restaurant window as she pulled away from the curb, her day had been strange and disturbing. And despite the post-traumatic stress that had plagued her after Brian's injury, she knew she hadn't been hallucinating that afternoon.

Because when she had pulled her BMW away from the curb in Little Havana, she swore she had seen Sam Wilson sitting in the window of the diner Ziggy had wanted to purchase.

CHAPTER TWENTY-SEVEN

"Why you wanna drag up ole history?" Chico Ramos kept his eyes on the oily red rag while he wiped his hands, then stuffed the rag into a back pocket of his overalls. He took a lamp and illuminated the underside of the car he had up on the lift in the service bay. Evidently finding what he was looking for, he hung the lamp and started toward the work bench holding his tools.

Brian handed him a wrench. "A new lead," he said.

Ramos' eyes narrowed, but he took the wrench. "What new lead?" He peered under the car before inserting and twisting the wrench hard a couple of times. "You're not with local cops, so why you so interested in finding Chad's killer?"

"Enough questions," Brian said. "What's it to you, anyway? All I want is for you to tell me where you were, and what you were doing. Who you saw hanging around."

"I told everything I knew to the cops back then." Ramos came out from under the car. "I don't remember details now. It's been too long. What? Twenty years?"

"Twenty-five. But unless you see murders on a regular basis, I can't see you forgetting much about that day."

"I've got a bad memory." Ramos sent a shrill whistle in the direction of a young guy hovering around another mechanic at the next bay. When the kid looked up, Ramos pointed to his car. "Ready. Get it out of here." He moved on to the next bay, picked up a clipboard and studied the scribble on a work order.

"You'd better recover your memory real fast," Brian said.

"Or what?"

Standing right beside the car, which was also raised up, Ramos was in a bad position to mouth off.

Brian rapped Ramos's head against a tire. "That clear things up for you?"

Ramos clapped a hand against his ear. "Christ, man. What the hell's wrong with you? Are you fuckin' crazy? The car could have come down."

"Bullshit."

"Hey, Ramos. You okay, man?" The mechanic in the next bay held a hammer in his hand.

"Yeah, yeah." Ramos waved away the potential offer to smash in Brian's head.

Brian followed Ramos over to a sink with a cracked mirror over it.

The mechanic looked at his head, washed his face and rubbed at the dirt with a paper towel. "That's gonna bruise," he complained. "Police brutality. I don't have to talk to you. Go find someone else to bully."

"Why would I, when you're right here?" Brian grinned. "Let's go talk in the office."

"No way, man; you're bad news." Ramos pitched the wadded up paper towel into a trash barrel.

"Take a break or get fired. Your choice."

"Son of a bitch, you'd fuckin' figure out a way to do that, wouldn't you?" Ramos glared before walking toward the wobbly stairs to the upper floor. "Okay. I'll take a break. You buy me a cup of coffee in the break room. That's it. Ten minutes. Then you're outta here."

"More than enough." Hanging onto the rail, Brian followed Ramos's battered steel-tipped shoes up the creaking wooden steps.

They entered a small room containing a couple of beat-up white plastic tables with white plastic lawn chairs grouped around them. The chairs were covered with grease smears, the table tops stained and scratched. Odors of oil, gasoline and hand cleaner mingled with stale coffee. Ramos ignored the vending machine, heading instead for an old electric coffeemaker. He poured a cup of what looked like turpentine into a Styrofoam cup, then sat in one of the chairs, his legs splayed out in front of him.

Brian knew Ramos expected him to balk at sitting on one of the greasy chairs. He sat opposite the glowering mechanic and slouched almost as low as his companion. "Start at the beginning of the day; don't leave anything out. I don't care if you think it's not important. I'll be the judge of that."

"You wanna hear how I brushed my teeth and took a shit before leaving home?"

"Only if it has some significance. Otherwise, I don't give a fuck about what you ate or how much you shit out."

They glared at each other.

"Fuck you," Ramos said, and then he laughed. "Goddamned Miami cop in your expensive shit suit. Bet you never worked hard a day in your life."

"This is my dead brother's suit," Brian said. "He was murdered almost five months ago. Start talking."

Ramos crossed himself. "Sorry, man." He sat up a little straighter. "Okay. I've got a good memory. But I'm not having my sister questioned about her relationship with that womanizing piece of crap, Chad Summerfield. I don't care what you say, or how much you threaten me. She's off-limits."

CHAPTER TWENTY-EIGHT

KAYLEN LOOKED through her office closet. None of the cocktail dresses hanging inside made her feel like wearing it, much less smiling for her customers. She should go home, she thought, but the freaked-out feeling she'd experienced the majority of the day had persisted, leaving her even less inclined to face an empty condo.

"Damn you, Brian." She slid the door closed.

If only it was last week and Brian hadn't yet gone to Tampa, or next week, when he was back in Miami. She'd willingly give up a week of her life to fast forward. She had already convinced herself that buying an airline ticket and going up to Tampa wasn't the best solution to her dilemma. If Brian had wanted her there, he would have taken her in the first place, or asked her to fly up when she talked to him earlier in the day.

She didn't want to be alone, but she didn't want to be at the club, where she'd have to socialize with patrons and oversee staff, however remotely. It was time for her to back off, allowing Rob to take the reins a majority of the time. She thought about calling Ziggy and taking him up on his dinner offer, but that reeked of desperation and even betraying Brian.

What would she tell Brian if and when he found out? That she was incapable of managing without him for a couple of days? That rather than tough it out, she went out with the first man who asked her to dinner? Neither of those options sounded even close to reasonable.

If she gave in to her fear and went with Ziggy, she couldn't keep it a secret from Brian. That would make her truly reprehensible. She'd made him swear never to lie to her. How could she not be as truthful? But if she told him, he'd be sure to think that no sooner was his back turned, she was out with some other man. And he'd be right.

Forget hiding it, she decided. He was way too astute. To him, she had become almost transparent. Being in this dilemma was her own fault. It was what she got for falling in love with a detective.

Her phone rang.

"Hi, it's Ziggy." His voice sounded so cheerful.

"Hi." Kaylen hated herself for feeling a little excited, and wondered whether he was intuitive or entirely obsessed and creepy.

"Louis has decided to become my partner," Ziggy said.

Kaylen allowed herself a moment to feel relieved Ziggy wasn't a stalker.

"His father has agreed to back us with whatever funds we cannot raise ourselves," Ziggy continued. "We're both selling our cars. They're almost new and were presents from our families. We can buy cheaper used models and add the remaining money to our trust funds."

"Well," Kaylen interrupted, completely surprised. "Once you made the decision, you really followed through."

"There's more," Ziggy said. "I've been planning to move out of my family's home, but instead of choosing an expensive condo, I'm going to move in with two friends. They have an extra bedroom they were planning to rent out. Louis lives in a guest house on his father's estate and doesn't pay rent, so we're already saving money. Everything is coming together. We just need to find the right space."

"I'm really happy for you. This is exciting news." Kaylen felt a lot less stressed. His enthusiasm was infectious.

"Will you change your mind about dinner now? I want to talk to you about the theme, and the size for a start-up, and where the best locations are. Should we rent in an outdoor mall or the smallest space in an upscale area? So many ideas are in my head, I feel dizzy."

"I know," Kaylen said. "With Bannisters; I felt the same way."

She wouldn't have to stay at the club or go home to spend the evening under a blanket with a glass of Chianti and take-out pizza. She wouldn't have to lie to Brian. This was a business meeting.

"Okay," she said. "You've talked me into going to dinner, to work on your business plan."

"Good."

"Why don't you pick me up at my condo? That way we won't take two cars."

"Excellent. Seven o'clock?"

"It's a date," Kaylen said, and then wanted to bite her tongue for the way it sounded. "A preliminary celebration combined with a business meeting," she added quickly, to clarify.

"It's a date," Ziggy echoed.

Kaylen gave him the address. She thought his voice sounded too excited for a business meeting, but she figured she would be able to re-emphasize her limited role in his life better when they were together. She'd already had some practice at turning down unsought advances, she thought, remembering her awkward exchanges with Sam when he had tried to become more than her mentor and friend.

Why couldn't men understand that not everything had to be about sex? She wondered as she took the side door out of Bannisters. She felt like a coward calling Rob from the road, but she didn't want to see the speculative look on his face when she told him she had other plans that evening. She'd have to tell Brian when he got back. He and Rob had become friends, and she definitely didn't want Brian to learn about her meetings with Ziggy from anyone but herself.

With no idea where they were going to eat, she dressed in black pants, a white shell and a turquoise shot silk jacket. She switched to a black beaded purse. Ziggy was taller than Brian. She pulled black high-heeled shoes from the back of the closet and dusted them off. She hadn't worn heels since Tim's death. Kaylen felt very tall and slightly wobbly, inside and out. The phone rang as she was putting on her lipstick. Ziggy at the buzzer entry system downstairs.

"I'll be right there," she told him, instead of allowing him access to the building. Looking at the photo of Brian on her nightstand, she stopped to touch his face with her fingers. "I need company this evening, and maybe a chance to prove I'm more than a one-hit wonder in the business world," she said to his image.

"You're taking a chance," she told herself as she glanced at her reflection in the hallway mirror. "I don't think Brian's going to like this at all."

She walked out into the corridor, closing the front door quietly behind her and making sure she had locked the deadbolt. On the short ride down in the elevator, her stomach fluttered in a disconcerting manner.

CHAPTER TWENTY-NINE

Brian caught Wally Malone on his way out of the building to go to work. They walked to the bus stop on the corner and sat in the shelter.

"I don't know what else I can tell you about that day," Wally said. "It was sunny and kind of hot, even for here. I had two part-time jobs at the time. Mornings I spent busing at the Hollywood Diner. Afternoons I walked two blocks to the Burger Shack, where I was a cook."

"How come you weren't a cook at the diner?" Brian asked.

"The owner said they made quality food there, not greasy spoon shit." Wally gave a half-smile. "Sorry for the language, but that's exactly the way he put it. I needed the extra cash to help my mom out. There were six of us kids at home and my mom couldn't bring in enough from her job. My dad was on disability from a back injury, and my mom worked at the Mega Groceries, which was where Best Pic is now."

"She worked with Chad Summerfield?" Brian was surprised Tab Benford hadn't mentioned that.

"He was promoted to assistant manager a few weeks before she quit. She'd found a better job. Retail, at a local mall. Regular hours with benefits, although it still wasn't enough to get us off food stamps."

"How come you never moved away?"

The bus roared up, smothering Wally's answer in a blast of hot air and a flurry of dust. Brian decided he'd better ride with Malone to his destination. The bus contained a half-dozen riders, spread out at the front of the vehicle. He and Wally opted to sit in the back.

"I couldn't hear you," Brian said. "What was the reason you stayed around?"

Wally shrugged. "I dunno. Habit? The neighborhood's home."

"But the rest of your family left."

"Yeah. Mom and Dad stayed with Gramma for a while, in a trailer park in Davie. Then they went to Texas. My brothers went their own ways. I had plenty of girlfriends, but none I wanted as a wife. Now it's too late. I don't look so good anymore, and I don't have much to show for being forty, either." He grinned. "Maybe the truth is I prefer my own space. Coming home from shift work and not having to talk to anyone. I can eat a burger, drink a beer and watch as many bad reality shows on TV as I want."

Brian thought how different Malone was from his last interviewee. "Did you go to school with Chico Ramos?"

"For a while. Until he dropped out or got suspended, depending on who you talked to."

"High school?"

"Last year of junior high." Malone's brow furrowed. "You think Chico had something to do with Chad's murder?"

"Nope. Just asking questions; trying to get a better handle on the way things were when Chad was alive."

"The neighborhood hasn't changed much since then." Malone ran big freckled fingers slowly back and forth across the top of his lunch box. "I guess people would say the crime's worse now, but I think it's better reported. Everyone and their mother's got a cell phone these days. You walk along the street the wrong way and they take your photo and send it off somewhere."

"You were a part of the group that tried to knock over a convenience store," Brian said.

Malone looked surprised. "Where d'you hear about that old business?"

"Asking the right questions. Well?"

Wally shrugged. "So, we were a group of stupid kids, scared out of our minds. Using a boosted car and a borrowed gun. Geez. You should have heard my mom when she had to visit me in juvie. She never got over it." He shuddered. "My parents picked up and left town soon after I got put there."

"So you all got caught." Brian knew that answer, but he wanted Malone's version.

"A couple of kids got away, one with his mom, of all people. He saw her, started screaming his head off, and then it was complete chaos. Ramos and I got the worst sentences because we were seen with the gun. I got two years. I came out, got a job through the back-to-work program. Factory job. I've been there ever since. Ramos was tried as an adult. He came out even harder and more anti-social, but he got his GED and went to school for auto repair. He's a good mechanic. We never hang out. No reason to. I don't own a car. Never did. The bus works fine for me...a whole lot cheaper."

"Who were the others involved?"

"Here's my stop," Malone said. "You getting off?"

"Yeah."

Malone and the bus driver exchanged pleasantries on the way out the door. "Gus's been driving this bus for fifteen years," Malone said as he and Brian walked toward a large plant. "I've worked twenty years checking out oranges on a conveyer belt. Any that don't look good enough to go to market get sent off for juicing. It's steady money."

"You didn't answer my question about who else was involved in that convenience store robbery," Brian said.

"Attempted robbery," Malone corrected. "We never got inside the place." He switched his black lunch pail from his right hand to his left and pulled out a badge on a lanyard from inside his shirt. "Tommy Spiro. He took the car without his cousin's permission, according to what the cousin said. Tommy couldn't get out of the car after crashing it. So much for him knowing how to drive. He took out a hydrant, went to the hospital and came out in handcuffs. Then there were the other two younger kids. One chickened out. He was younger than the rest of us. Acted like a freak as soon as Chico and I got out. He jumped out right after us and ran away. Then the other one saw his mom and started screaming. Thanks to all the racket he made, Tommy panicked and left us behind, so Chico and I went away for a while."

Wally grimaced and shook his head. "We were damned fools. Since then, we've all kept our noses clean. No more trouble. Spiro married and has a couple of kids. He works at Mama's Café. He's been cooking there for years. I eat there, sometimes. He makes a mean meat loaf." Malone stopped at the gate. "I've gotta punch in. You got everything you need?"

"For now. I know where to find you if I think of anything else." Brian pulled out his business card. "Same goes for you. Any information you have may help solve Chad's murder."

Malone glanced at the card before stuffing it into the breast pocket of his work shirt and getting waved through the gate by a security guard.

"What were you doing the day Chad got shot?" Brian asked, before Wally joined the throng of other workers.

Malone stopped and pivoted. "Sitting behind bars."

He turned and walked off, but not before Brian saw anxiety creep across Malone's creased face. Whether it was caused by memories of his own incarceration or some details about Chad Summerfield's shooting, Brian wasn't sure, and with the gate guard carefully checking IDs, he wasn't about to find out right then.

CHAPTER THIRTY

J<small>IM SENT</small> a text as Brian was finishing up a verbal report on his interviews into a digital recorder. He had purchased it a few weeks before, when he still held out hope that Hal was going to put him back on active duty within both their lifetimes. A real 'lefty,' despite hours of practice, he found scrawling notes with his right hand and using any mobile device that wasn't voice-activated both slow and frustrating.

'Where r u?' Jim's text read. '2 poss offices.'

Brian saw it was 6:00 PM. He wanted to talk to Tommy Spiro before one of the other men already interviewed got to him, but waiting another day to make decisions about the office was wasting valuable time. They needed space for the equipment and someone there to transcribe his lengthy verbal report.

'Back in 30' he responded. He finished the account of his conversation with Wally Malone and settled back to watch the scenery roll past the window of the empty bus. The driver had assured him Best Pic was on his route, and with only four other passengers, Brian figured it wouldn't take more than 10 minutes to reach his car.

"Best Pic," the driver called.

Brian realized he'd dozed off. He jumped to his feet, almost dropping the recorder. Thanking the driver, he practically ran off the bus. The door closed and the vehicle took off, leaving him alone on the sidewalk. His Mercedes sat isolated toward the back of the lot. Danny Cho's restaurant had its neon sign lit, with another flashing 'Open' in rotating green, yellow and red lights from the front window. Best Pic was fully illuminated, twilight fast turning to darkness.

Brian felt stiff and tired. It had been too long since he'd put in a full day's work pounding pavements. Out of nowhere, a flashback slammed him: Walking toward his Camaro in the parking lot at the marina and getting jumped. His skin prickled and his heartbeat picked up from slow and steady to more of a jogging speed. For a moment he felt the blows, and the gravel crunching painfully into his cheek...

Stop!

He fought back. Kept his eyes open, concentrated on that flashing neon sign across the parking lot. Assured himself he was in Tampa, not Miami, and the fight or flight response wasn't needed; wasn't there for any real, tangible reason.

Took a breath, then a deeper breath, accompanied by long, calming exhales. The neon sign grew brighter, more focused. He heard shouting across the lot. One man in overalls telling another several cars away that he was going home to his wife, not stopping at the bar again—she was already angry with him.

"What are you, chicken shit?" The other guy asked.

They both laughed and got into their cars. Doors slammed, engines started. Headlights pierced the gloom.

Brian unbuttoned his jacket, reassuring himself by the feel of the Glock in its holster. With a long history of detachment from threatening situations and cruelty, he was able to push back the images and ignore that rattled state. Unlike Kaylen, he told himself, whose vivid episodes of PTSD had awakened her sobbing in the night, and had even forced her to pull her car over to the side of road in the early days after his injury.

But as he picked up his pace and kept his hand on the butt of his gun, he decided that particular evening, making decisions over which office would work better and what to eat for dinner made more sense than trying to interview one more potentially unwilling and uncooperative cold case witness when his nerves were jangling like broken piano wires.

He listened to voicemails as he drove. A couple of Tim's tenants mumbled familiar lame excuses for not paying their rents on time. Another message reminded him of a pending appointment with Doctor Fleming the following morning at 10:30 AM.

Brian realized he had been so engrossed in his investigation, he had completely forgotten about the session. Deciding that swearing while alone in his car wouldn't be breaking a promise to Kaylen, he allowed himself the pleasure of reciting a mantra of obscenities before he used the Plaza's concierge services again.

"Can you book me on the first flight out to Miami tomorrow morning?" He asked when a cheerful female voice responded to his call.

"Certainly, Mr. Swift. Do you have a preference regarding which airline?"

Unruffled. Professionally pleasant. They were like well-mannered clones.

"No." He kept the needle on the speed limit as he navigated his way out of Best Pic's neighborhood and turned the Mercedes in the direction of the hotel.

"Do you need a rental car?"

"No."

He thought briefly about asking Kaylen to pick him up, but decided to take a cab and surprise her.

"Do you have a return date, sir, or will you be remaining in Miami?"

He'd definitely spend the night with Kaylen. Their reunion didn't need to be rushed. He could feel her body next to his already. "I'm coming back the following day. I'll need a reservation for mid-afternoon, preferably."

But he should have stayed to interview Tommy Spiro, damn it, regardless of his stupid anxiety attack.

"I'll call you if there's a problem, sir. Otherwise, the details will be placed under your door. Have a pleasant trip."

Brian heard the smile in the concierge's voice. "Thanks."

He swore again as he drove down unfamiliar darkened streets. He'd wanted to wind up the preliminary interviews that day, but he'd spent more time than he'd planned walking around the area and talking to the other witnesses. And then he'd left his car and taken a bus ride with Wally Malone.

But he'd also gained a better picture of Chad Summerfield in the process, and begun to wonder whether the murder was really a result of the robbery or whether a disgruntled family member had thrown the local cops off the trail by leading them in the wrong direction. Chad was very fond of the ladies, as Jim would have put it. He'd probably gained a fair number of enemies. Brian wondered if there were a few little Chads running around Tampa/St. Pete.

A hit would take a lot of planning and a devious brain, he thought, but if several people had been involved, then it might have been a little easier to work out all the details. Maybe that's why the original investigation had run into a wall. He knew sometimes he'd had blinders on when he first started investigating a case, but he'd come to realize pretty quickly that human nature rarely used linear thinking. A pact of silence in the local community would have removed a troublesome problem and kept them all out of jail.

By the time he arrived at the entrance to the Plaza, bathed in spotlights that reflected off glimmering gilt and lush greenery around the circular driveway, he'd recovered completely from his flashback episode. No doubt about it, he decided as he took his foot off the accelerator and coasted into the valet parking area, working a case again would get him over any residual issues related to his recovery. Working charters and dealing with Tim's tenants definitely wouldn't. He needed to be back where he belonged, and he hoped to convince Fleming of that at their next session.

A waiting valet opened Brian's door as soon as the Mercedes whispered to a stop. Brian tossed the keys to the young man dressed in a maroon uniform with gold braiding around the collar and cuffs before thinking the kid probably wouldn't know how to use the adaptive equipment. "I'd better park it myself," he said.

"No, sir, I've taken instruction on your equipment," the kid said. "All the valets at the Plaza have. We pride ourselves in catering to the needs of every guest."

Brian tipped him and walked inside to find Jim hanging out in the lobby. "I guess you're hungry," he said.

"Very." Jim got up from the leather couch he'd been occupying. "And

I took tours of those office spaces. I've got pictures on my phone and all the specs." He picked up a folder from the coffee table.

"Let's eat here," Brian said.

Jim nodded. "I figured we would." He looked at his watch. "Good timing. Our table's booked for seven-thirty. The restaurant instead of the grill. Want to hit the bar for a beer before we eat?"

"Sounds good." Brian realized he was hungry as well as tired. "Thanks, Jim. I'm really glad you agreed to come along. You're better than a partner. He wouldn't care if I ate or not, and he certainly wouldn't be checking out offices."

"My pleasure." Jim smiled. "I've got your back. Always."

"I know."

Brian felt uncharacteristically emotional. Jim now felt more than a good friend; he felt like…family? Brian wasn't sure, because he'd had so little previous experience of leaning on anyone for support.

They sat at a small table in the bar. A waiter brought mixed nuts, coasters and napkins. He took their orders and returned in moments with two frosted mugs filled with beer on tap. Brian initialed the tab and allowed himself to relax, feeling the tension ease out of his shoulder.

Jim took a long drink, smacked his lips and pushed the folder across the table. "Check these out. All the specs are in there. I've got my personal preference, but you tell me what strikes you. How'd your interviews go?"

The waiter returned at that moment. "Your table is ready, gentlemen." He scooped up their beers and placed them on a tray.

Jim tucked the folder under his arm. "Hold that thought," he told Brian as they followed the waiter into the dining room. "I'm sure you've got plenty to tell me over a couple of steaks."

CHAPTER THIRTY-ONE

"I MADE a reservation at Chez Bruno's," Ziggy told Kaylen as he drove his Jeep Grand Cherokee away from her condo complex. "I hope that is acceptable."

"Definitely." She smothered a smile. She wasn't sure whether his formal use of the English language annoyed or pleased her. "I haven't eaten there in a long time."

"You have not been out in your social circle since your former boyfriend died, so my friends have told me."

Kaylen wasn't going to comment on anything to do with her social circle or Tim's death. She watched as Ziggy maneuvered quickly but safely into traffic. "You'll miss this car. Are you sure you want to part with it?"

"Yes. I can get around very well in an older model, although I wonder whether you will want to be seen in it."

"I'm not into appearances so much anymore," Kaylen protested. "I could have been accused of that in the past." She drew her jacket tightly around her and raised the half-open window. "I won't be riding around in your car frequently, anyway, so whatever you're driving won't impact me, unless you break down on the way to a meeting. That would really cause some issues. I don't like being stood up."

She wished she had arranged to meet Ziggy at her office the following day. He was talking as though this dinner was a social event, not business.

"But really, it's a moot point," she said, to clarify. "We'll be meeting at the restaurant site, or with the planners at their office."

"Those might not be the only occasions," Ziggy said.

He didn't elaborate. Kaylen looked at his profile. He was intently watching the traffic. "What do you mean by that?"

Ziggy shrugged. He continued concentrating on his driving. "Only that taking one car is more efficient than taking two. We will have to continue meeting frequently if you are going to consult on this project, aren't we?"

"Well, yes." She felt a little silly. She'd misread him. "But it'll be a lot easier with Louis involved if we get together at a central location."

"He wants to be a silent partner for now."

"Why?"

"His father's wishes. In the event the restaurant fails, the Gilman name will not be associated with it publicly."

"Ah," Kaylen said. "Leonard's not at all sure you know what you're getting into and doesn't have much faith in your abilities."

"He has enough to allow Louis to place his trust fund money into the venture and to supply us with the remaining capital," Ziggy pointed out.

"That's true." Kaylen noticed his hands were gripping the steering wheel tighter. She didn't want to undermine what little confidence he had in himself. "You'll have to prove Leonard's misgivings are unfounded, that's all."

Ziggy shot her a sideways glance. "I hope that is a joke. I would like it to be. Otherwise I might get even more nervous about losing my shirt than I am right now. My father is going to be furious, and Apollo will be scoffing. I want to prove them wrong."

"You're bucking a lot of people who have little faith in your abilities." Kaylen tried to choose her words carefully. "I don't know why they feel that way." She paused to give Ziggy time to tell her why they shouldn't, but he said nothing. "You haven't let your family down before, have you?" She watched his shoulders droop and his mouth tighten.

"No." Ziggy shook his head adamantly. "I suppose I should tell you more about my background, so you will know why my father acts the way he does. My decision not to join the family business was a severe blow to him. He was already grooming Apollo, and even then, I felt inferior to someone who excelled at everything. Apollo was recommending changes to the menu, adding wines to complement the dishes and ordering the staff around while I was struggling to succeed in school."

"And your father encouraged him, I'm sure."

"Of course. With such aptitude, Apollo was a natural. I was not. I am more like my dear mother, who went back to Greece to care for her ailing parents and never returned."

"She died?" Kaylen's heart contracted painfully. *More death.*

"No. Worse." Ziggy smiled thinly. "She became involved with the man she had fallen in love with before her parents arranged her marriage to my father. She had an affair, refused to come back, and my father divorced her."

"Oh." Kaylen thought she might have found one reason why Peter Stavros had been so condescending and rude to her. His opinion of women in a collective sense was probably tarnished by bitterness over his wife's betrayal.

"My mother turned that affair into happiness, which she did not have with my father. She married her lover and remained in Greece," Ziggy continued. "Her parents had changed over the years. They saw how miserable she was with my father. They gave her their blessing."

"But she abandoned her children," Kaylen said.

"Not until we were grown. I was the youngest, a junior in high school. My father's least favorite, I suspect because I remind him very much of my mother. I asked to go to Greece. My mother and her family had offered to take me. He barely hesitated. I was skipping school, and it was a chance to get me out of his house and not deal with my failing grades and disruptive behavior."

"You? Disruptive?" Kaylen joked, in an attempt to lighten the atmosphere in the car. She felt for Ziggy. Her experiences paralleled his, except she had tried hard not to anger her father, only to do so on a regular basis. She had graduated from high school by the skin of her teeth, packed one bag and hitchhiked all the way from Maine to Miami.

She still wondered sometimes how she had survived that trip in one piece.

She wished the ride was over and so was dinner. Ziggy was doing way too much sharing. Kaylen felt distinctly uncomfortable.

"My grades radically improved in Athens," Ziggy said. "It was a much easier transition than any of us anticipated, partly because we had always spoken Greek at home."

His voice had regained its buoyancy and his grip on the steering wheel had relaxed. Kaylen felt relieved. "So, you were happy," she said.

Ziggy nodded. "I didn't think I would ever come back to Miami."

"But you did. What happened? Nothing awful, I hope."

"No."

They stopped at yet another red light. The traffic ahead was moving slowly, and the heat in the car had intensified. Ziggy flipped on the a/c and a welcome blast of cool air circulated.

"You will learn my entire life story if we keep moving at this speed," Ziggy said.

"I think so." Kaylen smiled, but wondered how much longer it would take to reach the restaurant. She took a surreptitious glance at her watch. They had been on the road over 30 minutes and they still had at least three miles left, which at the rate traffic was moving, could take another 30 minutes. She tried not to sigh.

Ziggy stopped talking and changed lanes. The other one was moving slightly faster. Kaylen wondered if he had seen her stifle that sigh. She felt mean-spirited. "So you graduated from high school and went sailing." she said.

"No, I was offered a full scholarship and completed college with dual degrees. That's when I chose to join a competitive sailing team. My father became extremely angry. Why did I want to throw away the previous six years of my life in order to sail around the world?"

"Dual degrees?" Kaylen raised her eyebrows as they stopped behind a long line of red tail lights. "What in?"

"Philosophy and journalism." Ziggy grinned. "My father was shouting so loud when I told him about my post-graduation plan, I think everyone in the neighborhood must have heard. He forgot his oath not to speak Greek with his family after my mother left, so at least the neighbors could not understand him."

Just then, the traffic started to clear. Ziggy drove past a vehicle being loaded onto a flat-bed tow truck and sped up. They arrived at the restaurant five minutes later.

He helped her out before giving the valet his keys, offered his arm and after a brief hesitation, Kaylen took it. She glanced around as they waited for the maître d', more from habit than anything else. Her gaze fell on two couples seated at a table not far from the entrance, and her heart sank. She knew them. The two women facing her exchanged whispers even as they smiled and waved.

She cringed inside. The gossipmongers would have a field day. Here she was on the arm of Ziggy Stavros, when she had just announced her relationship with Brian.

"What's wrong?" Ziggy asked.

Kaylen realized she had tightened her grip on his arm. "I know those people."

"Are you uncomfortable? Would you like to go somewhere else?"

"No." She forced a smile. "I'm not in hiding. I'll introduce you."

"Your table is ready, Mr. Stavros." The maître d' escorted them to a table on the other side of the room but well within sight of Kaylen's acquaintances.

She glanced over again. All four diners were staring; the men had swiveled around in their seats. She had come to despise some of the jet set she had associated with before George's death. Without a doubt, she would be social media fodder before morning. After all the trouble Brian had gone through to remain as low-key in her life as he possibly could, his anonymity would be only a memory. She'd get linked with Ziggy Stavros, and she'd have a lot of explaining to do, she thought, imagining Brian's reaction. He'd probably forget his promise and start swearing. She felt like joining him.

But if he didn't react that way, it would be a harder pill to swallow. Anger would be more welcome than complacency or ambivalence.

Mechanically, she took the menu the waiter handed her and hid her face behind it as she struggled with her emotions. Confronted with a test of her own making, she found herself as eager to avoid the public as

Brian had been to shield her from them. She bit her lip and struggled for composure before lowering the menu and smiling at Ziggy's troubled expression.

"I wonder what specials they have this evening?" she said. "I feel like having seafood."

CHAPTER THIRTY-TWO

KAYLEN'S DINNER ordeal ended when the foursome at the other table stood up. Both the women and one of the men headed for the lobby, while the last member of their group made his way toward Kaylen and Ziggy.

"Hello, Kaylen." He smiled brightly. His eyes flickered briefly to Ziggy. "So good to see you. It's been a while."

"Hello, Maurice." Kaylen smiled back, pleased at least to see a friend out of the group. "This is Ziggy Stavros." She turned to Ziggy. "I'd like you to meet Maurice Tauny, a friend of mine."

Ziggy stood and extended his hand. "Very pleased to meet you, Mr. Tauny."

"A pleasure." Maurice shook hands. "I heard you were dating a detective, Kaylen. Is that really true?"

"Yes," Kaylen said. *News traveled fast.* "He's out of town right now, so I'm having a business dinner with Ziggy."

"Kaylen is acting as a consultant for my new restaurant," Ziggy said.

"Is that right?" Maurice's eyebrows rose slightly when he looked to Kaylen for confirmation.

"It is." She nodded. "Ziggy's in the early planning stages."

"Well, when your plans are more advanced, we may want to talk."

Maurice glanced toward the lobby. "I should go. The others will be getting impatient. We've got tickets to a show." He bent to kiss Kaylen's cheek. "Don't be such a stranger. We're all anxious to meet your new boyfriend. What's his name?"

"Detective Sergeant Swift," Ziggy said before Kaylen could answer.

"Ah." Maurice looked perplexed. His gaze went from Kaylen to Ziggy and back again. "What's his first name?"

"Brian," she said. "His name's Brian Swift." She felt warm inside when she said Brian's name. She liked the sound of it. Direct and to the point. Nothing fancy or long-winded, very much like the man who owned it.

"I remember that name." Maurice's brow furrowed with concentration. "Didn't he get a commendation a few months back?"

"Yes." She nodded. "For valor. But he doesn't like talking about it."

"He got shot," Ziggy said.

Kaylen wondered if Ziggy had been scouring the internet to dredge up every piece of information he could find on Brian. But why would he do that? Brian's history had nothing whatsoever to do with her helping Ziggy become a successful restaurateur.

"That's right," Maurice said. "He did. I remember now." He turned from Ziggy to Kaylen. "How's Brian doing?"

"Good," Kaylen said. "He's doing well, thank you." *That was a lie.* Brian wasn't doing well at all some days.

"That was a tough piece of news about Tim." Maurice waded into dangerous waters.

"Yes." A lump came into Kaylen's throat.

"I'm sorry." A flush colored Maurice's cheeks. "It's difficult to know what to say."

Kaylen tried to smile but it wasn't very successful. "I had brunch with Angela Crossfield today, and she had the same trouble. It's probably best to move past the condolences. Tim will be missed by a lot of people, but he was a troubled soul, and he put himself into danger with his actions. No one deserves to die like he did, but it's over."

Maurice nodded again, his worried expression genuine and very welcome to Kaylen.

"Thank you." She grabbed his hand and squeezed it.

He squeezed back, gently but steadily. "I'll get the word out. None of your friends wants to make you uncomfortable. We want you back, Kaylen, and please bring Brian with you."

"I will. When we're both ready," she assured him. "It's a bit complicated. Brian and Tim were half-brothers, as you probably heard or read in the news. Brian's not only still healing but grieving. Me, too."

"When you're ready, we'll all be there for you," Maurice said. "No pressure." He kissed her cheek again and looked steadily into her eyes. "I mean that."

Kaylen felt a tear run down her face. She struggled for composure. The tear dropped onto her hand as she clutched her napkin.

"Nice meeting you, Ziggy," Maurice said. "Please, don't get up," he added as Ziggy started to get to his feet again.

Maurice walked quickly away. Kaylen looked across the table. Ziggy's eyes held warmth and understanding.

"Shall I take you home?" he asked.

"Please."

That one tear became two, then three. Her vision blurred, and for one dreadful minute, Kaylen thought she was going to break down. But she blinked her way through to clear vision with a couple of discreet dabs from her napkin

"Why don't we ask the waiter to box up our meals?" She suggested. "I'd like some company, if you don't mind eating at my place."

"Of course."

CHAPTER THIRTY-THREE

"You know," Jim said as he laid his knife and fork across his empty dinner plate, "you could take a flight back to Miami this evening instead of tomorrow. You can sign the lease for the office when you come back. I'll make calls tomorrow and see if I can get in touch with some more witnesses, or at least their families. I won't go talk to them. I know you don't want that."

Brian stopped pushing food around his own plate. He glanced at his watch. He could still make it if there was a flight around 10:00 PM. "Good suggestions," he said. "I'll go talk to the concierge right now."

He left Jim to sign off on the bill and scrambled to take his only option, which was a 9:15 PM flight. He didn't need to take anything back to Miami, but he worried the TSA might not like a lack of luggage, so he threw some items into an overnight bag. Refusing Jim's offer to drive him, Brian took a cab to the airport.

He appreciated his friend's intuitive meddling a whole lot when he buckled his seatbelt. As the plane taxied down the runway he closed his eyes, effectively shutting off communication with the man sitting next to him.

Once Brian knew he had to return to Miami, all he could think about was being with Kaylen. He allowed himself to dwell on how much he'd missed her, and it made him both excited and uncomfortable. He couldn't imagine his life without her, yet he knew he couldn't give her what she needed. Maybe Fleming would be able to fix him, he thought, leaning against the cold, hard window as the engines gained momentum and the plane gathered speed for take-off. Otherwise, he would have to let Kaylen go, much as it hurt to even think about that.

A churning started in his stomach at the thought of never seeing her again, but he refused to mess up her life along with his own. The elation that had filled him at the thought of seeing her again was damped down like a bucket of water thrown onto a blazing fire.

Smoke and ashes, Brian thought. Like the rest of his 39 years.

CHAPTER THIRTY-FOUR

"COME IN." Kaylen held her front door open for Ziggy, who carried two take-out bags filled with dinners, salads, rolls and dessert.

He looked around before setting the bags on the breakfast bar. "Very nice. Have you lived here long?"

"No." Kaylen tossed her jacket onto the back of a chair. "A few months, that's all." She walked past him into the kitchen. "What would you like to drink? White wine or red?"

"Red." Ziggy opened the bags and slid out black plastic containers with lids. "Do you want to eat off these plates or china?"

"China. We'll set the table like it was the restaurant." She took out plates, silverware, a white linen tablecloth and napkins.

Ziggy came into the kitchen and took them from her. Their hands touched. She pulled gently away to open the refrigerator and take out a jug of chilled water. She selected a California Merlot from her wine rack and placed it on the bar with an opener and the water.

Ziggy shook out the tablecloth and laid the table. Kaylen added glasses. He used the matches she handed him to light long blue tapers seated at the top of crystal candlesticks. A gentle glow illuminated the table.

Kaylen combined the salads in a bowl and tossed them with oil and vinegar, something she and Ziggy had both agreed upon at the restaurant. She put the desserts into the refrigerator and joined him at the table as he transferred their meals onto white plates.

His face, illuminated by candlelight, was young and handsome. Kaylen wondered why he was with her instead of a girlfriend on a Wednesday evening, even if he did want to discuss business.

"So," she said. "Couldn't you find a date tonight and arrange to meet me during the work day?"

"I didn't want to wait that long."

Ziggy seated her and shook out her napkin, placing it on her lap. He draped the other napkin over his arm.

"I am Constantine, your waiter for this evening," he said, smiling his charming smile. He opened the Merlot and poured her a generous serving, then one for himself.

"Please sit down," Kaylen said. "You're not getting a tip out of me."

Ziggy laughed, but he sat opposite her and put the napkin on his lap. "Salad?" He passed her the bowl.

Kaylen took a serving and passed the bowl back across the table. They both raised their wine glasses.

"A toast," she said. "To a successful collaboration."

"A very successful collaboration," he clarified. "*Salute'.*" They clinked glasses.

"Why would I want to spend this evening with anyone but you?" he asked. "You are now my friend and mentor."

"You're much too charming," Kaylen said. "I'd better watch how much I drink."

"You'll be perfectly safe," Ziggy said. "I promise."

"That's what men always say before they do something completely risky." Kaylen laughed. He was so very easy to talk to, she felt completely at ease.

"You'd have to do something risky right back," Ziggy said, and his laughter joined hers.

CHAPTER THIRTY-FIVE

BRIAN'S PLANE reached the gate at 10:45 PM. He caught a cab over to Bannisters, feeling anticipation far beyond what he'd ever felt before at the thought of seeing Kaylen and the surprise on her face when he walked into the club.

But when he greeted Rob, he found out Kaylen wasn't even there. She had gone to meet Ziggy Stavros for a business meeting and hadn't returned. Rob looked worried. A gnawing started in Brian's gut. He called her smartphone and was sent to voicemail.

He called her landline. She picked up on the 4th ring. She sounded like she'd had a couple of drinks and had been laughing.

"Brian!" she said. "I'm so glad to hear your voice. Just a minute." She covered the mouthpiece.

He heard her talking to someone, then the rustle of clothing as she walked and the sound of a door closing.

"I'm back," she said. "Ziggy Stavros is here. He got the funding he needed and a partner. We've been talking about possible locations for his restaurant."

Brian felt a surge of something completely alien to him: Jealousy. "I just flew in. I'm at the club. Rob was worried when you didn't come back. You should have called him."

"I don't answer to Rob." Kaylen's voice was uncharacteristically sharp.

"No, but I thought you'd learned enough over the past few months to keep someone posted about your whereabouts. Maybe you don't need to worry anymore, but I'm not altogether sure about that. While I'm not around, and with Jim up here with me, Rob's the one I expect to look out for you."

"I feel like a prisoner sometimes," she said. "Like right now. But I can't stay angry. You're back! Get over here. I'll send Ziggy home; he and I can talk more tomorrow. Use your key. I'll be in bed waiting for you."

Brian's disquiet eased at the thought of Kaylen in her bed. Especially if she was wearing the white silk gown with see-through lace on the bodice and spaghetti straps that slid off her shoulders with the slightest movement. He got up from the chair behind her desk and snapped off the lights before closing and locking the door behind him. Asking why Ziggy was at her condo until midnight could wait until the following day.

He told Rob to close up without waiting for Kaylen to return and took a cab over to her building. When he walked inside the condo, he found the lights turned down low and soft music playing. Candles cast flickering lights on the walls and ceiling of the living room. An empty wine bottle sat beside the sink with two glasses in the drying rack. The garbage can was filled with empty take-out boxes, the bedroom door ajar. He pushed it open and saw Kaylen laid out across the pillows, asleep.

Brian sighed. So much for romance. He blew out the candles, turned off the music and stripped off his clothes. But when he climbed in beside her, Kaylen made little contented noises and opened her eyes.

"Hi," she said. "What took you so long?"

"I wasn't long. You've been drinking, and you fell asleep."

"I had a glass of wine with dinner and a few sips of brandy with coffee and dessert. I'm nowhere near drunk."

"Did he try anything?"

"No way."

"Good," Brian said.

He took her in his arms and found she was indeed wearing that silk gown. The spaghetti straps conveniently slid off her shoulders, the swell of her breasts rising and falling in the soft glow of a bedside lamp.

"I'd have kicked him out," Kaylen said. She kissed Brian's neck and shoulder. Her hand drifted down his back and cupped his buttock. "Mmm." She ran her thumb from the base of his spine up to the nape of his neck. "I've missed you."

"I've missed you, too."

He rolled her onto her back and they kissed long, hard and deep before he pushed the straps of her gown down below her elbows, taking the bodice with them. Kaylen was so beautiful. He trailed his tongue between her breasts. She arched her back.

"If Ziggy Stavros lays one hand on you, he'll regret it really fast." He teased a nipple.

"I bet." Her hand slid around from his buttock to even more interesting and stimulating places.

Brian didn't waste another thought on Ziggy Stavros.

CHAPTER THIRTY-SIX

BRIAN PACED up and down Dr. Fleming's office the following day. "Look, how long am I going to have to keep coming here before you say I'm ready to go back to work?"

The psychologist watched, fingers tented.

"I feel ready," Brian said. "I'm working a cold case up in Tampa and making progress. It's good to be back where I belong."

"The chief offered you a permanent transfer, heading up the cold case squad here," Fleming said. "Instead, you've chosen to pursue a case out of town, where you don't have to be reminded of the fact that you're still on disability, and you don't have to answer directly to Chief Shaw."

"Wrong." Brian stopped in front of Fleming's desk and made direct eye contact. "I want to help my neighbors. They need to know who killed their son."

"And you're more qualified to do that than the Tampa Police Department?" Fleming took a sip of coffee from a Willow-patterned cup

Brian wondered why he knew it was a Willow pattern. He certainly hadn't looked at china patterns in any shape or form...ever. "I've got more time and a personal interest. Besides, it'll give me a chance to test drive the cold case position."

"Why, if you still want to get back to Homicide?"

"It may be better than waiting for hell to freeze over."

"So you acknowledge you may never be ready to resume your role as a homicide detective."

"The fu...the hell I do." Brian took a couple of deep breaths. "I'll never believe that. I don't think Hal does, either. But he's insisting I get back to the same physical shape I was before the injury."

"That may never happen," Fleming said.

"You sure know how to rain on my parade." Brian felt depression tug at him. He mentally shrugged it off. Fleming was a psychologist, not his surgeon. "My next follow-up with Dr. West isn't until next month. It's four and a half months since I got injured." He raised his left arm. "Does this look like I need to hang up my career?"

Fleming watched with a neutral expression. "You've made progress in all areas," he acknowledged in a flat tone. "Including here, although it's probably been slower than your physical recovery."

"I don't see the need to bring up my past," Brian said. "I aced all the tests I was given when I applied to the academy. I admit I've been a bit of a discipline problem in the past, but that's behind me. Why can't you leave things alone? What isn't broken doesn't need to be fixed."

"You know there's a lot broken," Fleming said. "It needs to be dealt with so you can move on with your life without the hang-ups and self-doubts. Without the anger and the need to isolate yourself from any relationships without blood ties. You told me you don't have any family left. You need to forge a circle of friends you can count on, regardless of what happens in your life."

"I have that. Kaylen. My neighbor, Jim. Rob, Kaylen's manager. Hal, in a limited capacity. His new position may change that, but life's all about change, isn't it?"

"How about your other coworkers?"

Brian ran through a list of them in his head.

"Tell me," Fleming said.

"Mills," Brian said. "And maybe Vickers. He lent us his apartment when Kaylen and I were homeless."

"Homeless?" Fleming's eyebrows rose.

"Yeah, me after my boat burned up. Kaylen when her condo got ransacked and her housekeeper was drowned in the bathtub. She didn't feel safe there after that."

"Ah." Fleming got up and poured another cup of coffee. "Do you feel settled in your new home? A boat seems to be another temporary Band-Aid. Why didn't you move into your brother's apartment?"

"I'm not comfortable there. I don't like Tim's furniture, and I don't want to put money into buying new stuff when the plan is to sell the place. My financial manager said that should happen within the next year. Property prices are rising. The area's ripe for redevelopment."

"But you won't move in with Kaylen."

"I like my space." Brian sat down. He realized he'd left his pills behind and wished he hadn't.

"You're in pain," Fleming said.

"It's that noticeable, huh?"

"Right now, yes. Are you weaning yourself off your meds?"

"Yeah. I left them in Tampa."

"Perhaps that will be a blessing in disguise."

"Or result in me losing my girlfriend when I snap her head off." Brian ran his hand over his face. He felt tired after the adrenaline rush of the last couple of days and barely sleeping the night before. He'd made love twice with Kaylen, and then they'd talked until dawn. She'd fallen asleep in his arms as the sun rose. Unwilling to disturb her, he'd held her against his chest while his right arm became numb.

"Let's talk about your career again." Fleming had settled back behind his desk. Brian hadn't noticed. He wondered if he'd been so absorbed with his thoughts, he'd blanked out. That wouldn't bode well for Fleming to recommend a return to the department any time in the foreseeable future.

"What d'you wanna know?" he asked, when Fleming didn't elaborate. "I thrive on nailing murderers. Whether Hal thinks I'll get the same satisfaction out of solving cases several years or even decades old, I'm not even going to try to guess."

"I've seen your impressive arrest and conviction record. But your methods have been forceful. Do you bully people, Sergeant Swift?"

"Bullying has nothing to do with it. I extract confessions. I close cases. I get the truth out of people."

"You never let your guard down, either in your professional or private life," Fleming said. "You refuse to discuss your childhood with me or your relationship with Kaylen Roberts, despite the conflict of dating and having intimate relations with the girlfriend of your dead brother."

"Kaylen and I are working through that. We both knew it could get complicated, but we're doing okay."

"Really?" Fleming took another sip of coffee, carefully placed the cup back on its saucer and dabbed his mouth with a paper napkin.

"Yeah." Brian refused to be drawn into a long discussion about Kaylen.

"Tell me about your mother," Fleming said.

"She worked hard. She brought home a paycheck that my stepfather drank away within a day or two every week of the year."

"So you've told me before. Tell me something new."

"She had curly black hair, like Tim's," Brian said. "And blue eyes."

"Was she attractive?" Fleming asked.

"Not particularly, but she worked long hours and didn't sleep much, so she always looked pale and worried."

"What brings you to make that judgment?"

"Ed either beat her up or if he wasn't too drunk, he wanted a lot of sex."

"You heard that."

"Saw it sometimes, too." Brian went over to stare out the window. There wasn't much of a view. A blank wall with windows, most blinds drawn. Sunlight slanting down but leaving the majority of the building in shadow.

"That must have been distressing for you," Fleming prompted.

Brian's eyes followed a crack in the brickwork up two stories, across the top of a window frame and into shadow. "For both Tim and me. We'd pull the covers over our heads."

"You survived your childhood, is what you're telling me. It wasn't an experience any child should endure."

"No." Brian turned away from the window. "And I left it there, in Baton Rouge, on Webber Street. Until Tim dredged it up, and now you. I don't want to remember details. It's not gonna get me back to work. It won't make my relationship with my coworkers or the chief any easier. It's not going to turn me into some guy who's found his vulnerable side and wants to bake cookies with Kaylen and become weak and useless."

"You think strength is all about force, don't you?"

"No. I think being a man is working through your fears and your anger and compartmentalizing them so you can get on with life and be successful."

"Do you love your girlfriend?"

Brian folded his arms across his chest before he could stop himself. His left arm shot sparks into his shoulder. "She loves *me.*"

"That's not an answer. But she's told you that?"

"Yes." He lowered his arms. The pain subsided.

"And you don't feel you can be the man she needs, do you?"

"No. I could turn violent. I could be abusive."

"You and I can work through that. If you're telling me the truth, and I believe you are, you've never shown violent tendencies toward women."

"No, but I have toward men. Even Tim. He made me so mad; I slammed him up against a wall one time."

"What for?"

"He'd gotten mixed up with a drug cartel. He was couriering for them. I wanted him to stop. He wouldn't do it, so guess what...he died. Stupid prick."

Fleming nodded. "Now we're getting somewhere."

Brian looked at the large Seth Thomas clock ticking away on the wall behind the deep and very comfortable-looking black leather couch he avoided sitting on during any of his sessions. Close enough to the hour. "You are. I'm outta here. Time's up."

"Not for five minutes," Fleming said. "Sit down. Tell me about Tim. You've never discussed your feelings toward him in such depth."

"Next week, doc." Brian headed for the door. "I want to spend more time with Kaylen before I leave for Tampa tonight."

"Sit down."

Fleming's voice hadn't raised; hadn't changed in tone, but Brian knew if he walked out the door, he could kiss an earlier return to work goodbye.

"Fine." He chose the chair opposite Fleming's desk and took deep breaths to calm himself. He wanted to slam out of the psychologist's office and never look back. But like Hal, Fleming wasn't going to put up with any physical displays, even if directed toward furnishings or doors.

The psychologist waited, his eyes unblinking behind black-rimmed glasses.

"I loved Tim," Brian said when he felt he could trust his voice. "He drove me crazy, but he was my brother. I feel like I let him down." His throat dried. He coughed.

"Why would you say that?" Fleming filled a glass with water from the carafe on his desk and offered it.

Brian took a sip. It threatened to choke him. He swallowed with difficulty. "We had a huge fight the week before he died." He rolled the glass around on the edge of the desk. "Biggest one we'd ever had. We both swore never to see each other again."

"But you did…"

"No, but he called me the night he disappeared. He sounded desperate. Not like him at all. He was always so much in control, or so he said and acted."

"So you went to meet him. How was that letting him down?" Fleming leaned back in his chair. "You did everything you could for Tim. He was an adult who made bad choices, as you pointed out a few minutes ago."

"I know. But that's my rational side talking. My gut reaction is to tell myself I could have done more."

"As his elder brother?"

"As a cop. Christ! I should've had him locked up. Would've been a whole lot better than him ending up in the morgue."

"You had no trouble loving Tim, who always tried your patience and even placed your career in jeopardy, and yet you can't love your girl-friend?" Fleming leaned forward. "Why not? What are you so afraid of?"

"I'm never afraid," Brian said.

"Anyone who lives has a time when he or she is or has been afraid," Fleming said.

Brian thought about that. "I *was* afraid," he acknowledged. "Of my step-father, Ed. In the beginning. Before I figured out fear was what he wanted. So I learned not to show it, and later, not to feel it. He could beat the crap out of me, but he couldn't break me inside. Not unless I let him."

"And you didn't."

"No. I was prepared to take the blame for the broken window the day I left home, but my mother was the one who insisted I leave. She was scared Ed would kill me."

"She wasn't afraid of that before?"

Brian shrugged. "I guess not."

"Why didn't she protect you?"

"She tried, at first. But he slapped her around."

"So she decided she'd rather see her son beaten?" Fleming's eyebrows rose for the second time. "What kind of a mother was she?"

"Helpless. Hopeless. Weak." *There. He'd finally said it. He'd held that inside for way too long.*

"Is Kaylen weak?"

"No way." That question surprised him. Brian stopped lounging and sat up straight. "Kaylen's nothing like my mother. She's strong and resourceful. She saved my life."

"Then she's worth loving," Fleming said.

"You're a bastard," Brian said. "You always manipulate a situation. Make me wonder why I say anything I do."

"I'm trying to present you with options other than black or white, yes or no. I'm trying to get you to think on a more emotional level, instead of being completely logically all the time. You can't continue weighing decisions in your personal life like you do the facts in a murder investigation."

"I don't."

"You do."

"Damn you," Brian said. He glared at Fleming. "Can I leave now?"

"Yes." Fleming nodded. "But I want you to think over the elements of this session and be prepared to discuss them further next week."

"Fine." Brian wasn't sure if he was ragingly angry or completely drained. His emotions were swirling at such a fast rate, he felt pressure in his chest.

"Give Ms. Roberts my regards." Fleming looked through trifocals with mild brown eyes. "I'd like her to come in with you next week."

"Like that's gonna happen."

Brian walked out the door, through the small reception area and into the corridor. When he got into the empty elevator, he laid his head against the polished wood and closed his eyes for the whole ride down to the first floor.

CHAPTER THIRTY-SEVEN

"LET ME COME BACK WITH YOU," Kaylen said, buttering a piece of toast. "I can be useful. I'll set up your office and organize the files ready for the temp."

"Jim's working on that." Brian wondered if he'd made the right decision after leaving Fleming's office by deciding to take Kaylen with him to check on the *NTK*. Hungry and emotionally depleted, he'd suggested they eat brunch before going to the marina. "He may've gotten the temp in by the time I get back," he added.

"So call him and check." She took a bite of her toast.

Brian watched her chew. He didn't want her involved in his investigation. She could've gotten killed the last time she'd helped him. He cared too much for Kaylen to place her in danger ever again. But he knew her too well to think she was going to drop the subject.

Against his better judgment, he took out his phone and called Jim, who thought Kaylen had a great idea.

Of course, goddammit.

He hung up in Jim's ear.

"He likes that suggestion, doesn't he?" Kaylen gave Brian a satisfied, smug little smile.

"If he'd already organized everything, he'd disorganize it to get you up there." Brian placed his phone on the table and aligned it with his unused knife. It gave him a chance to wipe the frustration from his face. "I've got reservations," he said. She wouldn't like it, but he had to say it: "I don't want you involved in any more cases."

Kaylen sighed, like she was the one who should be frustrated. "Do I have to remind you this one's a really cold case?" she asked. "So cold, it's frigid. Besides, what trouble could I get into setting up an office?"

"Hon, if anyone could, it's you."

"You talk like I'm a magnet for bad stuff." She looked offended, her bottom lip pouting prettily.

If only she wasn't so damned good at manipulating him, Brian thought. And she'd got Jim wrapped around her little finger, too.

"I don't want you even remotely near trouble," he told her. "I want you safe."

"Brian, I could get hit crossing the street. I could be mugged doing my grocery shopping…"

"You don't do grocery shopping," he said.

"I do, too. How do you think eggs, milk and bread end up in my refrigerator?"

"Your housekeeper?"

Kaylen pressed her lips together and gave a very unladylike snort, something she did rarely, but an indication she was getting more than irritated with what she called his over-protectiveness.

"I pay her to clean, not to shop."

She got up, balanced their plates effortlessly on one arm, scooped up cups, silverware and the coffee pot and took them all into the kitchen. The dishwasher racks slid open and she began loading, china clattering.

"Honestly, Brian, you must think I'm completely useless at anything except satisfying you during sex," she said, her voice muffled as she bent to put a platter into the bottom rack. She stood and turned, hands on hips. "I do that at least, don't I?" Her brows drew toward each other, a frown appearing on her forehead. "Well?" she urged, when he didn't answer immediately.

Brian decided to choose his words more carefully. His girlfriend was looking decidedly unhappy. "You do that and a lot more."

"Well, thank goodness for that."

She slid the racks back into place, filled slots with detergent and closed the dishwasher. Brian heard it filling. He watched Kaylen shake crumbs from the placemats into the sink and rinse it out with the sprayer. He walked to the edge of the kitchen but she refused to make eye contact as she dried her hands on a towel. Even in profile, she looked perturbed.

"I don't know why you're so argumentative today," Brian said. "I had a hard session with Fleming. I don't want another one with you. Can't we spend a quiet, uneventful day together for once? You can be rid of me this evening."

"I don't want to be rid of you. You need to change your flight." Still holding the towel, Kaylen turned and leaned against the sink. "So I have time to get packed and go with you. Rob can manage the club. He did it before, and that was opening week, for God's sake."

"And then you closed it for a week, because you couldn't be there," Brian reminded her. "Are you sure you want to abandon your business for the second time in less than five months?"

Kaylen bit her lip. "You're always so right, it's annoying, but yes, I'm going to take that risk. I'll call my backers and then hold a staff meeting; let them know I'll be out of town for a few days. I'd already decided I didn't need to be at the club all the time—it's thriving, and I'm getting bored. That's why I had that meeting with the Stavros family. I need a new challenge."

"What about opening another club yourself instead of helping someone else set up a potential rival for your customers?" Brian watched as her eyes flashed.

"Your logic's so sound, maybe you should open a club yourself," she said. "I thought you told me you don't have any business sense? You sound more like Tim than yourself right now."

"I guess that financial whiz I hired is rubbing off on me." He shrugged. "What's happening with my businesses has nothing to do with yours. I don't want you to jeopardize your club so you can go to Tampa."

"Bannisters will be fine. I've got every confidence in Rob. I want to help you and Jim. I know how to set up an office. I'll handle everything. I'll interview potential temps and make sure you get the right fit. If I don't, you'll scare off whoever takes the job on the first day, even if Jim's the primary contact."

"Why the hell would you say that?"

"After seeing what you did to the nursing staff at the hospital when you got well enough to open your mouth? *Please.*" She tossed her head. Her hair bounced, shining chestnut curls gliding across her shoulders.

She looked adorable and way more approachable than when she was cool and remote and completely beautiful. He walked into the kitchen, drew her close and ran a hand down the softness of her cheek. "Don't be mad, princess. I'll change my reservation and get you a ticket, too."

"Right next to you." She placed her hand over his. "That's where I want to be, even though you're not sure you want that, too."

"I do," he said. "But not all the time. I can't concentrate if I'm worried about you."

"You should be more worried about me when I'm *not* with you."

"Why?" He sensed trouble. "What's been going on?"

CHAPTER THIRTY-EIGHT

KAYLEN FELT like a load had shifted off her when she finished telling Brian about the incident at Mizelle's and seeing Sam. She wondered how many people he'd interviewed in the past had felt like she did. He had a way of drawing out the truth whether she liked it or not, and if she was totally honest with herself, she felt guilt along with the relief. She'd given him yet another burden to bear, like he didn't have enough already.

"You really think you saw him?" Brian looked like he believed her, but sounded doubtful.

"Yes. He was right in the front window of the little café. He was thinner and he had a beard. No comb-over. He had a full head of dark hair cut really short. But he was still hard to miss."

She felt cold suddenly, tremors moving through her at the memory. Then just as suddenly, comforting warmth. Brian's hand on her cold one. His *left* hand, she realized. She wasn't even sure he knew he was using it.

"I've been wondering if he knew I was going to be there, so he put himself where I would see him," she said, hesitant to air her misgivings. "I know that sounds paranoid, but I could believe anything of him after what he did to me...to you...to...to Tim..." She couldn't continue. Tears filled her eyes, choked her voice.

"I don't think you're anything close to paranoid." Brian kissed her lightly, reassuringly. "Super-sensitive, maybe, but I've made you that way. I prefer you over-react than wait too long."

He moved away to look out the balcony door, his back to her. Kaylen knew he didn't want her to see the expression on his face or the look in his eyes. But when he ran his right hand through his hair, a gesture she now knew meant he was angry and frustrated, she felt it was because he had left her, as he thought, unprotected and vulnerable.

"I don't know if Angela Crossfield would agree with you, or Mizelle or Dina, for that matter," she said.

Brian turned, his face completely expressionless. "Don't worry about that girl. She'll find another job. And Mizelle and Angela will be fine, too. I'm glad Angela was there. She sounds like she could turn into a good friend. You need that."

Kaylen still marveled at the speed with which he could control his emotions. "A replacement for Sandy, you mean."

She joined him at the partially-open sliding glass door. A chilly breeze wafted through the gap and encircled her bare legs. She shuddered. "Cold," she said, in case he misinterpreted her body language.

She closed the door and locked it, then thought better of that reaction. Who would climb four floors? She unlocked the door, thought about someone leaping over from an adjacent balcony or dropping down from the one above and relocked it.

Brian's eyes had narrowed.

He missed nothing, she thought with resignation.

But he didn't comment about the door. "I didn't mean for it to sound like that," he said instead. "I know you can't replace a best friend like you're changing clothes."

His arm slid around her waist. She leaned against him. He felt so solid, so safe. His breath tickled her ear. Tension flowed out of her. She turned to face him. He nuzzled her neck.

"I know you didn't mean it like it sounded," she said. "You're right, though. I do need a new BFF. Whether Angela's going to fill that vacancy remains to be seen."

"As long as Ziggy Stavros doesn't think he's taking that slot, then I'm happy." Brian's face was no longer expressionless, and his eyes held doubt.

"Silly," she said.

Brian shook his head. "Jealous. Stavros is so comfortable in your world. So much more your equal."

"So young and immature. So much less of a man."

She kissed Brian, long and hard. He kissed her back, holding her tightly against him. Encircling her with his warmth and security.

"You realize you're holding me with both arms, don't you?"

"Yeah. For the first time since my injury. I told Hal I needed to get back to work. See what happened when I did."

"I'm sure you'll let him know." Kaylen laughed, relieved to change the subject. "You never miss a chance to dig at him. And he puts up with it. He's a really great boss."

"Are you trying to make me feel guilty?"

"No, just kidding around. You're not very good at light banter, though."

"Never learned to be, I guess." He shrugged. "Don't know if I'm too old to learn, now."

"Maybe I can teach you." She held him close and felt a pang of sadness for him. From George and Tim she had learned life could be fun. Brian had experienced too little of that. She needed to show him how to relax and make jokes that didn't have a sarcastic edge.

"Maybe you can," he said. "But you've got your work cut out for you."

His misgivings rang true. "Well, hopefully, I'll have many years to accomplish that." She tried to keep her tone light, but in the back of her mind, she wondered whether he'd think she was trying to put a heavy chain around his waist and bind him to her. "Want to go over and check the *NTK* now?" She asked quickly.

But instead of commenting, or worse, emotionally withdrawing, Brian kissed her again.

Desire rose inside her, as it always did when they were together. "Or we could go later." *Damn, he was good at distracting her.*

"Better we go now and make love later." His hold on her loosened. "Much as I'd like it to be the other way around." He kissed the tip of her nose and stepped back. "You need to leave a note for Shelley Summer-field, so she can get started with her application."

"You're right; unfortunately." Reluctant to lose contact, she pressed up against him and felt his rapid intake of breath as that time, her arms wrapped around *his* waist. "I've missed you so badly over the last few days."

"That goes for me, too." He brushed the hair back from her face and kissed her again, that time much softer and sweeter.

Kaylen thought it was the perfect moment for him to tell her he loved her, but instead, he pulled gently away.

"What do you want to do, tuck a note and a business card in an envelope and leave it for her at the marina office?" He suggested.

"Probably."

Her arms felt emptier than they should have. Brian was only a few feet away, but Kaylen felt as though he'd already left the room. He was back to being himself...professional and distant. She felt colder than when the draft had slid around her legs.

Fighting off sadness, Kaylen went to her desk and pulled out a note-card, sat down and composed a short message telling Shelley she had heard she needed a job and there was an opening at Bannisters. Training would be provided and a good hourly wage, part or full time. She made Rob the contact person, dropped a business card inside the envelope with the notecard and sealed it.

Brian had turned on the TV and was watching a football game with the sound turned down low. Kaylen wished he was always coming home to her, but she knew that even if he did agree to it, he'd be gone frequently, either working or spending time on the *Need to Know*. A knot formed in her throat and for the second time that afternoon, her eyes welled up with tears.

"I'm going to get a sweater," she said, keeping her face averted. She walked briskly into the master bedroom, detoured into her ensuite bathroom and grabbed a tissue from the box on the vanity. She dabbed her eyes, freshened her makeup and tried to ignore the pinched look on her face. It seemed to be a permanent addition, and she had formed an affinity for concealer and blush of a deeper shade than she'd ever used before Tim's disappearance.

"Are you ready?" Brian stood in the doorway.

Kaylen jumped. "I hate when you do that."

"Do what?"

He grinned at her reflection; the old sarcastic grin that used to infuriate her, but now charmed.

"You know very well what," she retorted. "Let's go. What are you waiting for?"

"What a woman." He rolled his eyes.

Kaylen took up a jacket she had left lying on the bed instead of searching inside her closet for a sweater and grabbed her purse from the dresser. "Don't think you're getting anything else out of me after we get home," she threatened. "I'll be going straight to sleep."

"Promises, promises," he said. "Besides, I thought you planned to pack?"

When his hand brushed across her back on the way out the door, Kaylen knew she'd never be able to make that threat a reality.

CHAPTER THIRTY-NINE

"I'll make a couple of calls while you're in the office," Brian told Kaylen as they walked from the parking lot toward the dock at the Coconut Grove Marina.

"Okay." She squeezed his hand and released it before kissing his cheek.

Brian got a whiff of perfume, light and familiar. Before he could stop himself, she was in his arms and he was kissing her like it was the first and last time...hungry but bittersweet.

"Wow." She looked at him with genuine surprise. "What's up with you today?"

"Nothin.' You'd better head to the office with that note."

"Okay." Reluctance radiating from her, she left, but she kept glancing back over her shoulder.

He turned away, afraid of what his face might reveal. She was right; something *was* up with him. His emotions were churning, and he couldn't seem to control them. He took out his phone and got Jack Mills on the first ring.

Mills didn't waste time on pleasantries. He knew Brian never did. "What's up?"

Brian told him about Kaylen seeing Sam Wilson. "And I believe her," he added. "I know she has flashbacks, but never of Wilson. They're always about my injury, finding her housekeeper murdered or getting attacked in her condo."

"We've been getting intel he might be back," Mills said. "Hal didn't want you informed. He said you've both been through enough already without being told about unconfirmed sightings."

"Kaylen seeing Sam and not expecting it was a lot worse than being prepared for that possibility," Brian said. "But I get Hal's point."

He heard murmuring in the background.

Mills cleared his throat. "We've all been wondering at the squad when you're coming back, but all we hear is 'not yet.'"

"If it was up to me, I'd have been back weeks ago. Tell whoever's listening that Hal insists on me passing my goddamned proficiency at the firing range, and I missed it last time by a couple of points."

He heard Mills relaying the information and more murmurs.

"I'm stepping into the hallway and calling you back," Mills said.

"Okay." Brian wondered what Jack Mills had to say that he couldn't share with the rest of the detectives. His phone rang.

"That's not the only reason, is it?" Mills said.

Brian was taken-aback. "You're fuckin' direct today."

"I heard through the grapevine you've been offered a supervisory position."

"You heard right, but I haven't taken it."

"Doing what, and why not?"

It was on the tip of Brian's tongue to tell Mills to back off, but something in his coworker's tone stopped him.

"You belong at work." Mills sounded gruff. "I never realized what a damned good detective you are until you weren't here anymore. What's the chief want you to do?"

"Head up Cold Case."

"What?" Mills' voice held a note of disbelief.

"Yep. A fuckin' desk job."

"He thinks you'll never be ready to go back in the field," Mills said. "He should know better than that."

"Thanks for the vote of confidence. I needed that." Brian had walked the length of the dock as he spoke. He turned and headed back, debating whether to confide anything else in Mills.

"Why doesn't that shrink intervene?" Mills asked. "Tell Hal you'll do fine. I'd go out with you as a partner anytime, a few points shy of your proficiency or not."

"The shrink's a son-of-a-bitch. He's pokin' into my private life like he owns me."

"Bastard," Mills said.

"You got that right." Brian felt anger welling up and tried to tamp it back down.

"If you need someone to vouch for you, I'll do it," Mills said. "Any of us would, but I could sound more convincing."

"That's real comforting. Thanks, I think."

"We should get together, anyway. I can update you on your brother's case."

"Like there's anything new. If Tim wasn't related to me, you wouldn't even mention his name right now. Maybe I should take that position and insist on making his case my first. The bastards who killed him covered their tracks so well; I bet it's been hard to find any useful evidence."

"It's been difficult," Mills conceded. "But we're not giving up yet, and I've got a couple of things to run past you."

"What time d'you get off?" Brian walked slowly toward the *NTK*.

"In an hour."

"Why don't you come to my boat? I've got beer, and I'll order pizza."

"Okay. Sounds good." Mills grunted. "Pepperoni and mushroom?"

"Sure."

Brian watched Kaylen coming toward him as he put his phone away. Dressed in a pair of black pants and a dark pink jacket, her chestnut hair caught back in a ponytail, she turned all heads. His heart rate accelerated.

"Done," she said when she got close enough to speak quietly. "I called Rob, too. He asked for a raise. I'm not sure he was kidding."

"Even though he and I have become friends, I think he's still a bit pissed about me wrecking his cousin's car. Now we're asking him to do something else that could backfire."

"I don't know about him having reservations, but I do know his cousin still gives him grief about the LeSabre, even though it got replaced with a newer model." Kaylen took Brian's right arm. "Some people are never happy."

"You said it."

Brian thought of himself. He should be feeling a lot more optimistic. Life was getting better all the time, but he couldn't seem to enjoy it. The guilt over Tim's death oppressed him, and now Mills was coming to tell him they had followed up on yet more dead-end leads.

"Well, the locks don't look disturbed," Kaylen said.

Brian realized they were standing in front of the *NTK's* salon. He'd been so preoccupied with thinking about Tim again, his actions had become automatic.

He pulled out his keys. "I didn't expect them to be, but it never hurts to check after being out of town."

He unlocked the door on his second attempt and pushed it open. "I should complain to the boat builder about that awkward lock."

The interior of the boat smelled slightly stale. Kaylen stepped inside and took off her jacket, throwing it across the back of the couch.

"Coffee?" she suggested.

"Sounds good. I'll check the ropes. Jim's boat, too."

Brian made the rounds. When he'd satisfied himself the *NTK* and Jim's *Fanciful Folly* were securely moored, he took a look at the Summerfields' *Naughty Nautical*.

"Hello," Mel said from behind him. "Did I make everything tight enough this time?"

CHAPTER FORTY

BRIAN DECIDED Mel was all he needed that afternoon to make his brief stay in Miami even more complicated.

Sidling up next to him, she leaned over, hands on hips, giving Brian an excellent view down her low cut top as she looked at one of the lines. She definitely wasn't wearing a bra that day.

"You must be Mel," Kaylen called. "Why don't you have a cup of coffee with us?" She smiled down at both of them, a slight tightness around her mouth the only indication she might not be thrilled to see the eldest Summerfield daughter.

"Oh, and you must be Kaylen," Mel purred, returning Kaylen's smile as she took her time about straightening up. "I'd *love* coffee." She glanced up at Brian and winked before heading over to the *NTK*.

Great, Brian thought. *Coffee with his girlfriend and the woman who had been naked on his bed only a couple of days before.* He hoped Jack Mills would hurry. He'd need a six-pack of beer after Kaylen and Mel left.

He followed Mel's swinging hips as she stepped onto the boat. Her turquoise pants were skin tight. He decided she couldn't be wearing panties, either.

Like Kaylen, she took off her jacket, draping it across the back of the banquette. Her t-shirt clung to all the right or wrong places, depending on who was looking. Brian quickly averted his gaze from her nipples, standing boldly at attention, and concentrated on everything that was at eye level or above.

Mel hopped onto a barstool and swung it slowly back and forth with one hand on the counter. "I like mine with cream and sugar."

Kaylen checked inside the refrigerator. "You forgot to get milk," she said aside to Brian. "There's powdered creamer, if you can't face black," she told Mel as she slid a small cup of coffee across the bar and followed it with a canister of sugar and a spoon.

Mel wrinkled her nose. "Well, if there's nothing else, then I guess I'll take that."

Kaylen took a plastic container out of a cupboard and plunked it down beside the sugar canister. She placed a big mug of black coffee in front of Brian and clasped her own as she watched Mel stir sugar and creamer into her cup.

"I haven't seen you around for the last few days," Mel said to Brian, ignoring Kaylen like she was invisible.

Brian felt the tension and wondered what the hell to do about it. Tim would have managed the situation a whole lot better, he thought. Charisma and practice went a long way. He was short on both. He decided to keep his responses brief and to the point. "I've been out of town."

"Ah." Mel took a sip of her coffee and screwed up her face like she'd had a mouthful of brine. "This is really strong."

"The way we like it." Kaylen's voice had a decidedly icy tone. "Do you want me to make you tea, instead?"

"No." Mel took another small sip. "I don't want to put you to any trouble."

"No trouble." Kaylen ran water into the kettle and plugged it in. She took Mel's coffee cup away and tipped its contents down the drain. "It'll only take a couple of minutes." She leaned back against the sink, arms folded. "I hear your daughter's looking for a job. I left her a note at the marina office. My club's hiring wait staff."

"Oh." Mel stopped swinging the stool back and forth. Her breasts bounced to a stop, too. "That's really kind of you."

"Has she waited tables before?" Kaylen asked.

The kettle began making rumbling noises. Brian hoped it boiled real fast, so Mel would go pick up the note for Shelley and scuttle off home before Kaylen lost her cool and told Mel exactly what she really thought of her.

"Yes," Mel said in response to Kaylen's question. "Up in North Dakota. She started behind the counter at a fast food place, then worked the morning shift in a diner. Her last job was at a steakhouse. She made lots of tips."

"I'm sure she did," Kaylen said. "If she's anything like you, she would get a lot of those."

"I heard you used to wait tables yourself," Mel said.

She was good, Brian had to admit. It was a zinger disguised as a chatty piece of conversation.

"I did." Kaylen's face was impassive, her delivery smooth. "When I first arrived in Miami. I worked my way up from server to manager."

"You're talented," Mel said.

"You, too, from what Brian's told me."

The conversation was tipping from general barbs to the more personal kind. Brian wasn't sure whether to intervene or let things take their course, If Kaylen really let loose, Shelley certainly wouldn't be taking a position at Bannisters. He tried to catch Kaylen's eye, but the kettle went from rumbling to belching steam and then her back was turned to him. She filled Mel's cup with water and took out the tea box, filled with a selection of fruit teas, Earl Grey, Constant Comment and English Breakfast.

"Here." Kaylen placed both the box and cup of steaming water on the bar in front of Mel. "You get to pick from what's in the box. There's nothing else around here for you."

"Is that right?" Mel selected peach tea. She slowly opened the wrapper and dangled the teabag over the water before dropping it into the cup.

Kaylen closed the box and drew it slowly back across the counter. "Yes," she said. "Definitely not."

Brian drained his mug and took it into the galley. "Mills is coming over in less than an hour," he told Kaylen. "Are you going back to the condo before work or straight to the club?"

"The club, but I won't stay long. When Mills gets here, I'll take off." She looked straight at Mel, sipping tea and watching them over the brim of her cup.

"I should go pick up that note," Mel said, taking the hint. She put down her cup and jumped off the stool.

Brian hated himself for being such a guy, but he couldn't help watching to see if her breasts bounced on the way off the stool the same way they had on the way up. They did. He felt Kaylen's glare.

"No sense in waiting," Kaylen told Mel.

Her voice didn't sound smooth or silky. It sounded decidedly edgy.

"I'll be out of town with Brian for the next few days," she continued, as she watched Mel pick up her jacket. "Shelley doesn't need to wait for me to come back. She can call my manager and set up a time for him to do the interview. Make sure she takes verifiable references with her. At least three."

Mel nodded. She made a big production out of putting on her jacket, but Kaylen deterred Brian from going to speed up the process by glaring at him again.

"'Bye," Mel said. "Thanks for the tea...and the job lead for Shelley, of course." She smiled more toward Brian than Kaylen before sashaying out the door.

"Barracuda," Kaylen said. She took Mel's cup and threw it in the garbage. "Don't you ever..."

When she looked at Brian, her eyes flashed fire. He felt pretty good but a bit ashamed of himself. *Kaylen radiating jealousy? What a turn-on.*

"Wouldn't dream of it," he said.

"Not even." Kaylen looked at her watch. "Mills will be here soon?" Her hands ran over her hips and down her thighs, like she was either wiping off sweaty palms or caressing herself.

"Unfortunately." Brian thought he had similar unsettling urges. "Mel's having an effect on us both."

"Damn right." Kaylen drummed her fingers on the bar. "My God; the nerve of her! I've never felt more like scratching another woman's eyes out in my life. She's dangerous." She leaned her elbows on the counter and locked gazes with Brian. "You wouldn't, would you?"

Surprisingly, he saw uncertainty on her face.

"I'm a one-woman man," he assured her. "Not even one, sometimes, as you like to tell me."

"That wouldn't stop her." Kaylen looked toward the door, as though she expected Mel to reappear. "She wouldn't run from anything,"

Brian tried to make light of the situation. "I don't know…she might run from you."

Kaylen shook her head. "I doubt it. But something's off. It's like she's almost over-confident. She sure knows how to flaunt herself, that's for damned sure. And it must have worked for her a lot before."

"I'm sure it did. But she's gonna strike out with me. Let me assure you of that. I'll look, I can't help myself; after all, I am a man. But I'm not interested in what she's offering. I'm more than happy with you."

"Are you? I know you're most content when you're alone."

"I'm at my most comfortable; not necessarily my most content."

Kaylen gave him a weak smile. "We seem to be spending a lot of time discussing our relationship these days."

"Yes." He didn't elaborate.

What was he going to say? That she kept bringing it up? That Fleming did? That the run-ins with Mel were having a disturbing effect on him, and seemingly, on Kaylen, too?

"I'm not suggesting Mel or any other woman wouldn't throw herself at you," Kaylen said. She grabbed a sponge from the sink and energetically rubbed the bar. "*I* did."

"Is that what you think?" He took the sponge away and threw it in the sink. Cradled her elbows with his hands and made her look at him. "Why would you even go there?"

"I did," Kaylen said. Her brown eyes were troubled, her mouth pinched. "Because you wouldn't, and I didn't understand why. And now I wonder whether I pushed you into something you've regretted."

"Stop questioning yourself. That's my job."

"Questioning me?" She looked puzzled.

"No, of course not. Questioning myself. About a lot of things." He kissed her lightly. "I'll walk you to the car."

"You're not coming back to the condo?"

"No. I'll change clothes here and meet you at the club later. I can catch a cab."

"You're going there tonight?" She looked astonished. "Really?"

"Yeah. It's about time, isn't it?"

"It is." The clouds of doubt disappeared.

Her face was too close to resist. He kissed her and felt her instant response. Her lips opened. Brian's pulse sped up as her tongue danced against his, and he wished he'd never suggested the meeting with Mills. He wanted to take her to bed. Strip her naked and make her forget about doubting him…

"We don't have time," he said. "Dammit." He took her hand. "Come on."

He tugged her gently but firmly. Kaylen hesitated briefly before grabbing her purse and going with him. He helped her draw her jacket across her shoulders as they crossed the deck.

"Let's get you into your car before Jack sees a whole lot more of us than he ever should," Brian told her as he helped her onto the dock.

"I'll take a rain check." Kaylen slid her arm around his waist as they walked through the parking lot.

Brian held her close and wondered what was so wrong with him that he couldn't let go of the past and appreciate everything he had at that moment.

CHAPTER FORTY-ONE

Fifteen minutes later, Jack Mills arrived aboard the *Need to Know*. Like Kaylen and Mel before him, he tossed his jacket over the back of a chair before sitting next to Brian in the stern, facing the bay.

"Man, what a view." Jack loosened his tie. "No wonder you live on the boat. If I was you, I would, too." He took a pull from the beer Brian handed him. "Ah, that hits the spot. Good to see you. You look a helluva lot better than you did the last time I saw you."

Brian grimaced. "The commendation ceremony. I felt like shit. Must have looked like it, too. Now I'm almost back to normal. Whatever that is these days."

Mills looked at Brian's hands, the right holding a beer bottle, the left lying in his lap.

"Yeah," Brian said, before his coworker could ask. "I still don't have a good grip, but the surgeon insists I'm on track for a good recovery."

"Hal was pretty tight-lipped about your status, but he looked damned worried whenever he gave us an update." Mills turned sideways on the chaise, facing Brian. "How much was he holding back? He told us to give you space. I didn't feel good about that, but I figured you'd made it obvious you didn't want company while you were recuperating, at least not from the department."

Brian nodded. "That's true. Kaylen and Jim took care of me. They were the ones who should have gotten commendations."

"I can only imagine." Mills finished his beer and set the bottle on the table.

"Want another?" Brian pointed to the cooler on the deck close to their feet. "Help yourself."

Mills shook his head. "I'd better eat something first." He pushed back the lid on the flat white box sitting on the table between them, releasing an enticing aroma of pepperoni and cheese, and slid a large slice of pizza onto a paper plate. "Smells and looks great. Thanks, Swift." He grabbed a napkin and settled back. "I thought you were on the mend?"

"I'm doing a lot better now. For a while, it looked like I'd never use this arm again." Brian lifted his left hand, opening and closing his fingers.

"Damn." Mills looked down at his own hands. "I bet that made you think about what the hell you were going to do with the rest of your life. If I didn't have my job, I'd have very little else."

Brian realized he knew next to nothing about his coworkers. He found himself wondering how they successfully juggled careers and private lives. Or whether they didn't. He knew he was in the 'didn't' category. "I thought you were married," he said.

Mills put down the half-chewed pizza and used his napkin to blot up a spot of tomato sauce that had landed on his pale blue tie. "Damn, I'm a slob. Technically, I was still married when you were on active duty. The divorce became final last month. The second one. Two marriages, two divorces, one kid...a boy."

"I'm sorry to hear about that," Brian said mechanically, then decided he really was sorry, and had found yet another reason not to ever become a father. "How old's your kid? Do you get to see him much?"

Mills abandoned his attempt to clean up his tie and pulled it over his head, throwing it onto the deck. "I barely know Adam. My first wife got custody and I didn't make any waves when she moved out of state and took him with her. I paid child support until he turned eighteen. That was the last I heard from either of them. They were in Nebraska, living close to her family, and there didn't seem any point in trying to be part of his life." He finished the pizza on his plate with two big bites and took another piece. "Life sucks sometimes, as you know."

"We all have our problems," Brian said.

Despite having refused moments before, Mills put down his plate and pulled another beer out of the cooler. "Some bigger than others." He popped the top off the beer and took a swig. "I swore I'd never marry again, and then I went and did it out of loneliness. Number two was a cocktail waitress. Pretty as all get out. Really wanted to marry a cop, for whatever reason. Thought it would be exciting, probably. I never asked her. I didn't like the thought of her continuing to work and finding someone better than me, so I convinced her to quit. Then she found herself stuck at home and bored while I repeated the same pattern I'd had with my first marriage—not putting enough time into making it work. After we separated, I decided to marry my job instead."

"The job takes a lot," Brian said. "Until I got the boat I rarely thought of anything else, either, except when Tim derailed me."

He refused to even think about what could happen to his relationship with Kaylen when he went back to work full-time.

"Which he did on a pretty regular basis," Mills said.

Brian was thankful to break away from thoughts of Kaylen potentially confronting him as Jack Mills' wives must have done, angry at him for his long absences and his poor attention to anything but whatever case he was working on at the time.

"Yeah," Brian said. "Tim was good at disrupting things." He realized his voice had grown gruff and raw. Even that far from Tim's death.

Mills broke eye contact, turning to stare at the numerous boats coming back to harbor across the choppy waters of the bay. "I know you must miss him."

"Every damn day." Brian decided the beer was giving him a slight buzz on an empty stomach, and losing even a little control still brought his emotions to the forefront. He put down the bottle he'd been cradling and took a slice of pizza himself. "So, what's new on Tim's case, anyway? You haven't tracked down Sam Wilson yet, then?"

"No, damn it. Some people who knew him, at least slightly, have called the department. We've had reports on the tip line. A few described the paunch, the comb-over, the cigars, which were probably false reports, because the recent ones say he's lost weight and has dark, cropped hair. He may have gotten plugs and some plastic surgery. He was seen in a couple of coffee shops, then a restaurant in Coral Gables. Favorite hang-outs of his in the past, although by witness accounts, the last couple of months before Tim's disappearance and death, Wilson'd spent most of his time in his own restaurant."

"The Hideaway," Brian said.

Mills nodded. "We certainly know he can't go back there, since it got torched." He stopped to cram the rest of the pizza slice into his mouth.

Brian wondered whether his coworker was extremely hungry or filling his mouth as a punctuation mark. "I know what you're thinking. The *Destiny* burned as well, and three people died. Christ, those were difficult days." He watched Mills swallow with difficulty, like the pizza was sticking in his throat. "But they're over," he assured his coworker. "It's okay to talk about them."

Mills coughed a couple of times and took a swig of his beer. He wiped his mouth with another napkin. "I appreciate you telling me that. I only half-way told the truth when I said Hal had made it clear we should give you your space. He meant right after you got discharged from the hospital. I feel damned awkward sitting here. We didn't do enough. That apology we gave at Tim's funeral was heartfelt, but following up on his case…we've hit so many dead ends, frankly, the trail's been going cold."

"Until Wilson was sighted? That must have warmed things up."

"If we could substantiate those tips, it definitely would. No one has taken a picture of him. No one has called the precinct and said, "Hey, Sam Wilson's in such-and-such café right now. Go over there and pick him up."

"What about the two who killed Tim? You've got names and descriptions. What the hell happened to them?"

"They haven't been seen with Wilson. As far as we can determine, they're still out of the country. It looks like he came back alone."

"Hard to believe. He's a coward, and he likes an entourage. But I doubt he's got a lot of money to spend on a new protection squad, either."

"We're digging around, but we haven't found a source of income for him. He may have hidden funds before he skipped Miami. Could be disguised under a layer of other accounts. On the surface, it looked like he was close to bankruptcy. The feds are working on that. Then there's the payoff for his restaurant fire, but that's still up in the air. Definitely arson, and insurance isn't convinced he didn't pay to have the job done. Substantial rewards have been offered for information."

"If he's cartel-connected, it won't matter how big the rewards are. People don't snitch on those guys and stay alive."

"Which I always find damned annoying," Mills said without a trace of a smile. "Does the name Fontana mean anything to you?"

Brian thought for a moment. "No. Who's that?"

"He owns a piece of the Stavros family's business."

Brian sat upright. "The restaurant owners?"

"Yes."

"What's his connection to Tim? Or theirs, for that matter?"

"Maybe nothing. But we've been asked to check backgrounds on everyone related to or doing business with Kaylen."

"*What?*" Brian's head started buzzing again, and not from the beer. "Why the fuck would anyone start investigating her now? Because Wilson's back? She told me she'd seen him. She's not hiding anything." He jumped to his feet. "Who ordered this? Hal? The double-faced bastard. I'll…"

Mills threw up his hands. "No. God, no, not the chief. The new supervisor of Homicide. Name of Darrell Trehorn."

CHAPTER FORTY-TWO

"Where the hell did *he* come from?" Brian couldn't believe what he was hearing. "Why the fuck didn't Hal promote from within the squad?"

"Because I turned down the position and Hal said no one else was ready for it."

"He told you that?"

"In so many words. There was a staff meeting. The fall-out from IA's investigation, the mess over Tim and you…Hal had to shake things up and bring in new blood. We're all still under a microscope. One of the reasons I refused the position. I like field-work, anyway."

"Christ." Brian sat back down, picked up his beer and drained it. "The whole place has gone to hell, and it sounds like it's mostly my fault."

"Nah. You can't take *all* the credit." Mills gave a half smile. "Hastings and his squad fucked us all over. Hal knows you'd butt heads with Trehorn. I'd bet money that's why he offered you Cold Case."

He finished his beer and took the replacement Brian offered from the cooler.

"So he thinks he'll stow me in some shit position to keep me muzzled." Brian saw the inevitability of a career derailment, and for once in his life, felt completely powerless to prevent it. His personnel file held more than enough ammunition to put him wherever the chief wanted.

Despite a desire to use alcohol to take the edge off the resentment surging through him, he decided against another beer. He didn't want to arrive at Bannisters smelling like he'd been drinking and possibly acting like it, too. The information Mills had given him was already making his head spin.

Fortunate he couldn't drive a stick-shift, he thought. Otherwise he'd take the Camaro out for a long, hard ride. In his present frame of mind that would have very possibly resulted in a traffic stop altercation, followed by a night in jail. Instead, he'd have to curb his emotional response to being sold out, change clothes after Mills left and take a cab to join Kaylen at her club.

"How about some coffee before you get back behind the wheel?" Brian offered.

"You got any decaf? I'll be too spooled up to sleep, otherwise."

"Yep. No problem."

"Mind if I look around while you're making it? I've never been on a boat this big." Mills struggled a little getting off the chaise. "Comfortable but damn low," he said, looking at the chair.

"You're getting old and stiff," Brian told him.

"I think the word's gotten, not getting." Mills stretched, hands in the small of his back, and winced slightly. "I need to slow down."

Brian thought that if he ever seriously considered that Cold Case position, he'd ask Mills to join him. His coworker was astute and mature, two characteristics Brian knew he would need from anyone who worked in close proximity with him. Then he wondered what he was thinking, even considering the Cold Case position in the first place. He made his way into the galley and got the coffee going as Mills wandered in and out of the bedroom and the head.

"Trehorn's not showing any biases in his digging," Mills said when he came back into the salon. "He's going over everything again. Tim's connections, including looking at links to Hastings and his squad. Your place in all of it as well as Kaylen's. He said anyone who hasn't got the stomach for it can transfer out of Homicide or quit. All that shit Hal said about backing you up and pulling for you is going right out the window with Trehorn in charge."

"Fucker." Brian took mugs out of the cabinet above the coffeemaker. "But he's good. I'd probably do the same thing if I was in his shoes. He doesn't know what hell Kaylen and I went through, and he wouldn't care even if he did. He's got no emotional connections with any of us. Hal's picked the right man for the job. But my career's going to take a nose-dive again, right when it looked like things might start looking up."

"Damn." Mills looked surprised. "Not quite the reaction I expected from you."

"I know." Brian nodded, a little surprised himself. "Somehow, in the middle of all this, I must have mellowed." He poured the coffee and slid a mug across the bar to Mills, who had perched on the same barstool Mel had occupied only hours earlier.

"I doubt that." Mills chuckled. "But instead of your usual knee-jerk reaction, you showed insight. Good thing I never had aspirations of taking over Hal's position. When you come back, the rest of us can kiss that career path goodbye."

They fell into a discussion of what was lacking at the precinct, both in terms of manpower and support. Mills drank two mugs of coffee before standing up and yawning. "I'd better take off. I've given you a lot to chew on this evening. Sorry, but I thought you should know."

"Nothing to be sorry about. You were right, and I appreciate it." Brian got up and extended his hand. "No bullshit. Come over again soon. We'll take the boat out. Fish. Shoot the shit."

"That sounds great." Mills' grip was strong. "I've got some vacation time I've never used. Spending a day out on the water would do me good."

"I'll let you know when I'm back in town. I'm working a case up in Tampa. A cold case."

"Yeah, Hal told me. He said the day you ever follow his orders, he's going to retire."

Mills paused on the dock to wave before strolling through the parking lot, his jacket and tie over one arm and hands deep in his pockets. Brian watched until his coworker got into his dark sedan and cruised slowly out of the parking lot.

Fuckin' hell.

Brian gathered up the remains of their meal and threw it into the trash. He lingered on deck, reluctant to leave the peace of the marina for the crowded and noisy club, leaning back against the rail in the stern while he inhaled tangy salt air and watched twinkling stars sprayed across a sky as thick and dark as velvet. He wondered what was going to happen to the rest of his life. Nothing came to mind that was anywhere near what he had planned before Tim went missing. He'd been happy in his old life. No responsibilities except his job. No one to answer to except Hal…

Pissed at himself for lapsing into maudlin thoughts and inertia, and even more pissed at the thought of both Kaylen and himself being investigated yet again, he left his comfort zone for the bedroom, where he took a tux out of the closet, laid out a shirt, boxers, black socks and dress shoes. He looked at himself in the mirror and didn't like what was staring back at him one bit, but he'd used both hands to do everything since stepping onto the boat, and he was done with playing the victim role. Brian decided it was time to show Hal and Darrell Trehorn just who the hell they were dicking with.

He left everything where it was, got the keys to the Camaro and went into the parking lot, which was pretty deserted. He eased behind the wheel, having to push the seat back. His legs were longer than Jim's. He adjusted the mirrors while the engine warmed up, took a look around to make sure he wasn't going to wipe anyone out if he found he couldn't drive stick after all, gripped the gear shift, put the Camaro into reverse and with his heart beating a little faster than he liked, backed out of the parking space, shifted into first gear and headed down between the rows of neatly parked cars.

So far, so good, he decided as he moved into second gear and took the ramp out of the marina. He drove on SW 27th Avenue and hit all gears before taking the expressway. His left hand gripped the wheel firmly and he accelerated, feeling a sense of release. He would have liked to roll the window down, but he didn't want to push his luck. After months of missing his car, he felt like he'd just cleared another hurdle. He'd wanted to get the Camaro restored, and he had the time and the money to get the work done. He returned to the marina, decided to take the Camaro into the shop the following morning, and got ready for the club.

CHAPTER FORTY-THREE

By 6:00 PM, Kaylen had finished both her calls and a staff meeting. Backers and staff had been unanimous in demonstrating little to no enthusiasm about her leaving town, even for a few days. After eating three packets of crackers and drinking a Diet Coke, she felt less defeated and called Rob in to go over the details of day-to-day operations while she was away. His response reminded her quickly of why she'd had so much faith in his abilities. He could run Bannisters for a lot more than a long weekend. He'd keep it going if she was gone for months.

"I already heard from that girl you gave your business card to." Rob leaned back in a club chair and crossed his legs at the ankles. He jiggled one foot and rolled his take-out coffee cup between his palms. "I'll check her references tomorrow, as soon as I get here."

"Thanks for doing that. I really appreciate it. Hopefully, she'll work out well." Kaylen smiled at him. He didn't smile back. "I thought you wanted more autonomy here. Now you're giving me the distinct impression you don't. What's wrong?"

Rob placed the cup carefully on a coaster at the edge of Kaylen's desk. "I keep seeing that Stavros guy around here," he said after a moment. "And I'm hearing rumors you're partnering a new restaurant."

Kaylen thought about interrupting to clarify her relationship with Ziggy, but decided to let Rob finish airing his concerns first.

"This club's only been up and running a short time," her manager continued, his gaze candid as he looked straight at her. "I can manage the place, no worries about that, but I'm thinking of your clientele. They expect you to be on the premises. They come here because of you more than the food, Julio's bar concoctions or even the atmosphere. Bannisters isn't ready for you to run out on it again. We already closed for an entire week right after it opened. The public's fickle. Two other supper clubs opened as soon as this one was successful. When people hear you're gone again, they'll take their business elsewhere. They're not going to come here to see me, and Julio might be a great mixologist, but he'll never have the draw you do."

"You make me sound like a freak show." Kaylen felt defensive, which reminded her uncomfortably of Sam's increasing and unwanted interference in the way she ran the club and her private life.

"Not my intention," Rob said quickly. "But you *have* to know how popular you are. People want you to sit at their tables and talk for a few minutes, have a glass of wine. Makes them feel special. Gives them more of a reason to come here than anyplace else."

"I'd hoped they came here for more than that." Kaylen managed a smile she didn't feel.

Rob leaned forward. "If that were true, then the other two clubs would have beaten you somehow, but you're ranking number one with social media and the hotels. I've got friends at a lot of concierge desks— they recommend Bannisters when guests ask for a great place to go."

Kaylen shook her head. "That's not just because of me, Rob. It's a team effort. *All* the staff." She tried again to lighten the discussion. "That even includes Emrico," she added, knowing how much the head chef's bombastic nature rubbed against Rob's professionalism. "Even though he's the biggest pain in the neck, his meals are amazing."

"I get what you're saying." Rob fixed his gaze on the coffee cup. "But I've got to respectfully disagree…"

"I've got the picture," Kaylen interrupted. "You don't need to elaborate any further. I'd already planned to make this a short trip. Now after talking to everyone involved, I'm going to cut it even shorter. Four days, starting tomorrow."

"Is that what you told your backers?"

"Yes. They weren't going to get on board for anything longer." Kaylen shifted uncomfortably. She was done with justifying her behavior. "Time to wind this up. I've got to shower and change before the club opens."

Rob drained his cup and stood. "D'you want Marvin to bring you a meal before we open?"

"Maybe." Kaylen stretched kinked muscles. "Brian's coming. But he had a meeting, so he may have already eaten."

"Fast food, I bet." Rob smiled.

Kaylen welcomed the smile and the friendly dig at Brian's eating habits. Her manager seemed more at ease; more satisfied that she wasn't going to run out on Bannisters and leave him jobless when it closed as a result.

"Without a doubt," she said. "My man's consistent, that's for sure."

"He'd better watch out; all that fat and cholesterol are going into a middle-aged stomach now." Rob threw his cup into the trash can on the way out.

"God." Kaylen cringed. "Don't let him hear you say that."

Rob stopped in the doorway. "For someone who works out daily, runs miles and goes to P.T., you'd think Brian'd eat better."

"I'm hoping all the exercise counteracts the diet." Kaylen stepped over to her closet and slid one of the doors open, revealing a row of jewel-toned cocktail dresses, shoes lined up under each dress. "Now, I've got to decide what mood I'm in."

"Contrite?" Rob suggested.

"You'd better make sure you're indispensable after a remark like that," Kaylen told him.

He grinned before closing the door behind him. Kaylen heard him walking rapidly away, his shoes tapping rhythmically on the concrete floor. She took out a turquoise sheath dress, strapless and form-fitting. She'd better watch what she ate herself, she thought as she hung it on the back of the bathroom door.

CHAPTER FORTY-FOUR

BRIAN WALKED into Bannisters at 9:00 PM. To him, it seemed pretty crowded for a Thursday evening. It looked like Kaylen's club was even more popular than it had been the week it opened, judging by the horde clustered around the bar. Girls giggled over martini glasses filled with brightly colored concoctions while boyfriends looked down the girls' necklines or whispered in their ears.

Men dressed in tuxes talked with their peers over shots of whisky and bourbon, while the younger set laughed and raised bottles of beer. In the dining room, larger groups sat around big tables toward the back and chatted while servers with white napkins over their arms maneuvered deftly between the rows. Close to a crowded dance floor, small cocktail tables with lamps glowing in their centers were perfect for couples. The entire space was filled with elegantly-dressed people, many of whom Brian recognized from spending a couple of weeks confined to a hospital bed and watching TV news and entertainment shows. The A-Listers of Miami were very much in-the-house at Kaylen's club.

He decided his girlfriend was one shrewd entrepreneur. No wonder Tim had put her on his radar. Brains, a head for business, and beauty would have attracted his brother like a moth to a flame. When Tim discovered Kaylen was also sweet and vulnerable, he would have poised himself to reel her in and use her for everything she had. But somewhere along the line, Tim had fallen in love with her, and apparently, fallen hard.

Now, Brian thought, he was heading in the same direction. He wondered, not for the first time, what he was doing even hanging around the fringes of Kaylen's life. He didn't belong in her world. Never had; never would. Regardless of whether he dressed for the part or not.

He glanced down at his tux; another of Tim's retailored designer outfits. Brian knew he could have afforded a new one, but spending money on something he thought he'd only need temporarily went against his better judgment. Maybe that's why he kept skirting the issue of moving in with Kaylen, he thought. It was as though he was living in a dream world. And as soon as he woke up, he wouldn't own any of it...the Mercedes, the *Need to Know*, the investment properties, the money...

Despite his doubts, he continued pushing his way through the crowd. Kaylen was expecting him. He'd promised to go to the club, and he wasn't going to disappoint her. He knew she'd be mingling with her guests and thought he'd find her easily. *His mistake.*

He searched in vain while people bumped into him, carried drinks inches from his face or looked him over like he was a side of beef in a meat market. Just when he thought he was going to run out of patience and start shoving his way through the throng, he spotted Kaylen in the middle of a group of people close to the dance floor.

He managed to reach an empty space at the bar and took a moment to put his irritation under wraps. Was he actually feeling intimidated? He asked himself as the moment stretched into a minute and beyond while he watched her laughing and talking with her friends.

How was it he had no trouble confronting a group of heavily-armed gangbangers, yet he hesitated to meet Kaylen's social set? He watched her, appreciating how well she blended in.

The other women around her were dressed in what he guessed were probably designer outfits, but they were no match for Kaylen. She wore a turquoise form-fitting strapless dress, the bodice decorated with a row of sparkling beads that made her breasts look larger. Another row of beads encircled her waist. She'd told him rhinestones were her favorite decoration because they cut down the need for other jewelry. He thought she never needed anything to look more beautiful, but as he watched her in that moment, she took his breath away, yet again.

He doubted she was wearing high heels. In bare feet, he and Kaylen were roughly the same height, and she didn't like looking taller than him, even though he'd told her more than once he didn't care.

When she was dating Tim, she'd felt able to wear whatever shoes she damned well pleased, he thought with yet another twinge of jealousy. His half-brother had been lucky enough to inherit a gene that made him shoot up to 6' 3," a full four and a half inches taller than Brian. Tim had developed an annoying habit of standing over his brother until one day Brian had put him onto the ground so quickly, Tim had stopped his taunting.

Kaylen glanced over, waved and smiled widely. Brian returned the smile, pushing his way through the mass of humanity with as much restraint as he could manage. Kaylen excused herself from her friends and moved between people as though she had greased that rhinestone-studded dress in all the right places.

"What a busy night," she said when they finally arrived face to face. "You probably wish you'd decided to meet me back at the condo." She laughed. "I know how much you hate crowds."

"An occupational thing," he said. "Cops always hate crowds. I'd only do this for you."

"I know, and I'm grateful." She kissed his cheek before her lips slid closer to his ear. "You look really great," she whispered.

"Thanks. It's pretty easy to look good wearing one of Tim's hand-me-downs." He held her close as people pushed past, all elbows and feet.

"Those designer duds aren't anything close to that." She shook her head. "You're so self-deprecating."

"One of my charms."

Watching her happiness cloud over, he decided he couldn't be surly, even while being jostled, when he was with her.

"I'll try to be on my best behavior, tonight, don't worry." He held her tighter, his hands encircling her waist right below the rhinestones.

Kaylen ran her own hands up his back. "Good." She kissed him lightly, that time on the lips. "I want you to meet some friends. I saw them yesterday at dinner and promised to introduce you."

She tried to break free and take his hand, but he kept her close.

"You think that's wise?"

"Yes. And way past when it should have happened." Her eyes beseeched him. "Please. I don't want to keep our relationship secret any longer."

"I'm still not convinced this is the right thing to do," he warned. "But okay."

"If you don't do it now, they'll get even more curious about you."

"Fine. But first, we're gonna dance."

"We are?" She looked as doubtful as she sounded.

"Yeah." He steered her toward the dance floor. "I'm out of practice, but I still remember how."

By the time they stepped onto the parquet, the Bernie Draper Orchestra was playing the opening bars to "The Nearness of You," one of Kaylen's personal favorites. She had an extensive collection of old standards at home, and had told Brian her father's one weakness had been the music of the 30's and 40's.

Kaylen could and had sung that entire song while they cleaned up the kitchen after a late breakfast one Sunday morning. Brian fondly remembered the occasion. She had a sweet voice, and the sun filtering through palm fronds shading the living room windows had put golden highlights into the richness of her hair. She'd mesmerized him that morning, in the midst of that simple household chore set to music.

A pang shot through him and he held her as close as he dared in a public place, his cheek resting against hers, her right hand in his, his left hand on her back. He felt skin beneath that hand; warm and incredibly soft. He held her even closer, knowing everyone could see them, not caring suddenly. Physical longing conquered his desire to protect her privacy.

"Hmm," she whispered, her voice low, breathy. "This is wonderful." She pulled back a little to look at him. "I had no idea you could dance, and ballroom, at that."

"My mother taught Tim and me." Brian drew her close again and guided her around the floor. "I was in junior high. There was a school dance, and she said I needed to know how to waltz. I thought she was crazy, but I went along with it because it made her happy. When Tim saw us, he wanted to learn, too. She managed to teach both of us while Ed was working. He'd have put a stop to it if he'd been home."

"So, did you take a girl to the dance?" Kaylen asked.

"Nope. In the end, I didn't even go." Brian didn't care to elaborate. He hoped Kaylen wouldn't press the issue. Ed had chosen that week to fracture three of Brian's ribs.

Either she understood his reluctance to say anything else about the dance or she didn't want to break the spell. Whatever motivated her; she stopped talking and placed her cheek back against his, allowing Brian to enjoy the moment. As he felt the softness of Kaylen's body against his and breathed in her subtle perfume, he knew the old Hoagy Carmichael ballad was going to be one of his own favorites from then on.

The song ended, and the orchestra laid down their instruments. "Ladies and gentlemen, the band's taking a fifteen minute break," Bernie Draper announced.

A murmur of disappointment stirred through the couples on the dance floor. Kaylen took Brian's arm as they walked slowly back toward the bar.

"Are you still set on coming to Tampa?" he asked.

"For a few days."

Kaylen moved closer as a slightly unsteady couple passed. Brian put his arm around her. He worried about some aspects of her club—drunks, hidden weapons, drugs, even a holdup. She wouldn't hear about any of it. She felt safe with her security team in place and her trusted employees around her. Despite seeing the unpleasant side of Miami up way too close and personal after meeting him, she still retained a slightly unrealistic view of life and its inhabitants, he thought, trying to push aside irritation. Kaylen rarely listened to his advice.

"My backers are nervous about me going away, and Rob told me the club wasn't ready for me to abandon it again, too." Kaylen looked crestfallen. "I hate to say they're right, but I know they are. I can only spare four days to set up your office and find you a reliable admin assistant."

She looked around as they stepped off the dance floor. All eyes were on them...mostly on her...but a lot of Kaylen's patrons were looking at Brian with curiosity, too.

"I'm so glad you came," she said again, squeezing his hand. "Now, let me introduce you to a few of my friends..."

CHAPTER FORTY-FIVE

KAYLEN'S HEART pounded in her ears as she brought Brian over to meet those friends. Their curiosity was overshadowed by his reticence, and if her plan backfired, she would have no one to blame but herself.

"Hi, everyone." She barely needed to raise her voice, since Bernie Draper's orchestra had traipsed off to do whatever moved them during their 15 minute break. "I'd like you to meet my boyfriend, Brian Swift."

The group parted, like the waters before Moses' staff.

"Hello." Maurice offered his hand. "Pleased to meet you at last. I'm Maurice Tauny. This is my wife, Pamela."

Brian shook hands, keeping his left arm around Kaylen. She felt tension in the way he held her, but his face was Brian at his best—completely inscrutable. He smiled as he made the acquaintance of 16 people, whose names she thought he probably wouldn't remember afterward, although Kaylen wasn't so sure of that. Brian was trained to remember a lot more than any average person, she reminded herself.

The group's curiosity quickly brimmed over, and Brian was bombarded with questions: "Kaylen said you're a detective? How many years? How did you two meet, anyway? Where do you live? Would you like a drink? Champagne? Or are you on duty and you're not allowed to? Where have you been hiding all these months?"

She felt overwhelmed. This was a bad idea. She should have asked a couple of people at a time to dine with them somewhere, maybe at her condo. Brian might hate crowds, but he hated questions being thrown at him even more.

And then, out the corner of her eye, she saw even more potential trouble--Ziggy Stavros making his way through the crowd, heading right for them. Kaylen became aware that a sheen of sweat covered her brow.

What was that silly expression? Women sweat but ladies glow?

Well, she could forget about being a lady and settle for being a real woman in about two minutes, she decided as Ziggy drew closer.

"Hi." He gave his wide smile more to Kaylen than Brian and the rest of the group. "I hoped I'd find you here. What a delightful crowd." He turned to the inquisitive group, who were now primed for even more exciting revelations. "You must be friends of Kaylen and Brian. Let me introduce myself. I'm Constantine Stavros, but my friends call me Ziggy. So nice to meet all of you." In his friendly, polished manner, he managed to shake hands with all the men, kiss the hands of the women, and arrive at the other side of Kaylen, away from Brian, all in a matter of moments.

"Are you the youngest son of Peter Stavros?" Maurice asked. "I love the Corinthian. Pamela and I dine there at least once a month, if not more often."

"The very same," Ziggy said.

Brian's strength in his left arm had definitely improved, Kaylen thought. He was clutching her uncomfortably at that point. She found herself taking shallow breaths as the sweat from her brow started trickling down the sides of her face. Despite wearing one of her skimpiest and tightest cocktail dresses to look her best and most seductive for Brian, she felt totally overheated.

The Bernie Draper Orchestra had returned. The band struck a chord and eased into a rendition of "Stardust."

"Ah," Ziggy said. "One of my favorites. I must dance, and you must be my partner." He extended his hand to Kaylen.

She wanted to refuse, but all eyes were fixed on her. She felt a desire to kick Ziggy right in the shins with her Gucci pumps.

"Very well." She looked helplessly at Brian. "I'll be right back," she promised. She allowed Ziggy to tow her over to the dance floor, leaving Brian at the mercy of his inquisitors.

She watched him with alarm. He looked intently at her, then at Ziggy, and she thought she saw resignation more than annoyance in his expression.

"This club is brilliant," Ziggy said in her ear. "You have done everything I would want to do."

Kaylen ignored him as she tried to think of a tactful way to end their dancing. As Ziggy twirled her across the floor, she looked over to where Brian had been standing and was panicked to see he was no longer there.

Had he really left the club? She searched frantically as Ziggy continued to lead her toward the other side of the dance floor. Surely Brian wouldn't do that? Even when confronted with a bunch of overly-inquisitive socialites, he should be able to cope better than turning tail.

"I hope you don't mind—I stole Brian for a dance," Angela Crossfield said. "No one should be subjected to grilling when first introduced, especially someone who's going to become a friend."

Kaylen found Angela and Brian dancing right next to her.

"I told him he's a wonderful partner." Angela beamed first up at Brian and then over at Kaylen and Ziggy. "So light on his feet. But you two should really be dancing together." Her smile was bland, but her eyes twinkled. "I'd love to talk more with Ziggy, too, so why don't I cut in and let's switch partners?"

As she said the words, she followed through with the action. Ziggy, looking a little put-out, found himself dancing with Angela, while Brian led Kaylen right through the other couples and off the floor on the opposite side to where her group of friends still stood watching.

"I like Angela," he said.

"Me, too. Did you meet Jonathan? They must have arrived late."

Brian nodded. "Briefly. Angela saw Ziggy taking you away and took charge of the situation."

"Excellent." Kaylen laughed with relief. "I'll invite them to dinner next week, when you're back in town for your Thursday meeting. I think you'll feel comfortable with them. They're much more down to earth than the rest of my social set."

"I'd like to see that."

"Want to go home?"

"Yeah. That'd be great." He leaned in, his breath fanning her neck. "I love that dress on you," he whispered in her ear, "but all I've wanted to do since I saw you was get it off you."

"That's why I wore it. I thought it might have that effect on you."

"I was worried it might have the same effect on Ziggy." Brian followed her down the corridor leading to her office.

She noticed the lights were off again right outside the closed door to her office. She flipped the switch in the hallway, but nothing happened. "I paid an electrician to fix that short," she said.

"Better get your money back," Brian told her as they walked into her office.

He closed the door, pulled her into his arms and kissed her hungrily. His hands ran across her back, found her zipper and pulled it slowly down to where it ended at the small of her back.

Finding the dress too tight to slide down, he pulled it over her head, leaving her in a pair of skimpy white lace bikini panties.

"Someone might come in," she protested.

"I locked the door."

He led her to the couch and sat with her straddling him.

Kaylen arched her back as he caressed her breasts. She felt completely aroused, the excitement of Brian's completely unexpected seduction bringing urgency. Beyond the locked door she heard music and laughter, the bustling earnestness of the club. She unzipped his pants, pulled aside his clothing and lowered herself onto him, her panties pushed out of the way. They climaxed quickly, sweaty and breathless.

"My princess," he said, nuzzling her neck.

CHAPTER FORTY-SIX

"GLAD TO SEE YOU," Jim said when he picked them up at Tampa International Airport the following day.

Kaylen kissed his cheek. "Thanks, Jim. I've missed you."

He hugged her. "Missed you too, honey."

Brian felt like he was at a family reunion. There was a pleasant camaraderie and easy familiarity between the three of them. These two people who had been strangers only months ago had become his closest friends and allies. He marveled at that thought. Life had become more rewarding yet so much more complicated since Tim's disappearance and death.

"I'm riding in the back," Kaylen said. "I can check out the sights while you two catch up." She opened the door and tossed her jacket and purse onto the seat before sitting, her long legs gracefully following the rest of her as she settled in for the ride.

Brian watched those legs with distracted interest while he pushed aside thoughts of Tim and Kaylen together. The loss of his brother was still a gaping wound inside him, and even Kaylen couldn't always make him forget it. Sometimes, he couldn't control the jealousy he felt at the fact Tim had been Kaylen's lover before him.

Did she ever compare them, he wondered, hating himself for

allowing that question to creep into his head. He thought about her the previous evening, whispering his name, her damp hair clinging to her neck, her eyes locked with his. Not then, he vowed. Never then.

He realized Jim was staring at him. "Should I be suspicious?" he asked quickly, trying for humor. "Is there something you two've been keeping from me?"

"Nah." Jim's warm hand clapped Brian on the back. "Watch yourself," he told Kaylen before he carefully closed her door.

Brian grabbed Kaylen's largest bag, which he'd thought way too big and heavy for only a 4 day trip, but then, what the hell did he know about how many outfits and how much makeup she thought she'd need?

"Looks like she packed for the duration of a siege." Jim scooped up her carry-on and popped open the trunk. "I brought your firearms." He indicated Brian's gun case.

"Thanks." Brian stowed Kaylen's bag and retrieved his holster and Glock.

"You don't feel dressed without it, do you?" Jim looked at the contents of the case inside the trunk. "I thought it was pretty heavy to be carrying only your service piece," he said. "There's enough in here to take on a small army."

"I like to be prepared. Especially after being ambushed and shot."

"Not second guessing your reasons." Jim took a stick of gum out of his pocket, slowly unwrapped it and put it in his mouth. "I'm not much for firearms after my stint in Vietnam, that's all."

"Kaylen, neither. Apparently, she saw enough of guns when she went with her father on his hunting trips." Brian closed the case, spun the combination lock and closed the trunk. "If she saw what was in there, she'd give me a lecture. I want her to carry the Sig, but she won't do it. She's got it stowed in her desk drawer, for Christ's sake, like that's going to protect her in an emergency."

"We're not used to living on the edge, that's all." Jim chewed reflectively on his gum. "I debated carrying a firearm when I started working cases for that PI outfit, but they didn't require it, and I decided I'd rather use my wits than my trigger finger. Your situation's different…"

Kaylen leaned out the open window. "Are you guys going to stand back there yakking all day or are we leaving this airport any time before I have to go back to Miami?"

"We're coming already," Brian said.

Suddenly he felt like laughing. It had to be with relief. Again he felt a sense of familiarity and belonging. He thought back to the last time they'd all worked together, then shook off that memory quickly. Kaylen wasn't working this case in any shape or form. Except, she was…against his wishes. She'd managed to get as far as Tampa and within a half-hour, she'd be in his new office, sitting behind a desk and making calls that would impact his working life.

What a woman, he thought as he passed her smiling face, framed by the open window, the breeze blowing through that gorgeous chestnut hair and a definite sparkle of excitement in her eyes.

"That's more like it," she said when he and Jim were buckled in and they joined the traffic leaving the airport.

"Yeah," he said. "It is." And he felt like he was headed for a destination that he only had partial control over, regardless of what he did to try to influence the outcome.

CHAPTER FORTY-SEVEN

"I BOUGHT a whiteboard and set it up in the new office," Jim said as they cruised at a sedate pace down the freeway. "I started laying out the whereabouts of the witnesses, potential suspects, that sort of thing, at the time of the murder. I posted alibis, statements. Tried to organize things, so it's not so overwhelming. So much material, it's difficult to decide what could be useful and what's just taking up space."

Brian nodded. "Yeah, and sometimes it's the stuff you think's not worth anything that proves to be the most helpful, or damning, depending on what you figure out."

"This is our exit," Jim said. "The office is pretty centrally located between the hotel and the investigation area."

They took an exit ramp and merged onto a busy four-lane street lined with strip shopping malls, gas stations and office blocks. Brian saw the crowded parking lot of a small local home improvement store, a Publix grocery store, a number of fast food restaurants and coffee shops, including Peets, a liquor store, and a florist's shop as they passed by. Everything looked middle class, clean and well-kept. He thought Kaylen should be safe in that neighborhood, if she refused to stay in the office all the time.

"Did you put that two-bit slut on the board?" Kaylen asked from the back seat.

"What two-bit slut?" Jim asked. "What did I miss now?"

"Mel," Brian said. "Ted's oldest daughter. Kaylen thinks she's connected somehow." He tried to sound casual. He sensed any conversation where he mentioned Mel's name was a potential step into a minefield where Kaylen lurked, waiting for a wrong move.

"I'm hiring Mel's daughter, Shelley, to keep her under surveillance and see if Rob can find out anything that might be useful for us," Kaylen said. "I couldn't pump Mel for information myself. I'd make a lousy investigator where she's concerned. All I wanted was to scratch her eyes out yesterday on the boat."

"You did?" Jim glanced in the rearview mirror at Kaylen's reflection. "I thought you were more diplomatic than that."

"Mel came on to Brian." Kaylen's voice sounded tight.

"Oh." Jim glanced at Brian and didn't pursue the subject. He drew into a small parking lot in front of a two-story building. "This is it. Our office is on the upper floor. Midway between the elevator and the stairs, facing the parking lot."

Brian looked around. "Pretty good. The surrounding area looks okay, too."

"The owner was willing to rent it for two months, with a possible extension if we needed that. I guess either the market for leases is down or he's asking too much, but I knew you'd like the place." Jim opened his door. "The rented office furniture came yesterday afternoon, so now all we need is that assistant." He looked at Kaylen. "That's your territory, and I'm happy you'll be working on it."

"Yes; that *is* my job. The only purpose I have in coming here, according to Brian."

Brian sensed disagreement and disapproval in her tone, but Kaylen smiled and took his hand as they all strolled through the parking lot and up to the double glass doors of the building. Jim opened one of the doors and motioned them inside.

"He won't let me do anything else, Jim," Kaylen said as they stepped into the lobby. "He's laid ground rules for me coming here, even though he knows I could do a lot more in four days than hire an assistant."

"I'm not even going to comment on that." Jim threw up his hands. "I *know* better than to get in the middle of you two as a would-be mediator on some things, and this is one of them."

A shiny gray and white flecked marble floor led to a narrow table between two elevators. Beneath a list of tenants and their office numbers, a potted plant spilled over its container, shiny green leaves like a waterfall. Brian noted the names included a couple of attorneys, a weight-loss clinic, a financial counseling service and a party planner who appeared to be taking up two suites on the ground floor. A sunny atrium occupied what would have been an unassuming lobby seating area, complete with a small fountain burbling over rocks and tropical plants leaning close while palms reached toward the cathedral ceiling. The air felt slightly humid but refreshing. A grouping of beige chairs and a glass coffee table invited visitors to stop and rest.

"Very nice," Brian said. "Does the rest of the building look this good?"

"Yep." Jim pushed the elevator button. "I liked it immediately. Thought you would, too. Low key but professional."

The elevator door whispered open. The ride to the second floor was short and the trip to the office just as speedy. Jim unlocked a smoky-glass-fronted door with 'Suite 209' written across it in embossed gold letters.

"There's room for a plaque on the side." Jim indicated an open slot. "I wasn't sure whether you wanted anything printed up, so I told the building manager to hold off on that for now."

They walked into a small reception area complete with desk, chair, telephone, laptop computer and printer. Two doors flanked the back of the reception desk, and a bank of three chairs stood to the left, a teak coffee table devoid of magazines placed in front of them. A cabinet topped with a gleaming new coffee pot stood on the right side.

"I figured we might as well leave the coffee where we could all get at it," Jim said. "I took this office because we can put the files and white-board in one room and do interviews in the other, or whatever else we want to do in there. That way, no one who comes to visit will see what we're cooking up in the witness, suspect and location side of the investigation."

"Good thinking." Brian nodded his approval.

"The washroom's down the hallway. The only downside, but I think that's fairly standard for these smaller buildings. We can get a water cooler so we don't have to go out of the office to refill the coffee pot."

"I'll get that ordered while I'm here," Kaylen said. "You won't object to that, will you?"

She presented a guileless face to Brian, but he knew better. She was feeling rebellious, and he was on the verge of experiencing a mutiny. Once she saw that whiteboard, he sensed there would be no keeping her out of his investigation.

But without further comment, Kaylen sat behind the reception desk and booted up the laptop. "Password?" She asked Jim.

"Inside the top drawer," Jim told her.

She opened the drawer and took out a folded paper.

Jim showed Brian the office where they could conduct interviews. Utilitarian but with comfortable looking chairs both in front and behind the desk, and a view of the surrounding neighborhood roofs and back yards, it certainly felt more spacious and upscale than his desk in the squad room at the precinct.

"So, what do you think?" Jim asked.

"You did a great job. Exactly what we need."

Jim stuck his hands in his pockets and rocked back and forth on his heels. "Good."

"Let's look at that board," Brian suggested.

As they passed through the reception area again, Brian heard Kaylen starting her preliminary calls. Despite casual jeans, a navy blue hoodie and tennis shoes, she oozed professionalism and class. He brushed his hand across her shoulder as he passed. She glanced up at him and smiled, her hand briefly touching his.

He started by reviewing the board listing the results of Jim's meticulous work during the past forty-eight hours. In less than 15 minutes, Kaylen joined them.

"I've got coffee brewing," she said. "I contacted six agencies and gave them a stringent list of qualifications for their candidates."

"How many told you to forget it?" Brian asked as Kaylen linked her arm through his and propped one hip on the desk.

"One." She gazed at the board loaded with Post-It notes, photocopies both of faces and locations, and Jim's neat printing. "I gave the remaining five a deadline of two o'clock this afternoon. I want to start interviewing promptly tomorrow morning at nine. Not a minute to waste."

"I'm curious," Jim said. "What did you say you wanted?"

"Quiet, calm, discreet, flexible, highly organized, self-directed but not a free thinker. Willing to do whatever's asked without questioning the reason. I stressed nothing illegal's going on here, but if told to go home or come in early, the assistant's got to be willing to do it. I also warned there may be no set hours and working late can happen."

"That should cut the list significantly," Jim said.

"Yeah. Down to nothing." Brian shook his head. Those qualifications sounded unreasonable, even though he knew they were realistic.

"You'll be a demanding boss." Kaylen sounded a little defensive. "You won't suffer fools or slow-thinking people in any shape or form, so don't tell me you will."

Jim smiled. "That's the truth, buddy. She's got your number and no mistake."

"She does." Brian looked at Kaylen's perturbed face and pulled her close, giving her a companionable squeeze. She relaxed a little.

"So," she said. "Have you made any more headway in here? Jim, you're so organized. Brian's really lucky to have you." She smiled at Brian. "I hope you know that."

"Goes without saying, but she's right, Jim. You picked up at a moment's notice."

Jim shrugged away the thanks. "Wasn't doing anything constructive. The cases that agency dumped on me sure weren't giving a warm, fuzzy feeling. I've had more excitement up here in the past week than I've had in the last three months."

"Stick with me, and I'll show you a side of Tampa you'd probably never see otherwise." Brian gave Kaylen another quick squeeze before releasing her.

He needed to make light of things, in case Kaylen thought either he or Jim might get into trouble. He still wasn't sold on her staying the course when he started back on active duty. She worried about everything as it was, and when he was in the line of fire on a daily basis, she'd have a lot more reasons than she'd had since he was put on disability.

"I've gotta finish interviewing those three guys on the right side," he said, realizing that his attempt at levity hadn't drawn a smile out of either Jim or Kaylen. He pointed to three yellow Post-It notes clustered under a header that said "Pending."

"Did you think of talking to the girlfriends or wives of any of these guys?" Kaylen gestured toward the list of witnesses, which included the group Brian had already interviewed.

"Yeah," Brian said. "Next on my list once I've completed the pendings."

"It seems to me," Kaylen said, looking at the list, "that no one really liked Chad very much. Or, maybe I should clarify that statement: None of his male coworkers or the girls' parents liked Chad. The girls and the women seem to have liked him a little too much."

"You're right." Brian stepped over to the board. He moved a yellow Post-It from the left side of the board to the right. "Jim, can you call that couple who moved away? The two who worked at the grocery store and got married?"

"Why don't you let me do that interview?" Kaylen asked. "He's older, she's younger. I can relate. I'll mention to her that I was married to George. Maybe that'll bond us and she'll open up."

Brian shook his head. "Uh-uh. Let me say this again...you're only up here to interview potential assistants. Why can't you listen?"

"Do you really think you can tell me not to help any more than that?" She looked downright mutinous. "You know I'm good at wheedling stuff out of people. Most people," she added, when he gave her his 'I'm about to give you a good reason why I disagree with you' face. "Not Mel."

"No," Brian agreed. "Not Mel. Definitely."

"I do think she's hiding something," Kaylen said. "Why wouldn't she want you to try to find her brother's killer? What possible motive would she have? I don't believe that stuff she told you about saving her father from more disappointment and sending you off on a wild goose chase."

"Me, neither." He left the board and came back over to stand in front of the desk. Kaylen slipped her hand into his. "I believe she knows more than she's ever told anyone."

"You think she was involved with her own brother's murder?" Jim shuddered. "You watch yourself around her, honey."

"I don't think she'd even bother herself about me," Kaylen said. "She's really self-confident. Sure of herself."

"I thought that was considered a good trait these days." Jim said. "Women's lib and all that."

"Assertive, yes. Domineering, no."

"So what are you thinking?" Jim asked Brian. "Anyone pop out at you after a couple of days away from all this?"

"Not until I finish those last two interviews. Then I'll see if my conspiracy theory pans out. That bunch of kids hanging out, getting into more and more trouble. Chad, as Kaylen pointed out, making a few possible enemies of husbands, boyfriends, even parents, by having multiple affairs. Mel, his female counterpart, possibly acting a lot like her brother. We need to check into that angle more."

"I could do that, too," Kaylen said. "Women will talk to me."

"They talk to me all the time," Brian said. "I don't have any trouble getting them to open up."

"You, being charming?" Kaylen didn't quite snort, but it was close. "I find that hard to believe."

"I've got my ways. Let's get back to what needs to be done tomorrow."

"I don't like this desk," Jim said, completely changing the subject. "We need a table in here. Something we can all sit at and share information, files, photos or whatever else. I'll get the rental company to do an exchange."

"I'll do it," Kaylen said. "It's more befitting my female talents."

"Ouch." Brian knew for sure he was in trouble. She'd only appeared to be docile and in agreement with her role as temporary office manager while they were still in Miami. "If I agree to let you go with Jim to interview that couple, will you stop giving me a hard time?"

Her face lit up like he'd handed her a priceless gift. "Maybe. It'd help."

"I'll make some calls in the other office." Jim smiled and left.

Brian took Kaylen in his arms. "You're going to make me crazy if you keep acting like this. I didn't bring you up here to become an investigator."

"I know. But this is so exciting. I feel so much closer to you, not just physically, but emotionally," she said. "I promise I'll stay out of trouble. It's only an interview, and from what you said, these people aren't even close to being called suspects."

"Yeah, I don't think they are. But we're not setting a precedent here. I want you to know that. You're not going to be my sidekick. I've got Jim for that. You're my girlfriend, who is going to do very important things to help me get everything set up here, but not participate in finding a murderer. That's what we're doing here, Kaylen. You're the one who told me that—remember when you said the victim's still dead, just dead longer, that's all. Whoever killed him, unless they're dead already, isn't going to want to be caught twenty-five years later. They've probably made a life for themselves and put that crime right out of their heads."

"I know." She brushed one hand against his cheek before kissing him lightly. "I'm not here to get you worried about me, I promise. I'm excited to see you working a case again, though. You do it so well; I know you'll be successful if anyone can."

"Okay. As long as you understand and agree to the terms. No investigating. No getting into any situations that'll turn my hair white."

"I'll find you an assistant. I'll get the desk exchanged for a table. And if you let me do this one little interview with Jim, I'll go back to Miami without any complaints." She kissed him again. Harder. "I already ordered the water cooler. I'll get you guys some coffee, then I'll take the car and go to the grocery store I saw down the street so I can have cream with mine. You guys drink it black. I don't unless there's no other choice." She wrinkled her nose.

"Are you taking lunch orders, honey?" Jim asked as he came back into the room. "I could sure go for a smoked turkey on rye or whole wheat."

"Keys?" She held out her hand.

"Fine. Please give them to her," he told Jim. "I'll take a burger."

"I'm not going all over the place," she said. "And you don't need any cholesterol-filled meals, either."

"Christ." He wanted to tell both of them to stop telling him what to eat, but he didn't want Kaylen driving around looking for a fast food joint, either. "Okay. Get me a sandwich, too, then. Whatever you think's not going to clog my arteries. Can I at least have a bag of chips with it?"

"And a pickle." She laughed. "I'll be back in thirty minutes."

"She really is something else," Jim said after they'd both watched her leave. "Just what you need, buddy." He pointed to the box they had received from TPD. "I've got more copying to do. I'd better get started on it. I got hold of that couple. She took early retirement to nurse him. He's got lung cancer. She said we'd better hurry up and get there while he was still breathing. He's going on hospice today."

"Are they in St. Pete?"

"Clearwater. They moved closer to her mom, who isn't in great shape, either. She's got a lot on her plate. She said we can come tomorrow afternoon. He gets done with his nap around three. The mornings are rough."

"Fair enough. That'll give Kaylen a chance to get some of those assistant interviews out of the way. Maybe we'll get lucky and one of those'll work out. If she can get someone to start immediately, she'll go back to Miami faster."

The moment he said it, Brian felt a stir of something alien to him...anxiety. He wasn't sure if it was because of Sam Wilson possibly being back in town or another reason, like Ziggy Stavros being available for consultations or worse, dinner.

"I'll be in the other office, using the copier, if you need me," Jim said, breaking into Brian's thoughts. He picked up a stack of files and headed for the doorway, where he paused. "Is something worrying you, buddy?"

"Nah. Nothin' more than usual."

"Okay." Jim didn't look convinced, but he left.

Not the case, Brian thought. That wasn't bothering him at all. But Ziggy Goddamned Stavros sure was.

CHAPTER FORTY-EIGHT

BRIAN PARTED company with Kaylen and Jim after an early breakfast the following morning. They took the rental car and headed for the office, Kaylen for her interviews with the temps and Jim to prepare for the trip up to Clearwater. He wanted to take a list of questions and a stack of photos to maximize the time they had with Lester and Nola Chesney. Lester's input might be vital, but his poor health would limit the time they'd be able to spend with him.

Brian drove his Mercedes to Best Pic's parking lot, left it between the store and the Chinese restaurant and strolled the couple of blocks to the greasy spoon where Tommy Spiro worked.

"He's not here today," a big, burly cook said, his sweat-covered face peering between hanging tickets on a wheel and a heat lamp drying out several plates filled with withered hash browns, overcooked scrambled eggs and shriveled bacon strips. "Wadda ya want with him?"

"I need to ask him a few questions about something that happened a long time ago," Brian said. "Nothing to do with his job."

"We don't give out addresses or phone numbers," the cook said. "You'll have to come back when he's working."

"And when's that?" Brian wasn't ready to start pulling rank, but it was getting close.

'Tomorrow. Come back mid-morning. We're not so busy." He struck a bell with his palm. "Order up!"

A skinny waitress came running, her white clogs making her feet look enormous. Her stringy, dark brown hair was escaping from beneath a yellow headband. Her yellow apron sported a large coffee stain and her lipstick was smeared. She looked like she'd awakened five minutes before her shift and lived ten minutes away. She balanced three of the plates filled with overcooked food on her forearm, wincing as the heat from the china bit into her arm, grabbed the last one in her other hand and took off to a nearby table, where she laid the food in front of four workmen seated in a booth. They looked down at their less-than-appetizing meals and back up at her.

"How long's this been sitting up there?" One of them asked, his voice almost as loud as the cook's. "And where's my toast?"

The level of noise in the restaurant dimmed, and other diners turned to watch Rita's reaction.

"I'm sorry," she said. "We're shorthanded. I'm doing my best."

"Rita!" The cook's thundering voice boomed out into the restaurant like it was carried on sound waves. "You didn't put their bread in the toaster?"

"I'm sorry," she said again, wringing her hands and hovering. "I'm so sorry." She turned and fled past Brian, grabbed a loaf of bread, spilled half the slices onto the floor and finally managed to load six into a large toaster at the back of the bussing station.

"If you weren't the only one out there, I'd have you fired," the cook told her as she grabbed the coffee pot on the way back to the dining room. She ignored him, moving at a fast trot toward a booth filled with yet another group of men in overalls, waiting impatiently, flapping menus and looking around.

"Where's the rest of your crew today?" Brian asked the cook. "Two people for the morning rush?"

"Dunno." The cook slammed another set of filled plates under the heat lamp and shoved tickets under the plates. "Order up!"

Rita jumped. The coffee she was pouring splashed all over the table and the group slid out of the booth. "Forget this!" One of them shouted. "What the hell is going on in here today?"

The cook gave Rita a look worthy of turning her to stone. She burst into tears, put down the coffee pot and bolted for the bussing station, where she seized her purse and a faded blue denim jacket from a shelf. "I quit," she said, rushing out the door. She threw the headband on the sidewalk, tore off the apron and stomped on both of them before opening the door back up and throwing them inside.

"Guess you'll have to serve the customers yourself," Brian told the cook.

Rita paused long enough to pull a tissue out of her purse before crossing the street and sitting on a bus bench. Brian followed. When he reached her, she hugged her worn black purse against her chest and looked up at him with tears in her eyes.

"Tough day," he said.

She shrugged. "Same-o, same-o."

Brian thought she looked a little too calm for someone who had just walked off her job. "Did you really quit?"

"Probably not." Rita dug another tissue out of a pocket and wiped her nose. "Mark, the owner's away for a few days. He had to leave Van in charge because Tommy and our other waitress, Lolly, are both out sick. Big mistake. Van's a bully as well as a bad cook, and I can't manage the day shift by myself. When Mark gets back and hears what his customers have to say, I'll probably get a call asking me to put myself back on the schedule."

"This has happened before," Brian said.

Rita nodded. "Every time we get short-handed. We can't seem to find a waitress who'll stay and work for the low tips or a decent cook for when Tommy's off. They always find better paying jobs and quit. So we get days when I'm the only waitress, and we get stuck with cooks like Van, who mess up the food. The customers complain and threaten to go elsewhere, like that's going to happen in a neighborhood where their other choices are Chinese or dried-up hamburgers and hot dogs."

"What about the fast food chains?"

Rita shrugged. "We're too poor or something. People brown bag a lot around here. The only time the restaurant's busy is breakfast. For a lot of our customers, that's the only meal they have all day."

Brian remembered those days himself. Listening to his stomach growling at school because he'd given his half-sandwich of bologna on white bread, no mayo to Tim, who was always hungry. Knowing Ed Madison had spent their grocery money on beer and their mom had to make a bag of noodles, a loaf of bread and a packet of bologna stretch for the rest of the week. Scraping enough small change together for a hot dog at the end of the day when he first got to Miami. His uncle had moved and left no forwarding address, he'd found when he arrived with almost nothing in his pocket after the bus trip from Baton Rouge. He'd stolen food to survive when those small funds were depleted.

"Where's Tommy Spiro?" He asked.

"How would I know?" Rita avoided eye contact, peering down the street presumably to watch for oncoming buses.

"You work with him. I bet you've worked with him for years."

"Ten," she said. "On and off. Depending on whether we quit or get fired, then come back." She hugged the purse closer. "We get more than our fair share of complaints when Tommy's off."

"Where does he live?" Brian took out a twenty dollar bill.

Rita eyed the money with a tight mouth, as though it made her angry to think about selling out her coworker for something so crass. Then she grabbed it like a starving animal would take a chunk of meat, opened her purse, stuffed the bill inside and closed it. "With his wife, kids, and his mom," she said without looking at Brian. "Chestnut Street. It's less than a half mile from here. He walks to and from work."

"What's the address?" Brian took out his wallet and held out another $20 bill. "For the bus."

Rita paused briefly before taking the money. That time she shoved it into her pocket and kept her hand there so it wouldn't fall out or he didn't try to take it back. She gave fast directions, as though she knew Tommy's route to and from home by heart.

Brian left her perched on the edge of the bus bench as he walked the route Tommy Spiro would take on a daily basis. He didn't glance back, but he knew Rita watched him all the way until a bus passed and he spotted her briefly, gazing out the window at him. He raised his hand, but she didn't wave back.

CHAPTER FORTY-NINE

BRIAN WALKED past a convenience store with windows almost obliterated by signs for 99 cent sodas, hot dogs, and beer sales; a grocery store, its parking lot littered with battered cars, their owners loading brown paper sacks into trunks from shopping carts that looked as grimy and beaten up as their surroundings. Down an alleyway, overflowing and rusted dumpsters waited for pickup. A stunted palm tree struggled for survival on a vacant lot; weeds grew on easements; graffiti adorned walls, fences and even a couple of small trucks.

Brian wondered why the poverty bothered him. It never had before. He told himself he'd grown soft on his extended hiatus from everyday life. Hanging around Kaylen had made him dress and act like he was one of her jet set. Jim's influence must be giving him an aversion for anything that wasn't clean.

He found Tommy Spiro's home easily. The apartment building sported huge numbers outside, as though everyone who lived there must have impaired vision. He didn't need to get buzzed inside—the box was broken, its wires hanging out. He saw the printed apartment number beside Spiro and climbed the stairs to the third floor. Behind rows of brown doors, screaming children and exasperated mothers fought over a variety of issues: "Eat your lunch!" "Don't wanna!" "Stop fighting with your sister!" "I'll paddle you if you don't shut up!" Then the sound of the paddling. He walked faster, bare boards protesting under his feet, the smells of spicy cooking, cabbage and grease filling his nostrils.

Tommy's mother answered the door after he turned gentle knocking into pounding. She peered through the opening created by the limits of a thick chain.

Brian identified himself, showing his badge. "I need to speak to Tommy. It's nothing he's done wrong," he explained to her white, frightened face.

"Okay." She sounded doubtful, but she opened the door and let him inside.

The apartment was threadbare but clean. Sunlight filtered through net curtains. The scarred table top gleamed from recent polishing. The couch, arms frayed to the stuffing, hammocked visibly in the middle. A collection of toys hung out in an orange crate beside an old TV.

"Would you like to sit down?" Mrs. Spiro's shoulders shook as she peered up at him.

"Sure." Brian headed for the table after checking that the chairs had metal legs and looked capable of holding his weight. "Here's okay?"

"Yes." She followed him. "I'll get Tommy. He's been sick with the flu these last few days. Would you like coffee?"

"If you already have some made." He could smell brewed coffee, and the aroma was pretty enticing.

"I do." She twisted a kitchen towel between her fingers. "I'll see if my son is awake first."

"I'm awake." An apparition emerged from the darkened back hallway.

Mrs. Spiro started. "Tommy! You scared me. I thought you were in bed."

"I got thirsty." Tommy Spiro walked slowly into the living room. Short, stocky and with a dark complexion, he held a patriotic red, white and blue comforter around him. It hung down his back and dragged along the floor. He sniffed and wiped his nose on a wadded-up tissue.

"Tommy's been sick," Mrs. Spiro said again. "He shouldn't get too close to you."

"Maybe you could sit on the couch and I'll pull my chair closer," Brian suggested.

Mrs. Spiro took the comforter and waited while her son folded himself into the far end of the couch. She tucked the comforter around him and patted his cheek. "I'll make chamomile tea." She gave him a gentle smile and managed to keep it long enough to direct it toward Brian before she practically bolted into the tiny kitchen.

Brian took his chair over to face Tommy. "Brian Swift," he said. "I'm a homicide detective with Miami-Dade." He showed his badge. "But I'm here in a private capacity, investigating an old murder case."

"Chad Summerfield." Tommy pulled a box of tissues over and blew his nose.

"I figured someone'd tell you." Although Brian knew he'd lose the element of surprise at some point in his investigation, it still irked him that word had already gotten around his list of potential suspects.

"Rita called," Tommy said. "Told me you were on your way."

Brian felt a spark of hope. He hadn't given much information to Rita, and if no one else had contacted Tommy, he still wouldn't have had time to rehearse his shtick. "What can you tell me about the day Chad got murdered?"

Tommy shrugged and pulled the comforter up over his chin, almost obscuring his mouth. "Probably nothing different than you've gotten from anyone else."

Mrs. Spiro came out of the kitchen with two white mugs. She set one in front of Tommy on the coffee table and the other for Brian on a scratched-up end table holding a lamp with a ripped shade. "I only have black," she said. "I've got sugar if you want."

"Black's perfect," Brian assured her. The mug looked clean but chipped. She hovered anxiously, watching him. He took a sip. The coffee was strong and as good as it smelled. He smiled at her.

"Sit down, Ma," Tommy urged. "You're making us all nervous. I haven't done anything, and he's not here to arrest me. He's not even a local cop."

She burst into tears, patted Brian on the shoulder and pulled another metal chair over to sit beside Tommy.

"I did time," Tommy said. "It was harder on Ma than me. I cleaned up my act after that."

"I heard," Brian said. "You've worked at the diner a long time."

Tommy nodded and looked at his mom. "Yeah. Steady work."

"He got married, too." Mrs. Spiro dabbed at her tears with her apron. "Two kids. They're wonderful."

"Is that right?" Brian smiled at her. "How old?"

"Five and eight." She fetched a gilded frame from the top of the TV, handing it to Brian.

He saw two little girls in frilly pink dresses posing with their arms around each other. Both wore dark pigtails tied up with pink ribbons and lots of butterfly-shaped barrettes. Black patent leather shoes with white ankle socks. Big sweet smiles, the oldest with a couple of baby teeth missing, the younger one with a dimple in her left cheek.

"Beautiful," he said to both Spiros.

"They want to be nurses when they grow up." Mrs. Spiro had relaxed slightly, her hand no longer shaking when she took back the frame.

"Ma, how about going to the market and getting chicken noodle soup," Tommy said.

Mrs. Spiro carefully put the frame back on the TV. "I may have some in the cupboard." She started for the kitchen.

"You don't," Tommy said. "Take money out of my wallet and go. Get some crackers, too, and popsicles for the girls. Take your time. Make sure you chat with people and they know you're there."

Her hands started shaking again. She looked at him for a long moment before scurrying over to where his billfold sat on top of a rickety bookcase with more icons of the Virgin Mary than books. The Virgin in white, in gold, in white with a gold halo, in a blue cloak, her hand raised, her hands folded.

Brian looked at them all while Mrs. Spiro pulled on a raincoat and tied a scarf around her head, picked up her purse and opened the door. She glanced back at both men before stepping into the hallway, the door closing behind her. It wasn't actually slammed, but it definitely told everyone in the adjoining apartments someone was leaving the Spiros.'

"I don't want her mixed up in anything, or worrying about me or Marisa and the kids, neither," Tommy said.

"So you're not gonna give me more of the 'I don't remember' or 'I don't know nothin'?'" Brian wasn't convinced he was done with the run-around.

Tommy took a sip of his tea. "Ramos called. Told me to watch out. Chico's never said anything like that. When I saw you, I knew why he said it. Somethin' about you says no bullshit. Like you could make me regret it real bad."

Brian didn't comment. He didn't feel it was necessary. Since Tim's death there had been a shift inside him, and evidently it showed on the outside, too.

"I'm gonna show you somethin'," Tommy said. "It'll take me a moment to get it, because I've got it hidden from my family." He got up.

"Where?" Brian got up, too.

"In the bedroom." Tommy threw off the comforter. "You're comin?'"

Brian nodded. "I'll follow you."

As Tommy padded down the short, dark hallway in his bare feet, Brian unbuttoned his jacket and placed his hand on the butt of the Glock. His heart rate increased in an uncomfortable and unexpected manner. Annoyed, he took several deep breaths and the drumming in his throat subsided.

They entered a small bedroom dominated by an unmade bed, smelling stale. Clothes draped a chair in one corner; a pillow lay on the floor between the bed and a dresser. Tommy bypassed all of it and went to the closet. Brian tensed and put a slightly larger distance between himself and Spiro.

"I hid it in the ceiling, on one of the beams," Tommy said, moving slowly. He opened the closet door and pushed a tap light, which shed a feeble glow, illuminating an over-packed, bowing rail filled with clothing, a couple of old suitcases on a shelf above Tommy's head and a clutter of shoes he kicked out of the way. He pulled a step stool from behind his clothes, opened it and climbed up. He shoved up a small square of the ceiling. Brian got out of direct line and watched warily. Tommy felt around, slid out a small box and handed it to Brian. It didn't weigh much.

"No tricks, man." Tommy put the drywall back into place and climbed down. "We'd better go back in the livin' room. Light's no good here." He pointed to the overhead fixture in the bedroom. "It don't work, and the bulb went out on that, too, this morning." He jerked his head in the direction of an old floor lamp on the far side of the bed.

"You go first," Brian said.

Tommy glanced at the open jacket, said nothing and padded back to the living room. "Open the box," he said.

Brian cracked the lid and saw cards inside. "Here." He handed the box back. "You show me."

Tommy took out a stack, held together with a rubber band. "Mel Summerfield's family kind of paid me to keep my mouth shut after Chad got killed." He looked down at his feet. "Nothing' I'm proud of, an' I didn't ask them to keep doin' it, but the money will help send my girls to college. I saw Mel an' Chad in the storeroom. I heard her tell him she was pregnant, but the part I didn't tell was how mad he was with her. He slapped her and she slapped him back. Told him she wanted help, not a lecture. I was standin' out in the hallway when she said that."

"Did she tell him who the father was?"

"Not that I heard, but they were already arguing when I came through the back door." He handed over the cards.

Brian weighed them in his hand. "After keeping this secret all these years, why tell me?"

"Because you look like you're gonna solve this murder, and I don't want you thinkin' I was involved. I'm not goin' back to the joint for anyone. I don't make much at my shit job, but with what my wife brings in, we manage. My mom lives here and takes care of the girls. We're a close family. Now you're pokin' around, maybe Mel an' her parents will start talkin' too." Tommy cradled the box.

"Give me that." Brian held out his hand. "You know what you've been doing is called blackmail, don't you?"

Tommy's white face got even whiter. He pushed the box into Brian's hand. "I'll get you a sack. You come into the apartment with nothin;' you go out with a box? No way." He went into the kitchen and returned with a paper grocery sack. "I never asked them for nothin.' How's that blackmail?"

"Accepting money to keep your mouth shut's at least accepting a bribe," Brian conceded, watching the sweat roll down Tommy's face.

"You never told your family about this?" He pulled the grocery sack from Tommy's hand. "Going out with a bag isn't much better than going out with a box."

"What you gonna do?" Tommy wrapped his arms around himself. "You gonna arrest me?"

"Not yet." Brian dropped the box and stack of cards inside the bag. "But you'd better talk to a lawyer."

"Shit."

"You know damn well accepting money from the Summerfields for years wasn't because they wanted to give you a nice present every Christmas."

Tommy rubbed a hand across the stubble on his chin. "Cops. You always think you've got the right to judge."

"We usually do."

Tommy shrugged. "Guess I'll wait to see what shakes out." He blew his nose on a wadded-up tissue. "What if I gave the money back? Most of it's in a savings account. I spent it at first, but I could pay what I still owe in installments."

"Look," Brian said. "I'll talk to the Summerfields before I do anything else. They may want to keep this quiet, too, and if we prosecute, then it won't be. That's the most I can promise."

Tommy wiped sweat off his face with the back of his hand. "My fever's risin' again." He shivered. "Chills, too."

"I think your guilt's showing. Hopefully your conscience is making you sweat, you shit. Christ, you people are all fucked up." Brian walked over to the front door.

Tommy grabbed the comforter from the couch as he followed and wrapped it back around himself. "It's kind of a relief, tellin' the truth, finally." His teeth were chattering.

"Look at it this way, Tommy...when I figure out who killed Chad, then the rest of you can go back to whatever you were doing before I got here," Brian said. "I understand tight-knit and not snitching to outsiders, but I don't get withholding information that could get a murderer off the street unless one or all of you in your circle were involved."

Tommy shook his head emphatically. "We're got our own secrets, but not murder. No way, man."

"Talk to your friends. Tell 'em I don't give a crap what went on back then unless it involves this murder." He paused, thinking about Tommy's decades-long bleeding of the Summerfields. Tommy was beginning to look more hopeful, and Brian didn't want the guy to think he was going to get off scot free. "Except maybe for you accepting those bribes."

Tommy's face fell. He sniffled again.

"And the local cops can deal with that," Brian added. "I'm really only interested in who shot Chad, and why. I don't think botched robbery was the real reason, or I'd have gotten answers instead of stone-walling."

Tommy pulled up the comforter. Half his face disappeared again, but he looked squarely back at Brian. "No tricks, man. I'm done hidin' anythin' else." The comforter came down, settling across his chest. "I was shopliftin' when the shooting happened. It was the end of my shift. I had candy bars stuffed down my pants an' I was goin' for the snack cakes when I heard the shots. I ran out on the loadin' dock, candy fallin' everywhere and wondering what the hell to do next. I pulled the rest out of my pants and started chuckin' them at a bunch of empty cardboard boxes when people came chargin' out the store, falling over themselves to get away."

"So it was total chaos," Brian prompted, when Tommy's voice trailed off and he stood staring into space.

Tommy shook himself and nodded slowly. "Friggin' chaos is right. Screamin,' shoutin,' running…I stood an' watched like a dope. People were jumpin' over some little kid without even slowin' down. I grabbed him an' tossed him onto the boxes. That got me moving. I didn't know who else was comin' out of there. Coulda bin the shooter, all I knew. I ran all the way home. Right past my mom in the kitchen and into the bedroom. Same bedroom my girls sleep in now. She came an' tried to open the door but I'd locked it. "What you doin,' Tommy?" She asked. "What trouble you getting into, now?"

"Nothin,'" I said. "Nothin,' Ma. Leave me alone. An' I never told her what happened. But she heard about the robbery and the murder. Of course she did. An' I think she still wonders if I was involved. I never told her I was shoplifting. Maybe I shoulda, but I didn't want her knowin' her son was stealin,' even back then. I was the second youngest of our little friggin' gang. I thought I was such hot shit, man. Instead, all I was, was a friggin' little punk."

He shook his head. Brian waited him out. No point in interrupting Tommy's train of thought.

"I turned into a bigger punk," Tommy said. "Tried to jack a car two years after Chad died. The owner was in the back seat, sleepin' off a bender. He didn't want to wake up his wife an' have her start screaming at him for bein' a turd. He was a big guy." Tommy smiled ruefully. "He whacked me upside the head, got out of the car while I was wondering what the fuck hit me, dragged me out, kicked the shit out of me and hollered so loud, all the neighbors came out to see what was happenin.' His wife called the cops."

"So you didn't learn your lesson from the attempted robbery?"

Tommy shook his head. "Not until that guy about knocked my head off. His wife was gonna have him arrested for public intoxication or some such shit, but instead, I was the one who ended up gettin' sent away again. Five years that time. Straightened me up. I learned how to cook while I was in the joint. Got out in three for good behavior." He gave Brian the ghost of a smile. "Doin' time even gave me a way to pay bills when I got out. I became a short-order cook. Who would've thought?"

"Whatever it takes." Brian opened the front door. "I'll be in touch."

"Yeah, I know you will." Tommy leaned against the doorframe as Brian started down the hallway.

"One more thing," Brian said, turning on his heel to watch Tommy's reaction. "Exactly how much have the Summerfields paid you?"

Tommy's complexion paled. "I shoulda kept my damn mouth shut."

"If you don't come clean with me, you'll be doing a lot more than three years in the state pen. How much?"

"Fifty bucks a month to start out with, which was a lot for a young punk. It crept up to three hundred by last Christmas. I told you, it's in a savings account for my girls' college fund."

"How come it increased?"

"I told them I needed a cost of living raise."

"You're a blackmailing piece of shit."

"Your voice is gettin' louder." Tommy waved his hand. "Keep it down, man. Please."

Brian shook the bag and walked back toward Tommy. "I want your last bank statement. Right now."

"Okay, okay."

Tommy scurried off into the kitchen. Brian left the front door open and followed. Tommy slid out the bottom drawer of a cabinet, removed a slim manila envelope and handed it over. Brian found a current statement for a savings and loan in Clearwater. It showed a balance of $4,000. Hardly enough to send either of Tommy's girls even to a community college. He felt a stir of sympathy and quickly slapped a lid on it as he dropped the envelope into his bag.

Tommy looked crestfallen, as though Brian already had the cuffs out ready to clap them on.

"I'll see what I can do." Brian couldn't give out any more hope in this convoluted case filled with old secrets. He started back out of the apartment.

"I've come clean."

Tommy remained in the middle of the living room as Brian went into the hallway and shut the front door behind him.

Tommy's mom was slowly coming up the street as Brian exited the building. "Don't worry," he told her as they passed.

She looked at the bag in his hand, her expression filled with doubt and fear.

Brian didn't enlighten her about his conversation with her son. Tommy was going to have to decide what he was willing to share with his family. When Brian reached the corner, he glanced back. Mrs. Spiro was still standing where he had left her. He waved. Her hand lifted briefly before she turned away.

Brian walked briskly back to Best Pic's parking lot. He needed to get away from the poverty and the hopelessness for a while before he tackled the last interview on his to-do list. Memories from his own childhood continued to dog him. He'd felt a kinship with Tommy Spiro's situation, and he didn't like the empathy one bit. If he and Tim hadn't broken that window in Baton Rouge, forcing him to leave town before his step-father arrived home, his own outcome could have been a whole lot bleaker.

He took the manila envelope out of the bag and stowed it in his trunk before getting into the car. Maybe he'd make it part of the investigation and then, maybe he wouldn't, if it had no relevance. After all, he told himself, this was his can of worms, and he only needed to open it as far as he felt necessary.

That decision didn't sit well with him, but the alternative sat even less well. Tommy Spiro's family needed him more than the long arm of justice did. But Brian also had leverage now, and wouldn't hesitate to use it. If there was anything else Tommy Spiro knew about Chad Summerfield's murder, it would come out. Brian guaranteed it.

CHAPTER FIFTY

JACK MILLS CALLED five minutes after Brian got back to the office. He saw the caller ID and his heart gave an uncharacteristic lurch. It might mean news about Tim's case.

"How are things going up in Tampa?" Mills asked.

"Okay." Brian looked at the whiteboard in front of him. He'd moved Tommy Spiro into the "interviews completed" column and added a couple of notations, one to follow up on the money, another to re-interview Tommy after he had those results, and a third placed Tommy at the store as the stock boy. "Anything new on Tim?"

"Not much." Mills paused.

Brian waited.

"We've questioned yet another bunch of people who say they know nothing, or next to it." Mills sighed. "It's damned frustrating, but that's not the reason I'm calling. Gabe's about to quit."

"What?" That really was news, and not good for the department. Gabe Weston was one of the reasons Homicide stayed organized. His duties went way past his job description, and Brian for one was very glad Gabe kept on top of things. If he hadn't, Brian himself might not be alive. After he got shot, it was Gabe who had fielded Kaylen's frantic call and sent an emergency team.

"Trehorn doesn't like Gabe, and Gabe hates his new supervisor's guts," Mills said. "I've never seen Gabe come so close to losing his cool. Trehorn's got him so riled up, he can barely keep civil."

"For what reason? Gabe's always organized, professional..."

"Trehorn's making a lot of changes, and Gabe's job is one of them. Trehorn thinks it makes better sense to have the detectives answer the phones themselves. He doesn't take into consideration that we don't all know everything about each other's cases, even though we do briefings. Gabe keeps track of so many details for us."

"So what does he want to do with our clerk?"

"Move him to another department. Maybe down to the basement to catalogue old files."

"Cold cases."

"Yeah. Really cold cases. Trehorn wants our arrest numbers up. He said if we don't meet quotas, some of us are going to find ourselves canned."

"Sounds like a big shake-up."

"Yeah, with an emphasis on the shaking."

"So what do you want me to do? I'm not putting out a contract on Trehorn for you." Brian could imagine Mills' expression.

"Don't joke about that," Mills said. "Not even on my private line."

"Okay. So what gives? Why are you telling me all this? When I come back, I'll have to deal with Trehorn myself. Right now, I'm still involved with the case up here in Tampa."

"And that's why I thought of calling you. Can't you use Gabe for a while? He needs a time-out until things settle down here. They usually do. You know that old saying about a new broom—that's Trehorn. After what Hastings did to MDPD, they had to send in a ringer. Lots of noise, stomping around, clearing out staff, cleaning up. You know the drill. It's happened before. Just not to this degree."

"So who else is getting worried about their jobs?"

"Sanchez already transferred before he got asked to leave. He went to Saratoga. Browning decided he liked the sound of the Sheriff's Department."

"Christ. Trehorn *does* mean business."

"Told you."

"He's not making things tough for you, Jack, is he?" Brian couldn't imagine any supervisor even looking twice at Mills, whose steady work ethic, reliability and long list of arrests and convictions attested to the need for MDPD to retain him.

"Not yet, but that doesn't mean he won't in the future. He told us no one is immune to scrutiny. But Gabe?"

"Can't he take a sabbatical until things calm down? If Trehorn's on a fast track, maybe he'll be out of there in six months."

"Maybe." Mills didn't sound convinced. "But Gabe's going to need an income, Brian. He can't just take off and wait to see what happens."

Brian looked at the boxful of copying still to be done before all the material went back to Engelhardt and TPD. He considered the stringent requirements Kaylen wanted met in order for one of those temps to work with him. He thought about the six she had already rejected. All good workers, no doubt, but with flaws Kaylen had detected immediately.

Gabe knew him. He knew Brian's erratic work hours, his methods, his pet peeves and his temper. He never became flustered when things got stirred up or became downright hostile. Except, apparently, when they involved Darrell Trehorn.

"Have Gabe call me," he told Mills. "We need help up here in the office. Jim could be better used out in the field, not copying files. Kaylen's up here, too, meddling away as only Kaylen does. She wanted to come here for a couple of days to hire us an admin assistant, but she's already managed to talk me into letting her go along with Jim on an interview."

Mills' reply was faint but unmistakable snickering, as though he had his hand over the mouthpiece.

"Dammit, Mills, don't you laugh at me."

"Can't help it." Mills abandoned his effort to keep his mirth contained and laughed outright. "She's something else."

"You've got that right. If Gabe comes up here, that'll be one less reason for Kaylen to stay and get even more involved. I'm worried about her in Miami without me around, but I'm even more worried about her getting too close to some killer up here."

"You know, we can't always protect the ones we love," Mills said.

Brian thought that was a presumptuous jump, and way too early in his relationship with Kaylen.

"We're just dating," he said. "You know I don't want anything permanent. Never have."

"Life's all about change," Mills said. "Don't be so rigid that you miss out on something special."

"I've had enough changes lately."

If this was an example of getting closer to coworkers, Brian thought, it was excruciating. The only person he'd had to justify himself to was Hal, and then only in a professional capacity. First Kaylen had interfered with that status quo, and then Jim, quickly followed by Fleming, and now, damn it, Jack Mills.

But Brian knew Mills had a point: Kaylen was a bigger issue than anything but his damned arm. Or maybe the shrink. He waffled. Too many issues were complicating his life, which had been so much simpler less than five months ago. He'd found juggling arguments with his brother and bucking Hal while solving cases a lot easier than what was confronting him at that moment.

"She won't stay out of things," Brian found himself complaining. He thought of Mills and his two failed marriages. "I can't even imagine what a wife would do to a career like ours."

"Keep dating her and you'll end up finding out," Mills said.

It was like someone had finally let the cat out of the bag. Kaylen would be pretty angry about him calling her a cat, even mentally, Brian thought, but there were assumptions being made after the months they had been together. People were beginning to think, and even talk about, permanent changes to his lifestyle.

"Let's keep Gabe the topic of conversation," he told Mills. He knew he sounded defensive and snarky, but he figured his coworker knew him well enough not to keep pushing.

"Fine." Mills had a flat tone to his voice. The one he used when witnesses or suspects turned testy. "You want me to tell him to call you himself, then? Does he have a job offer?"

"Yeah, he does." Brian sat at the table Kaylen had gotten delivered that morning. "Have him call me, and we'll hash out the details. Tell him to work something out with the department, so he can keep paying on his benefits. Then he keeps his tenure with the department while he's working up here."

"Sounds like a winner to me," Mills said. "Thanks, Swift."

"Next thing, you'll be asking me to give you a job, too," Brian said, brushing the thanks aside.

"I might need to if Trehorn keeps weeding people out. I'm the one with the most seniority. He could save the department a bunch of money if he got rid of me."

"Our reps would love that." Anger stirred inside Brian. "They'd be all over it. I think your job's as safe as any at the department."

"Maybe." Again, Mills didn't sound convinced. "I'll be in touch."

Brian remembered Jim telling him to be more forgiving with his coworkers. Mills had touched a nerve with his comment about Kaylen and marriage, but Brian knew his intention wasn't to poke the sleeping bear. "Come over and have a couple of beers on the boat again when I get back into town," he said. "It was good catching up with you the other day."

"Look forward to it." Mills hung up.

Brian checked out the final name on the "Interviews pending" list and finished the last of his lukewarm coffee. Time to get back to work.

He wondered if Kaylen would be peeved about him hiring Gabe instead of one of her picks from the temps.

CHAPTER FIFTY-ONE

"THE HOUSE IS in the next block," Kaylen told Jim as they cruised slowly down a street in suburban Clearwater.

"Nice neighborhood," he said. "Retail must pay better than I thought."

"We don't know if they changed careers after leaving the grocery store." Kaylen checked the address one more time. She saw a yellow clapboard house with slate blue shutters and brushed nickel numbers beside the front door. "That's it."

Jim eased over to the curb and parked out front. A well-maintained yard with a curving flagstone path led to the front door. Kaylen thought the house pretty. She wondered whether, had she met Brian under different circumstances, they would have ended up in a similar little house. It lacked the picket fence she had once thought trite but now found charming.

Jim came around and opened her door. He helped her out of the car. "When does any man do that anymore?" She asked. "You're such a gentleman, Jim. I wish a few of your manners would rub off on Brian."

"No, you don't. Brian wouldn't be Brian, then."

"I suppose not."

Jim followed her up the pathway to the front door, which opened before either of them pressed the doorbell.

"You're on time," said a pleasantly modulated voice. The woman, in her early 50's according to Jim's meticulous notes, smiled at them and stepped aside. "Do come in."

Jim motioned Kaylen to precede him. Brian, in a protective mode, would probably have gone in first, she thought, but she didn't believe for one minute that the attractive woman with curly light brown hair and pale blue eyes was a murderer.

The woman extended her hand. "I'm Nola Chesney."

"Jim Paxton." Jim unexpectedly stepped forward to grasp her hand before Kaylen could do so. "And this is my associate, Kaylen."

Kaylen noticed he had left off her last name. She had pulled her hair back into a braid and only added a dash of lip gloss that morning in an effort to appear as conservative as possible. She'd chosen to wear black pants and a white scoop-necked shirt under a turquoise cotton cardigan. A quick check of Nola's clothing told her she had chosen wisely. Dressed in a pair of flowered capris and a yellow cotton top with a boat-neck and bracelet length sleeves, Nola oozed easy conventionality. She wore yellow slip-on shoes with cut outs exposing pale pink toenails. No jewelry except her wedding band and a watch. Kaylen was glad she had opted for a single strand of pearls.

"Lester's lying down. I hope you don't mind talking with both of us in the bedroom," Nola said. "Sitting up in a chair exhausts him pretty quickly."

"How about we meet Lester, then spend a few minutes with each of you individually before getting back together as a group?" Jim suggested.

"That's fine." Nola smiled again, but a little uncertainly. "This way."

She led them through a quiet house darkened by partially closed blinds that rendered the interior cool but gloomy. Kaylen saw traditional French provincial furnishings in the dining room carried through to the living room. Dark red floral material covered a couch and two side chairs. A vase of wilting flowers on the coffee table was the only sign it wasn't a home in order. She wondered how the kitchen looked. Did it reflect the turmoil that must be going on in this house where death hovered overhead? Her mood lowered with the gloom. She caught a faint whiff of stale air when Nola open a door and poked her head around it.

"Lester, honey, the detectives are here," Nola said. "Can we all come in?"

A murmured assent caused her to open the door wide. The master bedroom was bathed in gentle sunlight filtering between the leaves of tall bushes outside the window. Water reflected on the ceiling. Probably from an in-ground pool, Kaylen thought. The room was a little stuffy and smelled faintly of potpourri, probably in an attempt to disguise the sick-room odor that Kaylen remembered from George's last days. No matter how often she and the private duty nurse carefully sponged him off and changed his clothing and bed linens, George's sweat had exuded the same odor she found in Lester's room.

She looked at the bed, where a thin form lay covered in a sheet and a cotton blanket. Lester Chesney was propped up by three pillows and wore a cannula sending oxygen up his nostrils. Kaylen's memories of her late husband intensified. She wondered whether Brian's reluctance to let her go on this interview had more to do with his worries about the atmosphere than the actual words that would be said.

Lester raised his hand briefly before letting it drop back onto the bedclothes. "Come on in," he rasped, his chest heaving with the effort.

Nola hurried to his side. "Are you comfortable, honey? Can I get you some water?"

"Not right now." He looked first at Jim, then at Kaylen. "I feel so important, suddenly." He managed a smile even briefer than his attempt at a greeting.

Jim stepped over and took Lester's hand. "Jim Paxton," he said. "Glad to meet you. We really appreciate you both seeing us."

"I'm Kaylen, an associate," she said, stepping up beside Jim.

"They want to split us up and talk to us separately," Nola said. "Do you think you can handle that?"

Lester nodded. "Sit down, Jim. It'll be easier on my neck."

Nola started to pull over a chair from the other side of the end table.

Jim rushed to take the chair from her. "Let me do that. Why don't you and Kaylen go get acquainted for a few minutes?"

Nola nodded. She still looked a little uncertain about leaving Lester with Jim, but she gave Kaylen another quick smile.

"Let's go to the kitchen," Kaylen suggested. "Maybe I could help you get us all something to drink?"

"Do you like iced tea?" Nola hovered close to Lester, like a humming-bird desperately beating wings that were beginning to tire. Her face, in the brighter light of the bedroom, looked pinched and drawn. "Lester likes it, don't you, sweetie?"

Lester smiled up at her. "I do."

Still, she hovered.

"I'll be okay, Toots," he said.

Nola's shoulders lowered. The smile she gave him registered relief. "I know you will."

Kaylen's heart threatened to shatter. There was real love. No strings. No expectations. With that one pet name, Lester had reassured his wife he would be okay without her right at his side. They left Jim and Lester chatting like old friends and Kaylen followed Nola to the kitchen.

"How long have you been doing this?" Nola asked as she opened the refrigerator and took out a big pitcher of iced tea.

"Close to five months," Kaylen said without hesitation. From the moment she met Brian, she added silently.

"Do you like it?" Nola opened a cabinet and took out glasses.

"Some days more than others." Kaylen watched as Nola set the glasses on a tray.

"Do you have to carry a gun?" Nola took a container filled with ice cubes from the freezer.

"I have once." Kaylen took the container from Nola and dropped ice into the glasses. "But I didn't have to use it." She thought of Sam's shocked expression when she pointed Brian's gun at him. This role-playing wasn't as hard as she had expected.

"I watch reruns of 'Charlie's Angels' with Lester every week," Nola said. "It's an old series, but Lester really gets a kick out of seeing pretty girls chasing criminals. Is your job really like that?"

"No." Kaylen smiled and put the ice container back in the freezer. "Mostly, I get to ask questions. No running after bad guys with a gun in one hand and a hairbrush in the other."

Nola gave a quick laugh, like she hadn't used that in a long time and it felt weird, but the uncertainty left her face. "Darn," she said. "One illusion shattered."

Kaylen smiled wider, mindful of Brian's careful coaching the previous evening: Start slow, get the person you're interviewing to feel comfortable, and then get down to business. "How long did you work at the grocery store?" she asked, trying to sound casual.

"About a year. One of the hardest jobs I ever had. Pretty thankless, being a checker in a low-income neighborhood. People frequently put items in their baskets they couldn't afford. When they got to the checkstand and found out how much everything was going to cost, they started taking things back out of the bags. Or they argued over prices, like we were overcharging against what was listed on the shelves. We had one stock boy going around all day putting the correct prices back on the front of items because people kept moving them around."

"Sounds worse than waitressing," Kaylen said.

"Is that what you did before you got this job?" Nola looked Kaylen up and down with curiosity. "You don't look much like a waitress."

"I haven't done it in a while. But I can still balance plates all the way up my arm. It's one of the talents I list on my resume."

Nola burst out laughing. "You're funny. I needed this. Thank you."

"You're welcome."

Kaylen decided she had done enough easing and it was time to get into the questioning part of her time alone with Nola. She leaned one hip against the counter. "So, how well did you know Chad Summerfield?"

Nola took a packet of Pepperidge Farm Chesapeake cookies out of a cabinet, her back turned. She took a plate out of another cabinet before turning around to set it on the table. Kaylen took the packet, shook out the contents and fanned them artistically on the plate.

"Nice presentation." Nola nodded. "I should do that myself. It might stimulate Lester's appetite if I really worked on making the food look more attractive. Like in a restaurant."

"It doesn't take much," Kaylen said. "Just put a couple of sprigs of parsley on the edge of a plate or slice up a couple of cherry tomatoes and put them onto a lettuce leaf."

Nola nodded again, looking thoughtful. "To answer your question about Chad, I didn't know him well." She poured tea into the glasses. "He was the assistant manager, working a split shift from noon to close. I worked a register on the day shift, so we were only in the store together a couple of hours before I left at three o'clock."

"How well did he get on with the other employees?"

Nola shrugged. "Okay, I guess. I wasn't much for gossiping in the break room, so I didn't hear a lot. I ate lunch reading a magazine, then went out back for a smoke on the loading dock. That's how I met Lester. He was a smoker, too. Now look at him—dying of lung cancer, although he quit years ago. We both did." She took a napkin from a neat pile on the counter and wiped her eyes. "Look at *me*. I said I wouldn't get emotional and here I go again, crying at the drop of a hat." She blew her nose.

Kaylen wanted to reach out and tell Nola it was okay to cry. That she'd be doing it daily for quite a while, both before and after her husband passed away. But she wasn't there to do bereavement counseling. Brian would never send her on another interview if she didn't bring back something useful.

"It was a shock then when Chad got shot," she said, gently bringing the conversation back to Brian's case.

Nola blew her nose again and nodded. "If I'd had any idea what was going to happen that day, I'd have refused to go in on my day off and cover for someone who went home sick. But I was living with two other equally broke girls in a walk-up, and rent was overdue." She opened a garbage can and dropped the crumpled napkin inside.

"I arrived right before it happened. I was in the break room, putting my stuff into my locker. The robber came in at one o'clock. After the noon rush. Maybe he thought it would be quieter, and there'd be more money in the tills. But the strangest thing was, I heard he walked right up to Chad, told him it was a stick-up and then shot him. Chad never moved a muscle. He looked at the gun and froze. So the checkers couldn't figure out why he got shot. They were standing there, horrified, wondering who was going to be next, when the guy ran through the store and out the back, into the alley."

"What was he wearing?"

"A windbreaker, jeans and a ski mask, so everyone said." Nola shuddered. "Lester was on the loading dock when the guy ran right past him, so he was able to give a good description." She shook her head. "I can't believe Lester didn't get shot, too."

"He was lucky," Kaylen said.

"He was," Nola agreed. "And I was, too. I liked Lester a lot. He was so nice. Kind, sweet. I didn't care what people thought. What they said about our age difference, or the fact he was my supervisor. When he asked me out, I was happy to go. Our first date was a week after Chad's murder. Lester asked me if I'd go to the movies with him. He came and picked me up from the store. I had to work another extra shift because some employees quit after the shooting. They were scared because the robber hadn't been found."

"Was Chad dating anyone at the store?"

"Just about everybody who was under the age of twenty-five. That was his limit, I heard." Nola shook her head, smiling wryly. "So that cut me out. I was twenty-six. Lester was forty. Too old for kids, he told me. I wasn't sad about that at the time. Now I wish I'd pushed the issue. He'll be gone, and I'll be alone."

"No family?" Kaylen wondered about herself and Brian. They had no one, unless she counted her cantankerous father and his new wife and step-son, which she didn't. She'd spoken to the woman once, attempting to wish her a happy marriage, only to be rebuffed, like Kaylen was looking for a handout, or trying to get an inheritance that would cut into Preston Grant's new family's wealth when he died. Kaylen thought her father was so strong, he'd probably outlive all of them, out of spite.

Nola was shaking her head. "No siblings on either side. Lester's parents passed away. My mom's got a lot of medical issues. She's about to start kidney dialysis. Lester's got cousins, but he's not close to any of them, and they all live back East. Pittsburgh, mostly. We never visited. I moved here from Albuquerque with my parents when I was a senior in high school. My dad got a better job offer, and my parents had always wanted to come to Florida. My dad had a heart attack a year after the move. I felt resentful about everything. It's hard coming into a new school during the last year. Everyone else has friends and you're an outcast. Then after being dragged away from home with all these promises of a better life, the person who told you all this dies." She took a cloth and wiped a wet spot on the counter.

"I know what it's like to be in a new town and not have friends," Kaylen said. "I left Maine right after high school and moved down here. I was tired of snow, and Miami sounded so exciting."

Nola stopped wiping and looked up. "I thought I was going to get excitement, too. Reality was that without my dad's paycheck, we ended up living in the neighborhood around the Mega Grocery, and I worked there instead of going to college. My mom had to get a job, too. She became the receptionist at a local bank. We went from having a nice house in the suburbs to a third floor walk-up. Then she found a boyfriend. He and I didn't get along, so I moved in with those roommates. My dad had taken a big risk leaving Albuquerque, and he'd used up most of our savings. He had no life insurance. I guess he thought he wasn't old enough to think about dying." She sighed. "So did you do any better?"

"I started work as a waitress and ended up as a restaurant manager. Then I married an older man, like you, but he passed away two years later."

"I'm so sorry. What a tough road we both chose, huh?"

"I don't regret it," Kaylen said. "Not for a moment. My husband was wonderful."

Nola smiled. "Mine is, too. So much better than that Chad Summerfield. He was an incredible flirt. I heard stories that he got a couple of girls pregnant, but I think that was gossip. I never saw any proof. Lester said he was like a big tom cat, prowling around. He thought Chad had something wrong with him, like he needed therapy. Lester and one of the stock boys walked in on Chad having sex with one of the other employees in the stockroom one day. Her name was Cherry, Cherry Lauder. I remember that because I always used to joke with her about what was louder than a cherry. And the stock boy? Hmm...let me think...what was that kid's name?"

Her brow furrowed, and she tapped one finger against the counter, the nail showing chipped pale pink polish. "Sorry. I can't remember."

"So Lester thought Chad Summerfield had some sort of sex addiction?" Kaylen pressed. She felt icky, suddenly. Like she'd walked through a bunch of cobwebs and they'd clung to her. She wondered how Brian did this job on a daily basis. What awful things he must hear and see. No wonder he was tight-lipped about stuff and hadn't wanted her involved. But she was doing well at her interview, she decided. Nola was opening up. And maybe that was Brian's reward for digging into the dirt of people's lives...getting to the truth.

"You'll have to ask Lester," Nola said, breaking into Kaylen's thoughts. "We never discussed Chad after he died. It seemed disrespectful. The dead being unable to defend themselves and all that."

Kaylen nodded. Her phone buzzed in her pocket. She took it out and checked a text. "Ready when u r," she read. From Jim. "Shall we take these cookies and drinks in to the guys?"

"I take it you got a signal." The corner of Nola's mouth turned up. She slid the tray of drinks closer, ready to pick up.

"I did. Not so subtle, huh?"

"I think you did good," Nola said. "I'd hire you to investigate anything for me in a heart-beat."

"Thanks." Kaylen wondered why Nola would say something like that.

"When do they send you out by yourself with a gun?" Nola asked. "Do you have to work so many cases, or so many hours?"

Kaylen realized Nola thought she was a trainee. She felt defensive. "We frequently work as a team," she said. "Especially when we're interviewing more than one person at the same location." So much for patting herself on the back. Nola had her pegged for a rookie.

"You're wearing Ferragamo." Nola pointed to Kaylen's shoes. "Much too expensive on a private detective's pay, I would think." She pulled a Vogue magazine from under the daily newspaper. "I read about all the latest fashions. Those same shoes are in there."

Kaylen thought quickly. "I bought them at this really cool consignment shop," she said. "They were gently used. Aren't they fabulous?" She hoped Nola would look at the shoes and not the flush creeping up her neck.

Luckily, Nola did just that. "Oh, wow." She watched as Kaylen modeled the shoes. "They really are. How much did you pay?"

"Forty bucks. I couldn't resist." Kaylen tried to sound suitably awed.

The thought of Ferragamo at that bargain-basement price should be enough to excite any woman, even her. "I'm dating someone new, and I wanted to look really good," she threw in. At least *that* was partially true.

"You do." Nola nodded. "Did you get the rest of your outfit there?"

"Well, the pants and the shirt. I pieced it together. The cardigan I bought in a yard sale." Kaylen thought Brian's eyebrows would be up in his hairline if he could hear her.

"You should have a boutique," Nola said. "I'd shop there."

"Thank you. That's a big compliment." Kaylen giggled right along-side Nola as they took the drinks and plate of cookies down the hallway to the bedroom.

She'd like to see Brian bonding with Nola over clothing, she thought smugly. Ferragamo would turn any woman into putty in her hands, if she thought Kaylen had found a place that sold high fashion, gently used, at bargain-basement prices.

CHAPTER FIFTY-TWO

WITHIN 30 MINUTES of Brian's conversation with Jack Mills, his phone rang again.

"Hi Sergeant." Gabe sounded a bit hesitant. "How you doing?"

"Fine, Gabe. Yourself?" Brian poured another cup of black coffee. He didn't seem to be getting much done related to the case, he thought, glancing through the open door at the whiteboard, which was now covered with names on the left and sparsely populated on the right.

"Not good, as you already know."

"Yeah." Brian took his coffee into the conference room and sat, leaning back and putting his feet up on the table. "I talked to Mills. What's going on? You've always been able to work with anyone. Even Vernon."

"That was before our new boss arrived." Gabe's voice sounded distinctly hostile. "Detective Vernon's drinking binges and hangovers have nothing on this new supervisor. I called in sick today. The thought of another day with that man made me want to puke."

"Jack said there've been a lot of changes in the department."

Brian wondered idly whether the aborted convenience store robbery had anything at all to do with Chad Summerfield's murder, or whether he'd wasted two days interviewing all the perpetrators.

"*Too* many." Gabe sighed heavily. "And I'm next. I won't be sent to the basement. I don't deserve to be booted out because Trehorn wants to use my back as another stepping stone into upper management. He makes me..."

"Sick," Brian interrupted. "I get it. Mills feels you need a time-out until Trehorn moves on, which he thinks will happen fairly soon. I have a couple of things to run by you. If you come up to Tampa to help me out, you realize this is only a temporary fix for your problem? I'm not staying up here for months, trying to solve some old case if there's insufficient evidence or none of the ends tie together."

"Yes."

Brian decided he needed to go a second round with Rita Golding. She'd been too evasive, even if she was steaming mad about her job. He moved her name back under 'pending.'

"I'll pay you what you're getting at the department, but make arrangements to keep up your benefits while you're on sabbatical, or you'll lose a lot more than a few weeks' pay," he told Gabe.

"I'll do that."

"You'll have two bosses. My friend, Jim Paxton is up here with me, and whatever he says goes, too. Any objections?"

"No, Sergeant."

"Any questions?"

"What will I be doing for you?"

"Copying files and answering the phone, mostly, but you may have to run some errands, pick up food, whatever we need. Might be even more boring than that basement."

"I doubt that, knowing you. Detective Mills said I need to ask if I'll be doing anything illegal."

"Christ. What does he think I'm doing up here? Running drugs?"

"No, Sergeant, but we all know how tough you can be when you want results. Detective Mills wanted me to make sure I knew what I was getting into."

"Gabe, I don't even know what *I'm* doing up here half the time. This is the first cold case I've ever worked."

"I understand that. Detective Mills was just looking out for me."

"Jack Mills is a damn mother fuckin' hen."

Brian was more than ready to hang up and get on with his day. His mind had finished mulling over the problem with the convenience store gang. Those guys, who had once been tight-knit friends, knew something. He'd seen Rita's face when he mentioned Wally's name. It was the only time she hadn't either looked angry or bland.

But he had to continue trying to be more subtle than he'd ever been with suspects or witnesses before. Low key and informal was working better than badge-waving and threatening. Brian was beginning to believe Tommy and his buddies had made some sort of pact none of them was willing to break, but he was determined to sever that bond. Finding out what Rita and Wally had between them was one goal, and Rita's possible friendship with Mel was another.

"I'll drive up, so I'll have my car," Gabe said into his ear. "When do you want me there?"

"ASAP. I'll text you the office address. You'll need somewhere to stay that's close by. Ms. Roberts is up here for a couple of days. I'll get her to book you into a motel and text you the info." Brian walked over to the board and grouped Spiro and his friends under an umbrella that said 'Suspects.'

"Ms. Roberts doesn't need to do that." Gabe sounded less timid and uncertain. "I'd planned to make my own arrangements if you offered me a position. I can find a motel myself."

"What are you going to do about your apartment in Miami?"

"Sub-let," Gabe said without hesitation. "I already put out feelers to a couple of guys I know. Both have long commutes and want to rent my place until they find something closer to work."

"What if we wind things up here quick?"

"I'll take a vacation."

"Okay. You're hired."

"Thanks." The relief in Gabe's voice was profound. "I owe you, Sergeant."

"I think you'd better start calling me Brian."

"I don't know if I can do that. You kind of frighten me."

Brian had to smile. "You're safe, Gabe. If you hadn't made that call to Kaylen when I was shot, she might not have gotten help to me in time. I almost bled out as it was. I owe you, and giving you a job will be a good way of repaying you. I promise I won't yell at you."

"If Ms. Roberts is up there, I know you won't."

"Is that so?" Brian wanted to laugh. Kaylen had a lot more influence than he'd even given her credit for.

"I'll call from the road and give you a better ETA," Gabe said. "I made an appointment to talk with Trehorn. Originally, it was to give notice, but now I'll tell him I want the sabbatical, put it in writing, and send a copy to Chief Shaw, in case our new supervisor takes the opportunity to fire me. I don't think the chief would want that."

"Trehorn won't, either. He'll probably be relieved to get another potential problem out from under his feet without bringing the chief down on him. Keep me posted, and if things go sour, you let me know. I'll call Hal myself."

"Thanks. I really appreciate your willingness to help."

"You make good coffee," Brian said. "The only one in Homicide who does. But all joking aside, you're discreet and you don't get flustered. We'll be lucky to have you."

"I needed to hear that after the last few weeks."

Brian heard the emotion in Gabe's voice. Trehorn must be a complete shit-head, he decided. Their clerk was the last person who should be worried about his job. "Twenty-four hours? Or you need a couple of days?"

"I'll be there tomorrow," Gabe promised before hanging up.

Brian wondered how Kaylen and Jim were faring with the couple in Clearwater. As soon as Kaylen returned, he'd have her call the temp agency and cancel the interviews. Gabe was a much better choice. He hit every one of those bullet points on Kaylen's checklist.

Brian knew he could send her back to Miami any time now. But if he did, he couldn't keep an eye on her. Not only was he concerned about her possibly coming into contact with Sam Wilson, but he had an even bigger worry: What would happen between her and Ziggy Stavros if he wasn't around?

Glancing at his watch, he moved one more Post-It Note into the 'suspects' column on the whiteboard before shrugging into his jacket, picking up his keys and walking out the door...Tab Benford.

Hungry, he decided to stop for a quick bite at Danny Cho's Chinese Buffet and then catch Best Pic's manager right at the end of his own lunch break. It'd be a good time to find out what really went down between the convenience store fiasco and the murder at Mega Groceries. But before that, he'd cruise by the diner and find out if Rita had made good on her plan to return to work.

CHAPTER FIFTY-THREE

"Is THERE ANYTHING you didn't tell the police at the time of the murder?" Jim asked as he and Kaylen sat on the left side of Lester's bed, Nola on the right. Jim had, with the couple's permission, placed a video camera on the dresser opposite the bed. He was worried about not being able to prove anything Lester said that could be useful, with an acute possibility that Lester would have passed away long before anyone came to trial for Chad Summerfield's murder.

Nola held Lester's hand with one of hers. The other clutched a damp cloth with which she lightly but repeatedly blotted his face.

"Don't keep doing that, honey," he complained gently. "I can't concentrate or see Jim and Kaylen with a cloth over my eyes."

"I'm sorry, sweetie." Nola bit her bottom lip and dropped the cloth into a bowl filled with water.

Kaylen's heart went out to her. She remembered hovering around George in much the same way. When they left this house of sickness and got back to Brian, Kaylen swore she was going to hug him tight and take him back to the hotel, where they were going to spend a lot of time holding each other and reaffirming life.

"Anything," Jim repeated. "However minute. What was the robber wearing, again?"

"Jeans and a windbreaker," Lester said.

"And a ski mask," Nola added. "Don't forget that."

"I was getting to that, honey." Lester drew his hand out of hers, patted her arm and with a great deal of effort, pulled himself up higher on the pillows. "A red and white striped ski mask. In the middle of summer. He must've been sweating like a pig under that."

"He definitely wasn't dressed for the weather, then," Jim prompted when Lester stopped speaking and Nola didn't pick up, either.

Kaylen noticed Nola was watching Lester with her hands clasped tightly together. She probably wanted to fluff up his pillows and straighten the covers. But he'd asked her to stop fussing, so she was trying to control herself.

Kaylen could relate. Brian had been way more direct when she'd tried to fuss over him during his hospital stay. He'd told her to leave him the hell alone. But she had learned to look harder and to listen past his words. Brian's body language didn't reveal much, but his eyes did, if she caught the expression in them fast enough. She'd noticed pain there, and in the rigid set of his mouth. She saw similar emotions in Lester's face, as she knew Nola probably did, too.

"Dressed for the weather?" Lester's brow furrowed. "No, I guess he wasn't. Heavy jeans and that windbreaker on a sunny day. He unzipped the jacket as he passed me." He frowned harder. "He was wearing a belt with silver studs all the way around, and it was too big for him. The end of the belt hung down and banged against his legs as he ran down the alley."

"Did you tell the cops about that?" Jim asked.

Lester shook his head. "I don't think so. I was so shaken up by hearing people yelling about a shooting and then seeing him run out the back of the store with a gun. Right in the middle of a clump of employees and customers who were too hysterical to notice what was going on. That's how he got away so easily, I think. He got in the middle of the herd and kept on moving. The first thing I remembered was the ski mask, which he pulled off after he passed me. I reckon the rest of it came back to me afterward, when I heard what other people said. By the time the cops arrived, a big group of us were milling around, all excited and talking at once. We were all shouting above each other. Complete mayhem."

"Did you go back inside the store before the cops arrived?" Jim asked.

Lester shook his head. "I didn't know if the guy was alone. For all I knew, there could be more of them in there with guns, maybe taking hostages. I tried telling everyone to leave their shopping carts and their purses and stuff where they were, but it was useless. Too much hysteria.

People weren't making much sense. All I knew was, Chad was shot and we were all better outside the store than inside. I was real relieved when two patrolmen showed up. They'd been eating at the nearby Burger Shack when they heard all the commotion. Unfortunately, they didn't get there fast enough to save Chad or catch his killer."

"So what happened to all the people who ran out the back if you couldn't control them?"

"A lot of them kept on running. All different directions. Like I said, screaming and shouting. Tripping and falling. Some of them got trampled in the rush. The alleyway split in three different directions. Most of the people ran to the street. I'd lost sight of the robber by then, and I felt weak and shaky, so I sat on a milk crate. I guess I kind of blanked out, because the next thing I knew, a whole bunch of cops were there, patrol cars screeching brakes and blocking the alleyways from all directions. Then some detective shouting at me, asking me where the shooter went and what the hell was wrong with me that I couldn't answer him."

Lester stopped speaking. His chest was heaving, his complexion the color of putty. Nola had a handful of the blanket and Kaylen felt sure Nola was squeezing it much tighter than she had squeezed Lester's hand.

"That must have been terrifying," Kaylen said. She felt a little shaky herself. Brian was right. She wasn't ready for all the emotions that came with Lester's story. She'd only thought about getting information, not reliving traumatic experiences with witnesses.

Lester cleared his throat and accepted a drink of water from the bottle Nola handed him. "One detective took off down the alley that ran between the loading docks. He was shouting instructions to the patrolmen, telling them to search the buildings. Another detective stayed behind and started questioning me again. I'd pulled myself together enough to talk while I tried to smoke a cigarette. I remember it took a lot to light it and even more effort to smoke it, my hands were trembling so badly. My heart was pounding. And then suddenly, there was Nola, peering around the door and asking if I was okay." He smiled at her. "My own guardian angel. That's when I decided to heck with all those barriers I'd put between us, I was going to ask her out. Funny what facing death does to you. What thoughts pop into your head."

Kaylen could relate. She'd had uncharacteristic thoughts during the time she'd been on the run with Brian. And acted on them, too, she told herself, remembering how she had instigated their first sexual encounter.

Nola returned Lester's smile. "I saw you sneaking out for a smoke right before it happened. I was about to join you when I heard the shots."

"So you must have seen the shooter run past the break room if you were in there with the door open," Kaylen said. She felt proud of herself for thinking of that.

"No." Nola shook her head emphatically. "I dove under the table and closed my eyes, like an ostrich sticking its head in the sand. Just as stupid, because who wouldn't see me crouching under there? But I really didn't know where else to hide. If I'd tried to go out the door, he might have seen me and shot me, too."

Kaylen tried for another good question. "You were alone?"

"Yes. There were two other girls with me a couple of minutes before, but they both hit the ladies room. One was going off shift and another coming on."

"Do you remember their names?" Jim had a pen poised above the pad on his thigh.

"Mmm…" Nola tapped a nail against her front teeth as she thought. "Clarice was the one going off shift, and Shonda was the one about to start."

"Last names?"

Nola frowned. "I don't recall. Both girls were fairly new." She looked at Lester. "Do you remember, honey?"

"Maybe." He took another sip of water from the bottle perched against his side. "Clarice had a funny name…I associated it with something...like a rose." A dull red flushed his cheeks and he looked side-ways at Nola.

"Oh, Lester," she said. "She wouldn't even give you the time of day." She laughed, and it sounded like music in the midst of all the painful memories. "I guess I did know it, after all. It was Thorn."

The whole atmosphere had suddenly changed. The room felt brighter; not such a sick-room. Kaylen could see why Lester had been drawn to his wife.

Jim chuckled.

Lester looked relieved. "You're so right, honey. But I'm glad she didn't because I ended up with the right girl for me."

"Flatterer." Nola took his hand again.

"What about the other girl?" Kaylen prompted.

Lester shrugged, thin shoulders moving like twigs under his paisley pajama top. "I didn't see much of her. I remember she and Clarice knew each other out of work. I think Clarice might have gotten her an interview."

"If Chad was such a playboy, I wonder why any woman in her right mind would bring a friend over to work there," Kaylen said.

"Even he couldn't do much damage when he had things to wrap up before the evening manager came in," Nola said. "And we were too busy most mornings for any flirting activities." She shrugged, her gaze suddenly on the blanket instead of her husband. "I guess he must have done the most damage around lunch time."

"Ah." Kaylen wondered whether Clarice had told her friend about Tab and his reputation. She also wondered whether Clarice had been immune to Chad's overtures, and if so, why. "Was Clarice too old for Chad?"

"Yes, and she had a beefy husband, too," Nola said. "Clarice was definitely not someone Chad would go for, unless he wanted to risk a broken nose."

Kaylen watched the two witnesses and wondered what Brian's inves-tigative methods were, and how they differed from hers and Jim's. Were they getting as many answers as Brian would have done? Jim's approach seemed to echo hers...soft.

She remembered Brian telling her he busted heads for a living and thought warm and fuzzy probably were not words anyone would use after spending time under his scrutiny. He hadn't really scared her, though, she thought, when he'd questioned her, and he'd gotten a lot of information out of her when Tim went missing. Without exerting a whole lot of effort, either. She'd definitely be classed as a push-over. No grilling or intimidation necessary. Lester was pretty open, too. Nola, not so much, but warming slowly.

"I bet Clarice still lives in the neighborhood," Lester said. "Her husband worked at an auto repair shop close to the store. Her mom lived in the same building they did and babysat the kids after school, until Clarice got home."

"What was the husband's name?" Jim asked.

"Jennings," Lester said.

"And you can't remember Shonda's last name?" Jim looked from Lester to Nola.

"Not for the life of me." Nola frowned.

"Me, neither." Lester sighed. "Suddenly, I'm getting real tired."

Kaylen noticed Lester's already-noticeable pallor had increased, and a fine sheen of sweat had appeared on his face. She tapped Jim's shoulder. "Time for us to go."

"Okay." He stood. "We've worn you out, Lester. Sorry." He turned off the camera.

"I enjoyed the company, Jim." Lester gave a brief smile. "You want to come back tomorrow, that's fine with me. I'd enjoy talking baseball with you, and you could ask me a few more questions about the store, too, if you like."

"I don't know if that's a good idea, sweetie," Nola said. "You've got to save your strength."

"For what? A longer battle with the Grim Reaper?" Lester looked a bit rebellious. "How often do I get to talk baseball with anyone these days?"

"You don't." Nola pursed her lips. "I hate sports."

"Well, then." With a great deal of effort, Lester folded his stick arms across his concave chest. "I rest my case. Jim?"

"I'd be glad to," Jim said. "I'll call tomorrow and see how you're feeling."

Lester held out his hand. It trembled a little and started on a down-ward path. Jim clasped it quickly, before it dropped onto the blanket. "Pleasure meeting both of you," he said, looking from Lester to Nola.

"Me, too." Kaylen got up. "Thank you so much for your time. We really appreciate it."

Nola nodded. Her face looked pinched again. Kaylen wondered if she had some little secret she had never shared with Lester. A secret maybe about Chad, regardless of whether she had said she was too old for him or not.

She followed Nola to the door, Jim right behind her. Outside, light as yellow as citrus was a welcome sight. Kaylen stopped on the threshold and held out a scrap of paper on which she had scribbled her cell phone number. "Call me any time. I know what you're going through." She pressed the paper into Nola's hand.

Nola's eyes brimmed with tears. She nodded.

Jim guided Kaylen down the steps, away from the house where death hovered, and into a warm late autumn afternoon.

The door closed behind them.

"I doubt he's going to be around to talk baseball with you much longer," Kaylen said as they walked toward the rental car.

Jim looked aside at her. "I had the same feeling."

But as he opened the passenger's side door for her, Kaylen heard rapid footsteps tapping down the walkway behind them.

"Kaylen, can I talk to you a couple of minutes alone?" Nola asked.

"I'll wait here." Jim closed the door.

"I'll be right back." Kaylen joined Nola on the path.

"Let's go around to the side patio." Nola took a small path between plantings of Oleanders and Elephant Ears that led to a cool, shady area beside the living room. Chairs and a table sat in front of sliding glass doors closed against the heat.

"I had a feeling you had more to say." Kaylen took a chair opposite Nola's.

"I didn't want Lester to hear." Nola wrung her hands. "It would only make him mad, and all these years later, there's nothing he could do about it." She stopped, bit her bottom lip and took a deep breath. "I had a brief affair with Chad Summerfield. He'd meet me in the stockroom and we'd do it right on top of the supply boxes. He'd lift my skirt, pull down my panties and just go at it. He always came and I never did." Her cheeks were crimson.

When Nola stayed silent, her eyes downcast, Kaylen swallowed her own feelings of shock over images of Nola and Chad Summerfield together. "So what ended it?"

"I caught him and Mel in there." Nola looked up briefly before returning to staring at her hands, clasped tightly in her lap. "They were embracing. It revolted me. That sister of his was always flaunting herself whenever she came into the store. She wore tight blouses with the top buttons open and a push-up bra with her boobs half popped out. Tight pants with her butt wiggling around. None of the men could keep their eyes off her."

Kaylen thought how little Mel had changed over the years. She wanted to reach out to Nola, but she doubted a seasoned PI would do that, and she didn't want to act like the rookie Nola had accused her of being. Instead, she gave Nola a moment to catch her breath before urging her on with her story. "So you saw them...kissing?" she asked.

Nola looked up, her mouth held in a tight line of disapproval. "Well, not exactly, but they might just as well have been. He was hugging her and kissing her face."

"Do you remember how long that was before he got shot?"

"Not long. A few days. Maybe a week at most. Right at noon. No one went into the stockroom at that time of day. It was really hot in there. That's why Chad and I were never found together. I'd come in early again. Employees were always calling out sick at that place. I thought we'd have more time together. Maybe he'd, you know, make me enjoy it more." The crimson had blossomed right up to her forehead at that point. She took a deep breath. "I was wearing new see-through lace panties because I felt sexier in them, and I thought he'd really like them. Instead, I was made to feel like an idiot. I'd been thrown over for his sister."

Kaylen didn't want to interrupt, but she wasn't sure whether Nola was going to stop right there or say anything else. "You must have been completely shocked," she said, unable to think of a more appropriate or encouraging thing to say.

Nola nodded. "Completely. And then Chad saw me and smiled, like it was normal for him to be hugging his sister in the stockroom. He asked me to come on in. Meet his sister properly, like there was anything proper about her standing there with her low cut blouse and tears all over her face. I swear her boobs looked even bigger than usual that day. I turned around and ran out, got my purse from my locker and left. I lied and told Lester I was sick." She pushed her hair out of her eyes. "It feels so good to get that off my chest."

"I really appreciate you telling me all this," Kaylen said.

"You won't have to tell Lester any of it, will you?" Nola sniffed, took a wad of tissues out of a pocket in her capris and held them to her nose.

"I doubt he'll ever have to know." Kaylen couldn't stop herself from patting Nola's hand.

Nola grabbed her like a drowning woman clutching a lifeline and burst into a flood of tears. "I so love Lester. I don't want him to be hurt."

"We'll be discrete," Kaylen assured her. "Do you really believe you were the only employee Chad seduced in that stockroom?"

"I'd like to think so; it would salvage some of my pride; but probably not." Nola used the wad of tissues to brush away her tears. "I always wonder what would have happened if I hadn't run away." She sniffed again. "I felt really bad about myself. I was lonely and not very attractive, and it was flattering to be wanted so bad that Chad couldn't wait to take me someplace else. Then I began to realize he probably was never going to date me outside of the workplace."

"I can't imagine you being unattractive," Kaylen said.

Nola managed a watery smile. "Lester's very indulgent. He said he loved me the way I was, but he agreed to pay to get my big nose fixed and my tiny little boobs made larger. He said nothing huge. He couldn't see the point of more than a handful." She covered her face. "What's the matter with me? I never get crass like this."

"People do all sorts of strange things when a family member's dying," Kaylen said.

"Did *you?*" Nola took her hands away from her face.

Kaylen thought fast. "I lit candles all over the house when it got dark. The place smelled like a wax factory. My husband begged me not to do it, but I couldn't seem to stop myself. Then I noticed the ceilings had black marks on them and we were both coughing. That was what stopped me."

"Thank you," Nola said. "I keep baking cupcakes that Lester doesn't eat. I've made vanilla, strawberry, chocolate and even swirled chocolate and vanilla together. I've frosted them, put sprinkles on top, candied fruit, everything. He keeps telling me he can't eat them, but I go out in the kitchen and make another batch. I've had to drive over to the local mission and donate them every couple of days. I wonder whether all that unnecessary baking is giving me an excuse to get out of the house for an hour. Sometimes I really wonder what's wrong with me, when we've got so little time left together."

"We all cope the best we can," Kaylen said. "Don't be so hard on yourself."

"Thanks, Kaylen. You've been a big help." Nola really smiled that time.

"I should go." Kaylen got up.

"And I'd better get back to Lester before he wonders what's keeping me."

They walked in silence to the front of the house.

Nola paused at the front steps. "I hope you catch Chad's killer. Whatever he did, his family loved him and probably still misses him."

"Probably." Kaylen thought of the Summerfields, and Mel coming on to Brian on the *Need to Know*.

She vowed she would never, ever leave him alone with that barracuda again.

CHAPTER FIFTY-FOUR

Brian nixed attempting to squeeze any other information out of Chico Ramos. He reckoned he'd end up getting his head bashed in if he set foot into that garage again. But Rita had acted like she had something to hide. Leaning on her might get better results.

The diner was practically empty. A faint odor of burned toast vied with fried fish and greasy bacon. He was glad he'd skipped breakfast.

"You just missed her," a scrawny waitress with a bad case of acne told him. "She must have been running late for something. She bolted out the back door right before you came in the front."

Brian figured Rita had seen him. Walking back outside, he was in time to spot her flying around the corner at the end of the street, apron tucked under one arm, skinny legs moving like pistons. He ran after her, catching up as she stood waiting for traffic to pass before crossing the street to a bus stop.

She turned and saw him, scowling. "Don't you ever give up?"

With that, she darted into the street. Brian pulled her back as a van's horn blasted and brakes screeched. Rita made an exasperated noise and jerked out of his grip, but she stayed on the curb.

"I'm that scary, you'd prefer death over talking to me?" Brian watched her rub her upper arm.

She refused to make eye contact. "I need to be somewhere," she muttered.

"I'll give you a ride."

The scowl returned. "I'm not getting into a car with you." She held her purse across her chest like a shield. "You say you're a cop. I don't know as I believe that, badge or not."

"You wanna check me out, call Tampa PD and speak with Detective Fred Englehardt, or call Miami-Dade. Here, I'll make it easy for you. They're both on speed dial." Brian held out his phone.

Rita snorted. "I don't have time for this. I told you, I'm busy."

"Get un-busy. We need to chat. Right now."

She shot him a look filled with venom. "I don't have to talk to you. "

"Yes, you do, unless you're gonna hide behind a lawyer. Are you?"

"Well, no. I haven't done anything."

"Then stop throwing up a wall."

She looked like she was going to refuse again, but then she shrugged. "Okay. If I don't do it now, you'll probably keep coming back."

"Yep."

"But I don't want to be seen talking to you by anyone in the diner." She hovered, weight shifting from one foot to the other like she was still on the tip of running away, while worrying her bottom lip with uneven front teeth. "There's a park about two blocks from here. We can talk there."

She took off and Brian fell into step with her. "I want to talk about Mel Summerfield," he said.

"Why? You can ask anyone around here who knew her and they'll tell you the same thing."

"Which is?"

"She was ready to screw anyone and everyone."

"And did she?"

Rita colored up. "More than her share, from what I heard."

"Did you believe it?"

"Sometimes. She had a reputation she probably deserved, although she wasn't always that way."

"You went to school with her." Brian watched Rita's lips purse.

"Middle and high school, both. She wasn't that way until her sophomore year in high school. Something happened. I always wondered what. She had her sights set on one of the seniors. He played football, and he didn't pay her much attention, then he asked her to go to one of the dances. She was so happy." Rita smiled thinly. "I remember her mother wanted her to wear some frumpy dress she'd bought used. Mel said she wouldn't be seen dead in it. So she took a job sweeping up and shampooing at the local beauty salon and bought some short little dress with a low neckline. I told her it was too old for her. Too sexy. But Mel said I didn't know what men liked. She hid the dress from her mother and took it to school a couple of days before the dance. She kept it folded up in her locker. It got really creased up. She was so upset, I told her to bring it over and we'd iron it. My parents both worked evenings."

They arrived at the park. Rita made for a bench next to the brick wall of a warehouse. Shaded by a couple of spindly trees, it partially hid them from the street.

"So Mel got dressed up and went to the dance?" Brian prompted.

Rita nodded.

"And then what?"

"I don't know, but her dress was ripped when she came knocking at my window late at night." Rita looked down and ran the strap of her purse through her fingers. "Mel never said a thing about what happened. She was crying when she got into the frumpy dress and left. We barely spoke after that, not because I didn't try to be friends, but because she avoided me."

"You think she got raped," Brian said.

Rita shrugged.

"What happened after that?"

Rita shifted uncomfortably. "Do we really need to talk about this? It was so long ago."

Brian tried hard to make eye contact with her. "I need to know the truth, Rita. Chad got shot in cold blood in the middle of the day. I want to know why."

Rita stared at her lap for a good two minutes before she finally spoke again. "I heard rumors. Mel was pregnant."

"Who told you?"

"I don't remember."

"I don't believe you. She trusted you enough to go to your home and change into the dress her mother didn't want her to wear."

"Look, whatever I'm telling you, I'm not even sure it's the truth." Rita shuddered, like she had suddenly become cold.

Brian waited her out.

Rita rubbed her chin. "I don't want to send anyone to jail. Not after all this time."

"You think you know who the father of Mel's child is," Brian said.

"No. But I know who isn't." Rita massaged her temples. "Rita was going with Wally Malone's little brother before she got the big crush on the football player. Seamus was a sweet guy. A year younger than Mel and in a different school. One of those for special kids. Not special, like, you know…" She faltered.

"Not special needs," Brian interjected. "For smart kids. Gifted, they call it in the school system."

"Yeah. That's it." Rita nodded. "Seamus was the only kid around here who got to go there. We all knew he'd be the one to get out of this neighborhood. His parents weren't happy about him going with Mel. She laughed once and told me they thought she was distracting Seamus, like all he would think about without her around was his schooling. Mel said no boy would only think about that."

Brian smiled encouragingly. "Mel was right," he agreed.

Rita laid down her purse and her shoulders lowered. She looked less rigid and defensive. "The shit really hit the fan when Wally and Seamus's parents heard the rumor about Mel being pregnant. They were livid. Wally said their dad beat the crap out of his brother. But he kept telling them he wasn't responsible, and they finally believed him."

"You didn't believe it, either, did you?" Brian said. He watched her emphatically shake her head. "Still don't."

"No way. The Malones were strict Catholics." She managed a brief smile. "Wally said he had to save up and go buy a whore out of town to lose his virginity."

"So what are you saying?"

"That it sure wasn't any of the guys that tried to knock over the convenience store. They all got caught and were in jail at the time of the murder. It wasn't Mel, because she got packed off out of town to live with some aunt and uncle two days before Chad was killed."

She stopped and looked at Brian.

"Keep going," he prompted.

"Well it definitely wasn't me," Rita said. "I had nothing to do with Chad. He was way too old for me, and I was invisible to him, even when I went over to their house to hang out with Mel."

"What about Mel and Chad's parents?"

"Oh, her mom was a real peach." Rita made a face like she'd sucked on a lemon. "Mel's dad was pretty nice. He worked hard and wasn't around a whole lot. Chad had moved out on his own a few months before he was shot. Mel said it was after she and he had a big fight one afternoon. She never said what it was about."

"Are you absolutely sure she was dating Wally's younger brother?"

Rita nodded. "They started studying together because Mel needed help with math and Wally's brother was a whiz at it. He did it as a favor, because it was real easy for him. To pay him back, she took them both to the movies one Saturday. After that, they were an item. I think he was so brainy, she looked up to him. Maybe she even thought he was her ticket out of here. I don't know. He brought out the best in Mel. She always looked so cute when they were together. Very little makeup and no low-cut blouses, tight pants or short skirts."

"And yet when she went to the dance, she dressed like a slut, from what you've said."

Rita nodded. "I don't know what else to tell you. That's pretty much it."

"Did Mel contact you at all after she left? Did she come back for Chad's funeral?"

Rita shook her head. "Not a word from her. No cards, letters or calls. And there was no funeral for Chad. His parents couldn't afford it. They had him cremated and then they moved away."

"They had no other children?"

"There was a younger daughter, who was maybe ten."

"What else can you tell me, Rita?"

"Nothing. I swear." She avoided making eye contact as she stood up. "Can we be done?" She was finding her purse interesting again.

"For now."

The scowl was back.

"You should tell Wally how you feel," Brian told her.

Rita looked startled. "What do you mean?"

"I don't need to spell it out. He thinks he's too ugly to have a girl-friend. You need to set him straight."

"God, you really are a detective."

"Damn right."

Brian stayed on the bench and watched Rita until she was out of sight. She didn't run, but she definitely kept moving at a fast trot.

CHAPTER FIFTY-FIVE

THE CHINESE RESTAURANT was all but empty when Brian walked into the dining room.

"This is okay?" The hostess gestured toward a table near the front window.

"I'd prefer a booth at the back."

She bowed slightly, her face expressionless. Holding the menu against her flat chest, she continued on to the back of the restaurant, her high necked, form-fitting turquoise dress contrasting with the dim interior, illuminated only by what appeared to be paper lanterns hanging over each table. An elderly Asian couple with two small children sat at one table close to the center of the room, four men in cheap business suits huddled over bowls of soup at another table in the window, and a couple of men in overalls lounged with beers and broccoli beef.

"This is better?" The hostess gestured toward another booth at the end of the row, in the darkest corner of the dining room.

Brian noticed her brow was slightly furrowed. He figured with the noon rush over, maybe they only had one waiter, whose tables were not in the area he where he wanted to sit. Unless a bus filled with hungry tourists stopped by and they rushed into Danny Cho's restaurant within the next half-hour, he doubted whatever inconvenience he was giving the waiter couldn't be mitigated by a generous tip.

"Much." He slid into the booth.

She placed the menu in front of him and went to pick up a water glass, chopsticks and silverware from another table as the waiter appeared from the kitchen, carrying a tray loaded with steaming plates of food. He halted briefly when he saw Brian, glared at the hostess, and rapid fire conversation ensued, in what Brian thought might be Cantonese. He remembered a fellow detective who had spent years patrolling Chinatown in LA before leaving Tinseltown for Miami telling him that Cantonese sounded sharper than Mandarin, and those two were having a very sharp exchange.

Danny Cho materialized from the gloom like an apparition. A very solid and businesslike one. He descended on his two employees after a quick glance in Brian's direction. A few words from him and the heated discussion ceased. The waiter hurried to the businessmen, smiling and apologizing as he placed his loaded tray onto a serving table. The hostess returned to her post at the cash register, and Danny scooped up the items she had started to bring over to Brian.

"Hey, man. Good to see you again." Danny slid onto the bench opposite. "We've got a couple of specials you might like today." He laid Brian's chopsticks and water glass in front of him, opened the menu and presented it. "Kung pao chicken, dragon fried rice..."

"I'll take the broccoli beef today. You recommended it when I was here with Jim." Brian only glanced at the menu, noting stir-fried shrimp in garlic sauce and egg fu yong were also listed as specials of the day.

Danny smiled, evidently pleased Brian had remembered. He beckoned the waiter over and gave Brian's order. "Hot and sour or egg drop soup?"

"Hot and sour. White rice." Brian preempted the usual question over white or fried rice. "Iced tea," he added.

"I never ate lunch myself," Danny said. "Mind if I join you?"

"I'd like that. I've got a couple more questions for you." Brian watched Danny issue more orders. The waiter shot a sideways glance at Brian before leaving. He still didn't look happy.

"Rude," Danny said. "And his English is horrible. I apologize for speaking Cantonese with him, but he's the only one who applied for this position. I could hire a lot of other ethnicities, but I want Chinese wait-staff in a Chinese restaurant. Makes it more authentic."

The waiter bustled in with their soup. He spilled some of Danny's and made a big production out of mopping it up. Danny looked exasperated, but didn't comment until the man had left.

"As you see, he's not working out." Danny looked at his napkin, spotted with soup, lifted it up and waved it at the waiter, who had reappeared with a tray of water glasses. He brought over a stack of linen napkins and dumped them on the table.

Danny shook one out and placed it on his lap. "We do just enough business to keep in the black or I'd close this place." He tasted the soup and nodded his approval. "Biggest trouble with the afternoon shift is it doesn't bring in a lot of tips, so I can't keep good staff." He sighed. "Restaurants. A big pain in the ass."

Brian tasted the soup himself. It was even better than the egg drop he'd had the last time he'd eaten there. "You own more than one?"

"Three." Danny placed the menu carefully back into its place behind a red plastic tray holding a selection of soy and hot sauces. "Two in Orlando. I'd rather be there, but this was my parents' dream. We'd sell at a loss. Parents can be more of a pain than restaurants. You still have yours?"

Brian shook his head. "No. They've been gone a while."

"Sorry for your loss, man."

The broccoli beef arrived, steaming and aromatic. Brian was glad for the interruption. He wanted to get the conversation back to his investigation. He had no interest in sharing personal stories about family or business problems. His iced tea was already sugared. Another strike against Danny's waiter, but Brian was pretty thirsty and drank it right down.

"The big thing going for this restaurant is the lack of competition," Danny said as a bowl mounded with white rice landed on the table with a crash. He glowered at the waiter, who glowered back before putting the broccoli beef platter down slowly and quietly. "Everything else around here is either a diner serving meat loaf and gravy or fried chicken. Otherwise it's fast food...mostly burgers. Anyone who wants atmosphere and a bigger menu comes here."

Brian nodded and helped himself to the rice when Danny pushed the dish toward him. "I wanted to ask you more questions about the Summerfields."

"Sure, man. Anything."

Danny watched the hostess seat a couple of men in painters' overalls at a table close to the elderly couple, who started sniffing the air. He beckoned to the hostess, spoke in a low voice and had her move the painters to a booth. She got a couple of beers from the bar and delivered them to the tradespeople, who stopped looking disgruntled.

Brian watched the interaction between Danny and his hostess. "Does she know you're married?"

"Yeah, man." Danny took a large serving of broccoli beef. He leaned forward. "My old lady's gonna take a meat cleaver to me, she finds out, but she's busy taking care of our other restaurants. I can't afford to divorce her. She'd take half of everything. So I screw this one and tell the other one how much I love her. Life is fucked up, man."

Brian thought he'd just met the real Danny Cho, instead of the polite businessman who had offered him the daily specials. "You're right, there."

They ate silently for a few minutes.

"So, what can you tell me about Chad Summerfield and his family that you wouldn't talk about in front of my partner?" Brian asked.

Danny put down his chopsticks. "What makes you think I didn't tell you everything the last time?"

Brian shrugged. "Call it a cop's intuition. You and Chad were close in age and lived next door to each other. You must have hung out."

"For a while." Danny, who had been eating with gusto, looked down at his plate and pushed it aside. "One day he suggested something that I knew was wrong." He stopped, beckoned the hostess over and asked for a beer.

"What?" Brian prompted.

"Chad asked me if I liked his sister. I said sure. Mel was pretty, and she wore tight clothes. You could see her ass shaking in those pants, and those tits..." He shook his head. "They were big and I couldn't take my eyes off them. I'd wanted to ask her out, but my parents were real traditional and frowned on me dating white chicks."

The hostess brought him a bottle of Tsingtao and a frosted glass. "You sticking with that tea?" Danny asked, waving the bottle.

"Yeah, for now. But without the sugar, thanks." He looked up at the hostess. She nodded and went into the kitchen.

Danny drank half the beer without stopping, put the glass down and wiped the back of his hand across his mouth.

"Chad said he could fix us up." Danny grimaced at the memory. "Said Mel liked me, too, because I was different. She liked different." He finished the beer. "So I went over to their house one afternoon. Mel was in her bedroom. We started talking about music, but we moved pretty quickly into kissing, and then I started feeling her up and she didn't stop me. I was so excited. My culture, we barely even got to kiss before the wedding, those days." He shook his head. "I thought I was ready. I'd stolen one of my sister's bras and practiced unhooking it, but that damned push-up thing Mel had on, with the underwire getting in my way, like some friggin' piece of armor plating, made me fumble around like the amateur I was. I couldn't get in from the top or the bottom. Mel was laughing. She told me to pop the fastenings at the back and just get it off her." He swallowed hard. "God, I wanted that. My dreams were all coming true. I was sure I was about to lose my virginity." He sighed, his head down. "You want your first time to go like that."

Brian wasn't sure where this was going, but he waited Danny's silence out.

Danny looked up, his eyes haunted; his mouth a grim line. "And then my dream took one bad turn. Suddenly, the door opened and in came Chad, like he had been listening outside."

"That must have been one hell of a moment."

Danny dabbed his brow. "Yeah, man. All these years later, I still get a stab in my gut when I think of it."

He wiped his mouth again, that time with his napkin. His hand looked a little shaky. The once cool and calm restaurateur was squirming. The hostess had paused to watch him, but Brian knew Danny Cho was deep in his memories, and oblivious to his mistress's reaction.

"Chad started throwing punches, like he didn't know what would happen with me going into Mel's bedroom," Danny said, his voice low and strained, like the words were being dragged out of a deep, dark place inside him. He was staring at the wall.

Brian believed the middle-aged man had left the present behind and was reliving a pivotal moment in his past. The clatter of dishes and the low murmur of adult conversations, punctuated by high-pitched chatter from the two Asian children, contrasted with the mood hovering around Cho.

"I didn't realize how strong he was until he picked me up by the scruff of the neck, like some dog, and threw me out the door."

Danny's voice had gained strength. He waved his hands around, his tone angry. Brian kept quiet, and it seemed the diners and the staff were all waiting with him for the conclusion of Danny's story, as even the children were subdued, their grandparents gathering their coloring books and crayons as they stood to leave.

"I could hear him shouting at Mel and her screaming back at him while I was picking myself up," Danny continued. "I left that house and never spoke to either of them again. I heard she got pregnant and moved away." He threw the napkin down and looked at Brian for the first time since he had started his story. "I bet there were plenty of candidates for the father." He planted his elbows on the table and wagged one finger. "At least I wasn't one of them, man."

He beckoned to the hostess and she hurriedly brought him another beer along with Brian's tea.

Brian thought of Danny's humiliation. He thought of Mel and Chad. Of Chad maybe not understanding what his sister was until that day. Of Mel getting pregnant and possibly not even knowing who the father was. Of Mel moving away and staying gone for years, until she and her daughter lost their jobs and returned to the family home.

She must have thought the past was behind her when she came back to Miami. But then Ted had talked about Chad's murder with their neighbor, the detective with enough time on his hands to start poking around in a case that had long gone cold, and maybe Mel had become afraid that an old, buried secret might surface. Perhaps she even knew who had murdered her brother, or had taken some part in the crime. Brian well knew what rage at a sibling could do. The day he had pushed his brother into the dirt had been the first and last time he had touched

Tim in anger. Maybe Mel had found a different, deadlier way to stop her brother from meddling in her life.

They finished their food in silence. Danny ordered a brandy. Brian sipped black coffee that tasted like it had been scraped out of the bottom of the pot. Danny refused to let him pay and invited him to bring Jim back for another meal on the house any time. Brian got Danny to agree to make a statement to Fred Engelhardt.

But before calling Fred to update him on the case's progress, Brian was going back to Best Pic for that pow-wow with Tab Benford.

CHAPTER FIFTY-SIX

BRIAN PUSHED OPEN the door to Tab's little office.

Tab put down the remains of his sandwich. "You again. What do you want?" His chair scraped back on the worn linoleum and he stood, fear clearly plastered across his face. "Oh, God. They know, don't they?"

Brian realized Tab thought he'd been found out and his former childhood friends were coming to get him at any minute.

"No, they don't. Sit down. Relax." He wasn't sure if he found Tab's reaction amusing or sad. He'd never been afraid of dealing with anyone's attempts at retribution, and had trouble empathizing with Tab's fears. "I came back to clear up a few details, that's all." Without waiting for an invitation, he sat on the uncomfortable chair in front of the manager's desk.

Tab wiped both hands over his face. "You scared the crap out of me."

"My specialty. What can I say?" Brian shrugged when Tab gave him an incredulous look.

"I've never liked cops." Tab glared, as though to make sure Brian really understood that comment. "And despite what you said about helping me, I don't know if I believe you'll change my mind, especially when you pop in here unannounced. What details?"

Brian leaned back. "I interviewed the rest of those would-be convenience store robbers. A few things don't jibe."

"It's been a long time." Tab carefully rolled the paper back around pungent tuna on a hoagie bun and shoved it into the paper sack beside his elbow. "We've all got our own recollections of how things were. Sometimes I remember things differently than my wife. Especially arguments. She always feels like I'm in the losing corner. I don't."

"I'm not interested in what goes on between you and your wife. As far as that stick-up's concerned, those differences better not be poles apart." Brian watched Tab's face mask over. "That convenience store thing should have remained real clear in all of your minds, unless you planned to knock over stores on a regular basis."

"Not me. Hell, no." Tab's attempt to hide his expression fell by the wayside. He looked stricken. "I've told you what I know about the murder. I wasn't even in Tampa when that happened. And the stupid convenience store thing was a one-timer. I swear."

"I damned well hope so." Brian pulled his chair right up to the desk and leaned his forearms on it, pushing Tab's phone and pen holder aside. "I didn't hear anything that lined up. Makes me believe either one or all of you are lying."

"Not me." Tab's eyes were wide, like a startled rabbit's." I told you the whole truth."

"And nothing but?" Brian shook his head. "Let's get down to the real facts. How old were you again?"

"Thirteen," Tab said without hesitation. "For both the shooting *and* the convenience store."

"Which were only a week apart. Lotta trauma for a thirteen-year-old."

"Yeah. Mom was really glad she hiked me out of there when she did, even though we left everything behind. Looking back now, I realize there wasn't much to leave."

"Where did you say you ended up?"

"Living with my grandmother. She straightened me out. No more being unsupervised while my mom was at work. She rode me hard...homework, chores, cleaning my room. By the time Mom came home for supper, I was so tired I never gave her a hard time about my early bedtime."

"What was your name before your mom changed it?"

"Lonnie Fescue. Sounded like some new strain of grass seed. I hated it." Tab shook his head. "A lot of good things came out of that stupid hold-up attempt. Getting out of this neighborhood, getting a new name I halfway liked, although the Tab part sits better with me now than it did when I was younger. People have forgotten Tab Hunter for the most part." He smiled. "Except my mom. She still has a crush on that actor."

"Does your wife know about your past?" Brian watched Tab's mood deflate again.

"Not everything. She doesn't know about the stick-up, and I don't want her finding out from you, either."

"She won't unless I think it's absolutely necessary. But you'd be better off not keeping secrets. Things have a way of working their way to the surface whether you want them to or not."

Brian thought of his own circumstances, which were definitely working on cracking the surface. He felt dampness on his palms and wiped them on the knees of his pants.

"So," he told Tab, "let's backtrack. Did you see anyone acting suspiciously when you came to the grocery store in the weeks before the murder? Hanging around? Sitting in a car and watching the place?"

Tab shook his head. "All I had on my mind the two weeks before Chad's murder was a permission slip I wanted my mom to sign so I could go with my class to Busch Gardens. A trip we'd all saved our allowances for all year. I'd been doing extra chores at home and helping out some old lady with taking out her trash and going grocery shopping with her. I pushed the cart and put everything up for her. She paid me a quarter for the trash and fifty cents for the grocery trip. I thought I'd have enough saved, but I had a weakness for candy and ice cream." He smiled, apologetically it seemed, as though all those years later, he felt bad about his poor saving practices.

"I had a thing for corn nuts," Brian said. "I wonder I didn't break all my teeth."

"My sweet tooth resulted in cavities." Tab looked crestfallen, like he was thirteen again. "My mom wasn't happy, until she found a cheap dentist. That guy never used Novocain. She said that was my punishment. I've never eaten candy since."

Brian nodded. "So, you were distracted, and you didn't notice anything on the way to the store the day of the murder?"

"Yep." Tab leaned back in his chair. "I figured she'd say no. We had no extra money to make up the difference between what I'd saved and the actual cost. I'd flunked my math test, too. Bad grades really got her riled up. More than me hanging out with my friends after school and coming home late, even though she didn't much care for them. Chico in particular. Said he was too old to be my friend. I think she was afraid he was a gang member, too."

Finally, all the meandering around had reached a point Brian could use to his advantage. "Was he?"

Tab tapped a pen on the edge of his empty coffee cup, reminding Brian suddenly of Hal Shaw, who always tapped a pen against his desk when he was perturbed. But Tab's expression looked thoughtful, not angry.

"I don't think so," Tab said. "Although he'd already gotten a couple of tats, and he was starting to talk and act tough. Chico's home life was no walk in the park. He grew up in a rough, crowded apartment. His mom had a lot of boyfriends. According to Chico, half of them slapped him around or told him to get the hell out of there while they were visiting. He got food that was about to get thrown out of restaurants because he wasn't given any money when he was kicked out of the house. People saw him on the street so frequently, they thought he was homeless, which I guess he mostly was."

"So, he needed money. Was he the one who planned the robbery?"

"No. That was Wally. Chico used to go over to the garage where he works now and watch the mechanics fixing cars so he could get somewhere warm. He slept there sometimes. They'd close up the shop and leave him inside. He'd bed down in one of the cars and have coffee going when the owner got there to open up in the morning. He started handing tools to the mechanics. Pretty soon they were teaching him how to fix stuff. He really learned how to do things from the ground up. The owner kind of adopted Chico after that. Set up a cot for him in the back of the break room. Pretty soon Chico stopped trying to go home, and then he quit school and worked at the shop full time."

"So why the hell would he screw things up?" Brian felt genuine curiosity. A kid like himself, he thought, who got help in the right places and could have gone on to make something of himself.

"He had gotten some old car he was fixing up. I think he still owed the guy he bought it from, and then there were the parts from the garage to pay for. His back was kind of to the wall." Tab looked down at the desktop. "Ultimately, though, they all got screwed because of me chickening out and running off screaming."

"Sounds like maybe you did them all a favor instead," Brian said. "Stopped them from a life of crime and gang activity."

Tab's head shot up, his expression hopeful instead of grim and shuttered. "You think?"

Brian nodded, sitting back, arms folded. He stretched his legs out, making himself look relaxed and comfortable, friendly and non-threatening. One of his favorite interrogation tactics.

He had Tab in his pocket. The guy was so eager to make amends to everyone, he was as pliable as putty.

"If they'd carried out the robbery and gotten caught, they'd have done a lot more time." He leaned forward, putting an earnest expression on his face. "And what if the gun had gone off, even accidentally?"

Tab shuddered. "I guess you're right, looking at it your way. But those guys would never accept that excuse. They'd never forgive me."

"How'd you know? Did you ask them?"

"No way. What do you think I am, a complete moron with a death wish?"

"No."

Brian suddenly felt as earnest as his expression. Tab and his friends had really fucked their lives up, and unexpectedly, he had put himself in a position to maybe fix some of the issues. He'd never thought of himself as anything close to a social worker, but he no longer lived in an emotional void where anger was his only outlet.

"But," he said gently, mindful that Tab's emotions might be about as raw as his own when Tim died, "I think you've spent years blaming yourself for something your friends brought on themselves. Don't forget a lot of water's gone under the bridge since that day. The kids you knew may be a lot more mature than you give them credit for...you still think of them as teenage punks."

Fuck, he sounded like Fleming.

"Tommy Spiro's married with two kids. Chico's worked a steady job at that same place since he got released. I won't say they probably think fondly of you, but they might be willing to forgive.'

Shit, he was giving Tab the same crap commiserating lines he got from his shrink on a weekly basis. Was it really working?

"So what was the name of the other kid who ran away from the convenience store?" he asked casually.

Tab blanched. His fingers stilled, leaving curled edges on old spreadsheets he had piled in front of him. "What kid?" His voice was faint and held a slight quiver.

"Tommy said someone brought a gun. Chico didn't mention the gun. Neither did Wally. Was it yours?"

"No way!" Tab's demeanor completely crumpled. Sweat trickled freely down his face. "It was that other kid. Mix, or whatever his name was." He opened a drawer in his desk, pulled out a crumpled bunch of napkins and wiped his brow. "Some kid Wally knew, who was in some other school. He brought the gun because Tommy couldn't get one after all. Tommy's father had a gun safe and kept the key around his neck. Tommy thought his dad took it off at night, but found out he was wrong. He tried going into his parents' bedroom to cut it off, but his dad woke up and thought Tommy was trying to steal his wallet. Tommy got the paddling of his life. So we had to improvise. We all handled that gun so we'd know how to use it. I wonder we didn't blow our heads off."

"Yeah," Brian nodded. "I know how that goes. My brother and I did much the same thing with my stepfather's gun."

"We were idiots," Tab said. "Our only plan was to go into the store, point the gun at the clerk and tell him to empty the till. It was crazy. Tommy was waving the gun around like it was a toy. Wally took it from him and put it on the dash in plain sight. That's when that other kid got out of the car, said he was going around the corner to take a leak, took off running and never came back."

"He chickened out," Brian said.

"Or smartened up." Tab sighed deeply. "You'll have to ask the others what his real name was. More than one of them must have known him well, or he wouldn't have been included."

"Bringing a gun may have been enough to include him in anything."

"That's true."

"Did your mom see what was going on?"

"She saw enough to figure out why I was screaming." Tab rubbed a hand over his face. "She dragged me into a little shop. I'd never even noticed it before. Hardware. Narrow aisles with shelves full of tools on both sides. Looked ready to fall down if you breathed wrong. Mom ran me down one of those aisles with her fingers digging into me so hard I had bruises all over my arm. She got up to the counter and stopped long enough to yell about there being a robbery about to happen at the Mini Mart. The owner must have called the cops, or maybe the clerk at the Mini Mart did. Maybe both of them. Whatever." He wiped his face again. "Mom hauled me out the back of the store and kept going until we reached the bus station. She bought tickets on a bus that was leaving in five minutes and called my grandmother collect to tell her we were on our way and never coming back to Tampa."

"So what happened to the gun?"

"I heard Chico or Wally threw it in a dumpster while they were running."

"And the cops never recovered it."

Tab shrugged. "I never heard another thing about it."

"Then how come you knew about the gun getting thrown, and where the guys work now?"

"I had a friend, Billy Nixon. I called him while Mom and my grandma were at the movies. I was supposed to be doing chores and my homework, but I wanted to find out what had happened after we left town, so I went to the pay phone on the corner. That was the only call I made. I felt real bad about the guys getting caught, and scared, too. I figured they'd get out and come after me if they knew where I'd gone, but they didn't. Then when I found out I was going to have to come back here, I paid some private dick to find out where the guys were now. Cost me five hundred, but it was worth it. I can keep my distance from them that way."

Brian shook his head. "You really think they'd beat you up if they knew you were back in the 'hood?"

"Maybe kill me." Tab wiped his hands on his pants. "Chico looks like he could do it. The PI took photos."

"You were thirteen," Brian said. "A kid. This was over twenty years ago."

"Memories are long around here." Tab looked at his watch. "I've got a conference call in five minutes, and I need to take a leak. Are we done here?"

"Yeah." Brian stood. "Talk to them," he said. "Before you leave here. Don't let this hang over you any longer."

"No damn way." Tab got up, too.

"You ever see Chad's sister around here?" Brian asked.

"Mel?"

"Yeah."

"A few times." Tab headed for the door. "She used to hang around the diner where Tommy works. He used to wash dishes there after school."

"Did she have a boyfriend?"

Tab frowned with concentration either over the question or his bladder discomfort. "Yeah, I heard she did but I never saw her with him. I thought she was after Tommy. She sure used to flirt with him. We went to the diner for dinner sometimes as a treat, and I'd see her at the counter, swinging back and forth on a stool, her short skirt riding up. My mom caught me looking one time and made me switch seats so I couldn't watch."

Brian thought of Mel swinging on the stool in the *NTK*. She'd perfected that move at an early age and honed her flirting skills with a lot more guys than Danny Cho.

"Did you ever hear the name of that boyfriend?"

"Uh, uh." Tab shook his head. "But I think Chad's family didn't like her going with him."

"Why would you say that?"

"I heard her crying in the stock room one time. She was with her brother." Tab abruptly got up and walked toward the door. "I've gotta hit the head right now."

Brian followed him. "What were you doing back here?"

"The same thing I'm about to do now. I was in a hurry. All I heard was Chad telling her that's what she got for going with some hick. Then he said he was sorry for saying that and he was holding her tight and kissing her face. I thought it was gross."

He threw open the bathroom door and left Brian to watch the door swing back into place behind him. Brian stood in the hallway and wondered how reliable Tab's memory was all those years later.

As soon as he got into his car he called Jim. "Are you still with the Chesneys?"

"No, but we've got some bombshell news," Jim said. "We're only about ten minutes from the office. We're picking up lunch. You want a sandwich?"

"No, thanks, I ate Chinese." Brian pulled out of the parking lot. "I just wrapped up another interview with Tab. I can be there in fifteen." He heard Kaylen's voice in the background.

"She says there's a New York style deli a couple of blocks from the office," Jim said.

"Okay, but hurry the hell up," Brian said. "Sorry," he added. "I've got a breakthrough of my own. Don't let Kaylen get sidetracked."

"No way," Jim said. "She's as eager to spill the beans as I am, but we're both starving."

Brian wondered if the bombshell news was bigger than his own.

CHAPTER FIFTY-SEVEN

"Incest." Kaylen waved her turkey on rye. "If I wasn't so hungry, I'd be too disgusted to eat."

"Me, too." Jim put down the remains of his egg salad on wheat and dusted off his hands, like he wanted to brush something nastier from them than bread crumbs.

"I don't know how you do this day in, day out, Brian," Kaylen said. "I thought this was going to be fun, interviewing people and trying to shake loose old memories. I never expected Nola to drop that one on me."

"She wouldn't have dropped it on anyone else," Jim said. "You got to her." He looked over at Brian. "Kaylen was real good. Like a pro."

"Don't get any ideas," Brian told her. "One interview. That was it."

"I know; I know." Kaylen lifted her Diet Coke and took a long suck on her straw. "No worries on that score. Today was enough for me. You can be the detective. I'll be content to stick with being a club owner and social media fodder. And you didn't even need me to hire you an admin assistant." She raised her plastic cup. "Congrats on hiring Gabe. He's the best man for the job."

"You don't feel slighted?" Brian felt relieved when Kaylen smiled.

"Not in the least. Whoever I picked probably wouldn't have lasted more than a few days. From what you've told me about Gabe, he can hold his own with a whole squad of cantankerous cops."

"So what do we do now?" Jim tossed the remains of his meal into a nearby trash can. "Is it time to call in the cavalry?"

Brian nodded. "I'll call Fred Engelhardt, update him on what we found, and let him get written statements from all these people. Good job, Jim, getting that video-taped interview with Lester Chesney. But we're far from done. Mel had at least one boyfriend. Probably more. One of them was Wally Malone's little brother, Seamus. But Rita said he wasn't the father of Mel's baby. She said the Malones were strict Catholics. Tab said he heard Chad call the kid a hick. That was a strange thing to say about anyone in this neighborhood. Then there's the kid who ran off before the convenience store robbery attempt. According to Tab, his name was Mix. That's either one kid with two names or two kids with very similar names. Doesn't sit well with me."

"He's either lying and getting his names mixed up or his memory's just plain faulty," Jim said.

"Maybe a bit of both." Kaylen finished her soda and took another big bite of her pastrami on rye sandwich.

"We need to find out. Lean on him harder." Brian started pacing. "I need to find out more about Mel's love-life. Rita gave me a fair amount of info, but she was talking about Mel having a crush on some high school footballer, name unknown. The rest of the convenience store gang's stories don't completely match up. I got conflicting details out of them, and not one of them owns up to knowing what happened to the gun. They're all still lying, dammit." He ran his right hand over his face. "Christ, this is confusing and frustrating."

"You think the same gun was used to kill Chad?" Jim asked.

"I think it's highly likely. Supposedly Wally, or Chico, depending on who's telling the story, tossed the gun into a dumpster, where it could have been picked up later by whoever shot and killed Chad. Or maybe Wally or Chico told someone else where to find it. There's still a big piece of missing evidence, and it's the damned gun. All these years later, we'll never find it unless someone talks and tells us where it's hidden."

"You think it's still around?" Kaylen had finished her sandwich and was working her way through a bag of potato chips.

Brian wanted to smile. Funny how investigations could make some people ravenously hungry and others lose their appetites. Kaylen never ate junk food, other than packets of crackers. He watched as she finished her own bag of chips and looked over at Jim's open bag of SunChips. Jim slid the bag over to her. Kaylen dove in and started munching.

"Could be," Brian said. "Under floorboards; in someone's attic." He thought about Tommy Spiro hiding evidence in the rafters.

"One nasty souvenir," Jim said.

Kaylen's phone rang. She glanced at it and got up. "I have to take this. It's the club." She walked out into the reception area.

"I'm really glad Gabe's coming up here," Jim said. "I haven't made much headway with the rest of the copying, and I don't like leaving the office empty during the day, even if it's locked."

Brian nodded. "I agree. That front lock could be picked in a heartbeat." He cleared away the remains of Kaylen's lunch. He could hear a low murmur from the outer office. Evidently something was up or she would have been back already. "I still can't believe Nola Chesney gave Kaylen all that information."

"She was right about one woman telling another," Jim said. "Nola told Kaylen she hadn't even said anything to her husband." He shook his head. "Makes me wonder what secrets my wife kept from me. Better not to dwell too much on that. Nothing to be done now."

"You're right on that score." Brian sat and leaned back in his chair, staring again at the names on the whiteboard.

"Kaylen almost got found out as an imposter," Jim said. "Nola's a big fan of fashion magazines. She recognized Kaylen's high end shoes." He chuckled. "Kaylen told her she found them in a consignment shop. I always knew Kaylen was smart, but she outdid herself with that one."

"She's always surprising me," Brian said. "She's one of a kind."

Jim nodded. "That she is, buddy. You remember that."

His candid gaze made Brian uncomfortable. Sometimes what Jim didn't say was as powerful as what he did. The inference was unmistakable. Brian should be treating Kaylen much better and cementing their relationship a lot faster. Jim had told him before there would be no one better for him than Kaylen and asked what he was waiting for. She'd already given him an invitation to move in together. What the hell was he doing, living on the *NTK?*

The door swung back open. Kaylen stood on the threshold. "I have to go back to Miami," she said.

CHAPTER FIFTY-EIGHT

"ASAP," Kaylen said." I already called and got booked on a flight leaving in two and a half hours. Thank goodness I can afford first class, because that was the only open seat. Shelley Summerfield is as bad as her mother. Rob and Julio are already fighting over her, and both of them are threatening to resign. What is it with men? Can't they realize that a relationship needs more than a week to become something permanent?"

Brian thought about the speed with which he and Kaylen had fallen into their own relationship. He thought about the long hours Rob and Julio had spent at Bannisters, dedicating themselves to helping Kaylen build her business, and how important they both were to her continuing success.

"I have to call Fred Engelhardt," he said. "Then I'll take you back to the hotel to pack."

"I can do that." Jim got up. "You finish up what you need to do here."

"I'll only make a brief stop at the hotel. I can take a cab from there to the airport." Kaylen picked up her purse and sweater. "I'm not expecting either of you to drop everything. You've had a huge breakthrough."

"Are you sure?" Brian wanted to be supportive, but his work pulled at him, and the familiar tug felt like he was coming to life after a long period in darkness.

"Of course." She kissed his cheek quickly, her fingers resting on his arm.

At her touch, Brian felt more than a coming to life. The pull to be with her was almost stronger than the need to close Chad Summerfield's case.

"I'll meet you downstairs in a few minutes," Jim said. "I could do with a short walk. Stretch my legs." He left.

"He's such a wonderful man," Kaylen said.

"He's too old for you. Don't get any ideas about abandoning me. I don't care how old George was."

Kaylen giggled and slid her arms around his waist. "I won't."

Brian kissed her. He missed her already. He pulled her shirt out of her pants and ran his hands up her back. Kaylen didn't protest when he cupped her breasts. He slid her shirt over her head. Unfastened her bra and drew the straps down her arms. Cast the garment onto a chair.

"You'd better lock the door," she managed between kisses. Her breathing was as fast as his.

"You're sure?" He hesitated, fighting his need. In answer, Kaylen's hands ran through his hair and she pulled his head down, thrusting her breasts toward his mouth.

He wasn't sure what had come over both of them, but somehow he managed to get the door locked while she was caressing him and pulling down his zipper. He took her lying across the table, their pants still around their ankles, her skimpy white lace bikini panties ripped to shreds when they got in his way.

Afterward, he lifted her to her feet and kissed her softly. "Not a very romantic goodbye."

She kissed him back, a lot less gently. "Sometimes, when you touch me, I don't want romance. I need satisfaction, and you always give me that. Good God, you do."

She nuzzled his neck, her nails sliding across his chest and threatening to arouse him again. There wasn't time. They both knew that. And then there was Jim, walking around the parking lot...

Kaylen sighed and glanced at the clock ticking the seconds away on the wall behind Brian's head. "I have to leave. We never get enough time together." She looked down at the remains of her panties. "Well, these have seen their last wearing."

"Yep, they're ruined all right."

He watched her kick off her shoes and pants. She stuffed the tattered undies into his pocket as he picked up her bra.

"Something else to remember me by," she said, and then she laughed, her laughter as pleasing as a gentle shower of warm rain. She dressed quickly. Brian regretted the fact they couldn't be together that night.

"You stay away from Ziggy," he warned. "And although I know you'll fix things between Rob and Julio, if you need support, call me. Ask *them* to call me. No, forget asking. *Tell* them to call me. I'll threaten them or something."

"Don't you *dare*. I'll have the labor board on my back." She kissed him again, but chastely. "I'm really leaving this time."

Brian watched her with regret and longing as she pulled a clip out of her purse and caught her unruly hair inside it, anchoring the curls at the base of her neck. She blew him another kiss, mouthed 'I love you,' and ran out the door without a backward glance, her subtle perfume lingering.

She hadn't waited for him to tell her he loved her back.

He took a really deep breath before calling Fred Engelhardt.

CHAPTER FIFTY-NINE

KAYLEN TOOK a cab to Bannisters straight from the airport. She felt angry, exasperated and let-down. Rob had told her he could handle the club...endlessly told her...only to prove he actually couldn't handle anything at all. Even as she thought about firing him, she knew his behavior was completely uncharacteristic and wondered what it was about those Summerfield women that made them so irresistible.

Troublemakers, she thought as she paid the cabbie and stepped out in front of her club. She pulled up the handle of her carry-on bag and rolled it behind her to the side door, glad she had left her larger suitcase behind. Brian would bring it back with him on Thursday, and she really only needed her makeup and toiletries. She had showered and changed clothes quickly at the hotel, smiling to herself as she pulled on fresh underwear. She hoped Brian wouldn't forget the gift in his pocket and inadvertently pull out shredded bikini panties when he met with the Tampa detective.

Unlocking the deadbolt, she pushed the side door open and walked into the subdued lighting of the club. She had preferred to get a general feel for the atmosphere instead of announcing her presence by dragging her bag through the front entrance. Busboys and servers moved quietly between tables, laying cloths and tableware from carts piled high with snow white linens, silverware racks and chargers. Marvin was taking inventory of dishes and glassware, no doubt weighing whether he needed to order replacements for the breakages and losses that inevitably occurred in any busy restaurant. He looked up and nodded to her. No smile. He must know something was wrong, since she wasn't expected back for another couple of days.

"Hi, Marvin." She pulled her bag in his direction. "Where's Rob?"

"In his office, I think." Marvin put down his clipboard. "It's been a bit tense around here. I'm glad you're back."

"Rob called me. Where's Julio?"

"He said he had an appointment, but he'd be back in an hour."

Kaylen looked at her watch: 4:30 PM. "What time did he leave?"

"Twenty minutes ago. He said he'll be back before the bar opens."

He'd better, Kaylen thought. If he was off interviewing for another job, she'd be furious. Her highly-compensated head bartender needed to have a level of loyalty that transcended arguing with her manager over some server. She dropped off her bag and purse in her own office before walking across the hallway to Rob's. His door was cracked open. She gave a cursory knock and entered, finding him sitting behind his desk, his head in his hands.

"What's going on?" She sat on a chair in front of his desk.

"I'm really sorry…" he began.

"Don't give me excuses or tell me you're sorry, Rob. I want to know what happened between you and Shelley and Shelley and Julio that has you two guys fighting like a pair of adolescents."

Rob sat back. His expression shifted from contrite to angry. "She cried on my shoulder about her family. I felt sorry for her. I took her out to dinner and one thing led to another…"

"Spare me the details," Kaylen said. "You took her to bed?"

Rob nodded. "Totally out of character for me. I usually avoid entanglements with coworkers. I don't know what came over me."

"I can imagine what, unfortunately." Kaylen thought of Mel. She'd had less success with Brian, but then, he was made of something like forged steel. Rob had a softer heart and seemingly, less experience with manipulation. "So how did Julio get involved?"

"Apparently, Shelley did a repeat performance with him the following night."

"And you two compared notes?"

"No. Her mother came to the club and made an ugly scene. Said we had both taken advantage of her daughter. Then Shelley came in and it got even worse. Things got thrown…"

Kaylen thought of Marvin's inventory. "Let me guess…dishes, glassware…"

"Both. Then Mel said she was taking Shelley home and their attorney would be in touch. Sexual harassment, she called it. Julio blamed me. I blamed him. We shoved each other around. Marvin got between us. Julio said he was going to quit. I said he didn't need to do that. I told him as manager, I was the one who should resign. We haven't spoken since."

"And now he's at some appointment an hour before the bar opens." Kaylen got up. "I'm going to talk to my attorney, and then he can contact Shelley and Mel, if warranted. I've heard nothing about any suit, so I'm thinking Mel was blowing hot air. When Julio comes back, you let me know immediately. I'll meet with both of you. I can't believe I hired that girl and created such a mess for myself. I never should have done it. I was so stupid, thinking I could handle things without being here."

"I've let everyone down." Rob looked at an envelope sitting in the middle of the otherwise cleared desk. "You, your business, myself." He pushed the envelope across the desk. "There's no sense in you wasting any more time on this. Here's my resignation."

"Oh, stop being so melodramatic." Kaylen tore the envelope into pieces without opening it. "Get back to work and remember management can still be a learning curve. Heck, so can ownership. I'm not firing anyone or accepting resignations, except Shelley's."

She went into her office, closed the door and called her attorney, who assured her he would be happy to take care of matters for her, should they come to that. He suggested he accompany her to see Mel and Shelley. Kaylen wished Brian had come back with her, and told the attorney she'd call him back. She pulled up the staffing roster and found Shelley wasn't scheduled that evening. *Thank goodness for small favors.* After looking in Shelley's personnel file, Kaylen called her cell phone, which went directly to voicemail.

She left a terse message asking Shelley to call her back ASAP, then checked back in with Marvin and got a detailed run-down on some issues with the wait-staff. Never a dull moment in a supper club, she thought with a wry smile. She returned to her office and sat to regroup.

Drumming her fingers on the desk, she decided she'd have to call another cab to go home and pick up her car after meeting with Rob and Julio. Then she'd go to the marina. She could check the *Need to Know* and Jim's *Fanciful Folly*. If Shelley called back, that might also be a better place to meet than the club, as long as the girl didn't bring her mother along. Kaylen figured she'd be able to handle one Summerfield woman. She wasn't sure about handling two of them.

Kaylen checked her smartphone and realized she had forgotten to turn it back on after the flight. She sent a quick text to Brian, letting him know she had arrived back safely, and found two messages: Angela Crossfield and Ziggy Stavros. Angela wondered if Kaylen and Brian were available for dinner Friday evening. Ziggy wanted to meet when Kaylen had time. All the necessary arrangements had been made. He had leased the restaurant space and was ready to order equipment. Could Kaylen check in with him?

Kaylen sent a text to Angela. She wasn't sure if Brian would be in Miami on Friday, since he was still working his case in Tampa. She'd call Angela after taking care of some club business. She was debating on her best course for getting her car when Rob put his head around her partially-open door and mouthed that Julio was back.

CHAPTER SIXTY

"I INTERVIEWED FOR ANOTHER JOB." Julio sat back in his chair and crossed his arms. "Then I thought about how stupid I was, even considering going to work somewhere else, because Rob and I had a shoving match over a server." He looked at Rob. "What am I, eighteen and back in the barrio, trying to assert myself over a rival? I've got a future here, if I haven't blown it."

Rob returned Julio's gaze before looking at Kaylen on the other side of the desk. "I thought much the same thing," he said. "I apologize. I acted completely unprofessionally. I still think I should resign."

"Neither of you is resigning, or getting fired, either. You *are* getting written warnings placed in your files, though, and understand that if anything even close to this ever happens again, you're out of here without a reference. I'm firing Shelley as soon as I get hold of her. Before she came, there were no staff issues."

"She needs this job," Rob interrupted. "Again, this is all my fault..."

Kaylen held up her hand. "No interruptions. I just had a conversation with Marvin, and he had to counsel one of our junior servers for drinking on the premises. Ben said right before he went off shift, he had a glass of wine with Shelley from an open bottle that had been bussed from a table. She told him it would be okay, and then she kissed him

335

before she went home. Marvin told him he has to join AA and attend meetings every night he's not scheduled to work. Ben just turned twenty-one before he came to work here five months ago. Shelley's four years older and knows better. She's out to cause trouble, and that's not going any further."

"Thank you," Rob said. "That makes me feel marginally better."

"I'll second that." Julio leaned forward, his hands on the arms of his chair. "It's after five. I should go prove my value to you and the club."

"Fine." Kaylen nodded. "Go back to work. And keep your mind and your eyes on the bar. That means keep the flirting to a minimum. I don't want any gossip about your behavior with my female customers."

"Yes, Ma'am." He got to his feet and smoothed his tight pants.

Kaylen watched Julio's slightly swaggering walk as he left her office. "He's a handful," she said.

"A talented handful," Rob amended. "One of these days, he's going out on his own."

"So the other bartenders need to know how to mix every one of his specials."

"I'll make sure they do. Discrete observation," Rob said. "I should get back to my office. I've got some performance evals to finish up, then I'll bring them in to discuss with you. A couple of the servers need raises. Ben's training is about finished, but then there was that incident you just talked about."

"He's got a good future with Bannisters, as long as he doesn't make any other stupid mistakes," Kaylen said. "I hand-picked him. He was too smart and efficient to remain a busboy."

"I'll make sure Marvin takes him under his wing." Rob stood, and then hesitated. "If you don't mind me asking, how's Brian doing? I haven't seen him lately."

"He's doing well, still investigating a case up in Tampa." Kaylen smiled. "Getting back to work was the best thing for him."

Rob pointed to the little sink beside Kaylen's refrigerator and mini bar on his way out the door. "He must miss you."

Kaylen saw a large bouquet of red and white roses sitting in a glass vase, resting inside the sink. "Why didn't you put them on the desk?"

She realized she was talking to herself when she heard Rob's office door close. As she lifted the vase out of the sink, water flowed down the sides. Hurriedly, she stepped back before her clothes got splashed and poured some water out, wiping off the base with a bar towel before taking the arrangement over to her desk. Puzzled, she turned the vase around, counting the roses. A dozen red, a half-dozen white.

Brian would never give her red roses. That was the color Tim had always given her. Their heavy perfume filled her nostrils as she pulled out a small envelope nestling amongst the dark green leaves.

'For my princess,' she read.

Written in bold black letters, it brought a chill from the base of Kaylen's spine to the top of her head. She felt her hair stand on end, as though she had been hit with an electrical charge. Brian would never send a card with that name on it. He never called her 'princess' in public, and he certainly wouldn't write it on a card to be sent with roses. When he bought her flowers, they were always spur-of-the moment, hand-picked from a grocery store or a flower shop he happened to pass.

She looked again at the half-dozen white roses. *Sam,* she thought. *Damn him.* She hit the intercom. Rob answered at once.

"Did you see who brought these flowers?"

She took the key to her drawer out of her purse, unlocked it and took out the box with the Sig Sauer stowed inside.

"Some guy in a uniform. He had the FTD logo on his shirt."

Kaylen took the other key out of her middle drawer. Why had she decided to make that firearm so hard to get to? She was as stubborn as Brian about some things, she thought, angry with herself. She opened the box and took out the gun.

"From now on, no one is to come back here unless they're an employee," she said. "And when I'm not here, my office door is to be kept locked unless you tell me you need to get in here."

"What's wrong?" Rob sounded very worried.

"This bouquet may have come from Sam Wilson," Kaylen said, loading a full clip into the Sig.

Brian had her well-prepared for anything.

"I'll be right there." Rob said.

Kaylen carefully placed the gun and the card into her purse. She hurriedly slid the box back into the drawer as Rob opened her door.

"Did you call Brian?" He asked.

"No, and you're not going to, either." Kaylen put her purse over her shoulder, took the vase of flowers back to the sink and poured the water down the drain. "Come with me."

She walked out of her office and stopped beside the back door, Rob in tow. "Open it, please."

"I'm going first," Rob said. "Brian would never forgive me if something happened to you."

"Nonsense. He *knows* better than to think you're going to tell me what to do."

"Then let me have some peace of mind about my job security." Rob looked deadpan serious.

Kaylen wanted to be angry, but she couldn't after that comment. She managed a half-hearted glare. "You must have pulled that right out of Brian's playbook." She pointed to the door. "Help yourself, but I'm going to be right behind you."

Rob placed the doorstop used for deliveries and stepped warily outside, Kaylen following. She scanned the parking lot. No people; only neatly parked cars belonging to employees and on the far back wall, the dumpsters. Kaylen strode over to the bins. She motioned Rob to open the lid of the one closest to them and dropped both the flowers and vase inside. The trash had recently been picked up and the dumpster was mostly empty. She heard glass shatter.

She looked around, taking her time, surveying what she could see of the street, also empty except for more parked cars. "I hope he sees what I think of his stupid game." She stalked back into the club with Rob right behind her.

"I'll make sure everyone on staff knows to check with me before letting anyone but the regular delivery people in through the back door, and no one comes in the front without getting vetted by either Marvin or me, up until opening time," Rob told her. "The doorman and the bouncers'll take care of things from there, but I'll let them know that if any one of them takes a bribe or lets in an acquaintance without paying the cover charge and showing ID, then they're *all* fired. Deal?"

"Deal." Kaylen nodded. She watched Rob make sure the back door was completely closed and walk up the hallway toward the club before returning to her office.

She refused to be frightened. She'd already seen Sam in the restaurant Ziggy had thought he might purchase. Sam hadn't looked any more threatening than when he fell into the puddle outside his home the day Brian got shot. Brian had taken her to target practice. She knew how to handle the Sig, and she wouldn't hesitate to use it on Sam if he threatened her in any way, she told herself.

But there was no sense in placing herself in unnecessary danger, either, by going alone to the marina. She thought about calling Angela, but she didn't want Angela to think she was heading for a possible confrontation either with an untold number of Summerfields or a thinner Sam Wilson with a full head of hair. She wasn't about to take Rob out of Bannisters right before the club opened, but she wasn't going to wait until the next day to check both boats, either.

Kaylen sat behind her desk and rocked her chair gently back and forth. She thought hindsight always put a high beam on her stupid mistakes. She could have kicked herself for not going straight home in the cab, but then she'd have had to turn around and go to the club.

Damn Julio and his Latin temperament.

He had infuriated her far more than Rob, who wanted all the employees at Bannisters to succeed, as he had, climbing up in the course of his career from busboy to manager. He had been an easy mark, even if Shelley had been blessed with only half the skills of her scheming mother. Kaylen took out her phone and started flipping through her contact list.

As she scrolled past one name after another, rejecting every one of them, she realized how far out of touch she had become with her so-called social circle. Even before Tim's death, she had started depending on Sandy and Sam for most things. Since Tim's murder and her friends' betrayal, she had trusted no one but Brian and Jim.

With both of them out of town, she was really stumped, both for friends and for rides. She didn't feel she had any choice but to call Ziggy, even though she knew Brian wasn't going to like that solution. He'd expressly asked her to keep away from Ziggy Stavros, she remembered with a qualm in the pit of her stomach even as she called Ziggy, who picked up on the first ring, like he had been waiting for her call.

"Kaylen! What a pleasure to hear your voice!"

Kaylen explained she needed a ride to the marina. Ziggy said he'd be delighted to accompany her anywhere. He'd be over to pick her up in 30 minutes. She sat down to wait and looked through a small stack of invoices: The florist, the power company, the water bill. All regular operating expenses. Then she saw the bill from the electrician, which was higher than she would have expected for checking a recurring short in the hallway light fixtures. She saw Rob going back into his office and called to him.

"What's with this?" She waved the invoice at him. "What did the guy do? Crawl from one end of the attic to the other and replace everything he saw?"

"No, but he did look around over your office as well as mine, the hallway and the storerooms. He said that additional surveillance system you had installed is what's responsible for the power issues, and he might have to come back. He suggested next time you order equipment, you have the tech check with him before splicing any of the lines."

"What additional surveillance system?" Kaylen felt anxiety clutch her chest.

"Cameras, audio. Your office and mine. Covering the hallway and back exit in addition to all the other cameras that were installed before the club opened."

"I didn't have anything installed inside our offices." Kaylen found herself trying to suck in air and having little success.

Rob looked at her blankly. "You didn't? I thought you were keeping tabs on me."

She shook her head adamantly. "No way."

All her private conversations had been recorded. Employee counselling, business plans...

Oh, God! That's why the note said 'my princess.'

She felt dizzy. She reached out to grab the desk and missed. Rob caught her.

"Kaylen!" His voice sounded as panicked as she felt.

Whoever had that equipment installed had watched her making love with Brian on the couch...

"I...can't...breathe..."

Rob unceremoniously jammed her head between her knees. Brought her brandy and forced it into her. The black spots dancing in front of her eyes receded. She gulped in air as her heartrate slowed from a dizzying gallop to a painful trot.

"I'll be okay," she assured him as he hovered over her, his face white and strained. "But I've got to get to the bottom of this as quickly as I can. I'm calling the cops." She picked up the phone, but then hesitated.

Did she really want a patrolman taking her statement? Did she want to tell intimate details about her relationship with Brian to just anyone at Miami Dade Police Department?

"Aren't you going to call Brian?" Rob asked.

"Not yet." Kaylen shook her head. "I need a minute, Rob. I'm okay now. You can leave me."

He looked like he was going to argue with her, but stopped himself. He nodded tersely, his lips a thin line, and withdrew, closing her door.

She took out the Sig, folded her sweater over her arm to conceal the weapon, grabbed her phone and keys, and walked out into the back parking lot. A couple of busboys were smoking against the fence on the opposite side of the lot. Kaylen kept them in view as she debated who she should call.

Mills, she thought. Not Brian. Not yet. She'd ask Jack Mills to meet with her. To be discreet...

CHAPTER SIXTY-ONE

"Do we have a list of family members for the convenience store gang?" Brian asked as he stood with Jim and Fred Englehardt in front of the whiteboard at the office. "And what about Mel's boyfriends?"

"Everything you have is right here." Gabe had arrived, eager to dive right in. He brought in a banker's box from the outer office. "I've been making up separate files for everyone listed on the board." He turned the box to face Brian and ran his fingers along the edges of the tabs. "They're alphabetical by last name. Each name on the board has a file and inside those are all their contacts, family members and friends."

"There has to be a link somewhere in all this." Brian picked up Mel's folder and scanned the contents. He tapped the empty space below 'Friends.' "We can put Rita in that column and Seamus Malone in the boyfriends column, along with question marks for his brother, Wally, and the unnamed football player."

Jim looked over Brian's shoulder before taking Tommy Spiro's file. "We should be able to make a short-list of the most likely suspects. Tommy was behind the wheel, with the gun on the dashboard in front of him."

"Wally Malone was riding shotgun." Fred Engelhardt slid out Wally's file. "We interviewed neighbors of the Summerfields as well as the family. Mel had trouble keeping female friends...she always took their boyfriends."

Gabe added Mel to the 'suspects' list with a question mark next to her name.

"Mel would take anyone's boyfriend for the sport of it," Brian said. "But she had to have had at least one person she confided in. Rita said it wasn't her, but I'm not convinced." He turned to Fred. "What about all Mel's boyfriends, anyway? Didn't you even think about interviewing any of them?"

Fred looked sheepish. "We concentrated our efforts on Chad's acquaintances after we figured out robbery wasn't the motive."

"Which with hindsight may have been a mistake." Brian looked over at Gabe, busy at the board.

Without asking for guidance, Gabe had started two new categories: 'Mel Summerfield' and 'short-listed suspects' right next to it. He had put Wally and Chico's names under that heading. He stood, marker poised in hand. "Who else?"

"We can take Tab Benford out of the equation," Fred said. "He and his mother were on a bus before the rest of the convenience store group even got booked. Tab's mother registered him for school the following day." He sounded a little indignant. "We *did* access the school's records to verify that."

Brian nodded, aware that second-guessing Fred after bringing him in on their investigation might result in some defensiveness. "He's still a good resource. Jim, what about you go over to the store and pick Tab's brain instead of me? You'll make him less nervous. He was pretty observant and a lot more afraid of authority than his fellow would-be felons. Maybe he can give us some names for those boyfriends. Rita's information about Wally's little brother was pretty revealing, but she wouldn't give up anyone else."

"What do you want me to tell him?" Jim asked. "I'm your coworker?"

"Yeah, but don't go chatting about yourself—you're there to get answers. Find out if he knows Mel was going with someone in particular other than Seamus Malone at the time of Chad's murder. He's got a source in the neighborhood, but so far, I don't think he's really given me that person's name. He pulled some name out of the air. Tell him if he doesn't speak up, I'll go back myself. That should do it."

Fred Engelhardt shook his head and looked at Gabe. "Is he always like this?"

"Worse," Gabe said. "I'll go make another pot of coffee. Sergeant, do you want me to do more in-depth background checks than we already have?"

"Yeah. Let's see more of what they've all been doing for the last twenty-five years." Brian took the pen from Gabe and added Rita to the list of possible suspects. "I'm determined to find out what she's hiding, other than a jones for Wally Malone. I'm even wondering if she's Tab's contact. She didn't think much of me when I talked to her. She opened up some, but she was still withholding. Fred, you think you can try your luck?"

"I probably should have taken retirement before getting mixed up in this case again," Fred said.

"And miss all the fun?" Jim chuckled as he went out the door. "I'm off to terrorize Tab," he shot over his shoulder.

Brian pulled out another file. "I'm going back to talk to Danny Cho. See if he remembers more about Mel's friends, particularly boyfriends, since he lived next door to the Summerfields for a while." He thought he should tread lightly around Danny after Cho's revelations, but he needed to find out who else Mel had taken back to her home. "Then I'll go over to the plant where Wally works. He'll be coming off shift in a little less than an hour. I'll give him a ride home and get some more details on who exactly had the gun and where it was dropped, as well as leaning on him about his brother's relationship with Mel."

"Watch yourself," Fred said. "He was the soft-spoken one with the violent background."

"Hidden away in a juvie record, I suppose." Brian shrugged into his jacket.

"Yes, but I managed to get a look at it, anyway," Fred said. "He got probation a couple of times for purse-snatching, stealing bicycles, that sort of thing. He smacked some old lady around one time because she wouldn't let go of her purse and punched a kid who caught Wally taking his bike. He wasn't the best crook, judging by the length of the misdemeanors. But he never seemed to learn by his mistakes. His whole family was that way...his pop did time for breaking and entering, his older brother for carjacking. His mom and his younger brother were the ones who stayed out of trouble."

"What happened to them?" Gabe asked from the doorway. "There was nothing about them in the files, either."

Fred shrugged. "Dunno. I heard they moved out of state while Wally was incarcerated, taking the younger brother with them. Their eldest had already been convicted of manslaughter after a bar fight and did a dime before getting paroled. Last we heard of him, he was enrolled in a back-to-work program. IT services or something. He's in Jacksonville, or at least he was."

"Where did the rest of the family move? Do you remember?"

Fred shrugged. "No idea. We never had a reason to follow up on their whereabouts. They weren't suspects."

"Gabe, can you check on that?" Brian walked into the reception area.

Gabe looked up from his laptop. "I'll get right on it. And I finished those scans you wanted me to do. Nothing came up."

"Good." Brian felt relieved. At least Tommy Spiro didn't have thousands stashed in another bank account. He'd liked the guy. "Thanks, Gabe."

"That's what I'm here for."

"Maybe so, but I want you to know you're worth every penny."

Fred Englehardt joined them. "I'm going to find out where Rita is and interview her. No sense in waiting for her to prepare her responses again. From what you've told me, this group's tight and communicating regularly."

"I'll check for you," Gabe said. "See if she's at the diner." He pulled up a list on his laptop, picked up the phone and dialed. He told the person who answered the call that he was a regular customer and wanted to know if Rita was working that evening. "No, I wanted to surprise her," he said. "Thank you." He hung up. "She's at the diner, working an extra half shift to cover for a coworker who's coming in at seven."

Fred checked his watch. "Five-thirty. I'd better get on my way."

"Gabe, did you finish with TPD's box?" Brian asked.

"Yes, Sergeant. I can run it down to the detective's car, if you need me to."

"Stop calling me Sergeant," Brian said. "Fred, do you need a hand?"

"Maybe," Fred admitted. "My back's been tweaking lately."

Gabe grabbed TPD's box. "I've got it. Sorry, I can't call you Brian right now, so don't ask me. Maybe I can call you Boss."

"Maybe." Brian shook hands with Fred. "Thanks again for all your help."

"Anything I can do to get this case solved," Fred said.

Gabe had the front door propped open. "I wouldn't say that to the sergeant," he said. "You don't know what he's going to ask of you."

"Gabe…"

"Under oath," Gabe said. "Honest truth." He smiled guilelessly at Fred. "Ready, Detective?"

Fred nodded. "For anything, sounds like."

CHAPTER SIXTY-TWO

"I HAVE TO CHECK BOTH BOATS," Kaylen told Ziggy when he picked her up. "Thanks again for doing this."

"I was very pleased to hear your voice."

He sounded a little too warm and happy for Kaylen's comfort level. She tried not to look ill-at-ease when she settled into the passenger's seat of his Jeep. He flipped on the seat warmer.

She appreciated the gesture, but it reminded her of something else. "I thought you were selling this car?"

"I was, but I should have known better than for Louis to agree to anything that involved abstaining from his usual level of lifestyle. When he told his father of my plan, his papa met with mine. My father was predictably very upset about me going behind his back, but then he completely surprised me. After he found out how much work I had already done to secure the lease and the funding as well as receiving advice from you, he insisted on contributing, and he would not allow me to sacrifice my car. I think he would never have felt happy with his son coming to visit and parking a clunker outside his home, or at least that was Apollo's theory."

"How's Apollo dealing with this?"

"With somewhat bad grace, but my father told him to confine himself to all matters relating to The Corinthian and their new restaurant, which remains in the planning stages."

"What a relief for you." Kaylen smiled at Ziggy.

"Yes." He smiled back "My father is assisting me without being over-powering because Louis and his father are involved, but his money is financing a good portion of the initial outlay." He shrugged. "Part of me resents that, but not enough to bite the hand that feeds me."

"Common sense," Kaylen said.

"Very much so, but I still feel it cheapens my vision."

"Maybe, but you have to be realistic. Visions are all well and good if you have the money to back them up. If you don't, then you have to grovel around in the material world, like the rest of us." She thought of herself, benefitting from two years of being George's wife, and of Brian, reluctantly being drawn into Tim's vision instead of his own.

They drove along the McArthur Causeway, twinkling lights from the various marinas reflecting on the waters of the bay to Ziggy's left and street lights illuminating gently swaying palm trees, hotels, condos, and boutiques to Kaylen's right. She wondered what Brian was doing at that moment and felt a deep ache at his absence.

They led such dissimilar lives, she thought dejectedly. His was filled not only with the benefits of a large boat in a marina and more money than he would ever have wanted, but with the worries of keeping Tim's buildings solvent until they were sold for redevelopment. And then there was his own career, filled with sordid secrets, the worst of mankind's vices, and the deep sorrow of victims' families.

What an uneven balance with hers, which had recently involved nothing more exciting than mediating spats between employees, keeping her club in the black and pleasing her patrons, who could become fickle and bored with the 40's concept before winter was over. She felt shallow again and hated herself for it.

Then she thought of the bouquet of roses she had thrown into the dumpster, her call to Jack Mills and the gun in her purse, recanting the less exciting part of the equation. She'd begged Jack not to talk to Brian until he had more information about the surveillance equipment. She'd also begged him to keep any investigation low-key, and he had agreed to do his best.

Rob was to continue using his office as he normally would. Mills told her once she had reported the crime, she had to allow investigators into the building, but Kaylen refused to disrupt her business while the club was open. She swore they would have her full cooperation in the morning, before the employees arrived, and told him any attempts by whoever had installed that spyware would be thwarted by her own security system until then. She hoped she wasn't being overly-optimistic, when whoever had planted the equipment in the first place had been able to do so without anyone's knowledge.

"Do you want to pick up your car first or go to the marina?" Ziggy asked.

Kaylen was jolted out of her introspection. "I'm too hot. Where's the control? I want to turn off that seat warmer." She saw they were passing familiar buildings. "Slow down," she told Ziggy. "You're about to miss the turn-off for my street. Take a right after that restaurant."

He eased up on the accelerator and turned onto the small dead-end street with an exclusive boutique hotel and its parking lot taking up one side and the Buena Vista Condominiums on the other. He drew up to the little security booth beside wrought iron gates. Kaylen waved at the guard. He peered past Ziggy. "Ms. Roberts," he said. "Welcome home." The electronic gate opened soundlessly.

The Jeep rolled slowly into the parking lot. Ziggy looked around. "Where is your car?"

"In the middle of the lot. Front row." Kaylen pointed, and then noticed three other dark blue BMWs in close proximity to hers. "I must have a popular model," she said.

"And color." Ziggy laughed softly. "I thought you were more avant-garde. A leader of your social set."

"Obviously not in everything. You can stop right here."

Ziggy obediently applied the brakes. "Do you need to check your own home before you attend to the boats?"

"No. I'll have security walk through it with me when I come home tonight. I'll be fine." She didn't want him in her condo again. At least not right then. She felt slightly on-edge, which she thought was silly of her. She could handle Ziggy. She got out. "Why don't you follow me? You need a code to get into the marina."

Ziggy nodded. Kaylen kept his car in view as they drove over to the Coconut Grove Marina and parked. They walked side by side onto the chilly and silent dock. The damp night air felt like a blanket. Kaylen inhaled deeply. She loved the odors of the marina and the gentle sounds of boats rocking at their moorings. She understood why Brian spent so much time there. Solitude soothed his troubled soul. She wished it would do the same for her, but isolation had unnerved her since Tim's disappearance.

Ziggy stood staring at the *Need to Know*. "This is a very beautiful craft." His voice sounded wistful.

"I knew you'd appreciate it." Kaylen, still wearing the sneakers she had traveled in, stepped on board the *NTK*.

Ziggy removed his shoes and followed. "Black heel marks," he explained when she looked at his feet.

"Ah." She had to pull a penlight out of her purse to see where to fit the key in the lock. She fumbled around. Ziggy took the flashlight from her. Their hands touched. Kaylen dropped both the flashlight and the key. "Damn it." She felt like some ridiculous adolescent.

"Allow me." He scooped up both items, gave her back the flashlight and took the key, his fingers brushing hers again. "I've probably had a lot more experience with these, after my years of sailing."

Kaylen thought the first touch might have been accidental, but the second one wasn't. Her discomfort increased. She felt a need to justify her clumsiness and remind Ziggy of the boat's owner. "I've rarely opened this door, and only in daylight. Brian said the lock's awkward, and he's right."

She looked around, hoping none of Brian's other live-aboard neighbors were able to see them. She felt like a woman inviting a man home on a first date, which was crazy. She had asked Ziggy to check the boats with her. That was all. And if he made a move on her, she would tell him to leave and finish the job herself. In fact, she thought, now she had her car, after they checked the moorings on both boats, she'd tell him she was fine and finish looking through the *NTK*'s interior herself.

She turned around, almost bumping into Ziggy. "Let's go to Jim's boat first, instead," she said. "It's smaller and faster to look over. It's cold out here. After we finish there, maybe you could check Brian's moorings and then head out. I don't want to keep you."

"Are you going back to the club this evening?"

"No." Thankfully, she didn't need to...she'd brought a truce between her manager and her head bartender. And, she thought, maybe they needed to solidify that truce without her on the premises.

"Okay." Ziggy didn't sound pleased. He kept the key in his hand.

Kaylen didn't know how to ask for it without appearing to dismiss him, which would be rude after asking him to come there with her. He took her hand and helped her off the *NTK*. She lightly pulled her hand out of his as soon as she was back on the dock. Ziggy offered his arm instead. Again, Kaylen reminded herself Ziggy had European manners. She accepted the offer and they walked briskly over to Jim's boat.

Kaylen felt drained. She wished she could sink into bed and pull the covers over her head, but she knew she wouldn't be able to sleep, even if she did. Tired and jittery from the events at the club, she wished she had gotten more sleep over the past week. She certainly hadn't gotten much in Tampa. She and Brian had talked and made love half the night. Fatigue tended to jangle her nerves and make her hyper-sensitive. But she took comfort in the fact that she was beginning to feel anger and indignation more than fright about Sam sending her roses and having cameras installed to watch her. How dare he invade her privacy, like he owned her! Spying on her every move...

And then she wondered whether she was really alone at home, and the sick sensation she had felt at the bottom of her stomach when Tim went missing threatened to return. The dock, so friendly and familiar only moments before, looked darker and far more deserted now. A banner announcing charters flapped angrily and palm fronds rustled as though being parted by human hands. The wind lifted her hair and chilled the back of her neck. Kaylen found herself clinging to Ziggy's arm.

He glanced at her, concern in his eyes. "Are you okay?"

Kaylen nodded and tried to smile, but her mouth felt tight and unco-operative. "Let's get this over with," she said, tugging him along.

The *Folly* bobbed gently, lines tight. Kaylen took a brief look inside Jim's regimentally tidy living quarters. Nothing out of place or it would have stood out as though it had been coated with neon paint. When they returned to the *Need to Know,* Ziggy insisted on opening the door for her. She was beginning to shiver and gratefully stepped into the salon.

"How about a cup of coffee?" He suggested, rubbing his hands together. "That would chase the chill away."

Now she had no choice but to either be rude and refuse, or invite him into Brian's most private space.

She opted for good manners, even while internally cursing herself for doing so. "Of course, but it has to be decaf or I won't sleep tonight."

She should have been less of a coward and taken another cab to her condo.

If she had, she would have been dressed in jeans, a sweater and a jacket when she checked the boats. But she well knew how her PTSD surfaced in dark, deserted places. Ziggy's presence, although slightly disturbing, was a whole lot preferable to walking alone around the dock in the dark.

Kaylen turned on the heat and all the lights in the salon before going into the galley. She took out the canister of decaffeinated coffee and added only enough for two cups into the coffeemaker. She set out Brian's smallest cups. She'd try to get Ziggy to drink up and go home as quickly as she could get him back onto the dock.

The brewing cycle was in full swing by the time Ziggy had made a tour of the salon. He had poked his head into Brian's darkened bedroom and withdrawn it quickly, evidently feeling intrusive.

"This boat is even more impressive on the inside than the outside." Ziggy pointed to the TV. "Does this get good reception?"

"Yes." Kaylen took cream out of the refrigerator and set it beside the sugar canister on the breakfast bar. "Everything works in port or at sea. Brian spared no expense. He wanted us to feel at home here. It's much larger than his other boat...the one that got burned."

Thoughts of Sally rose to the surface. Sally, who had been murdered and whose body had been set on fire with the boat. Kaylen tried to push that thought aside. But her tired brain refused to be redirected. The *Destiny* was gone, it told her. Sally's remains had been shipped to her parents in Chicago. Kaylen had spoken with them on the phone, but had refused to go to Sally's funeral. Those were such difficult days...

Days that were over, she told herself as she watched the last of the coffee drip into the glass carafe. All those horrible memories belonged in the past. Now it was time for Brian and her to rebuild their lives...together.

Ziggy took a seat on the other side of the breakfast bar.

"You like yours black, if I remember rightly." She filled a cup and pushed it across to him.

"Yes, thank you." He took a sip. "Not bad." He nodded his approval. "But it's still not on a par with the espresso in Europe."

"You should try Cuban coffee. That's a lot stronger."

Ziggy made a face. "Too much chicory. You should taste the coffee in Greece." He put his thumb and forefinger to his lips and blew a kiss. "Hmm. Hmm."

"I've never been out of this country," Kaylen said. "George, my husband was going to take me, but even our honeymoon, which was meant to be in Italy, ended up as a week at Key West because he had some deal that had been delayed, and he needed to be able to fly back quickly to sign the contract. I've yearned to make up for that cancelled trip by going to Venice. I'd love to see Paris in the spring. The French or Italian Riviera in the summer. Maybe even Switzerland during the right season, but I'm not interested in seeing snow. I grew up in Maine. I saw enough of it there."

"So much of Europe is still slower in pace," Ziggy told her. "You would love it."

"If it's more relaxed, I probably would." She sighed. "In Miami it's always go, go, go." She stopped, surprised at herself for opening up to him about her secret wishes. She'd never told Brian any of this, not even lying in bed, when he was drowsy and holding her close.

"Come and sit down." Ziggy headed for the couch.

Reluctantly, Kaylen took her cup into the salon, but when she made for one of the side chairs, he raised his eyebrows.

"Are you afraid of me?"

"Of course not." She perched on the other end of the couch. "You're like my little brother. The one I never had."

Ziggy looked offended. "I thought I might look a little more desirable than that. You make me sound like a child. Dirty knees, socks falling down, a runny nose, that sort of thing."

Kaylen had to laugh. "Not at all. More like my protégé, on the brink of success. I feel a little maternal toward you." She put down her half-finished coffee.

"Maternal? Now I really *am* offended. I am only slightly younger than you. You have been associating with older men too much. I looked at the news clippings on Brian Swift. He's almost forty. You are continuing the trend."

Kaylen bristled. "Tim was only a year older than me, and look what that relationship did for me. I like men who know who they are and where they're going, if they haven't already gotten there, which George had. So has Brian." She felt a lot of anger toward Ziggy. "You have no idea what Brian's been through. How he protected me. Don't you dare tell me what I need." She jumped up and pointed to the door. "You should leave. Right now."

Ziggy's face registered astonishment. "I am so sorry. I had no idea you would react so strongly. I apologize. I have deeply offended you."

Kaylen found she was standing over him with fists clenched. She unclenched them. "Apology accepted with reservations." He was so untouched by the ugliness of life, she envied him. "You should learn to think before speaking. That was uncalled-for and rude."

Ziggy looked down at his feet. "I thought we were becoming good friends. I see now I made a mistake." He got up and made eye contact again. "If that's what you really want, I will leave, of course."

He looked like a contrite puppy. Kaylen's anger fizzled. Was she really willing to lose yet another friend?

"Don't go," she said. "We've had a misunderstanding. That happens sometimes, even with friends. And you're right, we *are* forming a friendship. Neither of us knows where the boundaries are right now. Or at least I don't with you." She managed a smile. "You just found out where mine are regarding my relationships with men."

"Did I?" Ziggy stepped around the coffee table and stood directly in front of her. "Are you planning to marry Brian Swift?"

Taken aback, she blurted out her deepest fear. "No. He's nowhere near ready for a commitment like that." A burning started in the back of her throat and for one dreadful moment, she thought she was going to start crying.

"I have no such reservations," Ziggy said.

His voice lowered and he cradled her elbows, much as Brian had once done on the *Destiny,* the first time he had touched her as more than a friend. Kaylen didn't know what to say or do. Her heart sped up and made her feel dizzy in an uncomfortable, shaky way.

"I am open to love and commitment." Ziggy's gaze, soft and warm, held hers. "I want marriage, and children, too, if that is what you would want in the future."

Kaylen found no words. She stood completely shocked and speechless as Ziggy moved closer.

"I want you to be with me," he said. "I have wanted that since the first moment I saw you. We move in the same social circles. I want to escort you everywhere you go. I would not leave you alone to face anything. I can learn to support your business as well as you, while giving you unconditional love and attention. This is what a Stavros man gives to his woman." He smiled his luminous smile. "I will even keep Apollo at a respectful distance from you."

And then Kaylen felt his arms go around her. She felt him pull her against him, and she saw his lips descending to hers. And she didn't resist strongly enough. She knew it, but felt powerless to stop him. Curiosity and doubt mixed with a stab of conscience that placed both her hands on his chest. But she exerted little pressure to push him away and her mouth trembled with anticipation while she hated herself for her weakness.

The moment their lips met, she lost all perspective. He pulled her close. Kaylen suddenly couldn't breathe. She opened her mouth to gulp in air and his tongue lightly touched hers. She worked harder to free herself.

Ziggy allowed her some space, but he continued to hold her loosely. "Is that really and truly your answer?" He whispered, disappointment in his voice as well as his gaze.

Kaylen felt confused and hated herself for it. "Yes. Please let me go." She gave his chest a good push that time.

He released her. If he hadn't, she wasn't sure what would have happened. "Thank you," she managed. She started to back away, but her legs bumped against the couch.

"I love you, Kaylen," Ziggy said. "I am proposing marriage." He drew a black velvet box from his pocket, popped it open and held it out to her. "I will not go down on one knee. I want to be the man in this relationship. You are a strong, very independent woman who needs to be adored and loved, but to have strength and fortitude beside you, not weakness."

Kaylen's own knees went rubbery. She thought she might be the one to end up in a kneeling position as she looked down to see at least a one carat diamond flanked by sapphires.

"I read everything I could about you, and I saw that you frequently wear sapphires," he said. "They are a demonstration of my love. The diamond is because that is traditional."

He closed the box back up and placed it in her palm. "I want you to take this proposal and the ring home with you. I do not need your answer tonight. I will make sure you get home safely."

Her trembling fingers closed over the box. Instead of fending off unwanted advances, she had been completely blind-sided by Ziggy's declaration. By his ring.

Despite wanting to believe his offer came strictly from his own wishes and desires, she had to wonder whether his father had planted any seeds during his heart-to-heart and donation of money to advance Ziggy's plans. It wouldn't hurt the Stavros clan to draw Kaylen Roberts, her successful supper club and her name into their empire.

She stood watching as Ziggy collected up the cups and took them into the kitchen. The coffeemaker was turned off, the cups placed in the sink. He was young, handsome and without hang-ups. He was going to be in the same business, and with him she could consider whether she did want to be a mother, which had never been in the picture with George, who, as a father of four adult children had no interest in starting a second family, or Brian, who barely managed to be in a relationship sometimes, much less wanted a child.

Ziggy returned and took the hand that wasn't holding the ring box. "Ready?"

Kaylen nodded and allowed him to guide her back to her car.

He kissed her again before she got into her BMW. She didn't resist him, but she didn't kiss him back, either. He didn't seem at all disappointed. When she was safely in her car with the doors locked, he smiled at her, waved and walked back to his Jeep.

Kaylen watched him. He was completely at ease with her friends and acquaintances. He was the perfect match for her...

If only her heart didn't belong to Brian Swift.

CHAPTER SIXTY-THREE

BRIAN LEANED BACK against the Mercedes and watched Wally Malone walk out the open factory gates toward the bus stop, only feet in front of the car's hood. Wally's steps slowed and his eyes opened wider when he saw Brian getting out of the car.

Swinging his lunchbox a little too forcefully, Wally stopped on the other side of the bus bench and jerked his chin up. "Brought your own ride this time, I see."

Brian opened the passenger's door. "Thought I'd take you home, since I was in the neighborhood."

"Sure you don't want me in the back?" Wally's face registered reluctance, but he walked over anyway.

Brian ignored the jibe. He watched Wally ease his big frame into the seat, closed the door and took his time walking around the car and getting behind the wheel. He noted Wally's knuckles were losing color as they clutched his lunchbox. "I wanted to ask you a few more questions," Brian said. "This seemed the easiest way to get answers."

"Yeah, having a captive audience can tend to do that." Wally put his lunchbox on the floor between his feet and adjusted the seat to give his legs more room as Brian waited for a gap in the traffic streaming out of the plant before pulling away from the curb.

Yeah, Wally was wary all right. "Quit with the references to being arrested," Brian said. "You've got no reason to be defensive unless you're hiding something." He moved into a space between an old white van with one red door and an even older white pickup with a crumpled grill.

"I'm not hiding anything. I don't like cops. Never did," Wally said, his voice filled with belligerence.

"You didn't act like that the last time we talked. I'm still not on active duty."

Brian wove around a knot of workers spilling off the sidewalk into the street. He decided sparring with Wally would only give the guy fuel to be even less cooperative. "Busy place at quitting time," he remarked.

Wally took a moment to reply, like he was fighting with himself to stay pissed, but losing. "Busy anytime. Don't you know at Morning Sunshine we're crushing and bottling Florida's gift and sending it all over the country, to quote the latest ad?" That time he sounded bitter, his gaze focused on the road ahead.

Something was eating him, for sure. Brian felt like he was climbing a steep hill, but he persisted, watching that his tone didn't match Wally's. "So, you said you stayed in the neighborhood because it was familiar. What happened to the rest of your family?"

"Moved out of state."

Brian looked at his passenger's profile as they waited at a red light. Wally's eyes were reduced to slits. Workers on the crosswalk spent more time than necessary peering at the occupants of the Mercedes. Wally slouched down and pulled the brim of his baseball cap over his eyes.

The light turned green and the workers were left behind in a little clump. When Brian glanced in his rearview mirror, they were still staring after the car. "Where out of state?"

"Houston. You already know that. What is this—some sort of test?" Wally had slouched down so low in the seat, his knees were close to chest level. He shifted uncomfortably. "A friend of my dad moved there. He helped Pop get a job at the power company."

"How long ago was that?"

"Twenty years, maybe more."

"You don't remember the exact year?"

"Nope. Don't keep track of shit like that."

More lies. Fred Englehardt had said Wally's family moved out of state while Wally was incarcerated. Wally's memory was that faulty? No way.

"You keep in touch?"

"Some. Ma mails a card at Christmas with ten bucks inside, like I'm a little kid she's sending ice cream money."

"What about the rest of your family?"

"What, my dad? He's still working for the power company."

They stopped at another light. "What about your brothers?" Brian glanced over again and saw Wally's lips purse.

"I've got a brother who's in some training program, and another who manages a big car dealership. He's done real well for himself."

"Older?"

"The one in training. The other's three years younger."

"Miss 'em?"

Wally shrugged. "Never was close to them, and I don't have money to burn, flying to Houston for some family reunion."

"Your brother couldn't find you a job in that big dealership?"

"Wouldn't want him to. Let's leave it at that." Wally tipped the baseball cap right down over his face. "I'm tired; been on my feet all day. Are we done?"

Brian missed the advantage of an interrogation room. Out in the world, he didn't have the leverage or the advantage of his badge. Frustrating, but not insurmountable, he thought, although he'd already struck out with Danny Cho, who had suddenly decided to take an impromptu trip to see his wife.

Danny's mistress at the restaurant said she had no idea when he would be coming back. She was hostile, and Brian was either going to have to get information from another source or chase Danny to Orlando. Now he was getting the cold shoulder treatment from Wally, who had been so open and friendly the last time they'd talked. Brian wondered whether he'd managed to stir up the hornets enough to get answers or send them all out of town.

He decided to have Gabe do an extensive search on what Wally's family had been up to since moving away and then re-interview to trip him up on his inconsistencies. "Yeah, we can be done. Where d'you want to be dropped off?"

"The market's fine." Wally pointed. "Turn right at the next block, then it's down on the left."

Brian eased the Mercedes over a cracked and pitted side street littered with battered grocery carts full of junk and a small homeless encampment. He sorely missed his Camaro, but reminded himself that when he got it back, fully restored, he wouldn't be any less conspicuous riding around in it. He needed to purchase a crappy-looking car with a great engine, or have one installed. When he got back to Miami, he'd start looking.

Wally's cap was back up where it belonged on top of his head. He nodded toward the homeless men staring at them as they passed. "They must stay for the climate. Can't be anything else. Panhandling around here can't bring 'em much."

The graffiti-adorned market was the same one Brian had walked past a few days before. More of a convenience store than a place to find a decent selection of groceries. Brian figured Wally was probably out of beer.

"What happened to the gun?" he asked.

"What?" Wally's hand was on the door handle. He pulled. Nothing happened. "Is this broken?"

"Nope. There's an auto lock mechanism. You didn't answer my question."

"What gun?"

"You know damned well which gun. Don't play games with me. I'm not the type to mess with."

"I threw it away."

"Guns don't get thrown out around here because they were used at a would-be stick-up."

"This one did." Wally's face had changed color to a dark red. "I had to ditch it while I was running."

"No. You gave it to someone."

A flicker of something close to fear showed on Wally's face before he turned away to push his shoulder repeatedly against the door, pumping the handle. "Open this fucking thing right now!"

"Or what?"

Wally turned, fists clenched, to see Brian sitting calmly behind the wheel, his Glock pointing at his passenger's mid-section.

"You *shit*." Wally slumped. "I'm sick of being cross-examined. I paid my debt to society, as you people like to call it. I've kept clean since I got out. Now all these years later, you're here poking your nose into things that need to be left alone."

"No, they don't. Chad Summerfield was murdered. I mean to find out who did it." Brian slid the Glock back into its holster.

"Chad Summerfield was a sick goddamned pervert. He deserved whatever he got."

"Maybe, but that's not for this community to decide; that's for a court of law. No one ever said a goddamned thing about what was going on in that store or at the Summerfield home. And then instead of going to the cops, some vigilante took it upon him or herself to take care of the problem, like this was the Wild West."

"Damn right they did. Whoever it was, and with whatever gun they used. That's all I'm gonna say about this. Live with it. Go back to Miami and stay there. Around here, we take care of our own. No one else does." He jerked his head back toward the homeless encampment, then pointed at the filth in the parking lot of the market. "This is what we deal with here. Real life and no help getting us out of it." He took out his phone. "Now, let me out of here or I'm calling 911 and reporting a kidnapping."

Brian popped the door lock. Wally got out, left the door wide open and stalked off without looking back

Brian had to get out himself to close the door. A couple of the homeless guys had sauntered over to add a little excitement to their lives, or Brian's.

"Don't even think about it," he said, showing his gun.

They backed off.

Real life, he thought as he drove away. A little *too* real for the inhabitants of that corner of Tampa.

He got Gabe on the first ring. "I want you to find out everything you can about Wally Malone and his family. Especially his younger brother."

"On it, Boss."

Brian glanced at his watch. 7:10 PM. "I'll be back at the office in an hour."

"I'll have everything ready for you."

He turned the Mercedes in the direction of the diner where Rita and Tommy worked. Time to call Fred Englehardt and find out how close Rita had been to Mel. Find out what Tommy really remembered about the day of the shooting.

He cruised past the diner and confirmed with a couple of tradespeople who had just come out that Tommy was working.

'Things cooking. Want to join you,' he texted Fred.

'Wait 10 mins,' Fred texted back.

'Find out if Wally owned silver studded belt.'

Brian picked up a local newspaper and coffee from a decrepit little corner store while he waited for another text. He briefly checked the headlines, made note of the editorial's disgust with the high crime rate and lack of jobs, scanned the ads, which were few, and sipped on yet another bad cup of joe as he waited impatiently, parked across the street from the diner, with the bus stop in full view.

CHAPTER SIXTY-FOUR

KAYLEN CLOSED and locked the front door of her condo, sat on the couch and placed the ring case on the coffee table.

She closed her eyes and felt Ziggy's lips on hers again. The fire and the longing she felt when Brian kissed her was missing. She opened her eyes back up. She knew she could learn to love Ziggy, but did she really want to?

She popped open the velvet box and took the ring out of its nest. Feeling like a traitor to Brian but unable to resist her curiosity, she slid it onto her finger. It fit snugly. Too snugly. She tried to get it off but it wouldn't budge.

"Damn it." She stopped tugging and sat back, holding up her left hand to stare at the bling on her fourth finger. She felt like a criminal. As though she had stolen it. Would she have to wear it all night and then get it cut off at a jewelers' in the morning? Horrible, but at least Brian was up in Tampa and Ziggy had gone home.

The phone rang. *Ziggy,* Kaylen thought, jumping up. *At the guard shack…coming to demand an answer after all.*

Fighting panic, she ran toward the kitchen, working the ring around and around her finger, her knuckle stinging then outright painful. She was being ridiculous. It was her cell, not the landline. In her purse. She pulled it out and looked at the caller ID. *Please, not Brian. He had radar where she was concerned...*

She breathed a sigh of relief and leaned her elbows on the cool granite. Thank God for small mercies...Angela Crossfield.

She hit the speaker. "Hi, Angela. How are you?" She twisted the ring again. Her knuckle had swelled and turned dark pink. She needed soap and cold water.

"I'm good. I called to see when you and Brian would like to have dinner with us. Jonathan's looking forward to it as much as I am."

"Er...well...Brian's still up in Tampa." Kaylen took the phone with her into the kitchen and laid it beside the sink.

"Oh." Angela sounded disappointed. "When's he coming back?"

Kaylen dribbled dishwashing liquid over both the ring and her finger, then started rubbing, easing. "He has to fly in for an appointment. He'll be here either Wednesday evening or early Thursday morning."

The ring popped off and fell into the sink with a clatter. Kaylen grabbed it right before it shot into the garbage disposal. The bottle of dishwashing liquid followed the same path as the ring, landing in the stainless steel sink with a heavy thud.

"What are you doing?" Angela asked. "Are you okay?"

"Yes. No. Oh, I don't know."

"Where are you?"

"Home."

"Alone?"

"Yes, of course." *Who did Angela expect to be there?*

"I'll be right over." Without waiting for a response, Angela hung up.

"Double damn," Kaylen said to the phone.

She fished the ring out of the disposal, put the strainer into the sink and ran water, washing Ziggy's ring and her finger until all the soap came off. She carefully dried his declaration of intent and put it back into its case before she did something else to it.

Feeling overheated and still slightly panicked, she took her phone with her and went out onto the balcony, gratefully breathing fresh air that carried a faint whiff of the ocean.

The phone rang again. "Angela?"

"It's Brian."

He sounded a little strange; as though he already knew something had happened and was calling for verification.

He really did have radar, she thought. His timing couldn't have been worse. "Oh, hi." She tried for bright and airy, surprised instead of freaked. "How *are* you?"

That was stupid, she thought. He'd know something was wrong.

"I'm okay." He sounded wary. "You?"

"Fine." She cringed. She couldn't have sounded less fine if she'd tried. "I'm home. Waiting for Angela."

"I thought you were staying at the club this evening. I called there first. Rob told me you had planned to go back, but he hadn't seen you. I got worried."'

"No need for worry." She felt like slapping herself.

"Good."

His sentences were even shorter than hers. Kaylen didn't know what to say next. She hoped Angela didn't hit any traffic and would arrive to save her before she said something she'd regret.

"How did things go with Rob and Julio?"

A question she could actually respond to without reservations. She felt a surge of relief and walked back inside, closing the balcony door quietly behind her. "Okay."

She needed a drink. Not wine, either. She got a bottle of Courvoisier out of the kitchen, passed on a snifter and grabbed a tumbler. "They're both at work. I left them to figure out the rest of it for themselves. I sent a voicemail telling Shelley to call me. It's her day off. I'll fire her as soon as I get hold of her." Kaylen poured a liberal serving of cognac.

"Good management tactics with Rob and Julio. I like that. Either they'll fight in the back parking lot or get over themselves." His voice sounded a little more relaxed.

Kaylen tossed back half the brandy in hopes of getting more relaxed herself. "Hopefully, neither of them reacts like you. You would fight anywhere, at any time, for the smallest reason." She couldn't help smiling. "It's so good to hear your voice." She tossed back the rest of her drink.

"I'm glad you tacked that comment on the end. I was beginning to think you were mad at me for some reason."

Oh God.

"No way." She took the Courvoisier and the glass with her to the couch. When she sat, she saw the ring case and pulled a stack of paperback books in front of it.

"So you and Angela are having a girls' night out?"

Kaylen put the empty glass onto a coaster but kept the bottle in her hand. "No, she's coming here. We're staying in. Probably we'll order a pizza or something." She upended the bottle and took a good swig.

"Is she going with you to check the boats?"

Of all nights, Brian who never chit-chatted on the phone wanted to talk. Kaylen took another gulp straight from the bottle. Warmth suffused her inside while a flush crept up her neck.

"You shouldn't go over there alone tonight," he continued. "Maybe not even with her. I'd feel better if you waited until tomorrow morning."

"I already went there." Kaylen felt like she'd blurted that out. *So much for seeking comfort in booze.*

She rubbed a hand over her face. It felt as flushed as the rest of her. Since Brian's injury, she'd rarely had as much as a glass of wine, because he couldn't drink and take his medications. She didn't think he was much of a drinker, anyway, which she liked. A beer or two with pizza on a Friday night would probably be his limit, she thought. She yearned for his presence and found tears rolling down her face. Great, now she was getting a buzz and becoming weepy. She got up to push the patio door back open. A brisk breeze entered, swirling around her, chilling her skin, cooling hot cheeks.

Why had she fallen in love with a detective, of all people? Why couldn't the love of her life be clueless, like some of her past boyfriends?

Tim hadn't been clueless, she thought. Neither had her beloved George. She'd never have married him if he had been...

She became aware of prolonged silence. Brian was waiting for an answer to what question? The boats, she thought. The marina...

"Everything was fine," she said. "No problems with the moorings or anything."

"Kaylen, it'd be better if you don't go near the boats until I tell you it's okay."

He sounded really worried.

"Why? What's up?" Kaylen felt as guilty as if he'd caught her with Ziggy in mid-proposal. *When Brian called the club, had Rob told him she had left with Ziggy a couple of hours before?*

"There's something really wrong with the Summerfields," Brian said.

Kaylen's agitation ground to a halt. "Wrong how? Worse than incest?"

"I can't tell you, but maybe. This case is going real active, real quick. Promise me you won't go anywhere near the marina while I'm gone."

"Okay." She closed and locked the patio door in an immediate gut response. "Am I in danger?" An all-too-familiar stir of nausea hit her, and not because of brandy on an empty stomach.

"No, I don't think so. But I don't want to take any chances. Not with all of them down there and me up here."

"I started carrying the Sig," she said.

"Why? Did you get spooked by something?"

"You know me way too well." *Wasn't that the truth?* "I was sent a bouquet of red and white roses today, before I got back. Rob had the delivery guy put them in my office. He set them in the sink. There was a card. It said 'For my princess.'"

"Shit! I *knew* something was wrong."

She could imagine him pacing up and down, running his right hand through his hair.

"I need to get back down there, but dammit, things are bustin' loose up here."

They're bustin' loose down here, too, she wanted to say.

"Can you go stay with the Crossfields?"

"I'm not going to hide, and I'm not involving anyone else. If this is Sam playing a prank, he won't harm me."

"Sam wouldn't do any of his own dirty work, but lucky for both of us, he probably doesn't have the money to hire anyone else to do it, either." Brian sounded like he had recovered some of his equilibrium. His voice was logical and calm. "He might try scaring you with pranks like this one. But I think you're right...he'd hurt the hell out of me, but he wouldn't touch you."

"I'm pretty sure that's true." She thought back to a flip remark Brian had made shortly after the first time they made love. He'd said if Sam knew what they had just done, her former mentor would arrange to have him shot. Now Sam had video showing just exactly what they did do when they got the chance. Her heart rate increased, and her breathing grew faster, too.

"Don't get panicked, hon. Not over Sam."

Brian's voice reassured her, despite the miles between them. She took a couple of deep breaths, willing her heart to slow down. It cooperated partially, and she felt less flushed. She'd tell him about the spyware when he got back. Otherwise he'd worry too much.

"Okay," she said, trying to sound a lot more serene than she felt. "I'll try not to. But you watch your back up there."

"Always."

His answer was too fast, as it always was when he wanted her to think there was nothing remotely dangerous about his job.

"You'd better mean that, Brian Swift. Don't be flippant. I'm asking you to be careful. I can't imagine my life without you in it."

Tears sprang into her eyes. She blinked them away. He frequently told her she had to get used to the thought of him being in some jeopardy when he worked. The months he had been healing, she'd been lulled into a false sense of security.

"You knew immediately those flowers weren't from me, didn't you?" His voice sounded soft and reassuring, calming.

Kaylen wiped her tears away. "Yes, because you never send roses, and you'd certainly never send flowers with a card calling me 'princess.' You know how much I hate that name."

"I haven't *always* used it sarcastically," he said.

"But you did in the beginning, and you meant it, too."

"I'm sorry. If you feel that strongly, I'll never use it again."

"Maybe you should, but only if there's a need. Like a secret word between us."

"That's a pretty good idea, princess."

"See, you're doing that again. Trying to make me mad so I'm not scared."

"Is it working?"

"Maybe."

"So why aren't you and Angela going out to dinner?"

The detective again. She was going to have to lie. She couldn't tell him long-distance.

"Oh, I think we're both a little tired."

She sat on the other end of the couch and immediately saw the ring box again. *Damn thing. She should have tucked it away in one of the kitchen drawers.*

"And I had cramps," she said, and then she really despised herself. She'd made him promise never to lie to her, and here she was, the biggest hypocrite in the world, telling one whopper after the next.

"Cramps? Your period was two weeks ago."

Damn his analytical mind!

Kaylen colored up. "Not *those* kinds of cramps. I must have eaten something that upset my stomach, or maybe it was the plane ride. It was a bit bumpy."

"Oh. Then pizza wouldn't be a good idea…"

Of course not. She gave herself a mental kick. "You're right. I'll talk it over with Angela when she gets here. Speaking of which, I've got to go." At least *that* was the truth.

"What's the hurry? You guys aren't going anywhere. You won't need to primp."

Kaylen felt trapped. "I'm in my bathrobe. I just took a shower." *Another lie.*

"Okay, hon." He laughed. "I'll leave you alone. Wish I was there, though. What are you wearing under that bathrobe?"

"Not much." She was going to get struck down by lightning if this kept up.

"Tell me."

"Oh, I was going to put on that black nylon set you really like," she said, improvising while hating herself. "But since it's only Angela, I was thinking of something more conservative."

"So you don't have *anything* on under the robe?"

"No. And I wish you were here, too." *That was a fervent wish, all right.*

"Soon, princess." He sounded really regretful.

"I love you," she said. "Go take care of your case. I'll be fine."

"You call 911 if anything, however small, seems out of place."

If she listened to that, she'd have to call right then and report Ziggy Stavros for kissing her and proposing.

"I will."

She waited. Nothing happened. No four little words that ended in 'too.'

"I've got to go," she said, and then she severed the connection, before his silence saddened her yet again.

"Damn you, Brian Swift," she said to the phone.

She opened the ring case and stared down at a possible future with Ziggy Stavros.

CHAPTER SIXTY-FIVE

BRIAN LAID DOWN HIS PHONE. Kaylen had sounded really off. Something was up, and he'd find out what as soon as he got back to Miami. But first, he needed to get to the bottom of what Rita and Tommy knew about Mel, the gun and Chad Summerfield's murder. Both of them had been holding out on him. Had Tommy given him that box of envelopes and the bank statement to throw him off the real trail?

Gabe had texted the info from TPD: No fingerprints apart from Tommy's. The envelopes were a dead end, except for Tommy's word regarding the amounts of money and the frequency. Brian watched Fred Englehardt saunter across the street toward the Mercedes.

"Making any progress?" He asked after Fred sat in the passenger's seat.

Fred shook his head. "Not much. Rita's closed-mouthed, all right. She said she never saw anyone with any silver studded belt. She pretty much denied knowing anything about the convenience store robbery or the murder. Deaf and dumb, apparently. "

"Wally, too." Brian felt like swearing; curbed it. "Suddenly, they're all denying they know anything, and the only progress we're making is to see more of what's confusing and not adding up."

"That's why this crime's never been solved."

Fred's grim expression looked too much like defeat for Brian. "Let's get more formal. Pick 'em up. Scare 'em a little. Maybe that'll shake something loose."

Fred's bushy eyebrows shot up. "You want me to take Rita and Tommy to the precinct? On what grounds?"

"No, not *that* formal, but put her into the back of your car. Ask what she thinks went on between Mel and Chad. Whether they had a good relationship or they were at odds all the time. I told you what Danny Cho said about Chad coming in and getting mad about him and Mel in her bedroom."

Fred nodded. "You think she had something to do with her brother's death? That's pretty damned cold."

"That woman'd be capable of a lot, even back then. We need to find out more about any other boyfriends. Rita doesn't think Seamus was the father of Mel's kid. So, then, who was?"

"Okay. Anything else specific?"

"See if Rita had a relationship with any of the convenience store gang or Chad Summerfield. Maybe that's why she's never tried to get with Wally Malone. I'll take Tommy." Brian checked his watch. "They both should be leaving work about now. Easier to talk with them when they're not on the job."

"There she is." Fred nodded in the direction of the diner.

Rita was wearing a pair of beige cropped pants and a bright yellow t-shirt. In one hand, she carried a large plastic bag with her uniform showing through. She walked rapidly down the street and into a dry cleaner's.

"Must have been one hell of a day." Fred pointed toward Rita. "Ketchup or tomato sauce, probably. Otherwise she'd go to a laundro-mat." He got out of the car. "See you back here in a few." He closed the door quietly and strolled after Rita.

Brian had to wait three more minutes before Tommy Spiro left work, wearing jeans and a black t-shirt. Instead of turning toward home, he took the same direction as Rita. *What the hell?*

The element of surprise was out the window. Tommy was sure to see Rita with Fred. But when Brian followed, he saw Fred hadn't gone into the dry cleaners. He was waiting patiently in the doorway of a neighborhood bar. Tommy, who either didn't know Engelhardt or didn't recognize him after all those years, walked right past him and into the shop. Fred happened to glance Brian's way and Brian gestured furiously. Fred joined him in the recessed entry of a shuttered store. A sign in the window announced: 'Lost our Lease. Thank you for your Business.'

They waited a couple of minutes before Rita came stalking out of the cleaners ahead of Tommy. He tried to take her arm but she jerked it away as she and Tommy moved closer to Brian and Fred.

"This is a bad idea," Rita said. "We can't keep on seeing each other like this."

"Why not?"

Tommy sounded angry. He had managed to grab Rita's wrist. That time, she wasn't pulling away.

"I love you," Tommy said. "I'll run off with you. Just say the word."

"And leave your wife, your mother…your *girls?*" Rita shook her head. "It's not going to happen, Tommy. We're never going to get out of this place."

"We can make it. Together we can do it. I've got money. I told you. I've been stashing it away for years."

"Keep your voice down," Rita hissed. "What's the matter with you? People will hear."

"Who? That old bitch in the cleaners? She's half-deaf and blind as a bat. And she's in the back of the place trying to get that stain out of your uniform. There's nobody here but us."

They stepped out of sight into the doorway of another shuttered store.

"Oh, you make me crazy." Rita's voice was muffled.

Brian took a chance and moved in closer. Tommy was holding Rita tightly and they were kissing like two teenagers in the back row of a movie theatre.

Brian crooked his finger and Fred Engelhardt joined him.

Fred's bemused expression turned to astonishment. "They're a couple?"

Brian walked right up to the lovers as they broke apart. "Did he tell you where the money came from?" He asked Rita.

Tommy flushed.

"Blackmail," Brian said. He figured he might have to explain extortion to Rita.

Rita stared at Tommy, then shoved him, hard.

"We're going to continue this conversation down at the precinct," Fred said.

"Is it really the Summerfields who've been paying you off, or the Malones, or both families?" Brian asked.

Tommy paled. "No, man, it's the Chesneys. He used to be the manager at Mega Groceries."

"I know who he is." Brian wanted to get physical with Tommy Spiro, who had dared to lie repeatedly about his blackmailing ways.

"Lester didn't want anyone knowing his wife had an affair with Chad. The old guy was worried someone might think she had Summerfield blown away."

Rita graced them all with the same glare. "Men! You're *all* lying, cheating bastards." She had her purse held across her chest again. "I'm done keeping secrets for everyone." She turned to Brian. "I've got the damned gun you're looking for, and the belt. You give me a ride over to my apartment; I'll give them to you."

"I want a lawyer," Tommy said.

"And I want a new life," Rita said. "Far the hell away from this damned place."

CHAPTER SIXTY-SIX

RITA HAD a dilapidated cardboard box hidden at the back of her closet, behind an old suitcase that looked like it might have belonged to her parents. "It's full of Wally's stuff," she told Brian as he pulled on gloves, carefully took the box and laid it on the bed. "His mom gave it to me before they moved away. She wanted him to have it when he got released."

"But you've still got it."

"I couldn't resist looking through it. I wanted to know more about Wally. When I saw what was inside, I couldn't give it to him. And since his family left town right after I got the box, I couldn't give it back to his mom, either." Rita folded her arms across her chest.

Brian recognized the defensive gesture. Rita needed someone to treat her right, he thought. He wasn't so sure it was Wally Malone at that point. He took the lid off the box and saw the belt, carefully rolled up, its silver studs darkened with age.

Rita pointed toward the box with one finger. "The other thing you want is at the bottom, rolled up inside a t-shirt. It wasn't a t-shirt Wally ever wore, and it was a smaller size, too." She worried her bottom lip with her teeth. "More Seamus's size," she muttered, eyes downcast.

Brian carefully removed the belt and a layer of photos, a couple of sports trophies for basketball, and a plaque for "Most Improved" that dated back so far, it must have been from Wally's kindergarten days. His mother had probably packed up everything she thought might be important to Wally when he got out of prison.

He saw the rolled up t-shirt. "You'd better step back," he said. "The gun might be loaded. Did you handle it?"

Rita backed up to the doorway of the tiny bedroom, her face a white blob above her bright yellow shirt in the darkness from the narrow hallway. "No. When I unwrapped it and saw what it was, I wrapped it back up and left it right where I found it. It's been at the back of my closet ever since. I couldn't believe his mother put that inside and gave it to me for safe-keeping."

"She probably didn't know it was there. I think the gun and the belt were added by someone else."

Brian carefully folded back the edges of the t-shirt until he exposed a Smith and Wesson .38 revolver. Rita hadn't done a good job of re-rolling, making it easy to unwrap the firearm, for which he was thankful. He was also thankful after he checked it over that neither she nor the Malone boys' mother had shot themselves. It was fully loaded except for two empty chambers.

Chad had taken two shots to the chest.

CHAPTER SIXTY-SEVEN

"I'VE GOT everything you want to know about Wally Malone and his family," Gabe said.

He'd had three mugs of coffee set out in the conference room when Brian and Jim came through the outer door moments before. Gabe pointed to the board, on which he'd placed a photo of a man standing under a car dealership sign.

Brian grabbed his coffee and looked closer at the photo. "That's not Houston; it's Miami. I pass that dealership all the time."

Gabe nodded. "Wally's brother has worked there for the past eight years. Promoted from salesman to manager a year ago. Sales manager, not general manager, like Wally told you. The parents are still in Houston. Annie and Patrick Farmer. They changed their names when they moved away. The brother's now Rick Farmer, with a wife, Lena, and two kids. Rick Junior's ten, Billy's six. The kids play softball in the summer and swim in the winter. The whole family vacations in Bermuda every year, where they have a time-share for two weeks in July."

"You *are* good," Jim said.

"Wasted as a clerk, I think," Brian said.

"I like my job, or at least, I did." Gabe grimaced. "*Damn* Trehorn. Research is candy to me. I would never want to be a detective. Asking people questions they don't want to answer, wondering if they're going to pull out a gun and shoot me? No thanks. I feel very safe behind a desk."

Brian took off his jacket and sat. He pushed the chair back and put his feet up on the table. His left shoulder ached and he felt tired. Gymnastics with Kaylen were taking their toll. He turned to Jim. "So, what's new with our friend, Tab? Any more enlightening memories?"

"He pulled a few more out, reluctantly. I told him I'd send you over if he didn't cooperate fully. That loosened his tongue." Jim shook his head. "What the hell do you *do* to people?"

"A lot less than you'd think." Brian took a sip of his coffee. It tasted remarkably like the precinct brew, and he wondered if Gabe had stowed a can in his trunk.

Jim looked unconvinced, but he opened the box of donuts Gabe had placed on the table, passed over all the more interesting ones in favor of an old-fashioned jelly, and took a bite. He chewed reflectively. Brian felt like taking the donut away from him, but Jim was probably savoring the moment, so he counted to 10 under his breath.

Jim swallowed. "Okay."

He didn't sound very convinced. Perhaps he had expected his friend to confess to pulling out the fingernails of potential suspects. Brian waited a lot less patiently that time, counting another 10 out in his head.

"Well," Jim said. "Tab said he'd spoken a bit out of turn the other day."

"Out of what friggin' turn? Is he going to recant on everything?"

"Not everything, but he revised the bit about seeing Chad and his sister in the stockroom. Tab said she was crying when she passed him in the store. When he went to use the restroom, he saw Chad comforting her. He thinks he heard her telling her brother she was pregnant..."

Brian interrupted. "Gabe, I need a copy of Shelley's birth certificate."

"Done." Gabe walked briskly out of the room. A moment later, sounds filtered in of a keyboard clicking.

"Tab said he jumped to conclusions, probably," Jim continued, as though nothing had interrupted him.

"No shit." Brian wanted to go over and pull out Tab Benford's fingernails just to hear him holler. "Here I was, thinking my boat was moored next to a group of incestuous perverts and telling Kaylen to keep away from all of them, based on what that shithead manager told me on top of what Kaylen had learned from Nola Chesney. Now he's telling you they were sharing a family secret?"

"Tab's terrified of you. He thinks if he doesn't tell you what you want to hear, you'll let all his old friends know he's back in the neighborhood."

"What a fuckin' crock of..."

"Kaylen told me to remind you not to swear."

"Oh, cut the crap, Jim." Brian got up. "That lying sack of shit. I'm going over there right now..."

"Perhaps you won't need to; I've got what you wanted," Gabe called out, his voice as calm as if he'd announced the dinner menu.

Brian headed for Gabe's desk, Jim right behind, carrying the box of donuts.

"Shelley Summerfield was born six months after Chad's murder," Gabe said. "There's no father's name listed."

"There wouldn't be." Brian shook his head. "She kept that secret. I bet that conversation in the stockroom set off a chain of events. Tab's the tattletale. I'm thinking he told the wrong person or people about what he thought he'd seen. Probably the father of Shelley's baby heard the first version, the one Tab told me, and concluded Chad was the father. And I'm betting the father's actually Wally. He didn't have to go out of the neighborhood and lose his virginity to a prostitute. He lost it to Mel, who was probably so pissed about Chad interrupting her with Danny, she got the next boy who would do it with her, and that was her boyfriend's big brother.

"And when Seamus found out about the pregnancy without all the right facts, he took the gun from the convenience store robbery and murdered Chad Summerfield. The rest of the community thought Chad was a pervert. He already had a reputation as a womanizer, so they closed ranks and refused to turn in the shooter. Wally's guilt must have been almost overwhelming. He would never turn in his own brother. I know all about that kind of loyalty. Christ, what a mess."

"Wally Malone's little brother isn't Shelley's father, but he's the shooter?" Jim looked befuddled.

"Yeah. Angry over someone else getting into Mel's pants while he was being a good Catholic. Furious that it was her own brother, or so he thought. Tab told me the other kid in the car, the one who chickened out in front of the convenience store, was called Mix, which I figured was some kind of nickname. But he also told me Wally called the kid a hick, which didn't sound like something that would come out of Wally's mouth. I bet that kid was Seamus, and Wally called him a mick. They're Irish."

"But wouldn't the other kids have known him?" Jim asked. "And why would *they* go to such lengths to protect him?"

"Seamus went to a school for the gifted, from what Rita told me. I don't think even when he started tutoring Mel and dating her that he really hung out with any of the other neighborhood kids. His family sheltered him and when Wally protected Seamus, Chico and Tommy evidently did, too. Damn good friends. Better than most of us have ever had."

"I don't think I was ever that close to any of my friends when I was in high school," Gabe said. "Not to keep something like murder under wraps."

Brian nodded. "Yeah. Makes me wonder what other secrets they're all keeping."

"So why would Wally bring his little brother along to rob that store in the first place?" Jim took another donut, that time a cruller.

Brian shrugged. "Maybe because Seamus managed to get the gun when Wally couldn't."

"That would make sense," Gabe broke in. "When I was transcribing your interviews, Boss, Tab said Mix brought the firearm."

Jim's expression cleared. "Well, finally Tab gave some useful information, as long as it's not more hearsay."

"I really feel this is the way it went down," Brian said. "Maybe Tab didn't get the kid's name right, but essentially everything else he remembered about that robbery attempt meshed with what I got from the rest of the convenience store gang and the police report."

"Okay, I can buy all that," Jim said. "But how did the gun get back in Seamus's hands?"

Brian pitched the rest of his coffee into a trash can beside Gabe's desk. "Seamus didn't run as far as Tab thought. Either he was going to hide and watch the robbery go down, or maybe he'd decided to come back before everyone else panicked and started running, too. So he either saw his brother toss the gun and picked it up or Wally gave it to Seamus as he ran past, and Seamus managed to get clean away."

"If Tab hadn't been assigned here right now to manage that store on a temporary basis, this crime might never have been solved," Gabe said. "No one else was willing to talk. Good job, Boss." He started chewing on a cream-filled donut with the relish of someone who was experiencing a severe sugar craving.

Brian shrugged. "I just did my job and got the facts lined up with help from both you and Jim. Don't forget Fred Englehardt, TBD and Hal all had roles, too."

"And Kaylen," Jim said. "Don't overlook her contribution."

"I won't, but don't you go giving her any ideas that she could get involved with any other cases going forward."

"She doesn't need me giving her ideas. She's got enough of her own." Jim threw up his hands when Brian glared at him. "Just saying."

"Tab's not going to get much in the way of thanks for helping solve this case," Brian said. "His panic in front of that store set off a chain of events that ended with Chad Summerfield's murder. It's like the glass staying half empty, regardless of how much water gets poured into it. I'll go back to Miami; try to get a confession out of Rick Farmer." He shook his head. "What a fucked-up case this has turned out to be."

Jim nodded. "I've got no disagreement with that. Good thing Kaylen's not around to hear your language."

"You're not the gate-keeper of my vernacular." Brian smiled when both Jim and Gabe stared at him. "I did go to college. I tend to let people forget that."

"Which we do." Jim tut-tutted. "No wonder you drive Kaylen crazy, buddy. But she loves you so much, she forgives you."

"Jim..."

"He's telling the truth, Boss," Gabe said. "On both counts."

Brian gave him a warning glare.

"I'm only clarifying what Jim said. In case you've got doubts or anything." Gabe no longer looked nor sounded anything close to hesitant or tentative. He looked completely comfortable in his new role.

"You two are ganging up on me." Brian had to smile. "Damn people." He took out his phone. "I'm going to call Hal and explain what's happened. Get him to agree to let me work with Mills in Miami. See if he wants me to call Fred Engelhardt to go back with me or how he wants to handle this."

"What do you want us to do in the meantime?" Jim asked.

"Make more coffee, for one thing." Gabe got up. "And order dinner. We all need something more substantial than a box of donuts. I'll get meals delivered."

"You also need to get me booked on a flight," Brian said. "If it has to be a charter, that's fine. Jim, can you drive the Mercedes back to Miami if I wind things up down there?"

"No problem."

"I've got to convince Hal to put me back on active duty. I want to extract that confession myself. I hope TPD doesn't want to wrap this case up as much as Fred does, or he'll be the one doing the interview, after they get us to hand Farmer over."

Gabe was back at his laptop and scrolling down a list of flights. "It'll be expensive. There are no available flights, but I have some contacts in Miami who know private pilots up here. I'll figure something out."

Brian pulled out his billfold and handed over a credit card. "Whatever. Just make it happen."

"I'm kind of sorry this may be over," Jim said. "Don't get me wrong, I'll be glad if the case gets solved after all these years, but I'll miss the investigative part and working with you. You've got one fine analytical mind, my friend."

"Thanks, Jim. The same goes for me, working with both of you." He looked over at Gabe, busy finding him a fast way back to Miami. "You've been everything I could ever have hoped for in a team."

Gabe was talking times and cost. He put down the phone. "It's going to cost you an arm and a leg, but they can take you out of here at midnight."

"Are we packing up and sending back the furniture?" Jim swallowed the last of his coffee.

"No. There's still plenty of work to be done here," Brian said. "Gabe, first thing in the morning, I need you to finish transcribing the interviews, then I want you to compare all the statements for discrepancies, inconsistencies. Pick out the facts and build a new timeline."

"Gotcha." Gabe scribbled a couple of notes. "I'll come in early and email you the timeline and any pertinent facts as soon as I'm finished."

"Great. We need to be able to present a case to the District Attorney, and I want it to be as tight as possible." He turned from Gabe to Jim.

"Okay, what's on my hit list?" Jim had his own notepad out, pen poised.

"I want you to talk to Tommy Spiro again. I'll call Fred and ask him to let you do the interview. See if he'll link Mel with Wally or his brother. Even both. Find out if he remembers the shooter wearing that distinctive belt, which I'm thinking was probably Wally's. Start out by asking if Tommy knows who had a belt like it before he gives you a description of what he remembers about the perp's clothing. Then take a trip to the diner and talk to Rita again. She was too shaken up after finding out the gun was loaded to try to give me much more info. Too emotional after the break-up with Tommy, too. Maybe she'll have calmed down enough to tell you more about the Malone brothers and how close they were with Mel. She's not the friendliest person in the world…"

"Which is why we needed to keep Kaylen up here," Jim interrupted. "She's got a real way with her. She got all that info out of Nola." He stopped. "Which reminds me…did anyone tell Lester he can stop paying off Tommy?"

"Check with Fred. Ask him if you can say anything about that or TPD's not ready. We're getting to the bottom of the dung heap, but those last few feet are the worst."

"I have a feeling you're right, there." Jim sighed. "Forget ordering dinner for me, Gabe. I've got a full day tomorrow. I'll order room service at the hotel and get an early night. You need a ride somewhere, Brian, before I go hit the hay?"

"I'll be the boss's driver," Gabe said. "I can leave and return to reports much easier than you fitting in an airfield trip, Jim. I'm going to work as late as I can, get a few hours of sleep and then finish up. My motel's close."

"I won't need my bag," Brian said. "But I'll pack it and leave it to go back with you, Jim. Kaylen left a bag that probably should go. She may give it to me if I don't drag that back to Miami." He looked around. "I'll be sorry, too, if this is all over, but neither of you should get too nostalgic. I can keep you both busy, back in Miami and elsewhere." He smiled when they both stared at him. "I've got some other plans up my sleeve."

After Jim left, Brian closed himself into the relatively unused second office and called Hal while he waited for the food to be delivered. He wanted to use Hal's personal cell, but he sensed going outside normal channels wasn't going to net him any favors, so he tried the office first. Surprisingly, Alicia Solis, Hal's administrative assistant picked up.

"I'll see if he's available." She sounded guarded, doubtful, and really tired. "We were about to leave the office. It's almost nine. We've worked late, and it's time for us to go home."

"It's really important, Alicia," Brian told her. "It's about me needing to interview a potential murder suspect in Miami on a cold case from up in Tampa. I need to problem-solve with the chief."

"Oh. Okay; I'll see what I can do." Alicia's voice sounded less stressed. "It might be better if one of us returns the call than you hold."

"Fine. I'll be waiting." Brian hung up. He didn't want to push Alicia, perhaps resulting in a stall either with her communicating with Hal or Hal deciding it wasn't worth his time to make that call.

Brian got himself a cup of freshly-brewed coffee and wondered whether Wally had called his brother to give Rick a heads-up. He called the car dealership in Miami. When he asked to speak to the sales team manager, he was informed Mr. Farmer had already left for the day. Could she take a message? The dealership was closing in less than five minutes.

"No," Brian said. "I wanted to say how pleased I am with my new car. I'll send him an email."

He listened while he was given Rick Farmer's email address, thanked her and hung up. He thought about Shelley and Mel, Rick Farmer's wife and two kids. One fucking great mess, he thought. Chad Summerfield may have died because some kid who wanted to be the big shot know-it-all around his little gang of friends had given them bad information.

Tab Benford was getting off light, shipped to the state of his choice by his company. But he might also spend the rest of his life watching his back after Wally Malone found out the truth.

Restless, Brian wandered back into the reception area to find it empty. Gabe had propped a note on his desk. He had changed his mind about getting food delivered. Instead, he was picking up burgers and fries for Brian and himself. For the first time in days, Brian was alone and in a quiet environment. He savored the silence for all of two minutes before his phone rang.

Hal ignored pleasantries. "What are you up to now?"

His voice didn't sound testy at least. Encouraged, Brian took more coffee with him back into the office, shut the door and brought Hal up to speed on the Summerfield case, his hiring of Gabe, and his thoughts on being considered for the Cold Case position if it was still available. He wanted to bring Gabe and Jack Mills on board, and use Jim as a civilian investigator on an as-needed basis. To his surprise, Hal actually agreed to pretty much everything he requested, although he did say Lieutenant Trehorn wasn't going to like three more of his staff members leaving.

"But I understand we were about to lose Gabe if another position wasn't found for him," Hal added. "He's a perfect fit for you. Mills, too. Voices of reason when you're going off half-cocked."

"I've stopped doing that," Brian said. "You can ask Jim and Gabe if you've got doubts. This case stayed unsolved twenty-five years, Hal, and I believe I can extract a confession from Rick Farmer."

"I could have Mills bring him in," Hal said. "But nothing's going to happen until TPD's been contacted. We're going through the proper channels on this now, whether you like it or not."

"Fine. TPD can send anyone they want, although I'd like Fred Engelhardt to be the one to help wrap up this case. He's vested in it, and I've kept him in the loop as much as possible. If TPD takes this out from under us, I'm going to be pissed."

"You being pissed is something I'm real familiar with." Hal's tone was tart. "Keep out of the negotiations over jurisdiction and all the other crap or I'll take you off the case instead of waiting for TPD to do it."

"I'm flying back tonight," Brian broke in, hoping to interrupt Hal's train of thought and deflect yet another discussion over his lone wolf tactics. "I want to start the conversation with Farmer at the dealership in the morning. If I'm wrong, the only thing his fellow employees will remember is a couple of cops came to see him. For all they'll know, it could have been about ordering cars for the department."

Hal mulled that over for a moment. "All right. I'll get that point across to TPD. But I'm still concerned that Farmer's older brother will call and he'll split."

"And take his family, or leave them behind?" Brian didn't want Mills or some rep from TPD initiating contact with Rick Farmer. This case was his baby, and he wanted to follow it to the end.

Silence assured him Hal was mulling over different scenarios. Brian idly counted out two sets of 10 in his head.

"If this backfires, Trehorn will fire your ass before I get the paperwork completed on your transfer," Hal warned.

"I'll take that chance. Jim and Gabe are staying in Tampa to wrap up details. Gabe's working on the timeline and making up a report of the evidence. I'll be ready to do the interview tomorrow. I want a confession out of Farmer, whether it's at his desk or the precinct. I can do this. You know I can."

"You make sure you have all the facts," Hal said. "Otherwise two departments are going to look like chicken shit."

"I'll take care of it," Brian assured him. "All of it, after you tell me TPD's in agreement with me handling the case along with Engelhardt, in a cooperative deal between the departments."

"You're a pain in the ass, Swift." Hal sounded amused more than angry.

"Thanks, Chief."

"Brown-noser." Hal hung up.

Brian breathed a sigh of relief and called Fred Engelhardt.

No sense in leaving the bureaucratic wheels to grind slowly to some possibly less-than-optimal outcome for either of them. As soon as Fred answered the phone, Brian began to lay out his plan. Sometimes, the brass needed a little push.

CHAPTER SIXTY-EIGHT

KAYLEN USHERED Angela into the hallway of her condo. When she locked the door, her fingers fumbled with the deadbolt.

"How much have you had to drink?" Angela asked.

"It's that noticeable, huh?"

"I wouldn't want to strike a match anywhere near you."

"Very funny." Kaylen turned and lost her balance. She reached for the wall and almost missed. Luckily, Angela was preoccupied with placing her purse and wrap on the hall table.

"Make yourself at home," Kaylen said to Angela's back. "If you want to join me, I can get another glass. It's Courvoisier."

Angela walked into the living room and came to an abrupt stop in front of the coffee table. "What's that?" She pointed toward the ring box. "Is that what I think it is?" She whipped around, eyes wide. "No wonder you've been celebrating! Brian proposed!"

"How I wish." Kaylen sat heavily onto an oversized side chair. "That's from Ziggy."

Angela sat, too. "No wonder you're tipsy." She looked at the Courvoisier. "You need something to eat."

"I was thinking of ordering pizza." Tired and unsettled, slightly dizzy from the cognac, Kaylen laid her head back and blinked away tears. "I've got to warn you, if you're thinking of staying, I might be a maudlin drunk this evening."

"No pizza," Angela said. "You'd probably get nauseated. Let's go to the little bistro on the corner, have a balanced meal and some mundane chit-chat, then come back here for the heart-to-heart. Big issues should never be tackled on an empty stomach and a snootful of brandy." She smiled.

Kaylen managed a watery smile in return. "Okay." It was an effort to get back up from the chair, and she stumbled a little as she leaned over to take her purse and jacket from the seat of a dining chair. Her jacket slid off and landed on the floor. "Damn."

Angela scooped up the jacket and took Kaylen's arm on the way to the elevator. "It'll work out. I'm here to help."

"I so need that." Kaylen had trouble swallowing a lump that had formed in her throat. "I've never felt so alone in my life. George and Tim gone. Sam, Sandy…"

Angela squeezed her arm. "I know. Jonathan and I have been waiting for you to reach out. We really care about you, but we didn't want to intrude. You had so many adjustments to make after George's death. Jonathan said the least he could do was give you some financial support for the club, but we wanted to do more, and then suddenly, there you were with Tim, that handsome boyfriend of yours, and your other close friends, and we felt like we'd be encroaching while you were building your new life."

"Tim." Kaylen leaned back against the elevator as it descended. She seemed to need physical support that evening as much as the emotional strength of a friend. "What a fiasco that relationship was. And now more of it, with his brother of all people. Why did George have to die? Life was easy with him. Predictable. *Logical.*"

"And now it's not." Angela smiled. "Now it's messy."

"Yes. That's what my life is right now. One big chaotic mess."

They strolled out of the building in silence. Kaylen tried to think how she could bring order back into her personal life, but didn't like the options.

Angela broke into her depressing ruminations. "I think I'm going to have the Alfredo. You don't mind walking, do you? It may help clear your head."

"That's fine."

Kaylen slid the strap of her heavy purse over her shoulder. She wondered what Angela would say if she casually mentioned she was packing heat. She waved at the gate guard as they passed. Welcoming lights from the bistro spilled onto the sidewalk a short distance away. A stiff breeze flapped Kaylen's open jacket. She shivered.

"Cold?" Angela asked.

"No, it feels good. Blowing the cobwebs away." Kaylen took deep breaths, drinking in fresh air.

"We should have Italian soda," Angela said. "No wine."

"Ugh, you're right there. I've definitely had enough liquor for one evening. But you can have wine. You should. You might need it after I'm finished unloading on you. By that time, you may need to finish the cognac, too."

A couple walked up to the bistro from the opposite direction, the man opening the door for his companion. He continued holding the door for Angela and Kaylen. "Well, hello. Fancy meeting you two here." He looked at Kaylen and his eyebrows rose slightly.

Phillip Sapperstein; the bigwig corporate attorney, at least in his own eyes. Yet another social acquaintance Kaylen would rather not have run into for a while longer. She wondered about those raised brows. Did she look drunk? Had she smudged her makeup and Angela hadn't noticed? She should have brushed her hair. It was probably sticking out all over the place after the walk. Dampness always produced even wilder curls, and here she was in public after an emotional meltdown.

"Where's Jonathan this evening?" Phillip followed the three women inside. His companion stepped closer to him and he helped her out of her coat.

"Home," Angela said. "He wanted to watch a game. I don't know which one. There are so many choices these days. We're having a girls' night out."

Sapperstein's companion extended her hand. "Good for you. I'm Felicity Hoffmeister."

"Oh, sorry." Phillip had the grace to look slightly embarrassed. "Where are my manners? Felicity, please meet Angela Crossfield and Kaylen Roberts."

"Hi." Felicity's handshake was strong and warm.

The maître d' appeared with menus. "A table for four?"

"Oh, no." Angela smiled broadly. She took Kaylen's arm again. "I'm sure Mr. Sapperstein and Ms. Hoffmeister would prefer to dine alone. Could you put us girls into a nice, dark little corner where we can gossip?" She winked at him.

"Certainly, Mrs. Crossfield." He inclined his head before turning toward Phillip and Felicity. "I'll be back momentarily," he told them.

"Enjoy your meal," Angela said over her shoulder. "I hate that man," she said under her breath to Kaylen as they followed the maître d' on a short walk to a table tucked into a space behind the partition dividing the restaurant's lobby area from the dining room.

"Will this be satisfactory?" The maître d' indicated the secluded table.

"Lovely." Kaylen sank onto a gilt chair with her back to the wall, where she could watch the entire dining room. She realized how well she followed Brian's instructions, even when she was a little tipsy.

Angela sat opposite and leaned forward. "So, first we eat. Then we have a delicious dessert and coffee boxed up to take back to your apartment. It'll make the true confession time a little more festive."

"Thanks, Angela." Kaylen tried swallowing the lump in her throat again, but it wouldn't budge.

"Of course." Angela spread her menu wide, but she smiled at Kaylen before turning her attention to choosing her meal.

Kaylen dug in her purse and produced her phone. "I've been expecting this to ring ever since Ziggy left this evening." She turned it off. "That's better. Now I can try to relax, at least until we've finished eating."

"What if Brian calls?" Angela moved her menu to one side as their waiter filled her water glass.

"The wine list, Madame?" He placed it on the table in front of Angela. "We have a couple of specials tonight: ricotta tortelloni with porcini sauce and a dash of balsamic vinegar, and pumpkin ravioli with a touch of Gorgonzola."

Angela glanced at the wine list, hesitated and looked at Kaylen.

"Do go ahead, Angela. I'll stick with mineral water."

"Okay, you've talked me into it." Angela gave the printed list a cursory once-over then looked up at the waiter. "I was going to have the Alfredo, but that tortelloni sounds wonderful. How about a good Pinot Noir to go with it? A glass, not a bottle. You choose."

The waiter looked flustered.

"Ask Gerard, if you're worried about which brand," she said, smiling up at him. "What's your name?"

He glanced toward the head waiter, who was deep in conversation with a busboy at the back of the restaurant. "My name is Alphon...Alan."

The maître d' reappeared, as though spirited in. "Is there a problem, Mrs. Crossfield?"

"Not at all, Henri. I was deciding with Alan's assistance which Pinot Noir would be best with the tortelloni."

"I can assist with that." The man's expression turned rigid as he looked at Alan.

"I think he was going to suggest either the 2012 Robert Goyette, weren't you, Alan, or the 2012 Argyle Reserve?" Kaylen broke in. "The Goyette would be *my* choice, but then I'm more familiar with the Sonoma Valley wines than those of the Willamette Valley in Oregon. What do you think, Angela?"

"Both sound like excellent suggestions," Angela said, catching on seamlessly. "But I'd like to try something different, so I'll go with the Argyle Reserve."

"Mesdames." Henri inclined his head and left.

Kaylen winked at Alan. "Great suggestions."

"Thank you." He let out his breath. "I'll bring your beverages immediately."

"Take your time." Angela waved a hand airily. "We're in no hurry. Really."

He left quickly, napkin over arm, back stiff.

"It's so hard, making the transition from a casual restaurant to some place like this," Kaylen said. "I feel like I should be keeping an eye on him. He reminds me of one of our own new waiters. He used to be a busboy, and still acts like one. Or maybe it's because he's still so young. Sometimes, owning a club feels like being a den mother."

"You're such a wonderful club owner," Angela said. "You look after your employees so well."

"Good training makes all the difference." Kaylen looked past Angela's shoulder and caught Sapperstein watching them. She moved her chair until his face was no longer in view.

Angela continued to peruse the menu, even though it had sounded like she knew exactly what she was ordering. "Do you want to make our meals take-out?" She asked. "Sapperstein's a notorious creep who always manages to bring grist to the rumor-mill. If Felicity goes into the restroom you let me know. I'll follow and warn her off him."

"Don't do that." Kaylen had to laugh. "Between the walk and seeing him, I've completely sobered up, and now I'm hungry."

"What are you having?"

"Antipasto misto. Share?"

"Absolutely. One of my favorites."

"Minestrone?"

Angela nodded. "Then the tortelloni for me. It sounds heavenly."

"I'm in the mood for manicotti, I think."

"A wise choice." Alan had reappeared with the drinks. He nodded his approval.

"An easy one." Kaylen sat back while Angela gave him the rest of their selections. He took a pencil from behind his ear and scribbled diligently on a little notepad he brought out of a pocket in his apron.

"Much easier than the other options in my life," Kaylen said after he left.

Angela took a sip of her wine. "This is really excellent. You'll have to try it yourself, sometime. Cheers."

They clinked glasses and toasted to world peace and some order in Kaylen's life as the antipasto arrived. Their meal was a leisurely, enjoyable affair during which they chatted companionably about Bannisters, Jonathan's latest business ventures and Angela's upcoming charity events. As they walked slowly back to her condo, Kaylen started filling Angela in on everything else that had happened since Bannisters opened. When she offered Angela a snifter of Courvoisier, Angela grate-fully accepted, but left the cognac untouched until Kaylen had finally brought her up to Ziggy's proposal that day. Then she drained her small serving in a matter of moments.

CHAPTER SIXTY-NINE

THE FLIGHT to Miami was completely uneventful. Brian thanked the pilot profusely and took a cab from the airfield to the marina. Knowing Kaylen was with Angela for the evening, Brian decided that after being around people without much of a break for the past two weeks, a night of solitude was far too appealing to pass up. But when he stretched out in bed, he found himself staring up at the ceiling with sleep very far from his mind.

Thoughts of the prospective meeting with Hal and Trehorn over his reinstatement to active duty and the Summerfield murder were already enough to give him insomnia. A confrontation with Wally Malone's little brother gave him yet another reason. Brian imagined Rick/Seamus working away at the car dealership the next day, completely oblivious to the fact that his life was never going to be the same again.

One senseless act on the part of a teenager had resulted in so many lives being affected. Maybe it was just desserts for Rick Farmer at this time in his life, and maybe it wasn't, but justice needed to be done at long last. Brian wanted it for Chad Summerfield and his family, although if Mel had been involved in the murder in any capacity, that justice was going to be bittersweet at best.

Tossing and turning, Brian's thoughts turned to a mystery much closer to his heart...finding out what had happened to his father and why his mother had burst into tears at any mention of Andy Swift's name. How could he move forward with Kaylen when he had no idea whether his father had been run over by a bus or was serving twenty to life for murder? Was his father a philanderer or a petty thief? Had he abandoned Maggie Brooks when she was pregnant?

After so many years of pushing away questions about his family background, Brian realized he was ready to know the truth. Kaylen already deserved so much more than he was offering in terms of emotional stability and security. Trying to make a life with her in the future would be impossible if he still wondered what might be hiding in his past. She already knew about the abuse and hadn't run the other way. Why did he continue to believe she would react differently to any other revelations?

Kaylen truly *was* a woman in a million. Tim had tried his best to give his brother a chance at happiness. Brian knew everyone else was ready for him to make his life with Kaylen. He was the lone hold-out, as the first one to f-up any relationship. If he didn't act soon, this one would be no different. Ziggy Stavros was poised, ready to swoop in and take Kaylen away. Brian knew it as well as he knew Rick Farmer had blown Chad Summerfield away that hot summer day 25 years ago, either in a fit of passion or because of blind rage and a misconception.

Completely unable to rest, he decided he didn't care if Kaylen was enjoying a girls' night out. He needed to hear her voice. Hell, he needed to *feel* her. It was close to 2:00 AM. He sat up, threw off the covers and reached for his phone.

He needed her. Period. In every sense of the word. He finally felt able to admit that he had made sure he flew back to Miami not only for his weekly appointments with Fleming, but to spend time with Kaylen. One touch from her, one of those intimate looks she gave only him, and he felt more alive than he ever had from the adrenaline rushes his job had given him.

There would be no going back.

The finality of telling her somehow didn't feel as apocalyptic as it had after Tim's death. If he was really honest with himself, the only thing he *would* have changed about anything that had happened in the last few months would have been Tim making it to Rio alive and well. Brian knew he'd even have taken that damned bullet again.

Abandoning his bed, he pulled on jeans and an old hoodie with a Miami Dolphins logo before leaving the *NTK* to walk the dark and deserted dock, oblivious to the drop in temperature.

He held his phone while he walked, still unsure what he was planning to say to Kaylen. He knew what he had to do: Keep her safe. If he didn't, then he knew who damn well would...Ziggy Stavros.

Jealousy ripped through Brian. Ziggy Fucking Stavros, taking care of Kaylen. *Sleeping with her.*

To hell with being noble and stepping away. His long strides took him up and down the dock at a fast pace. *To hell with feeling like he wasn't worthy.*

Kaylen thought he was. She loved him.

And he was a complete and total idiot for not admitting that he loved her right back.

Maybe he *didn't* deserve her, but then, who would?

He punched in her number, but instead of Kaylen picking up, he was told the subscriber was unavailable and he was sent straight to voicemail. "Kaylen," he started, and then faltered.

What *was* he about to say? That he loved her? That he wanted to commit to their relationship, but he was scared shitless for the first time in his life? Were those really words to be put into a message?

Brian hung up, not sure whether he was relieved or annoyed, leaving only recorded static and the sound of the wind.

CHAPTER SEVENTY

"So what are you going to do?" Angela asked, taking a sip of water from the bottle in her hand. Curled up on Kaylen's couch with her legs and feet tucked under her and her pale blonde hair hanging over one shoulder, she looked completely at ease.

Kaylen wished she was in Angela's shoes instead of her own that evening. "I don't know," she said. "I honestly don't."

Angela popped open the ring box and stared at the proof of Ziggy's affection. "It's really lovely. These look like very good stones. It must have cost him a packet."

"Or cost his father."

"You think Peter fronted the money for this?" Angela waved the box at Kaylen, the ring glinting as though it was a winking conspirator.

"I wouldn't put it past him. He's got a streak of ruthlessness that makes me wonder whether he isn't using Ziggy's infatuation to further his own business interests. It wouldn't hurt Peter if his youngest son were to marry the widow of George Bannister Roberts and gain an interest in her club."

"You'd make him sign a pre-nup. You had to sign one before you married George."

"A pre-nup wouldn't stop Ziggy or any of the Stavros clan from using my name, or George's, either, for that matter. They could secure bigger lines of credit. Get doors to open that have remained closed to them. You know as well as I do what the Miami business community is like."

"I know even more what the social community is like," Angela said. "We're all ready for you to introduce Brian. We're not ready for you to come back to us on the arm of Ziggy Stavros. He's younger than you and really immature. I could tell that in the short time I spent with him in Bannisters. He's totally charming, but he's not the man you're in love with, and frankly, if you put Ziggy and Brian side by side, Ziggy is not the one I'd choose, whether he's got more social graces or not. Good God, Kaylen. Brian is a man in every sense of the word. If I wasn't a happily married woman, I'd be fighting you tooth and nail for possession."

She looked so serious, Kaylen was taken-aback.

"You already had your mad fling with Tim," Angela said. "He had it all...the charisma, the height, the looks, you name it. But after George you went for the boys, and now you've got a wonderful chance to grab happiness a second time, with a man who's completely worthy of you. What do you want out of life? A repeat performance with Tim's double?"

"Of course not." Kaylen felt conflicted and more than a little defensive. She wanted so much to share her hopes and fears with Angela, but she had paid so dearly for that openness with Sandy and Sam.

"Come on, Kaylen. This is *me*. I have nothing to gain from you taking me into your confidence, and you need to reach out. I won't tell Jonathan any of what you share with me if you ask me not to."

Kaylen couldn't keep the dam closed on her emotions any longer. She burst into tears.

Angela slid closer and took her hand in a warm and comforting grip. "Let it out," she urged. "Tell me."

Kaylen took a gulping breath. "Brian won't tell me he loves me." She pulled a tissue from the box Angela held out to her and blew her nose hard. "He's had so many opportunities." Her voice quivered horribly. "He's not ready, Angela. I don't know if he ever will be."

"Men take longer than women to work through things," Angela said.

"They hold so much in. It's in their genes, I think, not to share their doubts and their troubles like women do."

"I thought I could wait."

The tears kept falling, like they had after George died. After Tim died. After Brian got shot. Her tissue sodden, Kaylen pulled a handful out of the box, wiped her face and let out a profoundly deep sigh. She felt physically depleted.

"That's what we all do," Angela said. "Sit around and wait while the men in our lives decide to make the commitment we're all looking for."

Kaylen shook her head. "I never have. This is the first time I've been on that side of a relationship. It hurts really, really badly, and I feel like a fool. I could be waiting forever, and I have a deep need to be loved and cherished. Not just by anyone, Angela. By Brian. But I can't wait much longer, if he's a lost cause."

Suddenly, her tears stopped. She knew the ugly truth: Either Brian was going to have to step up to the plate pretty quickly, or she was going to have to move on, alone.

"I can't be the perpetual girlfriend and settle for that." She knew that was the absolute truth. "Brian's everything to me. I want to spend the rest of my life with him. But it looks like I'm not enough for him, or his fear of commitment is so big, it's going to tear us apart, whether neither of us really wants that or not."

Angela took a moment to think before responding, her brow furrowed. She sat back and pushed her hair off her shoulder. "At least Brian didn't propose when you and he were barely out of the friends-only stage, like Ziggy just did."

Kaylen grabbed a throw pillow and hugged it to her chest. "That's true. But I'm so sick of being on the available list. Before Tim, men were hitting on me all the time, for the conquest. Just to say they'd been with me. I was devastated. I'm not flighty, and I was never cheap. I want stability and a loving relationship, like I had in my marriage. I miss George, damn it."

"I know." Angela leaned forward, forearms on knees. "We're all going through what you are: evolving, learning new skills, new roles. Me, too. 'Ang.,' Jonathan said to me a few months back. 'You can't be completely clueless your whole life. What if I died suddenly? Do you really want to have Dave Parkman the CFO running our company?'" She smiled, a little thinly. "As soon as he said 'our' it brought home to me that it wasn't Jonathan running *his* company but Jon running the company he'd inherited from his father and grandfather for *our* future."

"Oh," Kaylen said, thinking what a shock that must have been for Angela, who, like Kaylen, had made a career out of parties, social events and charity functions.

"And now Jon said he wants children." Angela threw up her hands. "When I met and married him, children were the farthest thing from his mind. So, my life is changing, too, Kaylen. I've got to learn the business and produce heirs, if I'm even capable. We're in testing. My fertility isn't great, and neither is Jonathan's. But we're remaining hopeful, and neither of us is against a surrogate, if that's what it takes. I'm thirty-nine. Jon's forty-one. We'll be middle-aged parents. That's a jarring thought." She smiled again, but there were tears sparkling in her big blue eyes.

"Angela, I don't know what to say…," Kaylen began, searching for appropriate words and coming up short. She suddenly had an idea her life and Angela's were on some parallel track she hadn't considered before that evening. But Angela wasn't finished, and rushed on, right over Kaylen's abortive attempt to console her.

"George didn't prepare you adequately." Angela pulled a tissue out of the box and wiped tears from her own cheeks. "He liked being protective, and he knew you were savvy as a manager, which is why he left you that property and asked Jon to invest when the time was right for you to open your supper club. But he didn't trust you enough with his own company, like he had Sylvia. And let's face it, after how wife number one took him to the cleaners, he wasn't going to do a repeat performance with you, wife number two."

"That's true," Kaylen admitted.

George had told her she didn't have the business sense to manage his affairs, and she'd accepted that judgment, signed the pre-nup and on his death, handed over George's business holdings to his ex-wife and their children like she was not only a second wife, but a second thought, and an appendage to George's shortened life. For the first time ever, she felt a spark of anger at his lack of confidence in her abilities. He'd thought her too young and green, she decided, to make a success of anything but the club, which was familiar territory for her.

Angela interrupted Kaylen's churning thoughts. "We all want the best for you," she said, her voice and expression radiating intensity. "Everyone in your social set. We loved George so much, Kaylen. You and he were a perfect love-match. But he loved you gently. I think all the passion you want is with Brian. I can see the change in you. You're not tentative or dependent anymore. You stand up to everyone. And yet there's an underlying softness and tenderness when you're with Brian. Even when you talk about him. Jonathan noticed that, too."

"I'm doomed, aren't I?" Kaylen shook her head. "Wanting more and getting less. What am I going to do? I've tried telling Brian how I feel. He's too strong for me to shake the truth of his feelings out of him." She smiled. "I think I'm a half-inch taller than him. Maybe I could put on my three inch heels and stand over him. Do you think he'd find that intimidating?"

Angela smiled, too, at that comment. "Not for a moment."

"No," Kaylen said. "Not even for the space of a heartbeat."

"Let's have a glass of champagne," Angela suggested. "I saw a bottle in your refrigerator earlier."

"What in the world are we celebrating?"

"You turning down Ziggy Stavros's proposal."

"But you shouldn't be drinking. You're trying to get pregnant. The testing…"

"No pregnancy this month," Angela said. "I found that out earlier today. So to hell with it tonight. Let's pop that cork."

CHAPTER SEVENTY-ONE

AFTER DECIDING he was in no fit state to start talking to Kaylen about anything, Brian went back to bed and slept restlessly, the *Need to Know* rocking on a heavy swell. Two weeks he'd been on land, and the boat already felt strange, as though he had just moved into it.

He was glad to get up the following morning. The rhythmic creaking annoyed him as he made his coffee, and even the coffee tasted bitter and stale. He threw the rest of the canister into the dumpster on the way to his car, and then remembered he didn't have a car. The Camaro was away for restoration. His license had been revised to reflect his disability. He wouldn't be able to easily rent anything on short notice.

He walked out of the marina, crossed the street and with great reluctance headed for Kaylen's condo. If she wasn't home he knew he'd be furious and more than a little suspicious. Conflicted over what to do for the best and feeling like a total coward where Kaylen was concerned, Brian stopped on the sidewalk and called Mills.

"Can you pick me up?"

"Good morning to you, too, Swift." Jack Mills yawned. "What the hell time is it, and where are you?"

"It's eight o'clock and I'm halfway between the marina and Kaylen's condo."

"What's wrong with your car?"

Brian explained his predicament.

Mills grunted. "I worked late and this was supposed to be my day off, before Trehorn told me to plan on a noon meeting."

"Go back to sleep, then. I'll call a cab." Brian wondered why Mills hadn't been asked to pick up Engelhardt at the airport. So much for extending professional courtesies.

"I didn't say I wouldn't do it." Mills sounded more awake. "I had to put in a token complaint before acting as your chauffeur." He yawned again. "Give me thirty minutes. I've got to shower and shave. You'd better have a cup of joe waiting. Where do you want me to pick you up?"

"The marina. I'll be at the entrance with your goddamned coffee."

"I like cream and sugar. Two packets in a large cup, and make it light. What are you cooking up? Anything you can share?"

"An interview with a murder suspect."

"That cold case you've been working on? Jesus; you've solved the damned thing?" Mills no longer sounded anything close to sleepy.

"Yeah. I think so. When I talked to Hal yesterday, I thought you were supposed to be brought up to speed and you were picking up Tampa's liaison from the airport."

"What? No one said a damned thing to me."

"I'm calling Hal right now. Find out what's going on. Hurry the f...hell up, Mills, and don't forget to brush your teeth."

Mills snorted and hung up.

Brian called Hal on his cell and got an earful of obscenities. He heard in no uncertain terms that he was overstepping his bounds.

Brian threw caution to the wind. He'd had enough of being kept out of department plans. "Not when you rained shit on me," he retorted. "What game are you playing? You told me yesterday you were gonna work on getting Engelhardt into town as the official TPD liaison and Mills and Gabe assigned to Cold Case. I just woke Mills up. He knows nothing apart from he's going to some meeting at noon."

"What? I told Trehorn what to do, and I left no room for error." Hal sounded furious. "Get off this phone and wait for my call."

Mills wasn't the only one in need of a good cup of coffee at that point. Brian felt the beginnings of a headache. He nixed both the local convenience store and a nearby Cuban coffee shop, deciding if Mills wanted his coffee pale, then he wouldn't want a dark roast full of chicory. Instead, he headed for Mizelle's. Kaylen frequently bought her own first cup of coffee there if she was rushing to a meeting at work. If he found her inside, then he would be forced to deal with her, too, but he wasn't going to walk all over the neighborhood to avoid her.

He checked his watch. He'd already used up half the time Mills had said he needed. Brian picked up his pace, the sign for Mizelle's coffee shop and patisserie in view a block away. He wondered whether Trehorn had tried to undercut or even sabotage his re-entry into MDPD, in hopes of either making his potentially-problematic detective look completely incompetent or incapable of pulling his shit together sufficiently to be placed back on active duty.

CHAPTER SEVENTY-TWO

KAYLEN AWOKE WEARING her street clothes and hanging half out of bed. When she started to sit up, a splitting headache made her change her mind. So much for drowning her problems in a bottle of brandy, she thought. And then she'd topped off the evening with champagne? What was she…crazy?

Pushing tangled hair out of her eyes, she rolled slowly out of bed and walked unsteadily into the living room to find Angela sprawled out on the couch, one foot on the floor. Kaylen knew that old trick. Keep a foot on the floor and the room stops spinning, at least theoretically. Maybe the same reason she had found herself hanging off the bed. She turned on the light over the stove and started coffee.

"Oooh, my head." Angela groaned, throwing a forearm across her eyes. "Can't you make that water run quieter?"

"No, unfortunately for both of us."

Angela slowly sat up, holding her head. "Oh, my God. I know I get a hangover from champagne, but that didn't stop me from drinking half a bottle. I need a lot of things this morning: A shower, clean clothes, coffee, water, and a strong pain-reliever. Maybe a new head. I should probably start with water and the pain killer, then work backwards on the rest of the list. Do you have any?"

"I do. Advil's on the bottom shelf of the cabinet to the left of the sink." Kaylen took mugs out of another cabinet above the coffeemaker and closed the door quietly. "I'll take some, myself. There's bottled water in the refrigerator."

"I'm getting too old for tying one on." Angela retrieved two bottles of water and the Advil, shaking two caplets out for Kaylen and another two for herself. "I had wine with Jonathan before I called you, then a glass of brandy, another glass of wine at dinner, and finished up with that champagne. Oh, I hate myself right now. I'd better call Jon and reassure him I'm mostly okay."

"I'm with you in the hate department." Kaylen swallowed the pills with half a bottle of water. "I acted like an idiot, but I'm so glad you came over." She removed the carafe from the coffeemaker and jammed a mug in its place.

"To share your pain?"

"Yes." Kaylen handed the filled mug to Angela before jamming another mug under the stream of coffee. "How do you take yours? There's cream in the fridge and I've got brown sugar or sweetener."

"Black this morning. Ugh, that shower's got to be next."

"The guest bathroom is to the right." Kaylen watched Angela walk across the room with her mug held out carefully in front of her. "There should be plenty of towels in there. And it's clean. Brian uses it when he stays here, so you might find a razor in the shower. But he hasn't been here in over a week."

"Good thing he hasn't." Angela paused in the doorway to look back at Kaylen. "I think Ziggy's enough for you to deal with right now."

"You're right, there." Kaylen took cream out of the refrigerator. "More than enough," she added to herself as Angela disappeared into the guest room and closed the door.

Kaylen had never been a big fan of black coffee, and with her stomach slightly queasy, she didn't think testing her dislike was a good idea. She did leave her coffee darker than usual however, sipping it while taking out clean clothes. She showered, dressed in jeans and a long-sleeved ice blue cotton top with matching cardigan. Forgoing makeup, she went back into the living room with her damp hair pulled back with a clip.

Angela was standing in the kitchen, leaning her elbows on the breakfast bar. She wore an overly-large white terry cloth robe with the sleeves rolled up. "Do you want breakfast?" She delicately rubbed the end of her nose with one French-manicured finger. "I drank most of the coffee already. I feel slightly better."

Kaylen managed a smile that didn't make her head thump harder. "I should think so on all that caffeine. You drank about six cups, you know."

"I know. I'll probably regret that in a while, too, but right now, it's clearing my head."

"Do you want to borrow some clean clothes?"

"Please. I didn't want to put back the stuff I slept in." Angela held out the coffeepot. "Refill? I think there's at least one cup left."

"Sure." Kaylen put her mug on the counter.

Angela drained the carafe and placed it carefully into the sink. "No sudden noises," she said. "I need food. Do you want to go to Mizelle's?"

"You think she'll lock the door and put the closed sign out if she sees us coming?"

"No way. She wants to keep her business." Angela up-ended her mug. "I'm sorry, I was a coffee hog, but I needed all of it."

"Let's find you an outfit, and then we'll walk over to the cafe." Kaylen tugged on Angela's arm. "If you promise not to get me drunk every time you come over, I'll let you be my best friend."

"Get you drunk? Girlfriend, you were already there when I got here last night. I'm sorry to say, I added to the experience. I can only promise not to do that again unless it's completely necessary. If you need a repeat performance after you give Ziggy that ring back, I'll come over and be supportive. I'll even hold your head if you need to barf. How's that?"

"Maybe the best I can hope for." Kaylen opened her closet. "Anything you want," she said. "But since you're several inches shorter than me, maybe you'd better stick with capris, unless you want to go around with the pants rolled up."

"I'm usually considered to be tall," Angela said. "But next to you, I feel like a shrimp. Five-seven's a good height for a woman."

"I'm *too* tall," Kaylen said. "It can be useful sometimes, especially in the business world, but in my private life, I've had more than my share of shorter men chasing after me. They really like the challenge of a tall woman." She nodded when Angela held up a pair of denim capris and a mint green cotton sweater. "Those would look good on you. How about underwear? I've got some new panties I haven't even taken out of the bag."

Angela looked at Kaylen. "Hmm...I'll keep my bra because you and I are definitely not the same size, but I'll take a pair of those panties."

Leaving Angela to get dressed, Kaylen took her cell phone into the living room and realized she had never turned it back on. When she checked her voicemail, she found Brian had called but hadn't left anything in the way of a message except a rushing noise. *Strange,* she thought.

Then she looked at Ziggy's ring and horror grabbed her heart. Brian had a key to her condo, which he rarely used because he didn't like to go into her home unless she was there. She felt the same way about invading his space on the *NTK.*

But what if he had come back early from Tampa to tell her he'd solved his case? What if he'd wanted to surprise her and walked into the condo while she and Angela were at dinner? He'd have seen that ring box, right in the middle of the coffee table.

Oh, dear God!

Kaylen felt lightheaded, her heart contracting painfully. "Angela," she said.

"What?" Angela's voice was muffled, like she was in the middle of pulling the sweater over her head.

"Oh, God, Angela! I think I've really blown it!"

CHAPTER SEVENTY-THREE

BRIAN WORKED on his relaxation techniques as Mills made short work of the trip to the precinct.

"Hal called me right after you did." Mills weaved in and out of traffic. "Asked me if I'd take that transfer to Cold Case. Warned me I'd have you as a supervisor." His expression was completely deadpan. "I asked him if he expected me to take early retirement after you gave me a heart attack."

Brian's apprehensiveness dropped a notch. Maybe Hal hadn't been screwing with him. "Mills, I…"

"I'm joshing you, Swift. I told him I'd be honored. He's putting through the paperwork. Told me Gabe's joining us."

Brian's world shifted back into focus. He let out a deep, cleansing breath and the tension that had held his left shoulder in a vice grip relaxed. "Thanks for the vote of confidence, Jack."

"Of course." Mills glanced over, and his expression changed to one of concern. "Bad time for a joke, huh? Seriously, I meant it when I told you I'd partner you any time. This is even better. You can tell me what to do. I know Homicide, but going over decades-old cases will be challenging."

"This one sure has been." Brian looked through the windshield as they slowed down and pulled into the precinct's parking lot, the sedan gliding past rows of cruisers to end up at the building's back entrance. "I've had a rough time these last few months, Jack. I can't even begin to tell you how much I want to get back to my job. I never thought I'd say this, but after working this old homicide, I know Cold Case'll be the right fit for me."

"The chief sounded pissed." Mills turned in his seat to face Brian. "Not at me, but in general. I'm glad I'm not the one going into an early meeting with him and Trehorn. After I drop you off, I have to pick up that Tampa detective you talked about. Alicia said they scrambled to get him on the next flight into Fort Lauderdale."

Calling Hal may have bypassed the chain of command, but it had also gotten lightning-fast results. "You'll like Engelhardt," he told Mills. "He's a straight shooter."

Mills nodded. "Good. That'll be a breath of fresh air around here."

Brian opened the door and started to get out. "Thanks for the ride, Jack. Yeah, and think yourself lucky you're the chauffeur, not the one going into this meeting."

"I'm to bring Engelhardt with me to Hal's office. Hope you're in one piece when we get there."

"I will be. Can't guarantee how good Trehorn will look." Brian heard Mills laughing as he backed his car out of the parking space and left.

It felt strange, walking into the building and taking the elevator to Hal's office floor, like he had become someone else during the past couple of weeks. Alicia looked up from her desk, phone to her ear, when he pushed open the door. She pointed to the small seating area. Brian sat to wait and glanced at the magazine selection: Back issues of Law Officer and Correctional News. He figured anyone looking for lighter reading materials, such as Better Homes and Gardens or Entertainment Weekly would be sorely disappointed.

Alicia put down the phone. The intercom buzzed once. "They're ready for you." Her usually wide smile was cut to a minimum, and even that appeared more than a little forced.

Brian wondered what had been going on before he got there. He walked past her into Hal's office, finding him seated across the desk from a sandy-haired man with a closely-clipped goatee. Brian figured this must be Trehorn. He looked to be in his late thirties, with pale blue eyes and a sizeable scar running through his right eyebrow. Brian closed the door quietly behind himself.

"Have a seat, Swift." Hal indicated the open chair next to the other man. "Darrell Trehorn, meet Brian Swift."

Trehorn extended one freckled hand, which appeared too large for his frame. Brian shook it, feeling strength in the warm, dry grip. Trehorn cracked a slight smile, which only lifted the left corner of his mouth. Brian noted the scar on his right eyebrow was echoed by another reaching from the corner of his mouth to his ear. Faded, but definitely visible against his freckled face, it left Brian wondering whether it was service-related or the result of some earlier accident.

"I've heard a lot about you," Trehorn said. His voice was deep, well-modulated and quiet.

"I bet." Brian sat. "My reputation precedes me everywhere in this department." He looked at Hal, who stared back, expressionless.

"We've been discussing your future," Hal said. "Returning to Homicide has been problematic, partly because of your injury, but also due to other factors—obviously, your brother's unsolved case, your tendency to work alone and frequently without notifying your immediate supervisor as to what you're doing; your angry outbursts toward personnel and the public."

Brian wanted to interrupt, but stopping Hal would only sound as argumentative as his reputation.

Hal paused, as though expecting that interruption. When Brian stayed silent, he turned to Trehorn. "But with all that said, Swift showed outstanding courage at a time when many others would have been brought to their knees. His ability to operate in the field while injured showed strength, tenacity and bravery above and beyond his training."

"Agreed." Trehorn nodded. "But regardless of those results," he pointed to a hard-copy on Hal's desk, "I still don't feel comfortable about him returning to active duty. He hasn't been cleared by the psychologist or his physician."

"Can I interrupt, since you're both talking about me like I'm not here?" Brian made sure he measured his words and took a quick, deep breath before they both looked at him.

Hal and Trehorn glanced at each other. Trehorn shrugged.

"Go ahead," Hal said. "But keep to the point."

Brian bit back a retort he knew he would have delivered less than a month ago. "I've made an appointment to see my surgeon this Friday." He raised his left arm. It moved in a continuous, fluid arc until it was above his head. He lowered it, exerting more effort than he would have liked to control its descent, but was moderately pleased with the result. He reached forward and picked up the fattest ballpoint pen he saw in Hal's coffee cup penholder and carefully wrote his name on a scratch pad. "I'm hoping he'll release me. Physical Therapy referred me to a trainer for on-going strengthening. I don't need to go back to the clinic.

"I'll be at my regularly-scheduled appointment with the psychologist on Thursday morning at ten o'clock. He's asked me to bring Kaylen Roberts with me, and I'm planning to do that, as long as she doesn't object. I want to continue my sessions to work through some issues that have no direct bearing on my job. After this upcoming session, I'm anticipating he'll also agree to me coming back to work."

He leaned back, hoping he appeared at ease. "And finally, in solving a case that's remained open for the last twenty-five years, in a collaborative effort with Tampa PD, I believe I've proved to myself and hopefully, to the chief and my new staff in the Cold Case squad that I'm fully committed to heading up that division and bringing some measure of closure and justice to those victims and their grieving family and friends." He surreptitiously let out his breath in one long, cleansing stream.

Hal looked at him incredulously, as though he was an imposter, sent to fill in for the real Brian Swift.

Trehorn blinked twice before leaning forward. "You're a slick talker, Swift."

"I'm laying all my cards on the table. No bullshit." Brian felt a cramp starting up in his left shoulder and sat up straighter.

"Better not be." Hal leaned forward, planting his forearms on his desk. "There must have been something in the anesthetic they gave you with the surgery," he said. "Slow-acting. You're rational."

"Yeah. Coming to terms with who I am, what I can do, and where I can go in the future."

Trehorn's face remained impassive, but a twitch started at the corner of one eye. "You really think you can change from some hot-headed renegade to a responsible supervisor, just because you got shot and lost your brother?"

It was a low blow. Brian almost caught it, but steeled himself not to react. Trehorn, for whatever reason, was trying to push his buttons, like Fleming had been doing for months. But the attempt failed. Brian wasn't sure if it was because he had grown another pair in the months since Tim's death or the never-ending waves of adversity had battered him so long and so hard that he'd finally become immune to the pounding.

"Yes," he said.

CHAPTER SEVENTY-FOUR

BENEATH A HUGE SIGN for "Barker's Buick, Cadillac and GMC," a slightly smaller sign announcing New Car Sales hung to the left of the buildings, and another, with an arrow pointing to the right, led to the Used Car Sales and Service Department.

Mills slowed down his black Buick Regal. "Left or right?"

"We'd better park in the first lot, I should think," Fred Engelhardt said from the back seat. "The sales offices are usually at the back of the showroom."

Brian's appreciation of Engelhardt's quiet professionalism had increased even further when they got underway to pick up Rick Farmer within minutes of a quick briefing at the precinct.

"Agreed." Mills drove onto the lot and eased the Regal into a space between a late model Honda and an older Toyota Camry with New Jersey plates, a sizeable dent and rust around the wheel wells.

Jack gave the dirty Camry a wide berth as he stepped onto the walkway leading to the showroom. "I bet that just made it down here," he said. "It'll fetch about a hundred on a trade-in, if the owner's lucky."

A smiling thirty-something guy in a shiny black suit strode out to greet them. Behind him, a cherry red pickup with a huge white bow on top of its cab gleamed from the other side of the plate glass window.

"Hard to imagine Christmas is right around the corner." Jack jerked his head toward the truck. "That would make one hell of a gift from some woman to her man."

"Then you'd better hurry up and find that woman." Brian watched the salesman extend his hand as he approached.

"Guy Buckman, at your service." He pumped Brian's hand energetically. "I saw you admiring the truck. Would you like to take a closer look? How about a test drive? It's on special. We can give you a good price."

Mills shook his head slightly. "My friend's thinking more about a sedan," he said. "Or maybe a van."

"Of course. For the family, no doubt." Buckman looked inquisitively at Brian. "Any particular model you're interested in? Is this a Christmas gift for your wife?"

"My girlfriend drives a BMW," Brian said. "I'm more interested in talking with your sales manager, Rick Farmer."

Buckman looked taken-aback. "Mr. Farmer's in a sales meeting." He drew himself up straighter. "I'm completely qualified to help you, Mr. ...?"

"Swift," Brian said. "It's a family matter. Urgent." He pulled back his jacket and showed the salesman the badge clipped to his belt.

Buckman's eyes opened wide. "Oh. Well, Mr. Farmer's actually not in a...ah...meeting. He's...ah...in his office." He hovered, undecided.

"Now would be a good time to take us to him," Brian prompted. Mills pulled his own jacket back enough to show Brian wasn't the only one with a badge and a gun.

"Er, yes. Yes, of course." The salesman turned on his heel and opened the door, gesturing for the detectives to precede him.

"Nope, you lead the way, and try to keep this low-profile." Brian grabbed the door when Buckman released it as though it had suddenly heated up.

They followed the salesman's brisk pace through the showroom to a door marked 'Sales Manager.' He knocked tentatively. Brian moved Buckman aside and opened the door to find Rick Farmer on the phone, a Styrofoam cup of coffee to one side of him and a half-eaten Egg McMuffin on the other, sitting on top of a take-out bag. Aromas of ham and cheese lingered in the air. Farmer looked even more startled than his salesman.

"I'll have to call you back," he said, then put down the phone. "What the hell is this, Buckman?"

"They're cops," Buckman said. "It's an urgent matter."

"Thanks." Mills nodded toward the door. "We'll let you know if we need you again."

Torn between obeying Mills and waiting for orders from his supervisor, Buckman hovered like an oversized drone.

"Thanks, Guy," Farmer said.

The salesman sped off, heading for the showroom. Before closing Farmer's door, Brian watched Buckman fumble around inside one pocket of his jacket and pull out a pack of cigarettes. He wondered how long it would take for the rest of the dealership to know Rick Farmer had cops in his office.

"I'm Detective Mills," Jack said.

"Sergeant Swift," Brian said.

Fred stepped forward. "And I'm Detective Engelhardt from Tampa. You might remember my name."

Brian watched Rick Farmer's face turn ashen.

Without waiting for an invitation, Mills pulled over another chair from beside the wall so all three of them could sit in front of Farmer's desk.

Fred glanced over at Brian and Mills. "We're investigating a cold case," he said. "In a collaborative effort between our departments. These officers are from Miami Dade. I'll leave the details to Sergeant Swift."

A flush started up Farmer's neck and quickly spread onto his face. His hands moved from the desk to his lap. "A cold case, you say?" He tried to settle back in his chair in an obvious and shallow attempt at looking less alarmed. "How would I be able to help you?" He swallowed, his Adam's apple bobbing like a floater with a fish on the end of the line.

"The case has been reopened, based on new evidence," Brian said.

He watched Farmer's blush darken, but Rick said nothing.

"I talked to your brother, Wally Malone," Brian said.

"My brother?" Rick's voice sounded like all the air had been sucked out of it, reducing its volume by a good half.

"Come on, Rick," Mills said. "Did you really think you could hide here in plain sight for the rest of your life?"

"I'm not hiding." Rick cleared his throat and managed to take a sip of coffee without spilling it.

Brian figured the only reason for that was the coffee cup was almost empty. "Sure looks like it," he said. "Otherwise, why'd you change your name?"

"Rick Farmer's a whole lot less ethnic than Seamus Malone," Rick said. "I wanted a fresh start after getting out of Tampa. My parents, too. I'm sure if Wally spilled the beans on my new identity, then he told you about my parents."

"Houston," Brian said, without confirming Wally as the informant.

Rick nodded. He carefully placed the coffee cup onto a pamphlet showing another bright red truck, gleaming black tires turned to indicate speed and handling prowess. "I've lived under a shadow for the past twenty-five years. I knew one of these days Tampa would catch up to me."

"Time to man-up," Fred said, leaning forward. "For the sake of the Summerfields, if not your own family."

Rick put his head in his hands. "I never meant for any of this to happen."

"I'm sure you didn't." Brian watched Farmer carefully. "Mel managed to persuade you, though, didn't she?"

Rick's head shot up. He looked straight at Brian. "Mel? She's the reason you're here? That little bitch..."

"The evidence is the reason we're here," Fred told him. "You messed up. People saw you, and they're talking. Not just Mel Summerfield."

"No one saw anything. I wasn't involved...." Farmer was regaining his equilibrium after the first moments of shock. "...in whatever you're saying I was involved in. I did nothing wrong. I never robbed any convenience store. If people are saying I did, then they're lying."

"Not the convenience store incident," Brian said. "We're talking about the investigation into Chad Summerfield's murder."

Farmer jumped to his feet. *"What?"*

Brian was on his feet, too, his hand on the butt of his gun. "Sit down."

Jack Mills got up slowly. "You don't want to ignore that order," he said, walking around the desk. He put his hand on Farmer's shoulder and pushed. "Sit."

Farmer sat. He looked rebellious, his mouth held in a tight line, his eyes darting to the door and back, as though weighing his chances of sprinting across the room against finding his route blocked by the detectives between him and the exit.

"If we're mistaken, you can tell your story, your way," Jack said. "At the precinct. Better to cooperate than add a charge of resisting arrest."

Brian had wanted Rick Farmer to confess of his own free will right there at his desk. He felt a shot of anger at Mills' interference, but he knew Jack's reasoning was clear: Mirandize Farmer and record his statement. Make sure this once-young killer didn't manage to slip through the cracks on some technicality. And don't muddy the waters with any resistance, either.

Brian remembered Kaylen's remark at Tim's gravesite. How Tim had left an indelible mark on both of them. Seamus Malone had done that to his family and to the Summerfields, in his own way. Before Shelley was even born, her life had been set onto a course that led to her own teenage pregnancy and out-of-wedlock child. And the Malone family's attempts to cover up and protect had now been blown out of the water.

"Stand up, Rick," Mills said. He had his cuffs out.

Rick's chair rolled back obediently from the desk and he stood, sweat shining on his brow and above his upper lip. "Can I call my wife first?"

"You'll get one call, down at the precinct," Mills said. "You can call her from there; ask her to get you an attorney. Turn around and place your hands behind your back."

Rick turned, breathing rapidly, head lowered.

Brian thought he could feel the disbelief radiating from Farmer. Twenty-five years since the shooting, and he was cuffed for Chad's murder.

"Rick Farmer, AKA Seamus Malone, you're under arrest for the murder of Chad Summerfield. You have the right to remain silent. Anything you say may be used against you," Jack said. He completed the Miranda as Fred Engelhardt opened the door and they escorted Rick out through the showroom. Staff and customers alike stopped and stared in silence.

Brian cast a look back as Mills loaded Farmer into the back of the Buick and Engelhardt climbed in with him. Stunned and inquisitive faces gawked through the plate glass windows of the dealership. A sense of closure swept through Brian. He was back where he belonged, and ready to make his own peace, both with his new career choice and with Kaylen.

He sent the same text to Jim and Gabe on the way to the precinct: "Done deal. Suspect apprehended."

CHAPTER SEVENTY-FIVE

THERE HAD BEEN no breakfast for Kaylen and Angela that morning. Kaylen had vomited three times after hearing Brian's vastly incomplete and unsettling voicemail. She made Angela go home despite all her attempts to stay. Kaylen needed to wallow in her own misery. At one o'clock that afternoon, she called Jim under the pretense of finding out if there had been any developments in the case.

"Brian sent a couple of texts. It's all over, honey. They arrested Wally Malone's younger brother. He made a detailed confession. Gabe and I are wrapping things up here in Tampa. Haven't you talked to Brian yet? He flew back to Miami last night."

Her worst fears were confirmed. Kaylen's misery knew no bounds. Although Brian was almost as bad at communicating as his brother had been, he wouldn't have blown into town and not contacted her unless something was really wrong. And she knew what that something was...

She took another shower and changed clothes, brushed her teeth vigorously, followed that with mouthwash and then picked up the ring box and put it into her purse. She had to find Brian and explain how wrong he was. She had to give Ziggy his ring back. Whether Brian believed and understood her explanation for its presence on the coffee table or not, she knew she would not be wearing that ring, ever.

Maybe Brian was at the marina. Or maybe he was at the precinct, going over the details of the confession. Kaylen decided to start with the marina, picked up coffee and drove over to find the Camaro gone from its usual parking space, which brought on another bout of nausea. Thoughts of regurgitated coffee gave her ample motivation to fight back the desire to heave. Brian had mineral water on board the *Need to Know*. She could rest a few minutes, sip the water and regroup. Call Brian. Make an appointment to meet Ziggy.

Wishing last night hadn't happened, Kaylen boarded the *NTK*, unlocked the door to the salon and stepped inside. She saw a coffee mug and the carafe sitting completely dry in a rack suspended over the sink. The bed was made, but in haste judging from the wrinkles in the comforter. Brian had definitely been home. She took a bottle of water from the refrigerator. It was marginally cold, telling her he hadn't been home long.

She dampened a hand towel and carried it outside with her water, where she sank onto one of the loungers in the stern and covered her face with the towel. She wished she could go back and start the last 24 hours over. Avoid the meeting with Ziggy altogether.

"What in the world are you doing out here?"

Brian!

She shot upright, the damp towel falling into her lap, and looked up at him. Her heart contracted painfully. He was wearing a suit and sunglasses. Obviously, he hadn't been hanging out at the marina.

"Waiting for you," she said. "I don't feel well."

"You do look a little green around the edges." Brian took off the sunglasses and smiled as he sat on the edge of the other lounger. "Seasick in port? That's unusual for you."

Kaylen saw the smile light his eyes and her stricken heart took a small leap of hope. She loved his eyes, the golden streaks against the blue. She couldn't imagine never seeing them again and blinked back tears.

"I've got a hangover," she confessed. "I had too much to drink last night."

"I'll have to chew out Angela and watch you two don't hang out too much, then." He took a deep breath. "Kaylen…"

"Brian," she interrupted. "I know you solved your case. I called Jim. But I have to say something before you tell me all about it…"

"The case can wait." He was no longer smiling. "I've got something way more important to talk about."

Forget crying. Her stomach flipped in an ugly manner. The nausea surged. She took a mouthful of water and forced it down. "I'm so sorry," she began, feeling lightheaded as well as queasy.

"Sorry for what?" He looked puzzled. "What's going on, hon? Is there another reason for you drinking?" He gave her one of those piercing looks that always made her squirm.

"Let's go inside." She struggled to get out of the lounger, and he gently pulled her to her feet. "I want to show you something." She grabbed his hand and started to tug him along.

"Not so fast." He tugged back. "I haven't even had a kiss, yet."

"You may not want to kiss me after I'm finished," she warned, sinking into his arms anyway. He nuzzled her neck. Kaylen's legs went weak. *God, she loved him!* The tears returned, welling up, threatening to choke her.

His lips met hers, and her mouth opened instinctively in response. She pressed herself against him, her heart rate rapidly increasing. Being as close to Brian as she could get felt like coming home, in a completely exciting and sensual way. Her tears spilled over.

Gently, Brian disengaged himself, holding her at arms' length, his brow furrowed, worry lines at the corners of his eyes. "What's going on?"

He cupped her face, his thumbs wiping away her tears with a gentleness she knew was only for her. She was going to shatter when anger replaced the tenderness. He'd tell her to leave and never come back. She wouldn't survive the loss. Couldn't…

"Has this got something to do with that damned Ziggy Stavros? Do I need to kick his ass?" Brian looked uncertain, like he hadn't since all the revelations about his brother.

"Maybe." She realized he was holding her face with both hands, and it hadn't taken any effort for him to keep them there. Something was new with him, too.

She took his right hand in hers and pulled him into the salon. "You started to call me last night, but you hung up without leaving a message."

"That's what I wanted to talk to you about."

"Did you go over to my condo yesterday?"

"No. Why?" His jaw tightened, so did his grip. "Did someone break in?"

He looked so worried, Kaylen hastened to reassure him. "No. Oh, God no. But something did happen. It was the reason I got drunk." She pulled the ring case out of her purse, held it up and opened it. "Ziggy proposed."

"That *bastard!*" Brian gritted his teeth. "I hope you didn't accept. You didn't, did you?" Suddenly, he looked really anguished. "I wanted to tell you something really important, but when I ended up in your voicemail, I couldn't just leave a message."

"No, I didn't accept. He kissed me. There was nothing there on my part except friendship."

Forget angry; Brian looked murderous. Kaylen knew why she had gotten drunk. He actually *was* capable of blind jealousy, and all those weeks of practice at the firing range guaranteed accuracy. She hastened to reassure him. Ziggy Stavros needed to live out his natural life.

"It's you I love," she said. "On whatever terms. I can't be away from you. Please don't make me."

"If you'll stop talking about Ziggy Goddamned Stavros and let me get a word in, I'll tell you what I couldn't on the phone."

Brian took the ring case out of her hand, snapped the box shut and threw it over his shoulder. His left shoulder; with his left hand, she noted with astonishment. The box landed with a clatter in the galley.

"If that ring came out of the box, we're going to have to find it," she told him. "Angela's opinion was it was worth a bundle," she added, when he looked like he was going to laugh at her.

"I've got more money than I'll ever need." Brian took her in his arms again. "If it went down the sink, I'll write Ziggy a check. Can we stop talking about him and his f'ing ring before I really start swearing?"

"Okay." She placed her fingers against her lips and made a zipping motion.

"Thank you. Honestly, do all women keep talking and talking like you do?" He waved his left hand at her. "No, don't answer that."

Kaylen wanted to protest, but she stayed silent.

He held her lightly but firmly, making it obvious he wanted her to stay exactly where she stood, a look in his blue eyes that she had never seen before, and had actually given up believing she would ever see. Her heart started pounding in her ears and she thought if he wasn't holding her, she would have fallen.

"Kaylen, I love you," Brian said. "I'm such a damned fool for not realizing it until I was away from you."

Kaylen couldn't get her breath.

His brow furrowed, and the look in his eyes faded. They turned murky, unsure. "But I'm worried..."

All the baggage had slid from her shoulders, and she had no plans to allow it to weigh her down ever again. "Oh, shut up yourself and kiss me," she said. "Let's work out the details later."

And he did. And he told her over and over that he loved her between kisses, and Kaylen knew she had finally left that dark and gloomy place she'd inhabited for too long.

"I've got to warn you," he told her after a while. "This doesn't mean we move in together, I give you a ring, and we start a family."

"I know." She snuggled up against him. They had ended up stretched out on the couch, the need for togetherness for once more emotional than physical. "Small steps, right?"

"Yeah. Starting with me getting to know all those people in your social circle and trying to learn some manners so I don't disgrace you."

"Brian, I don't want or expect you to be anything but who you are," she protested.

"Except for the swearing and the fast food parts," he reminded her, his smile wider than she'd ever seen.

"Except for those," she agreed.

"Maybe we could work something out so you spend more of your off-time on the boat? I don't mind staying a couple of nights a week at the condo when you're not working, but this arrangement we have isn't so bad. I've taken the Cold Case position, hon, so I don't know what my hours are actually gonna be until I settle into the job."

"Really?" She sat up and looked down at him. "You didn't take it because of me, did you? I don't want that on my conscience."

"No. Wrapping up the Summerfield case made that decision feel right. So did what you said, about people being dead longer, but their family and friends still needing justice. I want that, too, for Tim, and for me. Fred Englehardt personally broke the news to Ted Summerfield and his wife. I went to see Mel before I came here, to give her an update." He intently watched Kaylen's expression. "With Jack Mills," he added. "No barracuda visits without backup."

"Thank goodness." Kaylen felt overwhelming relief that he hadn't been near Mel Summerfield alone. Probably, she thought, akin to the relief Brian had felt when she said she was going to refuse Ziggy's proposal.

"There's a lot of confessing to do over there," Brian said. "Between all the players keeping secrets, it was one helluva case. I can't tell you anything more right now, or Hal will come down on me for leaking information. You might inadvertently let something slip."

"Doubtful, but I'm still learning how to be a cop's girlfriend." She was able to smile without reservations. It felt really good. "Speaking of kicking people's butts, I still owe Mel one in the rear end with my best pair of pointy Jimmy Choo's."

"No need for that."

Brian laughed, completely at ease. He ran his hands up her sides, a thrill shooting through her at his touch.

"Mel said it's time for her to take her licks; tell the truth to Shelley's father. That'll sure stir things up in Tampa, maybe for the better, maybe not. She said she'll convince Ted to moor their boat in a different marina. We'll wait to see if she follows through with any of that, but I do believe there'll be no more *Naughty Nautical* next to the *NTK*. Mel said seeing me on a regular basis wasn't gonna help any of them move on with their lives. She thanked me for what I did, but it was one of those not-so-great endings." He sighed. "Keeping secrets ultimately didn't help any of the people involved. In fact, it screwed them all up in so many ways. So many people affected. They may never get any peace, even if the shooter spends the rest of his life behind bars."

"I feel sorry for all of them." Kaylen smoothed the lines on Brian's forehead. There were more since his injury and Tim's death. Stress and pain had taken their toll. "Like with Tim, everyone talks about closure, but if whoever killed him gets brought to justice, will it really solve everything for you?"

"Probably not, but it'll be a good start."

Brian ran a finger down her face to the corner of her mouth. He traced her lips with his thumb, then pulled her down and kissed her again, lightly.

"Speaking of Tim, I'd like to do something," he said.

She felt she knew what he was going to say. "Go tell him?"

Brian smiled. Gone from his face was the pain she hadn't even realized was there from the moment she had met him.

"Yeah. You think that's weird?"

"No. I think it's a lovely idea." She kissed him again. She couldn't seem to stop doing that.

"I'm going to ask Jim to start investigating my background," Brian said as they got up. "I may be even more afraid of what he could find there than I was of telling you I love you, but it's gotta be done."

"You, afraid?" Kaylen shook her head emphatically. "Never, Brian. And whatever Jim finds, you won't be alone to deal with it, either."

"I'll hold you to that."

"Absolutely. Jim will say the same thing. We're your family now. You'll never be alone again unless *you* make it that way."

As they walked to her car, she held his left hand. They hadn't spoken about him using it to hold her, to open the door, or to help her off the *NTK*. She wasn't sure whether he wanted her to say anything. Maybe it was better to go forward from that point, instead of looking back and analyzing.

That would be plain sailing, she thought, watching a visual analogy of furled sails flapping against masts in the marina. Something she had always wanted in her life before Brian. But with him, she knew that wasn't what she was in for, and she hoped she would always be as ready for whatever life threw their way as she felt at that moment.

Brian took her keys. "I'll drive."

"You always do," she said. "Okay. I trust you."

"I know."

He drove out of the marina with Kaylen's hand firmly on his right thigh. She wasn't letting go of him for one minute that afternoon.

THE END

ACKNOWLEDGMENTS

To the members of the Novel & Fiction Special Interest Groups of the now-disbanded Alameda Writers Group in Los Angeles, a big thanks for convincing me to make *Indelible* into a series. It has been both a challenging and rewarding project to take these characters further on their journeys. Those group members included Bonnie Schroeder, Miriam Johnston, Terry Carr, Beverly Diehl, Vance Gloster, Tony Faggioli, Gayle Bartos-Poole, Jackie Houchin and many more who always gave thoughtful, in-depth and encouraging critiques.

To The Pacific Online Writers Group (POWG,) who continued on the journey after the demise of AWG, adding Christopher Page for a good part of this book. Bonnie, Miriam and Terry continued on for the duration, although Terry left us to pursue non-fiction and still owes me one last critique (LOL!)

I couldn't have done it without all of you. Although I moved to Portland, Oregon, we continue to support each other online, either through POWG, Facebook and/or emails. Tony sent me to his formatter, Jenn

Oliver, who saved the day when my publishing contract fell through and I was forced to wear yet another hat and wade into new waters.

Thanks to my friends, Anita and Kenny Sitomer, for providing me with opportunities to research and experience Miami, and to Anita's uncle, Murray, for giving me a great name for Brian's new boat in this book.

Thanks also, last but far from least, to Paula Johnson, web designer and all-round guru for all things publishing and self-promotion (mine as well as hers.) Her no-nonsense, plain-speaking ways force me out of my safe-zone for my own good. It's not always easy to go where I may not want to go, but the results are usually worth the experience.

ABOUT THE AUTHOR

Heather Ames knew she was a writer from the time she won first prize in a high school novel contest. An unconventional upbringing gave her opportunities to travel extensively, leading to nomadic ways and an insatiable desire to see the world in adulthood. She has made her home in 5 countries and 7 states (so far,) learning a couple of languages along the way. She is currently pitching her tents in Portland, Oregon, and after a long career in healthcare, has finally made her dream of writing full-time come true.

Heather is a member of Sisters in Crime.

Visit her website at
www.heatherames.com

ALSO BY HEATHER AMES

Mystery / Suspense series
Indelible (Book 1)

Romantic Suspense
All That Glitters

Contemporary Romance
The Sweetest Song

Upcoming Books
Night Shadows (Suspense) (Fall 2017)
Swift Retribution (*Indelible* mystery / suspense series—Book 3) *2018*